The Last of the Pascagoula

Rebecca Meredith

La Sirene Press

The Last of the Pascagoula is a work of fiction. The characters and places are, like Martha's art, part collage and part pure imagination, but I hope that anyone who knows Pascagoula and New Orleans and their surroundings will agree that the spirit in which they are depicted is true.

Chapel of Love
Words and music by Phil Spector, Ellie Greenwich and Jeff Barry
Copyright © 1964 UNIVERSAL-SONGS OF POLYGRAM INTERNATIONAL, INC., BUG MUSIC-TRIO MUSIC COMPANY and MOTHER BERTHA MUSIC, INC.
Copyright Renewed
All rights for MOTHER BERTHA MUSIC, INC. Controlled and Administered by EMI APRIL MUSIC INC.
All Rights Reserved   Used by Permission
Reprinted by permission of Hal Leonard Corporation

ISBN Number 9780615506371

Printed in the United States of America

La Sirene Press

For Marthas everywhere

Part One

2005

My sister Martha brought the little box in with the mail, when I sent her out to look for the royalty check. She dropped it onto my lap, said one word, and, just like that, began the destruction of a wall I had spent my whole life building around us. The word she said was "Tom."

She might have guessed from the fact that the package was from New Orleans, and that's the last place we knew he'd lived, but I didn't think so. Martha was like that. Sometimes, without me having any idea how, she would just know something. I thought it might be because, having given up talking for the most part, she had become more sensitive to the world. That and the fact that her heart was busted open so early in her life that she just didn't invest herself in the regular world the way most people did. But neither did I. In spite of having made a career out of finding things out for other people, I felt like I never really knew anything for myself. Except Martha.

Martha showed no interest in what was in the box. Instead, she went upstairs to her studio and closed the door. I could hear her pounding away with her hammer, the sound muffled by the burlap bag in which she put glass and pottery and anything that might fly around. She had a lot of sense about such things, even though she walked around naked unless I made her get dressed, forgot to eat unless I insisted, and was likely to steal or tear apart anything she might suddenly take a liking to and incorporate it into whatever artwork she was making.

I turned off the computer and picked up the box. My hands shook a little as I picked at its taped-up corners, making it hard to get

3

my bitten-down fingernails under the edges. If it really was from Tom Carmody, what on earth would he be sending to me after nearly forty years' time? Finally, exasperated, I pushed away from the kitchen table where I'd spent the morning working, and pulled a serrated knife out of the drawer by the sink.

Once the package hung open by a tape and paper hinge, I stuck my fingers inside. I tugged at a wad of red tissue paper, the other end grabbing briefly before it snapped free. An object fell onto the counter among the remnants of the breakfast that I'd eaten and Martha had picked at.

"Oh, my God."

It was a rosary, made of pink glass beads, the silver crucifix showing Jesus in his final agony. Beside Jesus' head hung a little silver cupid, bow drawn, as if either guarding him or trying to pierce him. The last time I had seen it I had been fifteen years old.

A slip of stiff paper hung from the cross. It read, "You said you'd always love me, no matter what. 504-555-9824."

I spent the morning staring at that string of beads, thinking about the boy that had bought them on the same say he'd begun the change that was to take him away from me and toward the life he needed to live. He and I had been friends in the way that only marginal children can be, joined by big hurts and the teeth-gritting determination to get out of them, to find something in ourselves to shake its fist in the face of the just plain awful that life had heaped on us. Tom had succeeded, I had thought. I'd spent all these years imagining him in some happy but essentially unchanged state, still the wry Bugs Bunny with the funny voice who could stick his head up out of things and wink at me like we were above it all, even when it seemed like the only thing we could count on was that the world was plumb crazy. Now here he was, casting the bait of "no matter what" my way, and I was full of delight and fear in just about equal measure.

I'd been in such a reverie that I jumped when Martha's paint-spattered hand reached around me and fingered the little cupid charm. "Hey," she crooned. I knew from her voice that she remembered when I'd given her a whole handful of them, nineteen in all, when she was eight years old and I was trying to make up for causing the accident that had made her the way she was. The one hanging with Jesus was the twentieth.

4

"You can't have this, Martha," I looked her right in the eye so she would know I was serious. If I didn't, she'd have the rosary so deep in one of her creations I might not even recognize it. As I put my hand under her chin I noted that her short, wild hair was grey at the temples. Though I knew that if I looked in the mirror I'd see my own grey-streaked braid, for the moment I saw us fifteen and eight, Kate and Martha Lynn, barely hanging on. What must Tom look like by now? I couldn't imagine him as anything but graceful and funny, smart and a little mean, doing his best in a time and place that couldn't have been less suited to him. I'd loved hell out of him then. I wondered if I still would.

I must have picked up the phone twenty times before I gave up and went to bed. I'd spent the brunt of the evening sitting on the front porch, wrapped in a shawl against the nighttime cool that had lingered into late August, sipping a couple of glasses of wine, though I knew the alcohol would make the night sweats worse and my joints sing and keep me from anything like a night's sleep. Not that it mattered; Martha would be wrapped around me like a human blanket before morning anyway, no matter how adamant I was about her staying in her own bed. It had always been that way and I guessed it always would. But as both of us advanced in age, and sleep, never one of my best things, was a skittery creature that I could never quite catch, maybe a little wine would bring me down from the ledge Tom's message had put me on and I could get at least a couple of hours. Maybe in the morning I could dial that number.

The next morning, as I made toast for Martha and watched her ignore it, I counted forward through time zones; I wondered if Tom kept New Orleans time, up until all hours and awake only after the streets had been hosed and swept and cleared of the detritus of the night before. He'd have taken to it, I imagined, unless he'd changed an awful lot.

The computer terminal sat waiting on the table. I had work to do. Martha needed to be cajoled into eating and coerced into a shower, only to have to be bribed and argued back out again and persuaded into panties and a T-shirt at least. I had a stack of research requests in my e-mail and, I expected, when I unlocked the desk drawer in which I kept it, the light on my answering machine would be blinking. Wearily, I poured myself a cup of coffee, picked up a pad of paper and a pen, and pulled my ever-present set of keys out of my pocket. Sure enough, when I opened the drawer the light was blinking. I sat down and pushed the button.

"Hi, Kate. It's Andy. Hope you're doing well. Saw the most recent Martha book; it's darling. I don't know how she does it. Anyhow, here's the latest. Can you find me something about wooden boat building circa 1970? Materials, design, stuff like that. Oh, and wasn't there a UFO sighting in that town you grew up in? I need some idea how police interviews for that kind of thing were conducted back then. Thanks, Kate. Call me asap, okay? Hi to Martha. Tell her I bought *Martha Bites the Moon* for my granddaughter's birthday and she just loves it. Bye-bye."

I scribbled while I listened, and then erased the tape, thankful that Andrea Gerald was such a Luddite. She didn't argue with the fact that I had an old-fashioned answering machine and no cell phone, like some of my clients did, and she hated the computer enough to write her novels longhand and never barrage me with e-mail requests. I'd even transcribed a couple of manuscripts for her, sworn to secrecy and pleased as could be that I knew the plot of the latest Andy Gerald novel before it went to press. In spite of the fact that I'd never laid eyes on the woman, and in spite of the fact that she was one of the best little-old-lady mystery writers around, I had a vision of her as wild-haired and a little bit batty, holed up in her house in Connecticut the way we holed up in ours on Whidbey Island, off the Washington coast and all the way across the continent from her. I'd never read any of her very popular books except the ones I'd typed up, and I felt a little guilty that she'd read Martha's, although "reading" didn't exactly describe what one did with Martha's work.

Even I didn't quite know what to call the Martha books, and I was more than a little responsible for their existence. I knew the checks we got for them kept us fed and sheltered far better than my research job could have, and that the time I spent sending the first of them out to agents years ago had given me connections that made my own work possible. When I wasn't chasing my sister around with clean underwear or following her like a scavenger hoping to snatch up some piece of work that I could incorporate into the narrative that I was building out of her Martha pieces, I did research for authors whose time was too precious for such things. It was a job I enjoyed; the internet had made it increasingly easy and allowed my sister and me to become more and more reclusive over the past ten years, after she'd been delivered to me one day by our father, who'd just learned he was dying.

"Don't you dare put her away, Kate Lynn," he'd said, his voice still able to touch the exact spot in my brain that made me want to run as fast as I could. "She ain't a danger to herself nor anybody else and I ain't got the money to put her anywhere that's not a rat hole. And God knows what she'd do if anybody tried to part her from that damned dog. She's your sister and you haven't put yourself out one bit for her since you left home. It's high time you did." Then he'd entered the base hospital in Spokane, refusing any treatment that might prolong his life, turned on the television to a daily fare of judge shows, baseball games and reruns of 1960's TV series, and completed the withdrawal he'd begun the day in 1967 that our mother had died. He seldom spoke when we came to see him, and in a few weeks he was gone. He died on a spring morning when I hadn't been to the hospital for a week.

Once the marriage I had thought was going to keep me safe fell apart from sheer lack of interest, I had been terrified I would never be able to make it on my own. Oddly, Martha and her incessant need to produce watercolors, collages, and mosaics made out of things in which only she could see the potential became the road to our survival. Every one of them centered on the adventures of a winged dog whose name was the same as hers. Once I'd realized that her pieces were telling a long and interesting story, one whose ending I might never know but whose episodes were as clear as any of the books I'd ever read, I began gathering, ordering and photographing them. Since in many ways she was my opposite, losing interest in a piece as soon as she was finished with it and moving on to the next, I had no trouble collecting the work. I knew from the start that it was remarkable; I just wasn't certain until I got the first call from one of the agents to whom I'd sent a small collection of the pieces that anyone else would respond to it the way I had. Then a second agent e-mailed me, and a third. By the time the fifth Martha book had come out I had been able to buy us a house in the woods on the pretty island off the Washington coast, as far away from Pascagoula, Mississippi as it was possible to get.

"Martha," I called up the stairs to the studio where Martha spent most of her time. I could hear the television in the background, static-laden murmuring that she liked to have on most of the time, even though we hardly had reception this far out. She didn't care what was on; if she watched at all it was, I had teased her, like a cat did, enjoying the motion and the crackling sounds but with no awareness of content. I knew it wasn't true. I could tell from the books that she paid attention. "Martha, I'm having a hard time deciding what to do about calling Tom. Do you think I should?"

I talked to her because I'd always talked to her. I talked to her the way Crusoe talked to Friday. Unlike Friday, she made no effort to create a language we could share, but in the way that lonely creatures come to know one another, we'd developed a kind of multisensory communication, a ballet that we performed constantly, that consisted of a word here and there, a way of occupying space, of leaving one another alone and yet never getting too far apart. Talking to Martha was like talking to myself, except that now and then she'd surprise me by answering and remind me that she wasn't stupid and she wasn't crazy. She just lived in Martha Land, a place the rest of us could only see through the intricate, deeply layered work she let fall from her fingers and left lying on the studio floor where I had to rescue it, lest she walk over it or tear it apart to make the next.

"Martha?" No answer. I was talking to the wrong person.

"Who may I say is calling?" It was fitting that a lovely, cheerily androgynous voice would announce my first contact with Tom Carmody in more than thirty five years. His own had been such a source of distress that I'd often wondered if he'd ever overcome it. I supposed I was about to find out.

"Tell him it's Kate Lynn. From Pascagoula."

"Oh, Kate!" The voice rose in pitch. "He's been on pins and needles—well, not literally, but you know what I mean, he's been itching—oh, let me just get him for you!" I heard the receiver clunk and the voice recede into the background, calling "Tom, Darlin', it's her! It's your Kate!" I smiled, imagining some sweet young man who was in love with my old friend, a possibility that didn't seem extraordinary at all. I imagined Tom indulgent and charming, his red hair now full and white, still decked out in the planter's hat he'd acquired on the same day he'd gotten the crucifix that I now held in my hand, but grown into the role of gentility he'd always been half convinced his family had fallen from. Tom, who had never really been young in the way most kids were, would make a fine older lover.

I heard a clunk and the scratching sound of the mouthpiece being pressed against something, then a short burst of words in a muffled voice before a long intake of breath whuffed against the microphone.

"Kate Lynn. It's about damn time."

It was a man's voice, soft and modulated, whispery at the edges as if not driven by quite enough breath, but so warm I could almost hear the smile. In spite of its maturity I knew it instantly. Unexpected tears welled up in my eyes.

"Tom. Tom!" I couldn't think of a single thing more to say.

"Yes, it's really me. Are you shocked, after all these years? Did my little present say it all?" Tom was as comfortable reintroducing himself as he had been on the first day he'd come tapping on our trailer door when I was fifteen, as if simply taking up where we had left off. I felt a rush of pleasure at that familiar characteristic. Its easy intimacy loosened my tongue now the way it had when we'd first met.

"It certainly did get my attention, if that's what you mean. Tom, how on earth are you? Where have you been all these years?"

"In New Orleans, of course. I've never been anywhere else; it's you took off, leaving us all to the whims of Pascagoula. I hated you for that. Good thing I loved you for so much else."

My head buzzed. Tom talked as though it had been mere weeks and not most of a lifetime since I'd seen him. I felt my life telescope down to the short, intimate time we'd spent together, and with the telescoping a tinge of old hurt rose to the surface.

"Now wait a minute, Tom. You were the one who left me."

"I beg your pardon. I didn't move out of Pascagoula until I turned eighteen."

"There's more than one way to leave."

He sighed. "You're right. But of all people you should know I couldn't do anything else. That's why I knew I could look you up. How's Martha, by the way?"

"Uh, she's okay." I played Martha close to my chest, the way I always did when I didn't know how much someone knew about us.

"From the look of things she's turned out to be quite the artist. I can't believe she turned that terrible little dog into something damn near magical. When I saw *Martha Land* on Amazon I knew it couldn't be anybody else. She could exhibit in any gallery in this city." He broke off, coughing, a soft, wheezy cough.

9

"Is that how you found us, through the books?" We'd gotten a quite a few letters over the years through Martha's publisher, but I'd worked hard at keeping our lives obscure. My lack of willingness to dive into publicity had driven Martha's publicist crazy until I'd invited her to come out to the island and stay the weekend. I was pretty sure pieces of her camera, her real Dolce and Gabbana sunglasses and her fake Cartier watch were still embedded in the mural on the north wall of Martha's studio, and though the woman had handled having her wander naked in and out of our conversation with a quiet aplomb that made me glad she was our interface with the world, she caught on right away that there weren't going to be interviews and book signings in our future.

"That and the services of a good internet detective," Tom went on. "You know, the 'find anyone for fifty bucks' variety. I hope you don't mind too much. You were pretty easy, no name change, good driver's license history." He stopped again, coughing. "Sorry."

"I'm not offended. It's a little ironic, since looking up things on the internet is a big part of what I do for a living."

"Really? Do tell while I swallow some tea."

"I'm a freelance researcher for authors. I check facts for historians, get the information, say, a mystery writer needs to make a plot believable, and I work like a mule for a few academics that write a lot and need sources for citations. It doesn't pay much of anything but between Martha's books and the research, and the fact that we don't have that much outlay, we hang in there. How about you? What do you do to keep body and soul together?"

Tom barked a short laugh, coughed again briefly and said "I am recently retired, as a matter of fact. Well, sort of. I own some property and I turned its management over to a protégé. I'm at leisure for the moment."

"Huh. I know you wanted to be Lord of the Manor but I can't quite get my head around the idea of you as a stuffy old landlord, Tom."

"Would you feel better if I told you I owned Miss Eddie's, which, in case you don't know, is one of the finest gay establishments in New Orleans?"

I choked, "Did you say 'Miss Eddie's?'"

"I did. Of course, when anybody asks me, I tell them it's after an old flame and act mysterious. No one asks more than one layer of questions in these parts."

"And Eddie? And your mother and father? How did they take it?"

There was a long pause. I had a moment of prescience, a prickling of the hairs on my arms. Still, I felt a pinch of sadness when he replied "Mother and Daddy never knew. They're dead, Kate. Years back."

"Oh Tom," the words came automatically, formally, as if for a moment we were strangers. It was what you said. "I'm sorry."

"Thanks. It was a long time ago." His voice had changed as well, the easy familiarity dropped. I decided to leave the topic of Eddie alone.

"Do you ever hear from Claire?"

"Kate, don't you want to know why I looked you up?"

I realized I'd been avoiding the question. Tom had found me easily enough; he could have sent an e-mail or a friendly "let's catch up" letter. The rosary and the "no matter what" had conveyed not only intimacy but urgency, and I was afraid. I'd spent most of my adult life avoiding both. I'd slogged through a few disappointed lovers and a brief marriage with a nice man whose last name I hadn't taken, and that had mostly left me confused and exhausted, as though there was something I knew ought to exist, that I longed for, but that I couldn't quite grasp. I lived in a sturdy, woodsy little house on a couple of forested acres on an island, locked to a sister who registered me as background noise, working for people that I never saw. Tom's message had reached out from a time when I had felt that there was something valuable that ran between me and the people I was with, a vital and tantalizing sense of becoming, of the possibility of escape from what I feared most—that the world had already beaten the life out of me at fifteen. Reconnecting with him just might be admitting what I'd been avoiding all this time, that my life had been nothing much. That whatever had made me afraid had won.

"Kate?" I thought about hanging up. Then Tom laid down his trump card. "Kate, they're here, Claire and the others. You're the only ones I haven't kept up with, you and Martha. I want you to fly down to see me. I'll buy the tickets and you'll have a place to stay. Will you?"

I laughed before I could stop myself. "Oh Tom, that's a very nice offer, but—,"

"It's not nice. It's important to me. I know it's a leap of faith for you to just pick up and come all the way down here, but—,"

"You don't understand, Tom. I mean, it's not just me. It's Martha."

"She wouldn't come? I could talk to her. I know she probably just barely remembers me if she does at all, but maybe I could persuade her."

I rubbed my forehead. Up in the studio, Martha was pounding away at God knew what. "No, you couldn't persuade her. Look, do you remember the last time you saw Martha, when Daddy came back, just before we left? Do you remember how she acted like he was another piece of furniture to walk around on her way to get to her art table?"

"Sure do. You said you thought he was going to have a stroke right there for hollering, trying to get her to look at him, and she just kept staring past him until he quit, and then went on to her pencils and paints. You don't mean she's still that way?"

"Still that way? In a lot of ways she's worse. She's not a little girl anymore; she's a middle aged woman. She sees everything in the world as either something she can use to make one of her Martha creations or as practically nonexistent. If she likes it, watch out. If not, it's not there. After we left Pascagoula Daddy tried taking her to doctors and special classes for a little while, but she didn't respond to therapy any differently than she did to anything else, and the things drugs did to her were worse than the way she was without them. After a while he just hired somebody to be sure she didn't accidentally kill herself or him, or walk out of the house naked—she's not much into clothes either when she can get away with it—and went on with his life. Never did remarry, retired from the Air Force eventually and near as I can tell sat in a Barcalounger while she did what she did. I got the hell out of there as soon as I could but she came back to me when he died. I guess none of us has ever been any good at being with anybody except us, so here we are. A plane ticket for Martha would only be useful stuck into a collage of some kind."

Tom whistled low. "You couldn't come without her?"

"Last time I tried leaving her with somebody I got halfway down the drive before she started screaming like she was possessed and thrashing so hard she had bruises for a solid month. Sorry, Tom."

"You mean you never leave the house?"

"Oh, we do. She likes the car, although I have to be careful not to let her steal the knobs off of the controls. And she stays dressed if I threaten her. But believe me, we shop on the 'net and get as much delivered as humanly possible. An airport is completely out of the question.

"Then I'll rent a car. Someone to drive you. I can afford it. Please, Kate. If there's any way you can come here, come. Please."

"Why? I mean, I'd love to see you too, but you have to understand how hard--,"

"I need you because of who you are, and who we were when we were best friends. Because of why we were best friends. Because I'm about to kill myself, and I need your help to do it."

Part Two

1968

Chapter One

I've always believed that if I hadn't met Tom Carmody when I did, I wouldn't have gotten out of Pascagoula Mississippi alive. One morning in the middle of a chilly, damp January, five months after my mother's death, a hired rig pulled the ramshackle trailer in which we had spent the last three years watching her die into Carmody's Trailer Park. My father, who was too old to draft but not too old to turn his career in the Air Force into an opportunity for escape from what he'd just lived through, had left the trailer, my sister Martha and me in his own mother's care, while he volunteered to spend the last years of the Vietnam war at a communications station at the edge of the war zone. He'd told us for months, and with some shame, that our mother's illness had kept him in a state of "compassionate deferment" and out of Vietnam. Still, the fact that we had waved him off to operate a radio in a jungle on the other side of the world so soon after her death smacked to me of volunteerism. Maybe, after watching cancer eat away a woman not even out of her thirties, an only semi-dangerous job in Southeast Asia looked like a reasonable way to get some thinking space. I might have done the same were I in his place. But I wasn't. I was in the place he couldn't bear to be. I was where she'd left us after using us nearly all up. I was in a world that, at fifteen, I had long ago lost faith in.

Martha, our grandmother and I stood in the street and watched as the trailer in which we'd gone through so much was backed and hawed into a parking space between a turquoise and white Marlette mobile home with a dripping air conditioner and a tiny, silver Jetstream. The tired arrangement of salt rusted mobiles sat near the corner of Little Red Road and Front Street, an intersection just a block away from the slow, broad river that flowed toward the Gulf of Mexico, which lay no more than two miles south of our new home.

We lived on the southern fringe of America. Sometimes it seemed that that part of Mississippi clung like a barnacle to the rest of the country, not quite a part of it but fiercely attached just the same. Mississippi coastal people were part Southern port culture, part ocean culture, part bayou culture, and that made us all water culture. The Pascagoula River, what we all called the Singing River, and the people who lived at its terminal, were to become a focus of our lives in a year when the country, particularly the Mississippi part of it, was going crazy, and Martha and I were going right along with it.

1968 was shaping up to be about as bad as a year could be, and it wasn't even Mardi Gras yet. We had spent the years of my mother's dying just a half hour away at the Air Force Base in Biloxi, but no one, not even my grandparents, had known what went on in that trailer during those years. They had come on weekends laden with leftovers from the Rebel Café, a tiny meat-and-three restaurant that hugged the fence of Ingalls Shipyard, Pascagoula's main industry and the source of income for most of the town. My grandmother had done what she could for us out of her own perpetual state of foot-shuffling exhaustion, but even at her sickest my mother's pride made her sit up in bed and swear that we were doing all right, maybe not as well as we'd like, but the Lord doesn't give anyone anything they can't handle, hallelujah. My father had the Air Force to answer to, and in his regulation ironed uniform and spit shined shoes he was indistinguishable, sometimes even to me, from every other sergeant at Keesler Air Force Base. Martha and I had gone to school in acceptable clothes and made acceptable grades, even if we never once participated in a club or football game or after school activity. No one thought to ask why, since we had, for the most part, not caused anyone any kind of trouble. In fact, until you got to know us we all looked passable. And so, like everyone else, my grandparents would go home, and the struggle would go on.

Maybe it was out of shame or just plain helplessness, but in spite of the obvious mark the disease had left on our mother, we hid the details of our losing fight with cancer well. It grew in the soft tissue of her belly and before anyone even knew it was there had gotten into her bones and lungs and everything. By the time she saw the Air Force doctors, complaining with some embarrassment of pain in her pelvis and her bottom when she sat down, there was nothing they could do that would cure her. They did the surgery anyway, and what they did was enormous. Afterward she hurt so bad that the pain and the drugs they had to give her made her half crazy. Sometimes they worked and sometimes they didn't, and the nights were the worst of all. At night she suffered and cried, and our father and I ran around like crazy people trying to take care of what was left of her while Martha staggered like a zombie, sucking her fingers, too little to help but too alarmed to sleep.

By the time we arrived in Pascagoula I really didn't know how to live any other way. I was a fifteen year old insomniac who had spent most of my teens working my own version of a hospital graveyard shift. I had lived those years like a zombie myself, missing a lot of school, forgetting everything except how to clean a feverish body without causing too much pain and dispense medicines according to a schedule, and in spite of the patient's pleading to either leave her alone or give her the whole blessed bottle and help her die. I learned about the world outside the trailer by watching the 10 o'clock news, curled up in bed beside a woman who hardly seemed to know I was there, while my dead-tired father snored from the living room sofa for fear of rolling over and hurting her in his sleep.

Even though I loved watching the news, it troubled me. I couldn't escape the fact that it spent a fair amount of time concentrating on what a horrible part of the country Mississippi was, and by my reckoning making a pretty good case for itself. Every night, it seemed, there were films of black men just like the ones I saw every day being beaten by the police. Little girls no older than Martha, in bright school dresses and carefully braided hair, were knocked to the ground by blasts from fire hoses. German Shepherd dogs jerked uniformed men toward women who lay down and screamed, grocery bags and purses erupting their suppers and their coin purses and their Kotex and their packs of chewing gum onto the ground. Young black men no older than I was had gone missing, or worse, been found hanging from the trees like the pretty blue bottles I had seen in Butch the café cook's yard when their old, beat-up car had given out and I had gone with my grandfather to give her rides home. As far as I could tell from what they said on television I was a product of the worst part of America. And from what I heard from the people around me every day, I figured it must pretty much be true.

Even the people I loved did things that didn't make sense. Those things got inside me and made me want to shrink away from my own skin. My grandparents, honest people who I knew loved me, and who'd kept Martha and me from being orphans for sure and without seeming mad about it at all, held onto feelings and fears that seemed strange when I heard them on the news but were everywhere around us. I'd seen Butch slide paper plates out the back door to her own husband and brothers and shoo them away like children before they could be caught loitering, and then laugh and joke with the white waitresses as though they were the best of friends. The only thing that seemed to scare people more than the way things were was the fear that they would change. Everyone knew it was crazy and everyone just kept their heads down and hoped nothing bad would happen to them. I seemed to be the only one who knew better. I knew nothing protected you from bad. Bad had already happened, and I couldn't imagine ever being safe from that fact again.

Between hiding the horror of what had happened to my mother and the terrible understanding that my people had done things I was afraid to even think about, I was pretty sure some big parts of me had faded away. By the time we moved to Pascagoula I felt bent and strange, I didn't know what to do with the rest of the world, and the only thing it seemed I could do was to stop feeling anything at all. The year before I'd started a diary, trying to find a way to write down what was going on inside of me. It lay at the bottom of the old toy box in my closet, under the pile of stuffed animals that I felt too old to sleep with any more but that I wouldn't have gotten rid of at the point of a gun. That book haunted me. Its mostly blank pages felt like the blank parts of me, longing to be filled up. Something was missing, some feeling that would connect it all together. I didn't know if I'd ever find it, whatever it was, and that thought scared me bad.

20

Chapter Two

Like me, Tom Carmody was an orphan of sorts, although his parents were both alive and living under the same roof he did. But his home situation had made of Tom a kind of beautiful starveling, a well-groomed, intelligent boy my age who was likely to show up at your house for supper and stay until people began to yawn and hint that tomorrow was sure going to be starting early and there were baths to take before bed. The Carmodys were Irish and Catholic, both common enough in Gulf Coast Mississippi, but in Thomas Mark Carmody the lineage came out particularly red haired, green-eyed and freckled. He was wonderful to look at, but more beautiful than handsome. He moved in a way I'd never seen anyone move before. It seemed that if he'd wanted to he could have walked on Pascagoula Beach without leaving a single foot print, he slid so softly through the world. In a region where bull necks and strong jaws were as highly prized as fine shotguns and new pickup trucks, the word I eventually discovered for Tom was "lithe." It was a pretty word for a pretty, half-grown boy. It fit him perfectly, a fact that kept him in constant trouble with the Copenhagen snuff-dipping crowd and would eventually bring us all up against his rage in a way none of us could have imagined. But for now, even my grandfather took one look at him and announced, with a typical gift for both perception and crudeness, that "That boy's a faggot sure as I'm sittin' here."

But Tom also had a wry, world-weary streak that I would learn to love. He reminded me of Bugs Bunny, smart and funny and a little above it all. The first evening he showed up at our trailer door, dark red hair wet and slicked down as though he had showered first in order to make a good impression, face so pale it looked green beneath the constellation of freckles across his nose, I thought he looked for all the world like he'd walked down off of a stage in the middle of a play, one about a place far different than the one that surrounded us. He knocked on the metal bottom half of the screen door very softly, a single rap, a pause, and then three more, as if we already had a secret code between us. In later months he would do the same with the small white shells that made the path beneath my bedroom window, tossing them up in the middle of the night, so softly that only the perpetually awake would hear.

Grandmother, a big, hard-working woman whom Tom was to spend weeks courting like a prospective bride so she wouldn't chase him away, was snoring denture free in front of the television. Her short, brassy hair, colored blonde from an industrial-looking bottle of dye not only because she was getting grey, but because she was ashamed of being part Indian and wanted to hide her dark features, was plastered to her temples with sweat. A scuffed white nurse's shoe whose back she'd mashed down with her heel so she could wear it like a slipper dangled from one toe. She still wore the white nylon waitress' uniform she'd spent the day in. It smelled like grease. I knew that two others just like it hung in the trailer's bedroom closet, alongside the soft, colorful dresses that my father had never given away, and that in the morning, for just a minute, my grandmother would smell just a little like my mother's perfume. Now, though, she'd sat down with a glass of cornbread and buttermilk and dropped off before either the early news or her supper was done. At the rap she snorted softly, once, but didn't move before the regular rhythm of her breathing took up again.

I made it to the front door first, slapping Martha out of the way at the same time I pointed a warning finger in her face, silently calling revenge down on her head if she so much as yipped. I don't know what I expected; my grandparents had never shown a sign of having the kind of friends who dropped by and the trailer park didn't look to be the kind of place where somebody would be coming over with a pecan pie or a pot of welcome-to-the-neighborhood gumbo.

"Hey." Tom stood in the February evening and squinted up the short steps at me. He looked neat enough for Sunday school. His pants were pressed khaki and he wore a short sleeved, striped, pressed cotton shirt. I could just see his bare ankles above the tops of oxblood loafers. In a backwater teenaged populace that was just barely beginning to discover fringe and paisley, and who embraced grubby blue jeans with a fervor that made the grownups half crazy, his only fashion rebellions were hair that brushed the top of his collar and an absolute refusal to wear socks.

At first word his voice sounded nice enough. I hadn't yet heard enough of it to understand the agony that the act of speech put him through, and how well he covered up the pain. His next sentence brought the problem into focus. "Mother said there was somebody new in the trailer park. I'm Tom Carmody. Come on out and I'll explain how things work around here."

I covered my mouth with one hand while swatting at my sister, who snorted with laughter behind me, with the other. Puberty had not been kind to Tom where speech was concerned. His voice started high in his nose and seemed to get stuck somewhere before he could push hard enough to make the words come out. When they did, they came in small, uncontrolled explosions. If I talked like that, I thought, I'd never utter another word. Tom, however, had a twinkle in his eye, as though he was in perfect control of the sounds that threatened to make me laugh right out loud, even as he practiced his deadpan delivery on us.

"I'm gonna get Grandmama," my sister hissed, giving me the option of persuading her out of it by her relative quiet. She was as interested in this stranger as I was.

"Shut up, Martha." I smiled when I said it but she knew I meant business. Turning back to the figure outside I said "My sister's gotta come. I'm watching her." I opened the door and shoved her into open space in front of me before she could protest the accuracy of either my statement or my aim. She did a little Wile E. Coyote scramble in mid-air and hit the ground hopping mad, not an unusual state for her these days. Martha had a hair trigger. Mad described her like numb described me. I envied her for it.

It was cool outside, and I shivered as I followed and sat down on the steps. "I'm Kate Lynn. This is my sister Martha." I extended my hand. Tom just stared at it.

"Did you know the handshake was invented by the ancient Greeks?" He gave an appraising look. "Although they didn't actually shake hands. Men grabbed each other by the testicles to show that they trusted one another."

I heard Martha's eyes bug out in the dark. Before she could squawk he said "Kate Lynn what?" It was the first of two questions I had heard a thousand times.

"Nothing. Just Kate Lynn."

"Like Loretta Lynn?" That was the second question. I scooted back on the step and sighed.

"Not if I can help it. I hate country music. It's just the name I got stuck with; that's all."

"Yeah, we Catholics get stuck with the names of saints." He nodded, ducking his head and thrusting his chin out before asking "So, what do you want to be when you grow up?"

I laughed, but his green eyes were as serious as a heart attack. I figured I might as well be serious back. "I have no idea. You?"

"Not one little daydream?" He wasn't letting it go.

"I don't know." In the distance I heard that diary heave a sigh. "I'd like to do something that will take me places. I've thought about writing news stories."

He nodded again. "What kind of music do you like?"

"Beatles. Doors. Motown. I like a lot of stuff." I shrugged but was happy to change the subject and liked the fact that he'd asked serious questions. There had been times when I thought the radio and the music I listened to from the AM stations off in New Orleans, WTIX and WNOE and whatever little crackly Cajun ones came in on my tiny transistor radio, were the only things keeping me alive.

"Beatles, here. And Supremes." He frowned, as if the subject required deep thought. "And Dylan. Dylan's very groovy." He sounded ridiculous saying that word, I thought. Nobody in Pascagoula said "groovy."

"Good songs. Bad voice." I stopped abruptly, afraid I'd said the wrong thing already. Tom continued, smoothly.

"And Sonny and Cher; they're great. Or she is. And the Smothers Brothers. I have to watch that show on the sly, though. It makes my brother crazy since he was in Vietnam. 'Course, everything makes my brother crazy." He abruptly shifted topics again. "Mother said you're here because your mother died and your daddy ran off. Is that true?"

I sighed. "True enough." I wasn't in the mood to talk about my parents. "He just went to Vietnam too, something about radio communications. Before that we were stationed in Biloxi."

24

"Ah, the Biloxi, sworn enemy of the Pascagoula. What grade are you in?"

"Tenth. You?"

"Tenth too. If I cared a good goddamn about football I'd tell you that the Pascagoula High Panthers take their rivalry with the Biloxi High Indians very seriously. Probably because they're not any better at fighting than the actual Pascagoula were. That's where they went in the river, you know. Just a little way down." He pointed in the general direction of his house, whose lights were just visible through the dense foliage that separated it from the trailer park.

"You tell ghost stories too?" I made a brief note of the "goddamn" and concentrated on the Indians. I had loved the story of the Singing River and the tribe that walked into it ever since I was a little kid. I loved it even more these days. That story had it all— Indians, love, kidnapping, and a mass suicide.

"Ever heard them sing?"

"Nooo—my granddaddy says he has, but he drinks a little." He drank a lot. It was one reason my grandmother was so worn out.

"You gonna kiss her, Tom? Go on. I won't tell. Go on; kiss her." Martha hopped around the bottom of the steps on first one foot, then the other. When I looked at her she puckered her lips and made sloppy sucking sounds. I pulled in a deep breath, ready to launch into my best imitation of a grown-up, knowing that no matter what I threatened I'd just be playing my part in a game that we'd invented long before Tom Carmody had been around. Before I could decide whether to use the one about snatching her bald-headed or knocking a knot in her tail, a shadow fell over us.

"Girl, what are you doing out here? Don't you have any shame a'tall? Who are you telling our business to?" Grandmother's broad shape filled the doorway above us. She'd awakened, found her dentures and was ready to light into us. In weeks to come Tom would describe her as a great ship, sailing through life behind her impressive prow, cutting through the rest of us like we were just water in her path. He liked her, but then he seemed to like all women over the age of fifty. For the moment, though, she was just putting an end to the first interesting thing that had happened to me since we'd gotten to Pascagoula and I hated her for it. "Get up here. And you," she looked at Tom as if she had caught him doing something nasty. "You get on home or I'll show you some kissing!" The door bumped my backside before I could stand, pushing me closer to Tom. He straightened and smiled, more relaxed than he had any right to be. Grandmother was mostly bluff, but she was big and could look far meaner than she was. She and I were just getting used to living with one another, trying to figure out how to renegotiate a relationship that had been good when I was small and the world was simple, and confused during the past few years, when we'd hidden ourselves from her so well. My father was her only child, and I had the feeling that raising girls wasn't something she took to naturally. Now that she was stuck with us, I figured I might as well just watch her for a while and see how things were going to be. Tom was direct enough to make me squirm.

"Hello Mrs. Lynn. Welcome to the neighborhood." He swept his arm toward the other trailers. "I'm Tom Carmody. Mother said to let you know the garbage man comes on Fridays and you can leave your cans out by the street. Two can maximum and no junk. And there's a milk delivery, too, if you want to get on the list. Just let me know and I'll tell him." I was impressed. Without a single squeak, Tom addressed my grandmother as though he was a man her own age, easy and familiar and sure she'd feel the same. He didn't know my grandmother. She glowered down on him, rattled the door once and stood back to let Martha and me pass.

"Thank your mother for me. Go on home."

"I could walk Kate to school tomorrow if you like, show her around." He raised his eyebrows and said, a little louder so that his voice strained and broke across the words, breaking the spell and making a kid of him once more. "I leave at seven forty-five."

"She knows how to get there, but I'll keep that in mind." Grandmother, who had always seemed a little afraid of "foolishness," let a little smile escape. I could tell already that Tom Carmody had talent that I would do well to observe. "Now go on."

I sighed, and, without saying good-bye, walked up the stairs, through the living room and into my bedroom. As I drew my covers over my head and turned on the radio hidden in my pillowcase, the last clear words I heard coming from the living room were Martha's. "Grandmama, that boy said 'testicle!'"

Chapter Three

Tom's enterprising mother had made the trailer park out of an old pecan orchard that took up the couple of acres behind the big, weathered house that the Carmody family had lived in since long before Tom's father was born. The house, which looked to my emerging gothic sensibilities like there must surely be a drooling great-aunt shut up in the attic, sat across a short strip of road from the bank of the Pascagoula River. Though it looked like it had been generations since the place had seen paint, it had a spooky kind of grandeur. It was surrounded by enormous, knobby live oaks that dripped grey-green Spanish Moss like mermaid hair. All the house's angles were a little off, as though it had gotten tired over the years and had slumped on its foundation, resigned to its decrepitude but holding onto some shred of dignity in spite. Leaded glass windows that must have once been beautiful and expensive reflected a distorted world, but the house's position under the massive trees and so near the river gave it a cool reserve, as though it was unconcerned about that world just the same. The front porch, which looked out over the river across the short dead end stretch of Front Street, had murky puddles of acorns in its corners that looked like they had been rotting there for years.

The Carmody house was the biggest house anyone I'd ever known had lived in, though as far as I could tell the only people who really lived there were Tom's mother Olivia and his older brother Eddie. Tom certainly spent as little time as he could there, and in the whole time I knew him I only saw his father perched on a stool behind the counter of the little bait shop, tilted on a rickety pier that jutted into the Pascagoula River, across the street from the house. I never knew him as anything other than Mr. Frank Carmody, the Bait and Tackle man.

Mr. Carmody had a leathery face that I could imagine hovering for hours over a fishing pole, and a sharp nose that emitted each breath in a long, high whistle. His hair was full and white, and he looked as though he had once been handsome. On the rare occasion that I accompanied Tom into the shop to get a Coke out of its musty cooler the two of them hardly exchanged hellos, and he ignored me altogether. If it hadn't been for the ghostly freckles across his nose's thin bridge and the clear green eyes I'd never have suspected they were acquaintances, much less father and son. He sat there day after day, surrounded by simple bamboo poles and flashy rods, reels and lures, under a wall filled with an astonishing assortment of mounted sport fish and the heads and bodies of myriad bayou creatures. They had all been stuffed, it appeared, a hundred years before, so that their fur had come out in patches and the eyes had collected a film of dust that made them look deader than dead. The radio was always on in the shop, usually tuned in to a baseball game that cheered out of the speaker like a message from a happy, tinny little world far away. Now and then someone, always male and usually smelling like my grandfather, a mixture of old sweat and Jim Beam whiskey, would come in and, with fewer words than I could have used to do anything, buy a bucket of night crawlers or a few bobbers and go out again. Mr. Carmody couldn't have made any money from the shop. After a while I figured it just gave him someplace other than that house to be.

Tom didn't seem to know his father any better than I did. Whenever I asked about his background he would shrug his shoulders, look a little tired, and say "You'll have to ask somebody who knows, and that sure isn't me," or some similar vague thing. I was never sure if he was joking or nicely telling me to shut up. There must, I thought, have been money back there somewhere, but if so it had disappeared a long time ago. Mr. Frank Carmody looked like a poor man in ways I couldn't exactly describe.

Tom's mother was another matter. Tom talked about her with a mixture of fury and adoration that made my chest squeeze tight. She had quit her job as a teacher at Central Elementary School when Eddie had come home a quadriplegic from the war. By the time I showed up she had spent two years doing little else but hoisting, bathing, feeding and figuring out ways to try to create a life for her immobile, angry and depressed oldest boy, while her youngest grew from her without her ever seeming to take notice.

Eddie had a big hospital bed set up in the living room with a TV at its foot, a variety of medicine bottles on a table beside it and a plastic, perpetually half-full bottle of urine hanging from one of its rails. A hydraulic lift hovered over him, with a system of pulleys and tackle that allowed Mrs. Carmody to move her son, in parts or as a whole, around in the bed. Whenever I went into that room there she was, flexing Eddie's limbs, massaging his slack muscles, adjusting him against the threat of bedsores, reading to him or changing the channel on the perpetually roaring television. According to Tom, Eddie himself never said a word unless it was to bark an order at her to bring something or change something. As I was to find out, that was a lie.

The first time I carried the rent check over, when we'd been in the park only a couple of weeks and the first of March promised a spring I was determined to hate, she met me at the door as though I was the first human outside the family she'd seen in a year, ushering me into the big room and shouting over the Dialing for Dollars movie roaring out of the television screen. "Look, Eddie dear! This is the young lady I told you about; Tom's new friend, the ones in the new trailer, what was your name dear?"

"Kate Lynn."

His eyes didn't move from the screen.

"Kate, that's right! Your grandmother's a lovely woman. I'm so glad such a nice family is living in the park! Isn't that wonderful, Eddie? Eddie, do say hello. He's surely glad to see you, Kate. He's just a bit worn out right now. We've had such a busy afternoon. It's bath and laundry day and it just keeps us hopping all day long."

Eddie didn't blink. I wondered simultaneously if he was paralyzed from the top of his head to the tips of his toes, and whether Tom was anywhere nearby and could rescue me. The room set off a clanging in my head that I had hoped I'd never hear again. I knew too much about sickbeds and television and distorted bodies. I didn't want anything reinforcing the visions I was giving all I had to try to banish. I'd have been just as happy if Eddie never saw me and I never again had to see him.

But a part of Eddie Carmody worked perfectly well. After a moment, the body on the bed drew in a breath so deep and sharp it startled me, turned its head and roared, "Mother, shut up! Shut the hell up! Shut up, Goddamn you! Shut up!" He didn't stop, and neither did she; she kept talking about the details of their day as though she just had to hammer it into somebody how great things would be if they just weren't a little peaked right now. The two of them got louder and louder, while I suddenly had somewhere else I desperately needed to be. I started backing up at about the twelfth "shut up," smiling and nodding, dropping the check on the sideboard and feeling for the front door at my back, while Mrs. Carmody and Eddie built to a crescendo. As I backed out the front door I smiled and nodded at her and she continued to say how happy she was to meet me and how lovely everything was going to be now that we were neighbors. Eddie's yelling had turned into a full-blown shriek, no real words discernable. I said it was nice to meet them and that I'd say hello to Grandmother and two or three other things that could have been "My hair's on fire and I eat pig turds for breakfast" for all they got through the noise. I closed the front door and sagged against a front porch post that looked like it might be able to take my weight. I was sweating like a plow mule.

"I see you've met Eddie." Tom's quiet voice beside me after the onslaught of his mother and brother made me jump a foot.

"Oh, yeah. Definitely." The shouting inside had stopped almost as soon as I'd closed the door, as though the whole eruption had needed an audience in order to exist. All I could hear was a voice from the TV saying that if nobody answered in two more rings the prize would go up to fifty dollars on the next call. "Uh, is it like that all the time?"

"Oh, on and off. Actually, he sounded like he was using company manners. He saves the best stuff for family." Tom led me down the mushy front stairs, both of us staying to the sides where the old wood was firmest, across the road and out onto the little pier beside the bait shop. "To tell you the truth, Eddie was a bastard before anything ever happened to him, and Mother's always thrown herself into things. Even me, when I was a little thing and didn't know any better. Hell, I spent most of the first ten years of my life a Mama's Boy, for better or for worse. But, believe it or not, she was kind of wonderful. She used to decorate that old dump six ways from Sunday for every holiday. She dressed so nice when she taught school that people stopped to watch us walk by. She took me to movies I had no business going to; I could quote Audrey Hepburn and Natalie Wood at length by the time I was in first grade. Good skills for a growing boy. I can't tell you how far it got me in my Boy Scout troop." Tom's face looked like he was joking but his voice quavered. He cleared his throat and dusted his hands together. "Anyway, that's them now. It's nauseating, but it's home."

"You're being kind of mean, aren't you?"

"Yeah, I am. I don't think I can help it. It's meanness toward them keeps me from being just like them. And darlin', if I was like them I'd slit my wrists and shit my britches." He picked up a few of the little shells that had worked their way out of the asphalt on the street and chucked them one by one into the river as he talked. "But, so far so good. I guess that's something you and I have in common. Your mother's dead and mine's locked away with Eddie, and somehow we're still here. 'So far so good' is about all we can claim right now." He turned and looked me full in the eyes, and I knew that, no matter what ever came or went between us, Tom knew just how loose a grip on you life could have sometimes. Just knowing that made me feel better, and worse.

Chapter Four

Before long Tom and I spent as much time together as my grandmother would allow or as much as I could steal. This meant some creative sneaking on my part, since I worked in the café before and after school, and spent more than a few nights piled up in the same bed as my sister. That left sitting on the trailer's steps, or now and then in the café after the afternoon shift under the scowling scrutiny of my family and the cloying curiosity of Linda the waitress and Butch the cook, who were likely to be hanging around grinning at us in a way that made us both nervous. It didn't take long before he suggested I come along on some of his nighttime walks. As soon as I got a taste of that freedom, I didn't care who I had to lie to, bribe or drug in order to get more. And that desire put me in direct conflict with my little sister and her dog.

Martha was a stringy, sallow eight year old with our mother's blonde hair and our father's dark-fringed eyes. While she wasn't anything remotely like cute, she had potential. Martha had also acquired two things during our mother's illness, and one since her death. The first two were a deep mean streak, and a taste for blackmailing me at every opportunity. Watching me and reporting on my every move had become her main connection, first to our mother and now to our grandmother. It was as if she recognized that in order to break through to either of these women, each preoccupied with her own brand of survival, she had to constantly come up with something dramatic and alarming. I provided the fodder for her relationships with the women in our family. "I'm tellin'!" had become her response to just about everything she saw me do. Her dresser drawer had filled up with the bribes I had to offer to keep her mouth shut, my half of the

Halloween candy, the little silver ring I'd gotten for Christmas, every hair barrette or Cracker Jack prize I had ever owned.

I worried about Martha, though, much as I hated to admit it. In all the years we were shut up with our mother and the terribleness of her disease, I'd never seen her shed a tear. She didn't cry when she was alive, and she didn't cry when she died. When she forgot, she sucked on her two middle fingers the way she had when she was a baby, but as soon as she realized she was doing it she yanked them out of her mouth with an expression that dared anybody to even acknowledge that she did it. I wondered sometimes how long Martha's meanness could hold out. Only once in a while could you see beneath it, and what I saw often made me come up with a tease or a little torture that put that meanness right back in place.

The third thing, and soon the most important thing in Martha's world, was a small, wiry haired black terrier that showed up at the trailer a few days after we moved to Pascagoula. The dog announced her presence under the front steps by rushing me, teeth snapping inches from my ankles, as Grandmother, Martha and I set out for the early shift at the café before school. I let loose a shriek, school books and papers flying, and launched myself from the bottom step up onto the hood of Grandmother's old tan Chevy, parked a few feet from the door. Martha, who had done little laughing of any kind since our mother had died, whooped until she bent double and ran back into the trailer for a piece of leftover pork chop from supper. I thought surely after such a vicious performance the little animal would growl at her, or at least slink away, but with me and our grandmother watching, mouths hanging open, the dog walked calmly to my sister and removed the meat delicately, the teeth that had nearly gashed my skin barely touching the outstretched fingers. With what I could have sworn was a sideways glance at me, she flipped the piece into the air, caught it like a lizard snatching a fly, and made it disappear. She gave Martha's hand a lick, they exchanged one long look, and then and there dared man or devil to keep them apart.

Tom said the dog had been born under a trailer that had sat on our little cement foundation two years before. She had never gotten much by way of attention, and had seemed uninterested in it up 'til now. When her owners had moved into a house ten miles away she had promptly disappeared and returned to the place of her birth, where she had only occasionally been fed. Instead she lived on what she

34

could root out of the garbage or catch in the brambles and along the river's edge, and had spent most of the winter avoiding human contact altogether. Tom said he'd seen her flipping rat bodies the same way she'd flipped the pork chop, slinging them to break their necks before tearing them apart with the teeth that had threatened my ankles.

Now, though, she attached herself to my sister with a ferociousness that even I had to occasionally admire. Grandmother, who generally eyed all non-food animals with a suspicion that made me wonder how much starving she herself had done as a child, had apparently fallen in with the "poor motherless thing" crowd where my sister was concerned. When Martha wrapped her arms around the skinny creature's neck and threatened to do herself harm if not allowed to keep her, Grandmother just let out one great puff of air and declared that if she saw one wet spot on the floor or one flea in the trailer the dog was done for. By some miracle, in an area that harbored more vermin than the weekly DDT trucks could fog out of existence, we saw not a single flea. Tom said either the steady diet of red beans and rice that Martha sneaked home to her from the café produced enough gas so no flea would get near her, or the dog was so crazy that none could stand to be on her. As for wet spots, my sister rode herd on her so closely that she'd have had to pee on the girl's feet to have done it inside, when my sister came home from the café and they reunited with a joy I'd only heard of with the word "prodigal" attached. Then the two of them would lie on the floor and stare into each others eyes like lovers, the dog pawing herself forward until they were nose to nose while my sister stroked her and crooned to her about what a pretty girl she was, what a special girl. Sometimes it went on for hours, girl and dog ending up dead asleep in a pile, locked together so that you had to step over them to get anywhere at all. I liked dogs, but the two of them made me nauseous.

In addition to filling us in on the details of her origin and speculating on her flealess state, Tom also swore the dog's name was Martha. I was pretty sure it was just his skewed sense of humor, but in the way that Southern people have of taking the strange not only as simple fact but dressing it up and running it up a flagpole, everyone treated the "coincidence" with casual approval. In the way that people let cars sit on their lawns until everything the environment could reclaim had rotted or scorched off of them, with the same laconic neglect that kept houses from being painted, diseases from being treated or long-lost cousins from being denied squatters' rights on the living room couch, no one questioned the name or sought to change it. Eventually they were treated as a unit by everyone, as though it was as natural as anything to say "Call Martha in for supper. And give Martha a bath; she smells like she tied up with a skunk."

Since the coincidence of the names made their lives one long running joke, people accepted the dog's generally unstable nature with benign approval. The fact that she was likely to launch herself at your knees, snarling and snapping, at the slightest hint of a threat that only she could discern, became just part of the folklore of Martha and Martha. I began to appreciate the wisdom of what Tom had done, since the other end of benign neglect gave quite a few of the town's more irritable folks the tendency to see animals the way my grandmother did. In a dog shooting town like Pascagoula I counted snarling, snapping little Martha's survival as nothing short of a miracle.

Martha became so loyal to Martha that she saw every little move as a possible threat to her new mistress. You couldn't get up to change the channel without a little black blur full of teeth slashing the air in front of your nose. Grandmother began carrying a flyswatter with her, waving it menacingly when the two of them were near, threatening to "tear that little booty up" if she got so much as a nick. It was clear from their combined response that, no matter which booty she was talking about, she would have to go through the other one to get at it. The only thing that kept my sister from having no human contact at all was the prohibition of dogs at her school and, on health department orders, at the café. Every morning began with the two Marthas locked together in a miserable embrace that only ended when Grandmother threatened to call the dog man and put an end to this foolishness once and for all. Every evening began with a reunion worthy of *Lassie Come Home* and went on until somebody couldn't take the staring and crooning any longer and chased them outside, or they fell asleep. I hated to admit it, but I was envious of the love they shared. But that didn't mean it made my life any easier.

Soon after I met Tom I was to find out that insomnia was another thing he and I had in common. Tom spent more time sneaking down from his second story bedroom and walking Pascagoula's late-night shadows than he did sleeping. He swore he had walked every inch of town, had done it once stark naked just because he was pretty sure he could get away with it. When he was outside in the middle of the night, he said, he felt like the last person on earth. Sometimes he liked that feeling, but sometimes he wanted someone else along, just to know that what he imagined, that everyone else was long gone, wasn't true. Eventually he came looking for me.

"Listen," he had said on one of the first afternoons he'd walked me partway to the café from school, "Just about the only time this town is tolerable is between midnight and dawn. If I come get you sometime want to go walking?" I did. I did more than anything. It was already clear to me that school wasn't going to be the center of my life here any more than it had been in Biloxi. I needed Tom to be my friend, to give me something to hold onto. The prospect of doing something as strange and forbidden as walking in Pascagoula at midnight made me feel happy and daring, two feelings that I hadn't had in years, and I carried the idea around inside like a wonderful secret, one that might make the days tolerable. I just had to figure out how to get away from Martha.

Although my sister and I had our own rooms in the trailer, she often insisted on sleeping with me, never admitting to being scared or lonely or wanting her mother, but just showing up with her chin sticking out and "I dare you to stop me" in her eye. At first I didn't much mind; after all, in spite of the way we treated one another in the daytime, if anyone understood how bad her nights could be, I did. All the things I had seen at thirteen and fourteen she had seen at and six and seven. I might want to strangle her, but we had the bond of shell-shocked veterans, and that understanding went a long way at midnight.

The problem was, once Martha the dog showed up she slept on my feet and growled any time I made a move to do so much as turn over in the middle of the night. It was Tom who came up with the idea of doping the dog with the bottle of paregoric that his mother kept for toothaches. Her ability to catch food in the air and swallow it in one gulp betrayed her in the end; whenever we had arranged for me to sneak out and join him for a midnight walk, I would lace a couple of my grandmother's Vienna sausages with the pilfered opiate and hide them, carefully wrapped in cellophane, in the center of the stretchy top of my pajamas, between my breasts. It was easy to slip them to Martha once my sister was asleep. Before long the little terrier would drop into a snoring slumber, not unrouseable but not interested in anything I might be doing either.

It was a testament to Martha's general hatred of me that she didn't start following me around and stirring up suspicion. A sausage snatched out of the air was one thing. Affection for more than one member of the race that had neglected her for so long seemed more than she could manage. I didn't care. All I wanted was to be free to meet Tom in the middle of the night and walk and talk about whatever came into our minds. Sometimes we talked about family and school and what we would do when we were old enough to leave Pascagoula, but neither of us seemed to believe it would really happen and so often we ended up just walking around in the dark, enjoying being strange and sad. Eventually we settled on a subject that we both liked a lot, and it became the basis for our friendship for weeks. What we could really relate to was death. If anything, Tom was more obsessed with dying than I was.

Of course, we covered the Singing River and the Indians first.

Chapter Five

Pascagoula was as proud of its resident spirits as any little Southern town. In an area of the country where the dead and the living shared space quite comfortably, separated by a veil that nobody seemed to think was all that impenetrable, the Legend of the Singing River could go toe to toe with any Southern tale of courthouse haunts or swamp fire spooks. I'd heard it first when I'd been about three years old, from my grandfather, who in his varying degrees of drunken friendliness could, as my grandmother often complained, "talk the paint off a wall." He'd told it to me about twice a year until we came to live so close, and about once a month ever since, bobbing his head and drawing me in with a crooked grin and a stringy, tattooed arm around my shoulder, beginning, as he began every story he told me, with "Now, Doll—." It was the same nickname he called Martha, marking him as the only one in the immediate vicinity who seemed to know her from her dog, a fact, given his dedication to Jim Beam, that I had considerable reason to doubt. But in his alcohol haze he did manage to do one thing that no one else in the family would do. As sideways as his approach was, in the wake of having the real thing rammed right down our throats, he didn't hesitate to tell me, again and again, a romantic and mysterious tale that made death sound like it could be more than just helplessness and pain.

"Now, Doll," the story would begin, and even though he pulled me into a circle of whiskey-tinged, unwashed funk that made me breathe through my mouth during the telling, I always felt a thrill of anticipation. Truth be told, my grandfather and I had adored one another for my whole life, and even though by the time I was twelve he embarrassed me and I did my best to ignore him most of the time, I loved hell out of him still. "Now, Doll, I go'n told you just like it was told to me, and you know I wouldn't lie to you now." For a man who wasn't himself a Cajun he had their way of talking down perfect. It stood to reason, since he spent most of his waking hours warming the barstools of every little bayou juke joint between Mobile and New Orleans. His cronies, as my grandmother called them, were legion, and in bayou country they were like as not to be Cajun. "Once upon a time this here river was where a tribe of Indians lived—the Pascagoula Indians. They was just as quiet a bunch of folks as you could want, didn't hurt nobody, minded they own business, just fished and trapped and lived on the water." I had a mental vision of the Pascagoula that went back a long way and was tinged by more television Indians than real ones, but I still thought of them as my Indians the way Pascagoula High School students thought that panthers were their panthers just because they had a school mascot of the same name. "Now, over 'bout where the Back Bay is nowadays there was a mess of wild Indians called the Biloxis. They was meaner'n snakes, looters and killers and what-not. Anyways, the chief of the Pascagoula Indians had a boy who one way or t'other caught sight of the daughter of the Biloxi chief, who was a pretty gal, and that boy decided right then and there that he wanted to carry her to his people and marry her. So he and his braves snuck over to the Back Bay and grabbed up that Biloxi gal and hauled her home. Well, when the Pascagoula all run out to see what the commotion was, the chief said 'We are done for for sure, because they are going to come over here and kill every blessed one of us, and take the young'uns to do the slave work for them. Ain't no apology going to stop it and ain't no giving her back going to stop it. So we got to decide right here what we're going to do.' And you know what they decided to do?"

I always shook my head "no," and even though the story had hardly varied a word to one side or the other of the legend in all the years I'd heard it, a part of me who had never quite stopped believing that my grandfather was somehow capable of the supernatural always thought maybe this time he would make it turn out different. "They decided that if they was go'n die anyway, they was go'n go out the way they wanted and not shot and scalped and their papooses taken for Biloxi slaves." Of course, he'd filled in the details of the well known legend in his own way. He'd had his own television influences to draw on, but the historical inaccuracies didn't detract from the tension one bit. I knew what was coming, and I loved it. "So they all joined hands, and took to singing their death song, 'Whooo—whoo—whoo—. Whoo—whoo—whoo," his voice dropped low so I would lean in even closer, "and man, woman and child, that Biloxi gal too, all walked into that river until the water took 'em and they didn't come up no more." Now and then he would choke on these last moments of the Pascagoulas' lives. I would fight back the urge to tear up with him, imagining those stoic, noble people singing their dignified way toward death rather than have it come and steal them. "And on some nights you go down to the graveline, on down the river a ways, you can still hear that 'Whoo—whoo—whoo—.' calling to you. Now you be careful, Doll," he would always add this last, "'cause you got Indian in you, so be careful if you go listenin' for them. They just might sing you into the river with them." In one fell swoop my grandfather had reinforced three of the most influential beliefs in my life: that stories were the most wonderful thing on earth, that my smidgen of Choctaw blood set me apart and a little above all my peers, and that too close an association with bodies of water was likely to end in death. In a land where dirt had to be dredged up and leveled off to make anything stick up above sea level, where the entire economic and recreational structure depended on the ocean and the bayous, I couldn't swim a lick. Neither could Granddaddy. But he sure could talk when the topic and the mood was right. I loved him so much I couldn't stand it, and hated the fact that the older I got the harder he was to be around. His stories had gotten more and more disjointed, and now and then I wasn't sure he even cared if I was there to hear them or not; he seemed to be talking to a whole world of people in his head and I was out here in the world he was drinking to get away from. But I always sat and listened to the story about the Indians.

Tom and I talked about the Pascagoula lots of nights, walking along the edge of the river and looking off toward the south where the tribe was supposed to have walked in, but in spite of the fact that both my grandfather and Tom swore they'd heard the river sing I tended toward only a feigned belief in the song's existence, much less its source. I loved the story, but I couldn't bring myself to actually believe it. I valued the Pascagoula purely for what they did for me; they made a bridge between me and my grandfather, and they created a way for Tom and me to talk about dying.

"Tell you one thing," Tom said as we sat at the end of the pier beside the bait shop on a purloined night and strained to hear something mysterious in the slow water and the breeze, "Those villagers knew there are things worse than dying. Lots worse. I mean, I'd rather be dead than live like my brother."

I thought for a long time before I answered. To tell the truth, Eddie wasn't the one that scared me. What scared me was Mr. Carmody and his silent spot inside the shop, and Mrs. Carmody with her frantic reassurances and her constant motion, and the way she never really looked at anything while she lifted, fed, washed, massaged and chattered. At least Eddie's anger at the world and at her seemed real. Mrs. Carmody gave me the feeling, a little like my grandfather when he was really drunk, that she was off somewhere and just her body was here, spinning like a top. She didn't even look at Eddie. It was as though she'd shut herself up inside of something that both bound her to and protected her from her broken oldest son and her broken life, and everyone—me, Mr. Carmody, and worst of all Tom, were shut outside. Tom fluttered against that barrier like a bird seeking company in its own reflection. Every step he made was defined by it, even though most of those steps were heading in the other direction. But even when he was most determined to be funny or smart or sly or even silly and girly, anything but lonely and aching, he kept returning in fact or in thought to hurl himself again and again against the glass.

Visiting the Carmody house wasn't so much hard as it was sad. Grandmother, who as far as I knew hadn't set eyes on Mrs. Carmody since we'd moved in, generally gave me the rent check to take over on the first of every month, which wasn't so bad since, after the first strange time, I could get away after just a brief hello. Tom would haul me there under some pretense like homework or even to just demonstrate that there was an important female his own age in his life, but I never did much more than smile and wave as I passed through the living room to the kitchen or the dining room or, more often, straight out the back door after grabbing or dropping off whatever had to be grabbed or dropped. I always had the feeling that Tom was just visiting as well. He'd bluster into the living room, making a show of it that I didn't understand until I realized that we were always in danger of catching her in the act of bathing, dressing or adjusting her inert son in his big hospital bed. "Hello Mother!" he'd shout as we came up the house's long front stairs, talking to me over his shoulder as loudly as if I'd been in the next county. She'd answer before we got into the living room, calling out "Hello Tom! Is that your Kate with you? Come in and say hello to Eddie, Kate!" Or she'd call, with somewhat more urgency, "Oh, Tom! Could you and Kate go around back and come in that way? I've just mopped the floor," or "Eddie's napping right now, dear. I'm sure he'd love to visit later." It didn't take me long to understand that this was code; Eddie couldn't have napped if he'd wanted to under the barrage of television and Mrs. Carmody, and the living room floor looked like it hadn't been mopped in years. The Carmody household was in serious disarray, a condition that embarrassed me mostly because it reminded me of how ours had been when we too had been consumed by trying to both feed and hide the monster that was the centerpiece of our lives.

When Tom said what he said, that he'd rather be dead than live like Eddie did, I thought it might be safe to ask him something that had paced like a hungry tiger at the edges of my thoughts for years, but that troubled me so much I hardly let myself think it, much less say it out loud. I didn't know how Tom would respond to what I was going to ask him, but it had been on my mind for so long it felt like an extra organ I'd grown, one that was there like a heartbeat whenever I stopped working really hard at drowning it out. "Tom, do you ever wish he was dead?"

He looked at me for a long time, not angry or embarrassed, just with his head cocked to one side, studying me closely. "Honestly, Katie, I think it was a lot easier to wish he was dead when he was just the pain in the ass older brother who treated me like I had cooties and told all his friends I kept Mother's old fox stole in my GI Joe duffel bag. Nowadays wishing him dead seems like mercy, like it would be scary for a minute but peaceful in the long run. I'm so mad at him for getting hurt I don't know if I want him to be peaceful yet." He sighed one of his deep sighs. "I'll tell you another thing. Him being dead might make it worse. I don't know if it would liberate my mother or kill her outright. There's all sorts of stuff so tangled up in that that you can't think about it and imagine you've got it all."

"It can make your head hurt, huh."

"Well you ought to know, girl." He leaned back against the side of the bait shop and I knew he was going to press something I wasn't sure I wanted pressed. "You don't ever talk about it."

"Talk about what?" I was going to try to dodge this, even as I felt my own wings batter against a too-familiar pane of glass.

"Kate, most of the time you act like you just dropped in here from another planet, like before you were in that trailer park you were nowhere at all. Like having a dead mother and a missing daddy just happened to be the way you showed up and we all might as well accept it. It makes me feel weird about getting all the attention, if you know what I mean."

"Like, you don't like showing me yours unless I show you mine?"

"Honey, I gave up on that kind of thing a long time ago. Mine just kind of hangs out there whether I want it to or not. These are my people, after all. They knew Eddie when he played football and went hunting and did all the things a good old boy does. When he was a native son of the South." Tom was right. This tangle was almost too big to think about. I knew he wasn't just thinking, he was comparing. "And they knew me from the time I first cried and begged not to have to go fishing with my daddy but to stay home and play loud music on Mother's hi-fi and dance the fox trot instead. In fact," his voice had been strong and soft up to this point, but now it broke with the force he had to use to get the words out, "you're asking the wrong question of the wrong person. Talk to my folks and ask them who should be alive and who should be dead. Then come back here and talk to me about who's showing what to who."

Suddenly I missed my daddy more than I had ever missed anything in the world. Not the one from the past few years, but the one before that. The one who, although he'd always been a hard man to get close to, had been big enough and tough enough to give me the feeling he could protect me from anything, and that he would throw himself between me and anything that could hurt me. As it turned out, I was wrong. What had come to us had hurt him too, had changed him and sent him packing, first in his mind and then for real. "You know how your mother is with Eddie?"

"Uh-huh."

"That's how my daddy was with my mother."

"Uh-huh."

"Only it wasn't just him." I felt as though I was underwater myself, trying to push the words against something heavy. "It was me too. In fact it was so much me that I can't hardly remember him. I

44

can't hardly remember anything. We were like," I waved my hands around, stroking the air as though trying to coax the sounds I couldn't make from it, "like we were asleep and dreaming two separate dreams but could kind of see each other in them. We were just sleepwalking and sleepwalking." My throat hurt but there was a part of me that this talking helped shake loose just a little, as if I'd been working forever on the hardest puzzle in the world and one tiny piece had clicked into place.

"Well it seems he managed to wake up long enough to leave." He'd never laid eyes on my father but I felt a rush of pleasure at the contempt in his voice. Part of me, though, couldn't help defending one of the only two living people other than me who knew what it had been like.

"I know. But you know that worry you've got about what would happen to your mother if Eddie died?"

"Uh-huh."

"Well, it happened to him. It was like—," I was reaching back into the dark, toward the lesser of two evils, to the parent who, for better or for worse, was still alive enough to get good and mad at. "It was like he ran down, all of a sudden, like the battery just ran out. I mean, he was a son of a bitch and proud of it when I was a little kid, and I mostly hated his guts but I was his. I knew him. After it was all over he'd go to work and come home and sit in front of the television and smoke cigarettes. That was just about it. He'd sit there and after a while he'd go to bed and then he'd get up and go to work again. Martha would go sit on his lap sometimes and suck on her two middle fingers like when she was a baby and he'd rub her head, just rub and rub, the two of them staring toward the TV like they were staring at a blank wall. He'd come to every now and then and ask me if we'd had supper or if we had clean clothes, but other than that, it was like he was trying to die right along with her."

"Who took care of you?"

"We did. It was easy." I sighed, rubbing my eyes and shrugging. "Compared to taking care of her, taking care of two healthy girls and one healthy man was a piece of cake. I gotta say, though, we could have used him. Heck, we could have used anybody. I swear, there were days when Martha went to school in holey underwear and socks that didn't match, and I remember going a solid week once in the same skirt just because I was too blanked out to wash another one.

45

By the time we moved out of Biloxi there were kids giving me the stink eye, but we didn't cause any trouble with the grownups until Martha had a meltdown right in the middle of giving a book report on "The Littlest Angel" at Christmas. Some kid snickered at her and she punched him right in the nose. She sat on the school nurse's office until they called me and I explained that our mother had died and we didn't have any way home until the bus came after school anyway. They don't let you get out of work early on an Air Force base for some little thing like your kid getting in trouble at school. By then we knew we were going to be moving to Pascagoula anyway, so we just stuck it out."

"And how are you now?"

"Me? Fine as frog hair," I laughed. "I'm thinking about taking up cigarettes and whiskey and moving to New Orleans."

"Well hell, Katie, that's the best idea you've ever had. Say the word and I'll go with you."

"We'll pool our vast resources and start a new life," I grinned and butted him with my shoulder. "I'll become a world famous writer and you'll find a sugar daddy that will keep us both in style. It's that or the river. Living or dying." I stood up and squinted downriver. "I wish I knew how I'm going to do either one. But I guess right now I better go home and sleep before I have to get up for the breakfast rush. You coming?" I jumped off the land end of the pier and started back toward the trailer.

"Not just yet." I could barely hear his voice, but could see his eyes glowing just a little, as if they were moist. It embarrassed me, so I waved and started to trot.

Chapter Six

There had been a time, when I was small and before the world had turned upside down, that I loved school. I loved the ABC's that lined the walls above the blackboards in first grade, the merry go round I got flung off of on the playground in second, the way my third grade teacher's arms had little bat wings made of flesh under them that I could feel wiggle when she hugged me. I loved the way I could rub two pencils together real fast, and the heat when I pressed them up against the little pit underneath my nose. I loved making Mardi Gras floats out of shoe boxes and house plants out of sweet potato eyes and carrot tops. I loved writing with my head so far down on my desk my teachers told me I was going to go blind, clutching my pencil so tight it raised a bump on my middle finger that never did go away. Most of all, I loved reading. From a time so far back I couldn't remember it I had read and read and read. Not only did I read, I remembered. Not only did I remember, I was eager to tell anybody who'd listen what I had read and what I thought about it. Until she got sick, my mother had looked at me with a kind of wonder, swearing that, granddaddy notwithstanding, I might have gotten the desire to talk from her, but that she'd never in her life talked about the kind of things I did. When I was little, she might well have liked me. But during the sleepwalking years she couldn't stand the noise. And after a while, neither could I. By the time I got to Pascagoula High School and my freshman year, I could have cared less about talking to most people, but I still read everything I could get my hands on, trying to figure out how anyone could create the miracle that was a book, and school was, more than anything, a place to be away from home. I wanted to travel to places

I'd never been and see people and places I'd never seen, just as soon as I was old enough. Until then, I was stuck.

PHS was hardly half a mile from Carmody's Trailer Park but there was the breakfast rush at the café to deal with before my school day even started. The Rebel was half a mile up Little Red Road and right on Canty, then a mile on toward the shipyard gate. Every morning we drove to the café and after the breakfast shift I had to walk the mile back in the early morning humidity. By the time I got to school my curly hair was frizzed to the point of nappiness and I reeked of bacon grease so badly I was sure that cats would follow me down the street. This was, I thought, the least of the burdens of being raised in the Rebel Café.

Every weekday morning we got up at five thirty, drove to the café to get the coffee going, greeted Butch, the beefy black woman who made the best peach cobbler in Mississippi and who never mentioned feeding her husband and two sons every day at the kitchen's back door, and tied on the change aprons in anticipation of the rush. By seven-thirty the smell of bacon and grits and hot coffee made me dizzy, and it was all I could do to keep from "accidentally" dumping one of those pots of hot liquid into the lap of one or another of the shipyard crew.

I hadn't worked in the Rebel Café before we moved to Pascagoula; I had just enjoyed being the favorite little girl of myriad shipyard workers when we visited. From age three to when I was twelve, when our mother declared that the Rebel was a bad influence and forbade me from hanging around in its cool, dark interior on hot summer vacation days, I had thought of myself as a kind of Shirley Temple, sitting on grown men's knees and charming them out of their pocket change. My tendency to be talkative to the point of exhausting my family had marked me early on as clearly my grandfather's child within the circle of my relatives, but when I was little I was right at home among the ever-shifting clientele of the café. No sooner would one begrimed welder heave himself up from the little cluster of tables in the back, where the hangers-around liked to watch me hold court, than a fresh set of ears would take his place.

Now things had changed, and not for the better. I didn't want to chatter any more, and if I had, the whole tone of my relationship with those men had changed. Although there were always the lifers, the men who spent twenty years going in and out that shipyard gate and

48

passing through the Rebel in both directions, most of the workers rotated in and out, moving on to the oil rigs out in the gulf or construction sites up North after a few months. Something about me having a chest that stuck out in front and hair that hung halfway down my back made the new crop of good old boys get stuck somewhere between thoughtlessly silly and downright mean. Like hyenas, they worked best in packs, and you could count on the same ones to sit together every morning and torment me. I couldn't pull the lever on the milk machine without some welder whining "Oh Baby, milk that cow!" to a chorus of laughs that would make you think the Red Skelton Show was on. My grandmother was useless at stopping them; they had a way of touching me just at the back of my knees as I walked by, making me jump so hard that I dropped whole orders of fried eggs and short stacks onto the café floor. I was too embarrassed to say anything to her about the things written in catsup on the plates I bussed, or the quarter tips stretched out toward me and dropped at the last minute so that I would have had to bend over to pick them up. I didn't do it, not once, but every time a quarter rolled across the café's sandy linoleum I quietly reached into the pocket of the change apron and slipped one from there into the front pocket of my jeans. I didn't care whether that tip quarter was ever found or not; the way I figured it I was owed for all I was going through, and if the change box came up short a few dollars a week then my grandparents could take it out of the Social Security check that they'd gotten every month since Martha and I had come to live with them. Besides, saving for my getaway, whether it would be to New Orleans like Tom and I talked about or not, was one of the things that kept me from going insane. I kept those quarters in a cigar box at the bottom of the old toy box alongside my journal, and now and then I'd go in and stare at them like they were leaves in the bottom of a teacup.

Pretty soon, though, I acquired something else that stood between me and, I was sure, some kind of home for teenagers who just lie down one day and don't get up again. I discovered there were ways of being a little nuts that not only weren't scary, they were downright fun. The thing that kept me together, other than Tom Carmody, was Claire Doucette and her very strange family.

Every morning after the breakfast rush was done I ran through my getting ready for school ritual. Even though I had showered the night before and was fully clothed, I always scrubbed the exposed parts of my body with soap and water from the café's kitchen sink, hoping to get the smell of the place at least tamed a bit. Then I grabbed a piece of ham, slapped it between two halves of one of Butch's mouthwatering biscuits, sneaked a Barq's Root Beer from the cooler under the counter and set out for school. I always met Claire on a little bridge that crossed over a swampy inlet halfway between our two houses and, on the route to school, and we planned our strategy for getting through another day at PHS.

Claire was to me what Martha was to Martha. The minute we set eyes on one another we knew we were kin, and that was that. Tom, who introduced us on my first day of high school life in Pascagoula, even said sometimes that he wished he never had, because if he made me talk, Claire made me laugh. It didn't hurt that the Doucettes were the kind of people you tell stories about years later and everyone believes you are an A-1 liar, because these things couldn't possibly be true. No matter how bad I felt, once I'd been introduced to the sprawling tumult of the Doucettes I knew I had a place to go where I could laugh. They were nuts, every last one of them, and being around them made me feel like I could breathe again. Even in the laconic South, the Doucettes stood out as a peck short of a bushel.

I never could figure out just how many of them there were. I could count Claire, like me the oldest daughter, but from a daddy that she claimed had taken off before she was even born and that her mother Jean simply refused to acknowledge. Then there was her brother Francis, a genuine child prodigy at fourteen, who played trumpet in the PHS Band, and in a jazz club on weekends that the band members had to sneak him in the back door of and pay off a couple of deputies in free beers to let him stay. Then there were sisters Regina and Marie-Therese, thirteen and eleven, who got sent home from school for wearing makeup about twice a week and were as boy crazy as any girls I'd ever seen, and Kenny and Keith, a couple of twenty year old twin cousins who had moved in one day last fall and never left. Add Jean and Jean's husband Richard and Jean's mother Gran'mere, and the friends and boyfriends and girlfriends that came and went as regular as the tide, and visiting the Doucette household was a lot like visiting a carnival.

The house had been added on to by Claire's daddy Richard, who was a carpenter and, according to Claire, could fix or build anything you could imagine. The original house had been a little square wooden bungalow with a little front porch, like half the houses in Pascagoula. Richard had added bedrooms like blocks on the sides and back, giving the place a cobbled together but sturdy appearance on its enormous lot. The house and yard, which backed up to a marshy little inlet with a willow tree that looked cool and inviting, and were surrounded on the other three sides by a smart chain link fence, would have been appealing inside and out, except for two things.

Adding to the chaos was what Claire sarcastically referred to as "the livestock." Although Jean Doucette swore, like half the middle aged women in the South, that she had been raised genteel, and that marriage to Richard Doucette had reduced her circumstances considerably, telling stories of her youth that sounded as though she had been given a pair of white gloves at birth and never removed them until she got trapped into mothering this motley brood, Jean had a passion for two kinds of creatures. One made getting into the house a study in fear and craftiness that kept Tom and me leaning on the gate discussing techniques for long minutes before ever making the attempt. The other made sitting down a hazard and coming out wearing a fur coat a certainty. Claire's mother had dedicated her life to raising watch geese and pink cats.

Jean said that her father had kept geese on his estate in Louisiana to keep thieves at bay. After the wedding, certain that his beloved daughter was going to be keeping company with lowlifes and thieves at best, he had brought her a pair of tiny, fuzzy pips and, in a frenzy of mothering that Claire swore had never extended to her or her siblings, the pregnant bride had cosseted the goslings as if they were her own babies. They had identified her as "mother" right away, and if parted from her set up such a strangled, desperate honking that she had set up her brand new baby playpen next to the bed so she and her amused husband could get some sleep.

"It's a wonder she didn't plop me in there with them," Claire commented in one of her long declarations about her early history, a story that endlessly fascinated and repulsed her, and that I found interesting enough to listen to even when it got repetitive. "She did get a little goofy with it for a while, sneaking a new fuzzball home every couple of months when the others started to feather out. Richard finally had to put his foot down," Claire grinned as though she could hardly imagine the lanky, easygoing man standing up to his wife. "She swore she'd never get another one but didn't figure on what horny little sons o'bitches geese can be. We've been eating goose eggs for breakfast as far back as I can remember and we still end up with a clutch or two a year. Thank goodness for the farmer's market or we'd be up to our asses in goose shit."

I'd often tried to count the flock that dominated the Doucettes' big fenced yard, but had never managed to get far since most of my counting was done at a dead run. As it turned out, geese really were good watchdogs. Not only did they set up a fuss at the approach of anyone not a part of the family, but let that someone open the chain link gate and start for the porch, and big, hissing males were on you like winged furies, followed by most of the ladies. "Ain't seen a Jehovah's Witness in ten years," Richard proclaimed proudly.

Luckily the Doucettes' screened porch had a door that opened easily. If you timed things just right and had a handful of white bread to toss around back of the house to distract them, often as not you could streak for that door and just make it through before something big and hissing grabbed hold of you and tried to beat you to death with its wings. Unfortunately, as soon as you crossed its threshold you were likely to find yourself tangled up in a pile of lazy, crazily friendly and eerily pink cats.

Jean had also owned the line from which the cats had descended since she was a little girl. They had started out, she said, as a pair of long-haired tabbies, male and female, pale gold kittens given to her by Gran'mere for her seventh birthday. She'd thought of them as living toys from the beginning, making doll babies of them while ignoring any of the practical implications of owning un-neutered, related animals that were beneath even the notice of her queenly mother and powerful father. According to Jean, she was soon up to her little eyeballs in red-gold cats, prompting their little household staff to attempt various drastic and traumatic methods to reduce the growing, hair-shedding, furniture shredding population. Jean had cried and screeched until Papa had finally listened, taking on the role of mediator and declaring that cher Jean could pick out half a dozen of her favorites, could keep two babies per year, and could not ask questions about the rest. Pink being her favorite color, the girl chose the youngest, most champagne colored of the lot, including a remarkable male and female whom she had named after her favorite movie stars. While she had lived at home things had gone according to plan. Once out from under her father's eye she had lost all control, and

52

over the ensuing years Clark Gable and Vivien Leigh and their assorted offspring had inbred with the reckless intensity of a train ripping toward an inevitable wreck. Now fully thirty years and fifteen generations later, the twenty or so feline inhabitants of the Doucette household were indeed a rosy shade of pink, were all named after Jean's favorite movie and TV stars, and were just about as unstable a pride as any normal human being could tolerate. The Doucettes' living room curtains hung in shreds, a catfight broke out every thirty seconds, and every surface not inhabited by something that looked like a hairy ballerina trying to lick her own crotch was coated in powder puff fine fuzz. The youngest litter, a troop of little hellions to whom vertical and horizontal seemed perfectly equivalent, and who spooked at the least change in the light, stalked everything that moved and made lifting one's feet off the floor fraught with the fear of bringing it down on a batting paw or flicking tail. Tom, who was as fastidious a male person as I'd ever met, tolerated the hair and the goose shit and the noise and the smells, which were considerable, because, he said, it was the most easygoing place he'd ever been in, and there was something powerful about living that close to the edge of total disaster and having fun rather than going right down the drain. Having spent considerable time circling that drain myself, I agreed. What had, in my mother's house, been chaos through desperation, this tumbledown assortment made look generous and interesting and warm. Crazy as a flock of coots, Tom said with wry joy, but better than what he faced at home by a long shot. I was glad he wasn't bent too out of shape by me loving Claire as much as I loved him.

Among her family Claire thought of herself as the normal one. She compared herself to Marilyn on the TV show The Munsters, the pretty, perky niece who lived calmly among the freaks and innocents without being affected by it at all. Maybe it was her conviction that she wasn't actually a Doucette, but the product of a short affair Jean had had before she married Richard. I didn't have the heart to tell her what I heard said behind her back, that she hauled the family around with her wherever she went and no amount of irony or smarts, both of which she had considerable, could hide the fact that she was pure Doucette and always would be. Luckily, she had the ability to walk through life in her own brand of oblivion, resulting in a kind of benign tolerance for both her family and the rest of the world. Clearly, even the idea of being a bastard kind of tickled her. I wondered if anything could knock her down.

One evening after dinner we sat in the living room watching television. Claire poked me in the ribs and whispered "Watch this," as though she was going to do a magic trick. She cleared her throat and turned to Jean, who lay stretched out on a daybed with three of her pink cats. "Mama, tell Kate about when you and my real daddy went to the amusement park on Lake Ponchartrain. I got created in the Laff in the Dark there, eh Mama?"

Jean, who had been stroking Elizabeth Montgomery, the resident queen of the cat clan, sat bolt upright, as though she'd seen her child struck by lightening. "Say what? What are you talking about, your real daddy? Richard Doucette is your daddy and I never went to Lake Pontchartrain with him nor any man. Not that I didn't get asked. I was as good as gold and never left my mama's side until Mr. Richard Doucette came and asked for my hand in marriage." She looked off into the distance as though seeing herself being given to the fine young man who had sought her out and asked for her. "Oh, he was a handsome Cajun man, and so sweet talking that my mama got over that he was a Cajun and poor to boot and said 'Why of course you can marry my Jean Josephine, but you be sweet to her because she's never been kissed nor hurt in her life. And you must promise not to take her away from me.'" She fell back on the daybed and sniffled, clearly in love with her younger self. "'Course he kept that promise, damn him."

That was true enough. Gran'mere was permanently ensconced in a bedroom that hung like an afterthought onto the back of the house. She had been there, Claire told me, ever since Jean's daddy had died some years before and it was discovered that the family outlay far exceeded its income. The servants had been dismissed and the old house boarded up and left in the middle of bayou country north of New Orleans until someone could figure out what to do with it. Whatever finery Gran'mere and Jean Josephine had had in the past, they were Doucettes now, and Claire's grandmother was with them for good. She was little and birdlike, white hair braided and coiled about her head, wrapped in a multicolored silk robe big enough to encircle her several times. She was, they said, a little touched, and so arthritic that she simply stayed in her room under a pile of cats who had discovered that she was a source of heat in the winter, and that tidbits of food fell regularly from her gnarled fingers. She spent her days watching soap operas and hollered out when she needed anything, which was, by my estimate, once every seven minutes. To make matters worse, Claire's brother Francis had gotten the brilliant idea of buying her a bullhorn so she wouldn't have to strain to be heard. Gran'mere had loved the notion of magnification but had never gotten the idea that she didn't have to scream into the thing, so that every few minutes a blast of static came from the room that sounded as if the police had surrounded the house and were making urgent but unrecognizable demands. Francis would grin and duck as a barrage of things were thrown at him by the other members of the family, and then someone would shuffle back to the bedroom to find out what it was she wanted. Since no one could understand her from afar the way they had before, his idea had neatly doubled the number of trips the family had to take to wait on her hand and foot. I figured it was a testament to how accustomed they were to chaos that nobody thought to take the thing away from her.

Claire wasn't about to let go of the discussion of her heritage. "Actually," she had somewhere acquired the affectation of beginning half her sentences with "actually." She seemed to think it made her sound like a fifteen year old sophisticate; I thought she sounded like Margaret Dumont from the Marx Brothers movies I had gotten fond of during my late night sessions with my mother. "Actually, I have a picture of Jean and my real daddy in New Orleans, her sticking out to there," she held her hand half a foot in front of her navel, "and him wearing a Merchant Marine uniform. He was blonde as a Norwegian, like me."

"And like me, I'll remind you," Jean had sat up again, ready to argue. "You got Gran'mere and my genes, and the rest got Richard's." They pronounced it "Reeshard," a sound I liked and rolled around in my mouth when I saw him out strolling around town pasting communist flyers on the light poles.

Next to my granddaddy, Mr. Doucette was the only grown man I knew who actually stayed home with his family. He didn't drink all the time like Granddaddy did, though. In fact, he was so clear-eyed, quick and sober that I always felt a little slow in his presence. He was always reading or writing, chain smoking and designing leaflets and posters that he turned out on a mimeograph machine that took up the dining room table and filled the house with a smell that I had loved since my first days of elementary school. When I asked Claire what he actually did for a living, she shrugged, flicked her blonde hair back out of her eyes for the millionth time, and said "When he's not carpentering he works for the people, organizes, helps the poor and downtrodden." For quite a long time I nodded politely and thought better of asking any more. It seemed to me that asking questions about the Doucettes just wore the luster off of them. If they were to get ordinary I didn't want to be the one making them that way. I liked them shiny and strange, and in Pascagoula, Richard was certainly both.

The first thing that stood out about Richard Doucette was that he was a bona fide Communist in Southern Mississippi. The second was that he was so charismatic that he wasn't shot on sight as he tried to hold rallies for the Negroes and the labor unions at the Pascagoula Beach Pavilion. If anyone had actually attended the rallies it might have been different, but the threat of communism was still so connected with the madness of civil rights as it played out in Mississippi that even the most ardent supporters of integration and equal rights avoided being seen in with him in groups of more than one or two. That fact had never dampened the Doucettes' enthusiasm for a rally. Twice a month the whole family would load up into the family pickup truck, which had a rickety, home-made wooden camper with big roll-out windows attached to its bed and served as a portable office, complete with mimeograph machine and a daybed for Gran'mere. They would troop out to the pavilion to listen to him speak about overcoming prejudice and giving the poor man a living wage. I loved the rallies; I went to them as often as I could lie to my grandmother about going over to Claire's to do homework. In the middle of the spectacle they created I could relax and disappear, because it was more than likely no one would ever see me. In spite of the fact that Richard, for all his radical leanings, was benignly tolerated much the way Martha and Martha were, when it came to the Doucettes' rallies Pascagoula wanted no involvement with them whatsoever, black or white, positive or negative. They could clear a park like a parade of lepers.

Being the only ones in attendance at these events didn't seem to bother the Doucettes a bit. Rather, they made family picnics of the rallies, packing ham and coleslaw and crawfish on ice and buying snow balls from the stand at the pavilion. In winter, seldom colder than fifty degrees, they built fires in the big stone grills and cooked hot dogs and beans. Francis would announce our arrival by bleating out a remarkably good version of "When the Saints Go Marching In" on his trumpet, followed by wildly embellished versions of songs like "We Shall Overcome" and "This Land is Your Land," trying, I guessed, to get the message across that we offered a little something for everyone. That "everyone," though, excluded nine tenths of the citizens of Pascagoula and, polite though they might be, they almost never hung around. I got great pleasure out of watching mothers swiftly pack up their bawling children while smiling and waving at us as though they were truly sorry we had showed up at the exact minute they had to get on home.

Tom, who never missed one if he could help it, saw the rallies as a way to go a little crazy. While Francis played, Tom took it upon himself to do his own version of a second line, the handkerchief-waving, butt-bouncing strut that was a part of every Mardi Gras parade and, he and Claire had told me, the more impressive funerals over in New Orleans. He was as good at it as anyone I'd ever seen, twirling and prancing with abandon, flashing that hanky like he was bestowing a blessing. Claire never failed to fall in behind him, her short paisley skirts and fishnet hose giving her the appearance of a Go-Go Girl let free of her cage. I held my place on the back of the truck, busily gathering the leaflets that would never be passed out, helping Jean herd the others, anything to keep from meeting Tom's eye. If he caught me watching he'd zero in on me, determined to make me dance, swooping and curling his body around mine, arms wild with the silliness of his mission. My feelings weren't in the least conflicted. I'd rather have eaten that beach sand than dance on it. But I did watch Tom and Claire and whatever Doucettes joined their display out of the corners of my eyes, and I never failed to be mad at myself for being mad at them for being able to play.

Claire took the same attitude toward education that she did about her family, the rallies, Tom, life, death and me, and so with her even school had its bearable moments. She hovered just a little above us all but relished us the way someone might relish a really great performance. She was hard to ruffle, carrying the weight and love of her family around as though she was part audience and part participant. It made her hard to tease, hard to hurt because she was just as likely to agree with you with a "well, whatcha gonna do," that placed you, what you were picking on her about and the whole rest of the world into the same category. I admired her. I'd have given anything to be like her, but when I said so she laughed. "Well, you gotta be you and I gotta be me and Tom's gotta be Tom. But it would do you some good to lighten up once in a while, no offence, Cherie." That was another thing. Claire could be as blunt as a bludgeon and never once expected that she wouldn't be appreciated for her insight and wisdom. I wondered if I would ever feel that secure in my life.

Chapter Seven

In March, Tom asked me to marry him and I turned him down. Even though I knew it wasn't even remotely possible, I also knew we both wanted something in our lives to be simple so badly that for a minute I thought about it, pretending we could overcome his liking boys more than he did girls, and my not being sure I could ever marry anybody.

It started when he sang to me and kissed me under the statue of the Virgin Mary at Our Lady of Sorrow. Pascagoula's churches were for the most part left unlocked, the threat of holy wrath being sufficient to keep most trespassers away. Going to OLS with Tom might make me a trespasser, but I reasoned that since the bible in both our religions said "Forgive us our trespasses," maybe I was just giving the Lord something useful to do. I wasn't sure whether I believed in God anyway, and even if I did now and then, my education as a Baptist had left out most everything about tolerance and understanding for other religions. My mother had told me that Catholics drank real wine in church and prayed to statues and performed all sorts of strange rituals that no one could understand, let alone use as the road to salvation. But she had never told me what those rituals were. It had never occurred to me before that she didn't know. She was my mother, and, having to find some mothering in her, I had taken her word as gospel. Now that she was gone I needed to doubt everything she had ever told me. If she was wrong, somehow she wouldn't be as gone.

Tom had been promising me that he would take me into OLS and show me where the graven images were. While everyone in Pascagoula except the third shift was doing the best they could to recover from the day's exhaustion, I gave Martha her Vienna sausages.

59

As soon as she, my sister and my grandmother were all snoring I slipped out and joined him under the live oak tree where Little Red Road met Front Street .

"You sure you want to do this?" Ever since I'd asked if I could see the inside of OLS and told him just what my people thought of his people, he had been bouncing with delight at the thought of transgression. "You aren't going to go all girl on me, are you?"

"Hell no!" Under Tom's careful tutelage I had been practicing some of the milder sins. Jealous of Claire's sophisticated look when she smoked, I had coughed and wheezed around my first cigarette before rationalizing my utter dislike for them by remembering that I shouldn't flirt with cancer in any of its forms. Now I was lying and sneaking, and I felt my father from a world away even as I reveled in the fact that even if I got caught he couldn't get to me for another year. But swear words still didn't roll off my tongue without sticking at the tip. Tom snickered at my delivery.

"HAY-ull no! Dammit to hay-ull gal, you goin' straight to hay-ull, you know that?" His attempt at talking like a redneck, delivered in that goosey voice, was as unconvincing as my swearing. In spite of his problems with pitch, Tom had always prided himself on having almost perfect diction. It was just one more thing that earmarked him as queer.

Before I could work up a sincere looking sneer, he grabbed my arm and began loping along the riverbank, toward the vague lightening of the darkness that indicated town. It was no more than a mile to Our Lady of Sorrow, even taking the dogleg route that ran along the river and up the short street that marked Pascagoula's core. The church was just off the center of town, underscoring the fact that the Catholics had been a part of Gulf coast culture long before the Baptists, whose churches were in the newer sections of the suburbs.

The night was full of noises, none of them human. Locusts thrummed in waves and now and then a distant dog would set up a high-pitched barking that would last a few minutes, cut off abruptly, and then take up again. The river was so close that we could hear the water like wind through leaves, whispering and rustling and now and then popping against the pilings of Mr. Carmody's pier. A chorus of deep bullfrog voices parted as we neared, and then came together again in our wakes. Things scurried, making me hold on tight to Tom, and to stumble as I struggled to see what we might be stepping on in the dark. I wasn't scared of much of anything; snakes or water rats or fire ants made little impression on me. But Pascagoula, like most Gulf Coast places, was full of palmetto bugs, and I'd almost run into walls running from them in the café and trailer at night. They ran into shadows, even if the shadow was a foot coming down to crunch them to greasy oblivion. They flew, taking off and ricocheting around to land on your head or in your supper. Palmetto bugs made me want to scream.

Tom, though, flowed along as though he had walked this path a thousand times and knew it with his body. Beside him I felt clumsy, a stranger who had thought him familiar, but had never seen him in his natural habitat. Even in loafers and no socks, he never slipped on the dew-sodden grass, never missed a step. As we left the river and headed toward town he seemed utterly unconcerned about getting caught crossing back yards and alleyways that I knew were under the protection of loaded shotguns and suspicious natures.

To my horror, in the stillness, he began to sing. "Benedictus qui venit inomine domini—."

I nearly yanked him off his feet as I stopped in shock.

"Do it again." To hell with shotguns. I had just found out that Tom Carmody, who couldn't say a complete sentence without making someone snort with laughter, had a singing voice that just about broke your heart.

"Do what? Let's keep going before we get dog bitten."

"Sing that song again. I didn't know you could do that."

"Altar boy. Choirboy. And years' worth of singing along with mother's hi-fi. I know the words to every old musical and pop song there is. I'll show you when we get there, okay?" He set off again as though a miracle hadn't just happened, as though we were the same as we'd been just a minute ago, before he'd made my heart hurt with a few words I couldn't even understand.

I kept quiet the rest of the way, absorbed in the shape and shadows of the approaching town. I could make out the Woolworth's that smelled like dead rats and ladies' face powder, where I sometimes sneaked breadcrumbs to the ragged little parakeets and goldfish in the back. It sat next to, and on the same foundation as, Miss Delaware's Stationery Store. Both of them had floors whose boards were so warped and far apart that you dared not carry your money in your hand for fear of watching it disappear forever into the mysterious darkness below. Martha had read a story in Ripley's Believe It or Not that Tasmanian Devils lived under the barn floors in New Zealand sheep farms and would gnaw the feet off of sheep unlucky enough to stumble and step through. Tom had told her that the owner of the Woolworth's had done just the same thing with alligators, and Grandmother had eventually given up on trying to get her to go into either store.

I could see Salmagundi, the store that had just opened in place of the old Blessings Hardware. Salmagundi sold things I had never seen before; incense, strings of little brass bells, carved wooden boxes that smelled like cinnamon, beaded curtains, candles shaped like African women. I longed to work there after school, not at the Rebel Café where I was surrounded by the sight and sound and smell of my own culture. Salmagundi made me feel shivery with desire. I was afraid it was a mirage that would one day disappear and leave me stranded in the Pascagoula ordinary.

"There she is—Our Lady." Tom's whisper pulled me back from my reverie. The church I had passed at least fifty times on walks to town stood very close to the street, no lawn, no trees between it and those that sought entry. Our Lady of Sorrows was small and white, old stucco patched with blotches of new that stood out in the artificial light. The windows were small and amber colored, giving the building a cool and mysterious look, as if anything at all could be going on within its walls. A faint but distinct glow shone from inside.

"You don't have a big stained glass window like we did at Calvary Baptist."

"Yeah, but wait'll we get inside. We've got you Baptists beat all to hell."

We paused at the bottom of the smooth white stairs that led up to the heavy wooden door. As Tom peered upward I recalled the first time I'd seen him, looking up at me from the bottom of the trailer's steps like a little kid who wanted a playmate so badly he would have accepted anything—open arms or a slap on the jaw—as long as it wasn't rejection. For just a moment all the sadness in the world washed over me. Then the look was gone and he grinned his best Bugs Bunny grin.

"Let us pray."

Although Tom had assured me that he came to Our Lady all the time and that no one was here and no one would object if they were, I had a terrible fear that the door would creak open. As far as I was concerned God's house was haunted. I was as afraid of what I would find inside as I would have been upon entering a tomb. My mother had so impressed me with her sense that Catholics were just this side of devil-worshippers that all the worldliness I could muster couldn't keep me from feeling that, once I entered Our Lady of Sorrows, I might never come out again.

The foyer was lit by small sconces, high on each side of the entry to the chapel. A big crucifix hung above what looked like a bird bath, until I remembered seeing people crossing themselves with holy water in movies on TV. To my surprise, Tom touched his fingers to the water's surface and did just that.

"Do I have to…" I wasn't at all sure what to do. Was it a sin not to do what a religion said you were supposed to do in that very religion's house? Or was it a sin to go through the motions when it wasn't your idea of God and religion anyway? Either way, if I was in a believing mood I stood a fair chance of having to beg someone's pardon for this whole enterprise. I had to trust Tom.

"No, darlin.' If you were a good Catholic girl you'd have to cover your head with a handkerchief, but I think it's all right. Just do what you'd do among the heathen Baptists."

He led me forward into the nave, from under the tiny balcony out into the big, dark room, softly illuminated by lights that shone upward from alcoves set high into the walls. At the front was another crucifix, this one looming above the altar and bearing a Jesus that was bloody and in obvious pain. Somehow, even though his body was twisted to one side and his eyes rolled upward, I wasn't the least impressed. This Messiah seemed to be a product of cheap theatrics and cheaper plaster. I hated to admit it, but I was feeling a little smug about the superiority of our symbols over theirs. Artistically, our crosses had them cold.

In fact, our crosses seldom had a Jesus on them at all. I had one on a gold chain in my jewelry box, uncool to wear but still a precious gift for my sixth birthday from a mother who had looked as though she was bestowing a blessing herself when she fastened it around my neck. It was simple and pretty, and when I was little I wore it with the same feeling I had when I carried my teddy bear. It meant I was all in one piece, that I was safe and that my mother knew where I was. I had stopped wearing it when it stopped giving me that feeling. Still, I felt a swell of emotion thinking about it, as though the idea of hanging a

63

simple, elegant cross around her child's neck was an idea my mother had thought up herself and just allowed the rest of Christianity to borrow.

Just when I was about to inform Tom that I was keeping score and that his team was coming up short, I saw the statue of Our Lady. It took my breath away.

This was no ordinary, mass produced icon. This Virgin Mother was carved of burnished wood that shone so warm in the alcove's light that, in spite of its uniform color, she looked warm and alive, as though real blood coursed through her veins. She stood, as tall as a real woman, just to the right of the altar, her bare toes so close to the alcove's edge that it looked as though she was gripping with them, slightly off balance, like a diver deciding whether or not to jump. She was dressed the way I would have expected her to be, long robes, head covered. No part of her body was visible except for her face, feet and hands.

It was the combined force of that face and those hands that caught me. My acquaintance with Jesus' mother had been mostly dictated by holidays; everything I had been taught about her seemed centered around her son's birth and his death, so most of the time I envisioned her either sitting placidly beside his straw-filled manger or weeping tormentedly but majestically at the foot of his cross. Even the statues I saw in front yard grottoes looked poised and serene, hands resting on a draped chest or raised toward an invisible God as though assuredly pointing the way toward something comforting and perfect. I had never thought about her as a mother, let alone a person who felt the way that any person might feel on any day of her life. I had never thought of her as a woman showing the most human of expressions— loss so great as to defy sanity.

This Mary wasn't young. In fact, her carved face looked like photos I had seen in the National Geographic at the library, pictures of women who had lived long, hard lives in the desert and showed every moment on their worn faces. Although handsome in an exhausted way, her cheeks were a little sunken, like my grandmother's at night after she'd taken out her false teeth. Her brow was lined beneath the robe and there was a furrow between her brows, as though she had spent all her life squinting at hot sun and arid land. I could imagine her dusty, bug bitten and with callouses on her feet and hands. She looked too real. She made me nervous.

Mary's hands were extended out in front of her and almost cupped together. She stared not at us, nor off into a peaceful distance, as most Virgin Mothers seemed to do, but down at her own hands. The look on her face held me suspended, afraid to look and afraid to look away. It looked as though she had held in those two cupped hands the most precious thing in the world, and had dropped it to shatter on the floor at her feet. Beneath the carved wooden halo that encircled her head and that, I thought, surely must offer some kind of protection against such things, Mary looked devastated.

"Isn't she beautiful?" I'd never heard reverence in Tom's voice before. Any answer I could give seemed inadequate, so in spite of my misgivings I simply nodded. I kind of understood, I thought, whether I wanted to or not.

"She's been here a long time, but they wouldn't put her up there until a little while ago. The story goes she came from Louisiana, from this crazy artist named Jeansonne who lived out in Bayou Le Coeur and mostly carved cypress knees back in the early nineteen hundreds. He was supposed to have been pretty good; people collected his stuff. He lived with his little boy after he ran his wife off from pure insanity, and he loved him more than anything else in the world. Only thing is, he was getting crazier and crazier, only coming out of the bayou now and then, and the boy was looking skinny and wild. One day when they were in town the local priest and the sheriff took the boy away from him and sent him to an orphanage that the parish ran. They said Jeansonne wasn't fit to raise him. When he finally found where they'd sent him he went there and the priests said the boy had died. They said the kid had been like an animal, had screamed and fought, and they kept him locked up and beat him to get the devil out of him. One day they opened up his door and found he'd broken the window and used the glass to cut himself up. And since he had killed himself they said he was in hell and hadn't buried him in consecrated ground. Jeansonne really did go crazy then. Went back to the bayous and never came out." My face must have betrayed my own horror and doubt. "Nice, huh? Do nothing but cause him hurt and when he can't take it condemn him for getting away from them. What bullshit— sorry, ma'am," he nodded toward the statue.

"He carved all sorts of things after that but they all had that look that she has, so sad you couldn't stand to look at them. People got spooky about them and wouldn't buy them. One of the priests that did

65

missionary work out in the bayous back then took a liking to him and helped him sell some things. They found her when he died, the biggest piece of cypress he had, his masterpiece, I guess. The father brought it here." Tom had sat down in the front pew, where the statue looked down on him. He seemed sad and comfortable at the same time, as though he and Our Lady had come through a long struggle and reached an agreement. I stood, knowing how much it would bother me to move into the circle of that gaze. "Poor thing," he went on, "she was locked in the church's storage for a long time because people didn't think she looked like the Virgin Mary ought to look. When I was an altar boy I used to go see her there when I went for supplies for Father Timothy. She and I had a few talks back then, kind of got to know one another. Then there was an accident a couple of years ago and the statue they had up there—a big old vulgar thing with lipstick and rouge, looked like a carnival prize—fell right off the wall. Some poor bastard— sorry, ma'am—will never get Virgin Mary cleaning duty again. The church didn't have a lot of ready cash, and Father Timothy suggested she be brought out." He straightened and laughed. "I was twelve. I remember that first mass, how shocked everybody was. They swore they'd get rid of her and get a new Our Lady—like they could just swap one Holy Mother for another. They ended up getting kind of superstitious, though. Wouldn't talk about it, but never got around to getting another one either. I think she's more perfect than anybody is ready to admit. She looks like a mother whose boy that she loved just died for a reason she can't understand, and right now, with the war and all, there's a lot of that going around."

I stood beside Tom quietly, until I remembered something. "Can I hear you sing again?"

"Oh. That." He paused for a long moment. "What do you want to hear?"

"I guess some church song. Can you sing regular music in a chapel?"

"Sure. Dixie?"

"Quit it. Something you like."

He paused and then breathed in, looking up toward the statue.

Spring is here, the sky is blue,
Birds all sing as if they knew
Today's the day we'll say "I do"
And we'll never be lonely anymore because we're

66

Goin' to the chapel
And we're gonna get married
Goin' to the chapel
And we're gonna get married
Gee, I really love you
And we're gonna get married
Goin' to the chapel of love.
Bells will ring, the sun will shine,
I'll be hers and she'll be mine
We'll love until the end of time
And we'll never be lonely anymore, because we're...

He stopped, gripping the rail as though he had suddenly gotten very old and needed it to keep from falling down. Then he turned and kissed me on the mouth. From the way he did it, he was no more experienced than I was, and I'd never kissed a boy in my life. His teeth bumped mine and in the instant the kiss lasted I didn't know whether to pucker like I did when kissing family or open my lips the way they did in the movies. Before I had time to decide, he pulled back and looked at me as though he was telling me goodbye forever.

"Marry me, Katie. Marry me some day, okay?"

I shook my head. "Don't do that, Tom; it's mean. You don't mean it."

"I do. No fooling Kate. We fit, you and me. We fit and we don't fit anywhere else. We could really do it, really go to New Orleans and never look back."

"Why would you want to marry me? I mean, don't you think you'd be miserable?"

"So we'll always take care of each other. So we can keep anything bad from happening to one another. So we'll never be lonely anymore."

He put his arms around me and his head on my shoulder. He was shivering. If I thought for a moment that I had done that to him, made him shake all over with the sheer power of the love he felt for me, things between us might have been very different. "I wish it was true," I said. "But bad things happen anyway, whether you're doing something you think will keep them away or not. I don't think I can keep it from happening to you and you can't keep it from me. Not with love or trying as hard as we can. I love you a lot. But I don't want to marry you. Or anybody. I don't want to end up like her." I nodded up at Mary, knowing from the stillness of his head on my shoulder that he was listening hard.

Chapter Eight

A few days later, while my grandmother snoozed in front of the evening news, a voice I'd been listening to on television for my whole life underwent a change that made my chest go tight. It sounded like it had sounded five years before, when Walter Cronkite had told me and my mother that John F. Kennedy had been shot dead in the middle of a parade in Dallas Texas. My mother, who'd been in the last months of a healthy life herself, sat beside me on our brown sofa and cried along with Cronkite, a man in whose voice I'd always found a warm kind of comfort even when he talked about the most disquieting things I could imagine, the Russians and the Cubans, and the terrible things going on around me in Mississippi. In fact, the way Walter Cronkite sounded as he followed the story of the assassination was more frightening to me than the events themselves. And though I was just a kid I knew from the way I'd always watched my mother closely that she wasn't weeping out of concern for our country. Her connection to John Kennedy was far more personal. She'd had a crush on that handsome man and his handsome wife from the first minute she saw them. She'd even taken to wearing straight skirts like Jackie's, and had bought herself a beautiful little blue pillbox hat, with a short veil covered in tiny white fake pearls, though I was the only one who knew it was way up high on a shelf in the bedroom closet. Loving a Kennedy wasn't a Mississippi thing to do. That handsome man had been called things by Mississippi people that worried me to listen to. People blamed him for everything from the jobs they didn't want but didn't want anybody else, particularly the Negroes, to get, to everything their children said that sounded different from what they themselves thought. John Kennedy was a Yankee, he was an idol-worshipper, he was rich and he wanted black people to invade places that they'd been kept out of forever. To my people he looked like the end of the world.

But my mother, in spite of quietly sharing some of those same feelings, looked at him and his elegant wife in the same way she looked at Grace Kelly, whose movies she never missed when they were on TV, and who'd married a real live prince. There were times when she didn't know I was watching that I caught that look on her face. When she was watching the Miss America pageant or looking at Princess Grace or First Lady Jackie on TV I saw something that looked a lot like the way Tom would later look in that church, like she was so lost and longing that she could hardly breathe, and that she wished somebody would take her out of there, and she knew it wasn't going to be my father. Oh, he'd been a little bit right, a military man who seemed like something wonderful in his dress blues, but there were times, like the day she'd shown me the little hat and then placed it lovingly into a blue hatbox and shoved it high up into the closet shelf's dark back corner, that I knew she was caught in a situation she would never get out of. Even when I was ten years old and Martha three, she still had that look, and sometimes seemed mad at him for not being what she longed for. So, while a good part of Mississippi had cheered as though everything John Kennedy had wrought was suddenly going to be undone by a single bullet, we held hands and cried together, both of us crying, really, not for John Kennedy or his pretty wife, but for her.

This announcement was every bit as bad as that other one had been, but I had changed. There was no one left in my family to feel sad for. This time Walter Cronkite, with that same tightness, that confusion that, when I was ten, had set me to reeling inside, was telling me that Dr. Martin Luther King Jr. had been shot dead on a motel balcony in Tennessee. I wondered what my mother, gone only a few months herself, would have thought. Then I wondered what I thought. I discovered I didn't know.

I wondered if Butch would come to work the next day, but when we arrived at the café she was there waiting in the passenger seat of her husband's old rusty Chevrolet. She didn't look like she had slept, though, and he pulled away without waiting for her to fix him a ham biscuit and coffee the way she always did, without a wave nor a "Mornin' Miz Lynn, young ladies," like he always did. He didn't say anything, and neither did anyone else. While my grandmother fumbled for the keys to the café door we all stared off in different directions, suddenly strangers.

"What's wrong with Mr. Butch?" Martha asked, causing my grandmother to hiss and Butch to frown down over her big, aproned stomach at the ground. I'd hardly had any sleep myself. I had sneaked to the living room to watch the late news at ten pm, to see reruns of President Johnson saying he hoped there wouldn't be "blind violence" and the reports that people were already rioting in Memphis. I was worried about school and what I could say to the few black kids that attended PHS rather than George Washington Carver High, and what they might say back. As the café's double doors swung inward, I heard Butch's voice behind us.

"Enoch Parsons," she said, walking around the three of us who had stopped still beside the counter where the cash register and the football pull tabs stood in the earliest dawn light. She didn't look back at us, but her words were firm enough for us to hear clearly. "His name is Enoch Parsons, and my name is Sarah. Sarah Parsons. They call me Butch after my daddy. He didn't have no boy to name after him so they always called me Little Butch. My mother's name is Carolina because that's where her people come from. Her grandparents was slaves on a Carolina plantation. My daddy's grandparents was slaves right up near Indianola. We's Enoch and Sarah Parsons." She stopped talking then and went on into the kitchen, pulling the hanging string that was attached to the overhead light and yanking the kitchen into light.

I was scared all the way through the morning rush, but I was thinking hard. The men at the Rebel Café's tables talked about the killing as though it was a good thing, a relief and a joke. It brought me up short. I thought about who I was and how I felt about what was happening. I thought about my people, both my family and the Mississippi that I heard about on the news. And I knew that even though I'd thought of myself as different from all those people and things, I hadn't given Butch's life a single thought. I liked her. We joked together as I made my passes in and out of the kitchen, grabbing up plates of the eggs and grits and short stacks with maple syrup and side bacon and country ham that she made for the men who were now joking about the death of someone who made her declare herself to us this morning. I was embarrassed that she sat in that kitchen, hot from the big ovens and the long, stainless steel grill and ate her own

71

breakfast afterward rather than come out into the air conditioned café where the rest of us ate. My relationship had been with Butch, the cook. I didn't know Sarah Parsons at all, had had no idea she was living inside the big, pleasant woman who made the best peach cobbler I'd ever tasted, and whose little shingle-sided house I'd hardly looked at when the rusty car broke down and we took her home. I hadn't known the name of the man she slipped a plate of dinner to when he showed up at the kitchen's back door every day at noon. I'd never thought about whether she was paid enough, what she thought about the way her children were treated in school, how she felt about cooking for crowds of men who thought she was less than they were. I didn't know how she really felt about Martin Luther King, even though I'd gone to all those rallies with the Doucettes that were about helping her people. And I hated to admit it, but if too many of her people had shown up at those rallies I might have been a little afraid of them.

I tried to catch Butch's eye but she wasn't looking up. So I did the only thing I could think to do to say I was sorry. At the end of the breakfast rush, when I took off my apron and hung it on its nail in the kitchen, she asked the same question she always asked me. "What would you like for your breakfast, Miss Kate?"

"How about if I fix you breakfast this morning?"

Butch stopped on her course toward the big grill and looked at me. She smiled a little, but shook her head. "No'm, I don't think so. I cook the breakfast. That's what I do." She went past me, but patted me on the shoulder as she did. "I don't know where you got such an idea. I'll fix you up a biscuit and you go on." Maybe she didn't blame me, but she wasn't up to being assuaged by a plate of eggs and grits either. This would take time. I didn't know what would come of it.

Chapter Nine

I needn't have worried about school. Before time came for me to leave, the telephone on the café's back wall rang. Martha jumped to answer, her face falling as she held it out to me. The phone rang so seldom that she was convinced that every call was our father calling from his radio communication station a world away. Even though hardly anyone else ever called, our grandmother insisted that the café phone was for business and forbade me and my friends from "tying it up." I reached for the receiver with a surprised frown.

"Hey Kate, you'll never guess!" It was Claire, breathless as if she'd run a mile. "No school! They cancelled the whole thing for the rest of the week on account of Martin Luther Bless-His-Heart-King! They're scared to death somebody'll riot. Don't tell your grandmother. Come on out and meet me and Tom at the boat. You can tell her you didn't know and stood around school talking to the kids that showed up. I've got something to show you. Do it, okay?"

Of course I'd do it. I needed Tom and I needed Claire to help me think.

I hung up the phone and grabbed my books, Martha eyeing me from behind a screen of suspicion. I hustled past my grandmother, saying, "Claire's on her period; I gotta take her some Kotex." It was the one thing I knew my sister wouldn't pursue. Somehow, after all she'd seen in her life, maybe because of all she'd seen, Martha nearly threw up at the very thought of menstruation. Lord help her, I thought, when she starts having her own. But I knew it wouldn't be the Lord or Grandmother or anybody else. I knew who she'd run to when the time came, and I knew I'd have to figure something out. I just hoped I had a few years to think about it. For the moment, though, I wasn't above

73

using her fear to avoid her questions. I circled through the bathroom of the apartment that was attached to the café, where our grandparents had lived before the trailer was parked at Mrs. Carmody's trailer park, and where our grandfather still spent most of his nights, sipping from a bottle of Jim Beam and dozing in front of the TV the same way our grandmother did at the trailer. Although it didn't really matter, I grabbed a sanitary napkin from the box I kept under the bathroom sink just in case, waved it in front of a slightly green Martha just to be mean, stuffed it into my purse and ran out the front door, chewing my ham biscuit and wishing I'd had time for a cup of coffee to wash it down.

The boat wasn't really a boat at all, at least not any more. It was a pile of pitted, half-rotted timber that sat at the end of Front Street, not far from Tom's house, beside the river and just inside the shipyard fence. Claire and Tom had cut into the chain link, bolt cutters, Claire said, being one of the things every good communist owns, in case of revolution or riot. The boat was a genuine historical artifact, had once been an important part of the Confederate Navy and had been sunk in the Mississippi. It had been discovered not long before and its pitiful remains hauled to the shipyard for restoration, though I couldn't figure out what they could do with it. The wooden part of it simply sat under a permanent sprinkler on this remote bit of shipyard soil. To me it didn't look like anything but a pile of rotten wood. No one ever came near it; it just sat under its metal awning as though it was waiting for something to happen. Tom and Claire liked sitting beside it, near the river, listening to the pump that pulled river water up and sprayed it on the wood and the surrounding sandy dirt in an endless circuit. I thought it was depressing, but would never have said so.

"Richard's gone up to Memphis," Claire began before I'd even sat down on the roots of the live oak tree that stood guard over the boat. Tom looked up and met my eyes with a smile that looked like he was in mourning. I knew it was a holdover from my telling him I wouldn't marry him, but Claire, caught up, rattled on. "He says if it was a conspiracy he wants to be there when it gets found out. He took the bus." She grinned and waved a set of keys under my nose. "That means nobody'll be using these. Jean's in bed with Gran'mere watching the TV and nursing a headache. I copped the truck. We have the whole morning to do as we please."

74

At fifteen, Claire was already a seasoned driver and a pretty good car thief. Not only was she good at hot wiring a car left sitting unlocked, as they tended to be quite often, her attitude toward car thievery was so logical that I had gotten lulled out of thinking of it as wrong.

"It's like this," she explained, the first time she suggested to me that we could get to the store and back in time to watch Dark Shadows if we just used the old Chevy sitting beside us in the afternoon sun. "This is Bill Whatcom's work car. He takes it to work and hunting, and he's on the graveyard shift, which means he won't even wake up for another three or four hours. I know because he cussed me out for waking him up when we were getting one of Richard's petitions signed for worker's rights last fall." She'd already opened the Chevy's door and, while I frantically looked up and down the deserted little alley behind Bill Whatcom's house, stuck her head under the dash. Before I could explain that, if I got caught, by some means I couldn't explain my father would be able to kill me outright from the other side of the planet, the engine groaned once and then snorted to life. "Shhhh—get in," she demanded, as if anything I could do or say would be louder than the sound of that engine in the quiet afternoon. But I'd slid into the musty front seat, tugging the door behind me quietly and feeling somehow guiltier for seeing the mounds of candy wrappers and beer cans piled around my feet like autumn leaves than for sneak-thiefing a sleeping man's car. Claire had thrown the lever on the steering wheel's stem into "Drive" and we'd slid away like the thing belonged to us. We'd made it to the Junior Mart on Highway 90 and back in fifteen minutes' time, Claire grinning at me and parking the car just far enough down the alley from where it had been to maybe make Bill Whatcom scratch his head and think maybe he should drink a little less before coming on home. She'd even added twenty-five cents' worth of gas from Junior's Regular pump. "It's the least I can do for my fellow citizen," she said as we settled on her living room sofa to watch Barnabas Collins suffer through another day of being undead, and pick cat hair out of our Jiffy Pop and Barq's Root Beer. Now, from the look of sly pleasure on her face, she was planning more than a snack run.

"You stole Richard's keys?"

"Right out of Jean's sugar bowl. The truck's parked at your trailer, seeing as how your family's all at the café. Comrades," she

75

grinned a conspirator's grin that thrilled me and scared me half to death at the same time, "we're going to the circus!"

I had no idea what she was talking about, but from the slow smile that spread across Tom's face I gathered that he did. "Yes indeed!" He jumped up and did a couple of dance steps that looked like a cross between the Mashed Potato and something the majorettes did when they marched in front of the PHS band. Whatever Claire had in mind, he clearly knew something I didn't.

"The circus is in town?"

"The circus *lives* in town." She started toward the trailer park, leading Tom and me along a path that skirted Tom's house and avoided Mr. Carmody's shop, though I doubted anyone ever looked out the windows of either. "Tom, you never told this girl about the circus?"

"Never did. Don't know what I was thinking."

"What circus? What are you talking about?" I'd been to a few fairs; we had even gone to Mobile now and then for the state fair when I was little. It had been impossible to get our mother's wheelchair through the shavings and straw, and she cried in crowds, so we'd given it up for the past several years. The closest I'd ever been to a circus was watching *Jumbo* and *Big Top* on Dialing for Dollars.

"It's a little bitty thing out Highway 90, over toward Ocean Springs. Good people and a lot of free thinkers among them. We get over there three, four times a winter. I've spent years afraid Jean would take a liking to those monkeys and talk Dan the Monkey Man into giving us one." We'd reached the truck and the moment of decision for me. Ocean Springs wasn't Junior's. It was a full twenty miles away, and if something went wrong I couldn't walk home. Tom's risk was a small one; Claire's nonexistent. I stopped, tugging at Tom's sleeve. Claire was already behind the wheel, grinning.

"Wait. Wait. I'll get in trouble. Somebody'll see, or the truck will break down or we'll get in a wreck, or—,"

"Cherie, get in the truck. Everybody in the world is off doing something important or glued to the news; we're just three nobodies doing nothing on a very strange day. You're too damned gloomy lately; it's time you saw a two-headed baby. Live a little, Kate Lynn, before you die. Tell her, Tom."

He was nodding, holding the passenger door open for me. "Do it, Katie. We'll take care of you. Nothing will happen."

76

"All right, all right!" I had to jump up to get my foot on the running board but I scooted across the ratty old blanket that covered the front seat and sat next to the gear shift. Tom leapt in behind me, whooping. Claire slipped the lever into drive and slid out onto Little Red Road and toward Highway 90. It was warm for March and the windows were down. Tom fiddled the radio dial to WTIX. Otis Redding was singing. Tom sang along.

"Sittin' in the morning sun, I'll be sittin' when the evening comes. Two thousand miles I roamed, just to make this dock my home." He leaned back and closed his eyes, that beautiful voice filling the cab, and before I knew it Claire and I were singing along, in a moment so out of time I knew it would stay with me forever, "Sittin' on the dock of the bay, watching the tide roll away. Sittin' on the dock of the bay, wastin' time."

We drove onto the Singing River Bridge, headed west, toward Ocean Springs and Biloxi and New Orleans and California and every place I ever thought about, for better or worse. Tom put his loafered foot on the dash and Claire lit a cigarette, the ash blowing around us like Mississippi snow. Under the tires the metal bridge sang. I imagined that beneath the river, the Pascagoula stirred and, for a moment, missing the world and its beautiful mornings, hummed along.

I counted landmarks along Highway 90 as though I was seeing them fresh. It was the first time I had been anywhere in a vehicle completely free of adult supervision, and I felt drunk and nervous and full. Claire smacked the wheel with her ring-bejeweled fingers, shouting the words to songs more than singing them, only getting quiet when the news came on.

"Turn it up a little." She leaned forward as the announcer told again about the shooting. Martin Luther King had just been standing on a balcony outside his motel room when someone had picked him off like a squirrel on a pine branch. I shuddered, feeling the vulnerability of being right out in the open. Tom seemed distracted, as if he'd rather think about other things. Claire, though, teared up and shook her head, angrily flinging the tears away with the back of her hand.

"Sometimes you just want to give up, I swear. You should have seen Richard this morning; he didn't know whether to shit or go blind. I know I pick on him a lot, but he's got a lot of guts to go up there right now. I hope he comes home okay."

I felt sad about the things that were going on too, but even more I felt envy for the tenderness Claire felt for her daddy. In spite of the fact that she disclaimed him whenever it amused her to, I'd never seen a real harsh word between them. Something about Claire's family made them trust one another to be good people, to deserve respect. I knew that, even if she drove the truck off into a ditch and had to call home to get us rescued, no one would say she was worthless or stupid when they got there, just as no one would tell Richard he was foolish to walk into the teeth of the racial storm in Memphis. I couldn't imagine what it must be like to have such freedom. Claire had to steal the truck because she was too young to drive, but she didn't have to steal herself from anybody.

When we'd been driving for about fifteen minutes, Claire swung the truck hard to the left and we headed down a short stretch of ambiguously paved road. "There she is," Tom punched me on the arm and pointed. My mouth couldn't have dropped open any more if I'd seen a UFO sitting on a scrub lot not a quarter mile off the highway.

"How long has this been here?"

"Years, but sort of in bits and pieces. The people who don't have some other place to go are here in winter and spring but it all joins up and travels around in summer, then they come back after fair season." Claire was talking as if she was on intimate terms with the place. "I can't believe you've never been out here; it's the coolest place on earth. And they'll be the first to tell you so." She hit the brakes as we turned into the crushed shell parking lot and leapt out, holding the door open for me and smiling. "Come on, Gomer. You look like you've never been to town. I hope Gator Bill is around. He'll let us do pretty near anything." Tom, who was standing beside her by now, kept nodding and pulling at her, clearly eager to get going.

I couldn't stop gaping like an idiot at the entrance to the place. It looked just like things I'd seen on television. I couldn't figure out how it had been here, even in bits and pieces, for years, without me knowing it. It was just the kind of thing my grandfather would fall in love with and my grandmother would forbid him to haul Martha and me off to see. But I hadn't heard a word about the Biggers Brothers Circus.

A wide entryway with a turnstile sat in the middle of a series of wildly garish paintings that promised, in huge, painted words, "The Fantastic, the Bizarre, the Terrifying!" Underneath that proclamation was a row of characters right out of "The Greatest Show on Earth." A wild-eyed gypsy stared out over a crystal ball beneath the legend "What Does Your Future Hold?" A fiercely grimacing man's torso ended in the long, scaly hind legs and tail of an alligator. Above him the banner screamed "Half Man! Half Reptile!" A woman who looked as though she was naked except for the uncountable number of snakes coiled around her, gyrated under the words "The Dance of the Seven Serpents!" They all looked likely to be pure hokum, except for one that looked to me like it had definite possibilities. Beneath the legend "Titans of Africa!" was an elaborate painting of two elephants, standing trunk-to-trunk on their hind legs, while a beautifully costumed girl stood, one foot on each trunk, arms held high and smiling bright as the sun. I wondered if there really was a girl behind that gate who could stand up on such huge creatures, comfortable and self-assured as though she knew that, for all their size, their whole purpose was to support her little frame. A girl like that would be something to see.

"Hey Tom," I nodded toward the girl in the garish painting. "Is she in there?"

He and Claire exchanged a glance. "Might be. Kate, there *is* something you ought to know. This," he swept his arm across the wild, oddly beautiful panorama, "is advertising. It's not a lie, but it's not quite the truth either. Felicia—that's her on the elephants—is probably here, but you might have to squint a little for her to look like that. And as for Gator Bill," he waved toward the alligator man, "the truth itself isn't near that strange, but he's a cool guy. You know, it's a circus. It's all spit and baling wire and paper mache and keeping things dark enough so you imagine more than you see. You gotta believe to enjoy it." He winked at both of us. "Just like everything else."

"You'd have made a lousy talker, Tom," Claire cleared her throat, reared back and began to bray, "On the inside! On the inside! We got more excitement than the law allows! We got the strongest, handsomest men and the purtiest, nekkedest women in the state! We got wild animals and wilder humans, and some that's a little of each! If you are weak of heart or feeble of mind do not, I repeat, do NOT enter these golden gates, for you may not live to see the light of another day! Come see the Ten-in-One!"

"Not bad. I keep telling you you ought to sign on and we'll let you try the tip between turns in the kitchen." The voice from the other side of the turnstile was gravelly and a little wheezy, like its owner had smoked a lot of Lucky Strikes in his lifetime. I peered around Claire, who'd stopped her spiel. I couldn't quite make out the man the voice came from. In the warmth of the spring day he wore a long sleeved, high buttoned shirt and a fishing cap pulled low over sunglasses. All I could see was a long, rough-looking jaw that might have had a good day's beard growing on it. The figure stepped back and beckoned for us to enter the gate. "Come on in, Miss Claire. Good to see you, Tom. And I see you brought company. You start hauling field trips out here I'm going to have to start charging you like we do the rubes."

"Bill! How are you doing?" Claire bounded through the gate, the turnstile clicking as she shoved it forward. "Jean says why haven't you all come picked out a kitten for Felicia yet?" She sounded as though Jean knew about and approved this excursion. I thought I could take lying lessons from her.

"This is Miss Kate Lynn, Bill," Tom swept me in front of him and pushed me through the gate. "She lives in the trailer park since January."

"Hello Miss Kate Lynn." Not knowing what to do, I held out my hand. It was quickly seized and pumped up and down. Something in my brain went a little haywire; it felt as though my hand was enveloped in an SOS Pad. Before I could look down, the grip tightened and Gator Bill stepped forward, whipping off the glasses and the fishing hat.

"Gator Bill. Pleased to make your acquaintance."

I blinked when I saw him, before a feeling of calm settled over me like a cool mist. I twisted my hand away and fought the urge to wipe it on my shirt, but if Gator Bill had expected me to squeal and run back out to the truck, he didn't have a clue. I'd seen scarier things than him in my own living room. In the shadow behind the entryway billboards, as my eyes adjusted, I looked at Bill and he looked at me. After a minute, he winked. "Steady as a rock, this here one." He turned and walked out into the sun, calling back over his shoulder, "Come sit awhile. Felicia's got some sweet tea'll set your teeth singing. We've all been sitting around thinking about the sad state of the world this morning."

In the light, Gator Bill's skin was tinged a faint grey-blue. His head was smooth, bald, and appeared to be made of scaly pieces that didn't fit together well. Although his face wasn't as affected as the other visible parts of his body, it still had the appearance of horny plates, with lines etched in unusual places. He looked like a jigsaw puzzle. Just looking at him made me itch. I remembered the steel wool feel of his hand and surreptitiously ran mine down the front of my shirt. Not only was his flesh different from anyone's I'd ever seen, but his teeth were short and pointed, as though he'd taken a file to them. He did, indeed, look a lot like an alligator. Claire had dashed up to walk beside him, chatting as if they were old friends, a little too softly for me to hear. I hoped she wasn't apologizing for me.

As we started across the big open space, I looked around. Three enormous semi trailers were strung near the back of the lot, all painted with the Biggers Brothers logo, a brilliant red and yellow scroll with the name and various clowns, acrobats and the twin elephants splayed across their sides. Each trailer had a door set into either end of its side and a short stair leading down, making it possible to walk in, straight through and out again at the other end. A generator sat between two of them, ready to bring them to life at any moment.

At least a dozen travel trailers and as many pickup trucks and old cars were clustered nearby, among the tall pines and the occasional Spanish Dagger. Rough picnic tables sat around them. A few men and women, whom I tried hard not to stare at to see if they shared any of Gator Bill's peculiar characteristics, were draped over the tables with coffee, cigarettes and newspapers. Some wore work clothes, some looked as though they'd just climbed out of bed and thrown on robes for breakfast. They all looked morose. I could just hear a voice coming from a radio sitting on one of the table tops. A pack of little dogs, shaggy looking poodles and mutt terriers like Martha, begged around the tables' legs and chased one another around the assembly. A snotty looking toddler in a diaper, tiny tennis shoes and an oversized, bright red pajama top staggered after whichever dog was in closest proximity, giggling and clutching at the adults, who reached out to steady it and pat its head without looking. Men with the normal kind of dark, leathery skin, the kind I saw every day in Pascagoula, strode around the lot with purpose, carrying things I couldn't identify. Then I widened my gaze out to take in more of the place, and shivered with pleasure at what I saw.

This wasn't really a circus, not in the big tent, cotton candy, Eighth Wonder sense of the word. This was more of a circus autopsy, the guts of the thing spilled out all over the sandy scrub, its bones exposed and scattered in the sand. An enormous, open sided metal shed was filled with rows of what looked like porch swings but could only have been the seats of a Ferris wheel. They leaned like fallen dominoes toward the back of the shed, where I could make out a bright, sparking light that I knew well. I had seen it through the shipyard fence, way up in the distant skeletons of ships. Someone was welding something, maybe one of the seats or maybe something vital, something that, if broken, would cause someone to fall to their death. My stomach did a short dance of fear and delight before I made myself look somewhere else.

A pile of metal rods and a disk that I thought must be fifteen feet in diameter sat alongside a motor whose belts and gears looked greasy and tough. I didn't recognize anything about it until I saw, stacked against the outside wall of the big welding shed, row after row of painted wooden horses, legs bent and hooves arched as though in mid-stride, as if a stampede had suddenly fallen over, turned to immobile statues. I'd grown up loving the carousel at the beach pavilion, my grandfather using his drinking buddy status with its operator to get me free rides as long as I could stay upright without throwing up. I'd spent long afternoons on that carousel, in my own world, playing *My Friend Flicka* or pretending I had given Black Beauty the wonderful home he had been searching for. I hadn't ridden a carousel since I was younger than Martha, but seeing this one, splayed out and reduced to its fundamental parts, made me want to hide my eyes. I wanted to know these things, and I didn't.

Then the elephant walked around from behind one of the trucks.

"Look! It's an elephant!"

As soon as the words left my mouth I felt like an idiot, but I couldn't have held them back if I'd had to. There was an actual elephant not a hundred yards away from me, led by a girl who looked no older than I was. She was dressed normally enough, in rolled up jeans and a short sleeved shirt, but she seemed to have white greasepaint all over her face and arms. She must have been rehearsing her act, I thought. Before I could ask she looked over at us and whooped "Hey! Tom! Claire! It's about time you showed up! Gimme a minute; I'll be right there," before grabbing the animal's big trunk with both hands and tugging it toward a slab of cement set into the ground a good distance from the rest of the people and hardware. A clawfoot bathtub sank into the sand beside the slab, the pile of hay and vegetables beside it attracting the giant creature and making the girl's task considerably easier.

"Felicia! Hurry up! We can't stay too long!" Claire literally skipped beside Gator Bill, who hadn't broken stride, as she waved with both hands to the girl. "We've got jail bait with us so we have to get back before her folks find out!"

Jail bait. That was me. All of a sudden I wasn't one of them anymore; I was just some dangerous cargo they were hauling along that was likely to get them in trouble with the law if we got found out. As we neared one of the trailers I saw the girl pick up the end of a massive linked chain and wrap it around the animal's hind foot. The elephant seemed oblivious; it had begun rooting in the hay with its trunk and thoughtfully chewing mouthfuls before she'd finished. As we reached the picnic table that sat in the shade cast by the short, white trailer, she dropped the chain and bounded toward us.

The nearer that girl got the stranger looking she got. At a distance, with the elephant taking up all the scenery and my imagination filling in the rest, she'd looked like she could easily be the girl on the poster, covered in clown paint but ready at the blare of a big top trumpet to bespangle and prance herself into the role of glamorous tamer of the Titans of Africa. By the time she flung herself at Claire and they exchanged the kind of hug that long lost sisters might, I realized I had been completely wrong about what I had been looking at. It made sense that I would try to think in terms of make-up. I understood make-up. I had never in my life seen a real live albino.

If I hadn't been so eager to meet the lovely, wonderful girl in the poster I'd probably have just been embarrassed at my own desire to stare. As it was, I stood and worried what I would do when we were introduced, whether my face would say something I didn't want it to. The girl pulled back from Claire and dove at Tom with the same fervor, the two of them hugging and murmuring words I didn't quite catch, while I perched uneasily on the corner of the picnic table.

"Felicia," Claire turned her toward me. I didn't know where to look. Under hair that looked like the soft, yellow down on a newborn chick, Felicia's face shone like a searchlight. She was beautiful, and yet the fact that I couldn't look at her without words like "Fairy" and "china doll" shouting in my head troubled me. I had to either look at her or away from her with a deliberateness I couldn't feel good about either way. It was strange; with Gator Bill I'd stuck out my chin and refused to be startled. He was a grown man, maybe thirty, already alien, someone I couldn't envy or fantasize about being. She was close to my age, too close, too much like me and not enough like me. Claire went on as though I wasn't about to fall down from shock. "This is Kate Lynn—that's her last name, Lynn. She's the first person that's been worth dragging out here to see your sorry little dog and pony show, so you know she's something. Kate, meet Miss Felicia Devore, animal trainer, and the only reason Bill's survived this long." Bill nodded and smacked his hand on the table in agreement.

"Pleased to meet you," I held out my hand but, after only a second's hesitation, she stepped forward and enveloped me in a warm hug. She smelled sweet like hay and sweaty like work.

"Oh, me too. I hardly ever see anybody when we're in town and I get lonesome. Have a seat and I'll get y'all something to drink and we'll catch up. Come help me carry, Claire." She spun on her heel and went up the steps of the trailer, Claire tossing me a look before following. I followed Tom and Gator Bill's example and sat down on one of the benches, worried that the heat in my face showed as glaringly as I felt it.

"You all not in school?" Bill's raspy voice was casual. Now that I thought about it I imagined that both he and Felicia were used to being looked at. Heck, his teeth were pointed, and who'd do that to themselves if they didn't want to be stared at? They probably knew I'd goggle a little, and maybe were willing to take Claire's and Tom's word for it that I was, as she'd said, worth bringing.

"School went all spooky at the thought we might have a race riot about Martin Luther King," Tom answered. "Have you heard anything about what's going on up in Memphis? Richard took off up there last night and even if she's not saying it I think Claire's worried."

Bill rubbed a bluish hand over his chin. It made a sandpapery sound. "It sure is a hell of a thing. People have gone plumb crazy, killing one another over something should have been settled a hundred years ago. If it wasn't so damned cold up north I'd leave this part of the world, not that it would do me any good. 'Course, everybody around here don't feel that way." He nodded toward the little group at the other tables. "We just about had a riot of our own last night. Somebody cried and somebody cheered and then a few folks got to drinking and arguing, and before you could stop 'em Big Jay busted some roustabout's face and sent him off under the threat of a good nut-crushing—sorry Miss Kate; I hope you aren't offended."

I shook my head. I was still trying to get used to just where I was. These really were circus people; there was a full grown elephant eating whole cabbages and splashing water a few yards away. An albino girl was bringing me tea while a fellow who told folks he was half alligator chatted about the goings-on on the lot. I was sure sorry about Martin Luther King, but I had to admit it had turned out pretty darned good for me. They could kill me when I got home for all I cared.

Claire came down the trailer steps followed by Felicia, each of them carrying glasses that clinked ice cubes in amber liquid. I took the one Felicia held out and sipped, sighing as the cold, thick liquid slid down my throat. She did indeed make a good sweet tea. She also set a pile of home made cookies in the center of the table. "Girl, you're going to give me the sugar diabetes yet," Bill smiled happily as he bit into one. She nodded, winking one ice blue eye above her upturned glass before she set it, half empty, on the wood.

"Well, tell me what's been happening with you all—what's kept you away all winter? I ain't seen you since, what, November? You know I need good gossip more often than that. Claire and I been catching up while we were getting the drinks. Bill, she tell you about Richard? How's your mama, Tom? How's Eddie?"

" 'Bout the same." Tom shrugged. "Kate here's the news. She moved in about the first of the year and we've been introducing her to the finer points of life in Pascagoula. She gets kept pretty close to home though, so we didn't have much of a chance to get her out here. Thought she might want to see the show while everybody's all cockeyed over the assassination."

"Terrible." She shook her head. "Bill wants to go somewhere else, out west somewhere, and see if we can hire on with another show, but I don't. I like it here, even if it is crazy about half the time. Other places it just pretends to be better." She turned to me. "Who are your people, Kate? Where were you before Pascagoula?"

I snorted. "Not far. Over at Keesler for years. My daddy's Air Force."

"Ever go to any other countries? That's what I'd like to do."

"No. My father's in Vietnam now. Not in the fighting, though, whatever that means."

"That's awful anyway."

"Well, we didn't get along." Tom wasn't the only one eager to leave family out of the conversation.

Bill reached over and patted the pale hand that lay on the table. "Felicia always wants to know about everybody's relations. I guess it's because she doesn't have any around here. Just me."

"Oh," I looked from one of them to the other. Maybe there was some genetic link between their conditions. "You two are related?"

"We're married, Miss Kate."

"But—," I looked around, waiting for someone to crack up, to make a joke of the new girl. Instead, I was met with open faces, Felicia's bobbing up and down as unselfconsciously as if she was telling me about the events of her ordinary day. "But you're not old enough, are you? And you're—,"

"Older'n hell." Even without his strange skin Bill's expression would have been unreadable. I couldn't tell if he was regretting his age or reveling in it. "But we're sure enough married, have been for about two years, since Felicia was fifteen."

"Don't get a headache over it, Cherie," Claire talked around a mouthful of cookie. "Felicia's folks signed the papers and that was that. Richard and Jean even came to the wedding. Had it right after a union rally. Francis played 'Here Comes the Bride' on the trumpet."

"Your parents let you?" I wondered what kind of people would let their daughter marry a man twice her age at fifteen. I couldn't even date, and I knew that if our lives hadn't gotten so out of control I wouldn't have the freedom that I did; my parents would have known where I was every hour of the day.

"My parents are practical people, Kate. They're circus folk. They look like me, and they like Bill. I grew up with the show ponies and the elephants. I like what I do and don't much mind what I look like, but I don't have much desire to go out among the population, if you know what I mean. Hell, we used to be a family act, The Yeti Family or The Cannibal Albino Family, Mommy, Daddy and Baby. Mother's mother was a Circassian Beauty, billed all over the country as a favorite in the court of kings. Mother and Daddy broke off from the show and retired in Florida, and I wanted to keep on working. I know how to do this. And Bill understands a lot that most folks don't." She sucked her teeth. "Ever hear stories about albino people?"

Of course I had. I was embarrassed about it, but when I'd been little and things had been more ordinary than in the past few years, my friends and I had scared each other in long summer twilights telling albino stories. They'd been boogey men, baby eaters, ways to make the little ones cry and to sweat over ourselves late at night, staring hard at the windows of our bedrooms for ghostly white faces and shining red eyes.

"Thing is, Kate," she went on smoothly, though she clearly recognized that I knew what she was talking about, "here we get to just be us. Outside we get looked at and sometimes picked on, and there's no stopping it. Here," she gestured around the lot, "we're all the same, more or less. Even the ones who look ordinary out there are here for a reason." She pointed toward a bulky man in a flowing robe, who leaned his chin on his fists as he listened closely to the radio's news. "See him? You know what a hermaphrodite is?" I did. I felt myself blush. "That's George; we call him King George. Reason why is he's king of the blow-off, the show after the show, if you know what I mean." I shook my head. She went on, explaining as simply and openly as though she was telling me how to understand a math problem. "See, people only get goosey when we're close enough to them so they have to think about us like they think about themselves. I'm albino because my folks are, but anybody can have an albino kid, just like anybody can have a hermaphrodite or a dwarf or a thalidomide baby with no arms and legs. That scares hell out of people. But put us on a stage or behind a curtain that says "X Rated" and they can get all excited and look at what they want to look at without it being too close to home. So we take their money, spend it to make good lives, and we get a lot better laugh at them than they do at us."

Gator Bill chimed in. "Not that we don't want it to be different sometimes, Miss Kate. Felicia and I talk all the time about quitting, but she was born into it and I just plain got drove into it when I was about y'all's age. You ought to try to get a date in high school when you look like I do. Anyway, like King George, we have a good trade, and most of us take one another for what we say we are. He's got man and woman parts but he's a man to himself, so he is to us. He's just an oddity to outsiders. By the way, when he's not in the blow-off he's a hell of a good cook. Miss Claire'll be working for him when she decides to join up. Unless she ends up the ringmaster." Claire looked like she liked the idea. I was wondering something else.

"What do you do? Other than, you know—."

"Don't be afraid of it. I'm Gator Bill, half man, half reptile, and then again I'm not. I'm a man with a condition. Ichthyosis—it means something like 'fish disease.' Don't sound near dangerous enough, does it? 'Catfish Bill?' But you're right, that's not all I am. Come on; I'll show you what else I do." He got up and Tom leapt up to join him, rubbing his hands together in delight. Felicia waved hers lackadaisically.

"Go on. I've got ponies to work. Come talk to me, Claire; you've seen his critters. I'll let you hold the lunge line while I ride. Bring them back to the ring when you get done, Bill." They linked arms and started off, quickly disappearing behind the truck once more. I was torn. I got the feeling I was being treated, but I longed for girl company, for gossip and that particular kind of laughter that I never got enough of and didn't quite feel comfortable with when I did. Still, when Bill went to the generator that sat between the semis and yanked it to noisy life, bringing a chorus of complaints from the little crowd trying to listen to the radio, I realized we were going to go into one of the semi doors.

Bill went first. Tom swept me in front of him as we went up the few metal steps and into the trailer. Once there, I had to stop for a minute as my eyes adjusted. The inside was dim, and stank slightly, a strange combination of chemicals and barn. Once I could see I got at least some idea where the barn smell came from. We were standing in a wide aisle that ran down the middle of the trailer, and the space on either side of us was fenced and filled with clean hay. The pens were empty, but each had a poster with a lurid legend and a big, painted version of what I guessed must inhabit them when the circus was in full swing. The one on the left said "Push Me Pull You in the Flesh!" and had an illustration that looked like it came right out of Doctor Doolittle. I cocked an eyebrow at Bill. "A real Push Me Pull You?"

"Well, more like a two-headed goat. But he's a beaut, just the same. The live critters are farmed out when we're not on the road; they live longer that way. We've got a six legged sheep, and a calf with a spot looks like a map of the United States. Got a monkey with no arms, uses his feet for hands just fine. Nature's mistakes, the talkers call 'em. Some farmer's always coming around with something

Mother Nature made unusual, and management pays pretty good money." He beckoned us forward, past the pens and toward the door in the wall that divided this section of the trailer from the next. "But Mother Nature's got nothing on Gator Bill. Come see."

At first I thought the room held nothing more than musty taxidermy, like Mr. Carmody's bait shop, and I couldn't imagine why Tom would give a rip about it. There were shelves stuck to the trailer's cheaply paneled walls on either side at staggered intervals, and each shelf had some sort of stuffed and mounted creature on it or hanging above it. I wasn't excited about stuffed things; it seemed everybody who had the money had some kind of head sticking out of the wall or a big, shellacked fish bent into a shape that suggested it still had fight left, long after it was dead. In fact, they made me a little nauseous. I didn't like their dead eyes and I didn't like their dead smell, and I didn't like the way dust seemed to know they were dead and collected on them in a way it didn't collect on things that had never been alive. There was something about dust on eyeballs that made me want to shrivel up. I tried to think about anything but the fact that preserving people wasn't that big a leap from preserving raccoons and red tailed hawks, and my brain shut down entirely before I could draw much of a line between what I expected to find on those shelves and the woman who looked nothing like my mother, lying in a coffin at the front of Calvary Baptist Church. Then Bill flipped a switch beside the door, and each of the displays was bathed in its own individual light.

"Oh! Oh, Jesus!"

I was looking at the impossible. Light shone up from the base of the creature on the first shelf, set higher than my head on the right wall, casting on the ceiling the perfect shadow of a dragon in flight. I flinched at the eagle claws that clutched air just above me as though it was diving straight for my head. Above them the head of the eagle, beak open as though frozen mid-shriek, shone green and golden in the light. Enormous, shining wings stretched and curled as though scooping the air. The thing looked alive.

Even if the trick had stopped there it would have been a thing to admire, but just behind the unfurled wings was where the impossible began. Feathers blended into pelt, claws into arched body and haunches that ended in wide, firmly planted paws, around which curled a sinewy, tufted tail. The whole thing was gold and sleek, and indescribably beautiful.

"Behold the Gryphon, legendary guardian of the divine," Tom whispered in my ear. I caught a look of wonder on his face, not that different from the look he'd had when looking at the statue of the Virgin Mary at Our Lady of Sorrow. Past him I could see other equally fantastic creatures on the other shelves, all shining under lighting that made them look as though they were alive and we'd caught them in the middle of cavorting all over the room. I had the sense that, when we left, they'd start right up again.

Bill led Tom and me down the aisle as proud as a father showing off his babies. "Think there's no such thing as a unicorn, Miss Kate?" He gestured to a tiny goat kid with curly white hair and a single horn protruding from its forehead. One polished hoof was lifted as though it was about to spring away. "And here, here's Pegasus, ready to carry the gods across the sky." It was a white foal, curled up and in the pose of sleep, wings folded forward underneath its soft muzzle. I could almost see it breathe. "And here, you know about Cerberus, who guards of the gates of Hell? Here he is, all three of him." The dog looked like a mastiff; it stood a good three feet high at the shoulder, the head that stared at me savage eyed and with its dewlaps drawn back in a snarl. It actually looked like it was drooling. The other two heads matched perfectly, one at an angle of rest and the other sniffing the air. I couldn't imagine anything getting by it. "But this here," Bill indicated the last in the row of wonders, "is my favorite, although," he chuckled, "it scares the wits right out of a lot of the children."

I could see why it would. The last shelf, set just shoulder height for me but impressively looming for someone, say, Martha's size, held a winged monkey straight out of The Wizard of Oz. It sat crouched and ready to take off, wings at the ready and knuckles pushing against the base of the display. It was even dressed like the creatures from the movie, and the leer on its face was gleeful and malevolent. I shivered in spite of myself.

"You made these?" I stood in the middle and turned round and round, things I'd read about in mythology books and seen on midnight movies about Jason and Odysseus all around me. "They're just beautiful, Bill. They're not what I would expect from—well, you know."

"Not cheap carnival gaffs? 'Course not. I won't mess with pickled babies or half mummified remains of God knows what, put together with spit and baling wire. This is my self-respect. I want to do something that'll make people believe things like this just might have existed one time, like all the old stories come true."

Bill's gravelly voice had a note of pride and challenge, an invitation to believe that these creatures he'd made were real, that magic was here in the room with us and not some claim that was just plain cruel for being a lie. But the more I stood there looking at his marvels, the more I felt a war starting inside me, between the romance of something that you could pretend had been wonderful, and the reality of death that I knew all too well. These pieced together things weren't the Pascagoula Indians. They weren't here willingly. They might look good enough to fool the public, but they weren't fooling me. As much as I might want to let go and be like a little kid, to shiver with happy fear and be enveloped in Bill's and Tom's delight in the magical creatures he'd made, I couldn't do it. And the fact that I couldn't felt like a broken place inside. When I felt broken, I got mad.

"It's a little gross, isn't it? How do you get the bodies to sew together?" I saw the shift from pride to hurt in Bill's eyes. It felt like a fish hook in me, but I couldn't stop. "I mean, you make them look wonderful all right but they're just pieces of dead animals." I flicked at the Pegasus' soft ear. I knew my voice was getting higher and tighter, but I kept on. "These look like swans' wings; are they? What are they all stuffed with? Did you ever kill any of them yourself? Like this baby horse, did you just go out and buy one and kill it?"

"Kate." Tom said my name, loudly and forcefully, no honking, no hesitation. What he was really saying was "Stop. Right now." He didn't have to say anything else. I'd broken the spell Bill was trying to weave, out of something mean that I didn't want to admit was inside me, but that protected me as sure as Martha's meanness protected her. There was a voice in me, one that never shut up, that said to keep my eyes open and my back against the wall, not to let anyone tell me that things could be put back good as new or better. I didn't want anything pretty to come out of dead things and body parts. I wanted the dead dead and the living living, and no in between about it.

"Tom, I have to go home." I groped toward the door that led outside, past the winged monkey and the gryphon and the hay-filled pens and on out into the sun and the generator noise. I didn't realize I was running until a few heads at the picnic table turned my way and

91

grinned. They thought I was just a scared town kid, an outsider who'd been shaken up by Bill's art. They had no idea who I was.

"Claire! Claire, come on! I want to go home!" I covered the ground toward the entryway like I was running from the devil; I could hear Tom's and then Claire's voices shouting at me to wait, but I couldn't. I pushed at the turnstile, becoming even more frantic as I realized it only turned one way and my escape was blocked by metal rods. As I was readying myself to climb over, Tom, Claire, Felicia and Bill caught up with me. Felicia pulled me back as I tried to bat her away.

"Here now. Here now. It's all right. Be still. Be still." She stroked my sweating, shaking arms with her pale hands, soothing me as though I was a frightened animal, never raising her voice much above a whisper. "You don't have to worry; we know what it's like to be in a place that takes a lot of getting used to. It's okay; you didn't do anything wrong, Bill just didn't know about your mother. He didn't know you had a tender spot about dead things." Claire had been talking, I figured, but there was a lot Claire didn't know.

"It's the truth, Miss Kate," Bill patted me on the back with his rough hand as though I was a baby. "I didn't mean to upset you; I thought you'd like my critters."

I relaxed just enough to be afraid I was going to start sniffling and further my disgrace. "I did like them, Bill. I did. But only when I didn't think about how they used to be. I mean, when they were alive they were ordinary, but they were alive. You did such a good job I forgot to be sad they were dead and taken apart and put back together with parts missing and parts that weren't where they should be. It's like trying to make it okay to be dead if you're part of something else that goes on and makes people happy. I mean, Martin Luther King, he'd be better off just being a live guy, don't you think? Wouldn't his wife and children like him just plain old him and not a real good story they grow up telling? I don't mean you did anything wrong; they're wonderful, but—oh, I have no idea what I think. About any of it!"

Bill barked a laugh. "Welcome to the circus, Miss Kate."

Chapter Ten

We were home by noon. We had listened to the radio on the way back just as we had before, but this time no one sang along. On the drive I caught sight of my face in the truck's rear view mirror. My eyes were sunken and my face pale. My throat was so tight from holding back tears that it hurt. Every now and then Tom cleared his own throat and started to say something, but his voice had started betraying him again, and after a few attempts he propped a loafer on the dashboard, sighed and slouched down beside me in the seat, shaking his head. Claire smoked and concentrated on her driving. I was scared to death that neither of them would ever speak to me again, but when she swung the truck back into the spot in front of the trailer, she cut the engine and turned to me.

"You all right?" I nodded, but both of them looked dubious.

"I'm sorry." It was all I could choke out. To my surprise, she reached out a long finger and poked me in the shoulder.

"Shoot, it's no big thing. I do wish you'd waited another fifteen minutes before you freaked out, though. I nearly had Felicia talked into convincing King George to show me his privates." She rubbed her nose and gazed out the windshield. Among the three of us only she seemed content that things were basically okay, that I'd be okay, and that life would go on. I'd have given anything to have been Claire Doucette at that moment. "Well," she slapped the seat with her hand, "what now?"

"I think I'd better go on to the café," I said. "They'll find out about school sooner or later and I might be able to convince Grandmother that I spent the morning just hanging around. If I get

93

back in time to work the lunch rush she'll be so glad she won't ask too many questions. What about y'all?"

Tom shrugged. "We figured we'd steal the truck, elope, upstage Richard and take everybody's mind off their troubles."

"Hah!" Claire looked as thought she might just be willing. I wondered if Tom was paying me back, both for turning down his proposal and for ruining our morning. "Tom, if you and me get married then we could run off and join the circus ourselves. You could be the Barking Boy and I could do The Dance of the Seven Veils! We'd get rich and retire and both afford all the men we could ever want."

"Hell yeah, sister," he opened the truck door and moved to let me slide out and down onto the crushed shell drive. "We'll make a fortune and support Miss Kate here in whatever endeavors she sees fit to pursue. And we'll never be lonely any more." As I slid past him he kissed me on the cheek, quickly and with a loud smack. And I burst into tears. I grabbed him and hugged him, burying my head briefly in his shoulder and reaching out blindly for Claire. She took my hand and I squeezed hers hard, let go of the both of them, and, without another word, turned for the café with the barest possibility that Claire was right, that it was all fundamentally okay, tickling the edge of my thoughts. Just before I rounded the corner I heard Tom yell after me, "Hey! You got snot on my shirt!" But I knew I was forgiven.

Chapter Eleven

Tom brought Martha's unusual habit up first. It was a surprisingly muggy Saturday afternoon in April, and we were sitting on the trailer's front steps eating the Nutty Buddies that I'd swiped from the café's ice cream freezer and brought home for the weekend. I was watching him out of the corner of my eye because the way Tom ate made me want to scream. He picked and nibbled, scraping the nuts off of the top of the chocolate and delicately biting them off of the tip of his fingernail, then quickly tried to catch up with the stream of ice cream that melted down the brown cone in the eighty degree heat. As soon as he managed to corral the mess he went right back to picking. In spite of the constant danger of the dripping chocolate and vanilla, he never got a drop on either his face or his crisp shirt. Tom ate everything with the same neat, fussy concentration, turning things over with his fork, pushing them around and taking delicate little bites. It galled me under most circumstances, but his added refusal to appreciate the happy messiness of eating a cone in the late spring heat brought out the animal in me. I could only watch him for a minute before having to fight the urge to mash the whole thing into his face.

Martha, who was sitting on the gravel driveway in front of us, had finished hers quickly, sharing it with Martha, who licked happily at one side while she licked at the other. Between my irritation at Tom's fastidiousness and my revulsion at Martha's comfort with dog spit I mostly kept my eyes focused off into the distance and enjoyed my own perfect method for eating Nutty Buddies.

"Don't you think that's just a little, you know, strange?" Tom nudged me and whispered into my ear. He nodded toward my sister, who'd made a circle by kicking gravel and dirt into a ridge that extended around her at leg length. She'd brought out her little collection of dolls, one genuine Barbie and a couple of cheap knock-offs that she'd managed to wheedle out of our grandfather at the Dollar Store when they went to buy the cheap shorts and halter top sets that she wasn't old enough to be embarrassed to wear. She'd placed an empty cigar box from the café in front of her, and was holding a beauty pageant with it as the stage. She'd made dresses for the dolls by wrapping them in old bits of cloth from our grandmother's occasional attempts at sewing, and one strapless evening gown from a worn yellow sock with the toe cut out. When Tom poked me the bathing suit competition was in full swing, the three dolls parading as well as Martha could manage it with two hands. Since she had neither an interest nor skills in sewing herself, the bathing suits were truncated forms of the evening gowns, scraps of the brightest cloth she could find wrapped like bath towels around her beauty queens. The dolls, Barbie and the two knock-offs, pranced back and forth to Martha's tuneless singing of "There she is, Miss America" over and over again. She only knew the one line, so the pageant had the feel of a desperate attempt to find an elusive quarry rather than to elect a queen—"There she is, Miss America. There she is, Miss America. There she is, Miss America—." I figured that was the weirdness that Tom was talking about.

"I'll throw a party if she ever learns the rest of it," I said.

"Not that," he was watching her so hard it was embarrassing. I knew what he was looking at. It was a fact that I, along with everybody in the family, had ignored ever since she'd started doing it, shortly after our mother had died, before we'd moved to Pascagoula. Martha had ripped the right leg off of each of her dolls, leaving them truncated and hopping in her hands.

."Oh. Yeah," I said. "So, want to go watch American Bandstand?"

Tom cocked an eyebrow my way while never taking his eyes off of the pageant. "Is this some sort of crippled beauty contest? Miss One-Legged America?"

"Quit it, Tom."

"Honey, me not mentioning it does not mean it isn't happening. Your sister's gone a little Wednesday Addams, don't you think?"

Martha hadn't missed a beat in her song, but after a few more passes back and forth across the stage she dropped the two Dollar

Store dolls and concentrated on the real thing, a gold cigar band now perched on her head, who had clearly won the title and the crown. Miss America turned and twirled, bowed and raised her stiff arms toward an imaginary audience. Now and then Martha would stop singing and pronounce "Thank you! Oh I can't believe it! I love you!" as her winner basked in her moment of victory.

The Barbie had been a Christmas present when Martha was four years old, and looked it; the blonde pony tail had frizzled until it looked like a yellow Brillo pad stuck onto the back of her head. There were smudges on the arms and, when the doll was undressed, red dents at the tips of her hard breasts, where Martha had tried to make nipples with a red Bic Pen. I remembered how she had sat in our mother's lap and watched the real Miss America Pageant, holding onto that doll when it was brand new and had a real gold evening gown and not just a yellow sock, and our mother had had a lap to sit in. It was a thing the two of them shared the way I shared the Kennedys with her. In the midst of the disintegration of our lives I was the only one that knew that Martha had stolen the old high school annual that held the photograph of Miss Homecoming, 1951, a pretty, golden-haired, small town girl in a homemade evening gown, whose teeth were slightly crooked but who smiled like an angel from the yellowing page. She'd swiped it a couple of years into the disease, when our mother had begun to get hysterical whenever she saw it. Martha squirreled it way under the backmost corner of her bed, knowing that in her condition Miss Homecoming, 1951 would never be able to look there. I'd found it one day while trying to hunt down the stray laundry from the pile that Martha slept under rather than fold and put away. The annual was part of a stash she'd started accumulating after the operation that had changed Miss Homecoming so much that neither of us recognized her any more. If she'd blackmailed things away from me, from our mother she'd simply stolen. I might have felt some obligation to mention it to someone except that no one missed any of the items—a pair of high heeled pumps that had been rendered as useless as if they'd been stilts, an empty prescription pill bottle that said "Darvon" and another that said "Demerol," and a Mother's Day card that Martha had made in school the year after she'd come home—a carefully traced copy of a little girl with her face half buried in her mother's skirt that I recognized from a book of children's Bible verses our mother had read to each of us in turn when we were very small. Inside she had started to write, but had only gotten as far as "Happy Moth" before stopping. Our mother had never known about the card, and I wasn't going to be the one to tell her. Martha's cache had remained untouched for months, but it was clear from the way that Barbie kept thanking her audience and saying "I love you! I love you!" over and over again, that Miss Homecoming wasn't far from her mind. She put on a pageant a couple of times a week, sometimes more if the week had been a hard one. With our father a world away, Grandmother either working or in a dead sleep in the living room, and Granddaddy immersed in his drinking and rambling, no one paid my little sister any attention when she wasn't actively clamoring for it. I didn't do it either; I just didn't want to. I was tired. I wanted it all to be somewhere else, shut away in the past or exorcised into someone else's life. But it wasn't. Watching Martha with Tom I felt torn. He was right; it was creepy. But he hadn't been there. He didn't know what it had been like.

"She reminds me of Mother," he murmured.

"How's that?"

"She's kind of on automatic. Look at her. We could be shouting in her ear and she wouldn't look up. It's like she's trying to do something we can't see."

"Like make your son be the way he was even though you know it won't work? Like spending your entire life trying to undo something so bad that people can just barely stand to be in the same room with him?"

From the look on Tom's face I knew he felt the same kind of embarrassment I did, but it was nice to be talking about what was really going on, instead of just watching it and feeling as if I was hallucinating something that no one else could see. But I wasn't yet willing to tell him what had happened to Miss Homecoming, 1951.

Chapter Twelve

I was shocked when Tom took me to pick up dog shit at the graveyard, though when I thought back on it I shouldn't have been. Something had been up, some things had happened. I just hadn't put two and two together. If I had, I'd have crawled over glass rather than be a part of it.

" 'S go," he walked by the step where I was sitting at PHS one afternoon, the end of the school year three weeks away, trying to come up with an excuse for missing the three-thirty rush at the café. I'd been thinking of getting Claire to forge a note from my English teacher saying I had to make up a test I'd missed a couple of weeks before, when I'd had cramps bad enough to keep me curled up in bed with a heating pad and a bottle of Midol for the day. I'd planned to hide out in the library and read the book about dreams that Sigmund Freud had written, and that I couldn't believe was even in a high school library. But that "'s go" of Tom's, a condensation of "Let's go" accompanied by a jerk of the head that disallowed any disagreement or hesitation, usually meant something interesting was to follow. Even Sigmund Freud couldn't compete with him for the ability to make me look forward to the afternoon.

"Where are we going?" I ditched my books under the steps where I could pick them up them later, and fell into step beside him. Grandmother was going to be madder than a wet hen, but it had been a wet hen kind of week and I couldn't think of any reason to miss out on something interesting for fear of just more of what I was getting used to anyway.

"To the graveyard."

I perked up at this information. The place he was referring to was a genuine historical landmark, with a plaque mounted on a big live oak tree, and a tiny iron fence that wouldn't have kept anyone from wandering among the few dozen graves inside. "What're we going there for?"

"To pick up dog shit."

"Of course." Tom had long since lost the power to surprise me. Once we'd realized the same things impressed us we both found a comfortable camaraderie in just going along with whatever scheme the other presented. My only problem was that I didn't have any schemes. Tom, with his relatively undeterred freedom to wander, had far more understanding of what he called "backstage" than I did. Backstage was what lay beyond the everyday, the internal workings and the off the beaten path underpinnings of Pascagoula. It was something he and Claire had in common, the appreciative intimacy with the funny little quirks in what, to me, seemed an unbearably dull place. Both of them had grown up there and had a proprietary attitude toward every nook in the town that I both envied and didn't want to acquire. The circus had been there all along and I'd had no idea. So had the boat. I knew that, had they not pulled me into their way of making those things a special and interesting part of their lives, I would have walked right on by, caught up in my sleepwalk, hardly aware the world was there. I was surprised that Tom found me halfway as interesting as he did Claire, and when the three of us were together I was embarrassed at how much I watched every look that passed between them. So far, though, it seemed I had something that held him in a stronger grip. I hated that it was the hard things that bound us, but would take it when nothing better was offered.

By the time we reached the little side road that led back from McIlwane Street between two of the neat, deeply shaded houses that ran along its wide front I was sweating and gasping for air. Tom seemed to be oblivious to the humidity and heat. Although his red hair was plastered against his head, and his striped cotton shirt and khakis stuck to him as much as my blouse and frayed jeans did to me, he didn't seem to feel the need to slow or fan or complain. I wasn't going to embarrass myself by straggling if I could help it, but I was happy to see the deep shadows under the old live oaks as we began to weave back among them toward the small group of graves.

The graveyard occupied a peculiar little plot of land at the intersection of four back yards, in a respectable old neighborhood a few blocks from the beach pavilion where Claire's family held their rallies. It was clear that it had been there far longer than the neighborhood that had grown up around it. In fact, it was older than the country that had grown up around it. Here in the middle of what I thought of as a dead boring, embarrassing little town, a little bit of history and mystery lay beneath the sandy Mississippi soil.

Tom didn't bother going around to the gate. The iron fence was short enough for even me to step over. It sat bent inward in some places and outward in others, as if it had been stumbled over by people going both in and out. I imagined that over the centuries quite a few drunks and lovers had lain on the graves and felt something important was happening there, but I also liked to think that maybe just once in a while the dead themselves got up and escaped, to look in peoples' windows and marvel. If Tom had ever had a similar thought he didn't let on. He seemed to be on a mission.

"Here, hold this." He held out a paper bag with one hand, while fishing in his pants pocket with the other. The bag was limp with moisture from the same sweaty pocket that now produced a plastic soup spoon. Tom didn't give me any more instructions, just held the open bag toward me and gave it a little shake as if to tell me to hurry it up. For the first time I realized that his lips were white around the edges, as though they had been compressed tightly together for a long time.

"Something wrong?" I took the bag and held it open.

"What could be wrong? What could possibly be wrong on this fine day?" He scouted around the graves, passing the toes of his loafers through the ragged tips of the grass and then setting them down carefully. I strained to read the inscriptions on the sagging tombstones, most so timeworn that they had become nearly invisible.

"Look here, Tom," I felt the need to chatter, made uneasy by the graves and his odd demeanor. "It says '*Mellisande DuChamp, b. 1769, d. 1787. Beloved wife.*'" I was careful not to stand on the spot where Mellisande lay under the ragged grass. "Jesus, she was eighteen. How do you think she died?"

"Who knows. They mostly died of living back then. Mosquitoes, snakes, infections, Montezuma's Revenge, they got everything we get but didn't have jack squat to deal with it." He sounded as though Melissande had died to spite him. "Aha!" He bent down and extended the spoon to a spot next to a tilted slab that bore the name *"Jacob Ferrier"* and a pitted patch where the record of his birth and death had once been. Tom scraped at the roots of the scraggly grass and lifted a dark chunk toward the lip of the bag that I held at arm's length. "Looks like the Thibideaus' Beauregard to me. Merci beaucoup, Beauregard." He bent back over and brushed more grass. "Mm-hm, looks like we got us a sale on Gravy Train this week. Lots of red in the mix." I felt a wave of nausea. The heat didn't do much for the smell that was now coming out of that sack and I was beginning to get mad at not being told what Tom was up to.

"Tom, I got better things to do than hold sacks of dog doo—."

He straightened up with his hand at the base of his back, like an old man, and flashed a grin that had a certain grimness to it. "Remember that little incident with Cash Collins last week?"

Boy did I remember. If Tom Carmody's life had been a comic book, Cash Collins would have been Doctor Doom. For one thing, he was a year older than most of the kids in tenth grade except for the dumb ones. For reasons nobody was quite sure of, but most thought had to do with his mama being a little crazy, he'd started school late, entering first grade at seven and then some, and it had had a bad effect on his personality from the get-go. Cash was big and mean, and smart enough to make his perpetual anger work. He stalked the halls of Pascagoula High like the point of an arrow seeks a target, with a wedge of worthless hangers-on trailing behind just because he was a constant source of risk-free excitement.

The crazy thing was, Cash was handsome as hell, with an intelligence and charm that let him get away with things that a dumber, uglier, less interesting being would have been brought up short for. He had black hair and a swarthy complexion that could have been Indian or Cajun or both, and perfect timing, so that even I had to laugh at some of the terrible things he said, some of his spot on imitations of people who showed their weak places too much. And it wasn't just me. The trail of wilted and sobbing girls he left behind gave sad testament to the kind of boyfriend he would have made, but it seemed that even the ones who scattered like chickens whenever he came near for fear of having their weight, their periods or their family histories become part of his snide running commentary closed ranks behind him and sighed a little after they were safely out of range.

102

Perhaps predictably, Claire Doucette was the only girl at PHS who was completely immune to him. She'd pass him in the hall with a flip of her blonde hair and a smile, saying "Hey Cash," the same way she said "Hey" to everyone else. If he called her Comrade Claire she raised her left fist high in a revolutionary salute, and went on. If he shepherded his goons onto the auditorium steps and clapped and whistled and sang "Backfield in Motion" as she passed, loaded down with schoolbooks, on her way home, she did her best approximation of the Watusi and, with a bow that barely broke her stride, she went on. She didn't let him or his followers upset her, she didn't retaliate, and although I worried constantly that he'd find some way to up the ante until he found a tender spot, she always nudged me away from any barb he threw my way with "C'mon Cherie; think of the cross he has to bear. With his life it's a wonder he don't just full out explode."

As much as I hated to admit it, the thing that humanized him was pretty awful. Claire and Tom had filled me in on his history before I'd ever laid eyes on him. Cash Collins' cross was his helpless love for a mean, drunkard father who, when he was twelve, had finally hit him so hard that he'd had his jaws wired shut for a month, and his genuine humiliation at having had a mother who was so in love with Johnny Cash that she called her only son, whose real name was simply James, "Cash," even hinting that the music legend might be the boy's natural daddy. A big, housedress-clad woman whose mousy brown hair never seemed to be released from a set of bright plastic curlers, she oohed and aahed over the Man in Black at every opportunity. You couldn't start a conversation about the weather with Mrs. Collins without it leading to "and it looks like a fine night comin' did I ever tell you about the night I hung around with Johnny Cash after the outdoor concert at the fairgrounds in Mobile in nineteen fifty-one?" In a town the size of Pascagoula, talking incessantly about even a well-respected country music star was sure to get you snickered at behind your back. Swearing your baby boy was the spitting image of a world famous celebrity with a wink and a spookily seductive grin was enough to keep Cash on the attack, I figured, just so no one else could bring the matter up for fear of retribution. Besides, Cash's mean streak kept anyone, student or teacher, from asking about his bruises.

There was one more thing about Cash, something that helped to keep his minions in his wake, girls clinging when he did everything but put fish hooks in their skin, the cooler kids from being quite able to reject him outright, and lent a terrible credence to Mrs. Collins' fantasy. Cash Collins could play the fire out of just about any musical instrument you could name. Claire told me it had just always been that way; even in fifth grade he'd pounded out a respectable enough boogie woogie on the music room piano to make Mrs. Sawyer, the widowed music teacher who hadn't gotten most of the class past "Peter and the Wolf," turn herself inside out trying to convince his parents to let her give him some real training. She swore that with his talent she could teach him Chopin and Mozart, and he'd be the next Liberace for sure, maybe even Floyd Cramer. But, Claire said, after a few after school lessons where Mr. Collins, reeking of Wild Turkey and slouching red-eyed over his back, slapped the grim faced boy upside the head every time he hit a bad chord, she couldn't take it anymore. She just found a way to leave the music room door unlocked after school sometimes, and could be seen standing outside it, listening to Cash trying to pound his way through "Tutti Frutti" or some New Orleans jelly roll, her hand over her mouth, her eyes closed tight.

Cash stayed away from guitars and Mississippi's love affair with country music for obvious reasons. The last thing he needed to do was to add fuel to his mother's fire.   Instead, when he'd gotten to junior high age he'd decided to take up the saxophone, a good jazz section being the spine of any band between Mobile and Houston, and Francis Doucette having a solid trumpeter's lock on the future of any high school ensemble that Cash might hope to be a part of. Playing with the band was about the only time Cash acted like a member of any kind of society, taking instruction surprisingly well and even being generous when others got the lead in a song. It was so clear that he was a racehorse among mules that he could, maybe for the only time in his life, relax when he played with the PHS band. Even the people who wouldn't get near him for fear of being impaled on the spear of his sarcasm would stop and listen when he soloed on "Just a Closer Walk with Thee" at halftime. His ability came as close to elevating the jazz band to real excellence as anybody ever had, and the pleasure in his eyes when they managed, with his standout solos, to blat out an acceptable version of most of the songs we all claimed as our heritage, was wonderful and awful at the same time.

Cash might have found a reason to like himself and everybody else through that horn, but even then his family threatened any real pursuit of excellence, his mother waving her handkerchief and carrying on so at any PHS band performance that she, and not he, became the center of attention, and his father snorting and declaring that his boy "wan' no nigger and wan' goin' to be spendin' his life playin' nigger music." We might have taken delight in seeing Cash's pain and frustration, except we knew that somebody, sooner or later, was going to pay. What none of us knew was that he would turn that horn into a weapon, and would use it against Tom.

Tom had good reason to hate Cash if anybody did. It was a fact that most of the students at PHS were just trying to get through their lives. There were kids who lived in the really nice houses on Beach Boulevard, kids who lived in the long tracts of ex-Navy housing that had been converted into featureless suburbs, kids who lived in varying forms of freedom and decrepitude in the bayous around Pascagoula, and kids who lived in the many apartment buildings inhabited mostly by shipyard workers just hanging on for a little while before moving on. Some of them took college prep classes and most didn't, some ran for student council and most didn't, some were the football players and cheerleaders and band members that defined the PHS Panthers and Panther Pride, and most weren't. Some, like Tom and Claire and Cash Collins, had been in Pascagoula for their entire lives, going from first grade right on through high school in the same, well established order. They interacted like siblings in an enormous family, their reputations made and most of the kinks worked out in elementary and junior high, long before I'd come along. I might be accepted, like Martha and Martha were accepted, but I knew I was in many ways new blood and that there were relationships, even among those I liked, that I would never understand. I felt it. I understood the kids of the just-passing-through variety and doubted I'd ever expect to feel permanent anywhere, no matter how long I might stay. It felt light, as though I could pack up any time and wave goodbye without a second thought. And I thought I'd surely die if I had to do it one more time.

Tom saw it differently. He told me on an almost daily basis how good it would be when he could finally light out for New Orleans, and Cash was one of the reasons why. "For somebody as good as Cash is at knowing where your skin is thin," Claire told me in one of the long talks where she tried to explain Pascagoula teenaged society to me, "Tom's about as natural a target as you're going to find. And," she went on, "Tom's always been pretty much like he is right now; you tell him his shirt's ugly and he'll spend half his life looking for an uglier one, just to prove he can. He's always been the kind who everybody knows is like to go for boys, but he's smart and funny and hasn't put his hand on anybody's knee, and generally people like him. These days a lot of people feel bad about Eddie and leave him alone for that. But our whole lives, every time Cash calls him a queer, for about a week he gets a whole lot queerer, just to piss him off. It's a wonder nobody's given him a worse time than they have." There had been months-long truces over the years, she said, usually when things were going pretty well for Cash and he didn't need anyone to make a fool of in front of his buddies.

But Cash had turned sixteen not long before, and to celebrate, his daddy had done two things. First, he bought him a loud, run-down Impala with a frame so badly bent that the rear wheels didn't follow in the tracks the front made, but just a little to one side. "It looks like some old dog trottin' down the road," Cash had declared, and "The Dawg" it became. It was no time at all before Cash had his buddies piled into the back of the Impala, and, in imitation of the shipyard workers, they spent their spare time driving around and catcalling anybody who was young and unprotected and fool enough to walk Pascagoula's streets. Not many things could make me sprint for the café after school, but Cash and The Dawg could.

The second thing Cash's daddy did to celebrate his sixteenth birthday was to throw him out. If Cash ever told anybody what had happened, they didn't spread it around; he just kept coming to school and driving that car, and after a short while Mrs. Sawyer, who'd never lost her hopes for him, let him sleep in a spare room off the carport her husband had used for his ham radio before he'd died. "The fact he hasn't dropped out is a testament to human determination," Claire had declared one afternoon as she, Tom and I had watched from the safety of the honeysuckle covered fence beside the school parking lot, while The Dawg, loaded with whooping teenagers, peeled rubber at the end of a long day.

Tom snorted. "That's a little like asking Satan to give up hell and all his little demons and go to work at the Five and Dime, isn't it?"

"Well, I didn't exactly expect you to kiss his feet."

"Well, don't, because he's mean just waiting to happen."

And Tom was right. The thing that had brought us to the graveyard, him angrily scooping with his plastic spoon and me holding a bag full of turds with one hand and my nose with the other had

106

happened in front, not only of our whole school, but a respectable number of parents, students from Ocean Springs High and a bored reporter from the Pascagoula newspaper.

Debate was an elective that only a few PHS students had an interest in, public speaking being just about the last thing any of us wanted to do. And the team wasn't much, being too steeped in lassitude to advance to any real level of competition. There were, however, a few who were naturals, picked in one way or another by talent or plain fearlessness. They were the smart ones, those on the college track when most of us, Tom and Claire and me included, weren't even completely sure what that meant.

Everybody who took debate was a natural arguer, some were hams and some were smart alecks. Tom Carmody fit into all three categories. The fact that he had the strangest sounding voice in Pascagoula High didn't faze him; in fact, he looked at it as an advantage. He'd joined, he said, because it was a lazy man's way to get credit. He got the same classroom preparation as everyone else on the team, but his unpredictable squawking and honking so unnerved Mr. Bailey, its coach, that a plague would have had to knock out half the team before he ever saw time at the podium.

"It's a fairly sweet deal, actually," he said. "I'm sorry I can't do it professionally, like the last guy on the bench at a Celtics game."

Then the plague hit. Not a real plague, just a run-of-the-mill flu that dropped just enough students so that, in the last meet against Ocean Springs, Tom found himself sitting onstage with the healthy remnants of the team, ready to argue the position that the Vietnam War was good for the Gulf Coast economy. We'd laughed at the irony of that, but Tom said he figured his taking a stand for the war when even the opposition knew what it had done to his brother might give him an advantage. Now, though, I wasn't sure anything would. In the few months I'd known him, I'd seen Tom in lots of emotional states. This was the first time I'd seen him look afraid.

Claire had dragged me down to the front row, "to give the boy some friendly faces to look at." I could see that his dark red hair was shiny with sweat and his complexion was a little bit green under the freckles. But he caught my eye and winked, and I thought he might be relaxed enough to get through sounding halfway normal. "Please," I prayed silently to the God I didn't believe in, "let him be as fine as frog hair, as smooth as peanut butter pie."

Eventually, Tom's turn came. He stood at the podium, gripping its sides and sweating, taking deep breaths. Other debaters had made their points, decisions had gone both ways. Tom and his opponent, a sallow girl with braces, who perched like a coiled spring on her chair, rebuttal notes in hand, were the only two left. All the bored PHS students who'd been promised extra credit at the end of a long semester knew what the reporter and the Ocean Springs students did not, that Tom was in danger of real humiliation. We sat as one on the edges of our seats, Claire smiling a million kilowatt smile up at Tom and me praying "please please please." With a final straightening of his shoulders and swooping intake of breath, he opened his mouth to speak.

"HAWWWWNNNNKKK!" The note bleared so loud through the PA system that we clapped our hands over our ears. Then, utter silence. All of us, the speaker and the spoken to, looked at one another in confusion, we in the audience murmuring to one another in wonder. I heard "feedback" in the murmur and took that to be the case until Mr. Bailey stood and spoke clearly through the microphone in front of Tom, quieting us and patting a shocked but still slightly amused Tom on the back and saying "Go on, son," before resuming his seat. Tom scooped another lungful of air.

"SCREEEEAAAAANK! SCRAAAAAWWWWNNNNNK!" It dawned on us all at the same time what we were hearing, even as the noise stuttered to a series of mule-like brays and silence descended once more. The saxophone player must be somewhere nearby, patched into the auditorium's picayune sound system, watching Tom carefully and timing his blares to coincide with his every attempt at speech.

The audience divided abruptly into three neat factions. One consisted of me and Claire, horrified, paralyzed, gripping one another and unable to completely absorb the situation. One included the reporter and the Ocean Springs crowd, still concentrating on the debate and looking annoyed at the interruption. The third, and the most terrible, exploded into laughter as Tom stood stock still, alone at the podium. The laughter pushed the horn player, and we all knew who it was by now, past all restraint and into a whinnying version of "I Feel Pretty," causing the laughter to broaden and deepen until even the kids who wouldn't dream of doing Tom harm got caught up in it, hiding their helpless giggles behind notebooks and hands, ducking their heads down below the seat backs. The song went on and on, until Mr. Bailey turned off the microphone, leaving nothing but the laughter.

Tom didn't try to say another word, he just stepped away, stonefaced, from the podium. He walked calmly, arms straight down at his sides, down the steps at the side of the stage, passing me and Claire as though we weren't there, up the center aisle of the auditorium and out the big doors at its back. Claire and I took off after him, catching him at the corner, still walking, spine stiff, straight toward home. We could still hear the chaos behind us.

"Tom, are you okay?"

"Course I am." He was smooth as peanut butter pie. Too smooth.

"That bastard. We've got to do something!" My voice rose in contrast to Tom's dead calm. Claire hadn't said a word.

"What difference would it make? We do something and then he does something and before you know it, we're good for the goddamn gulf coast economy," Tom said. He smiled the most terrible smile I'd ever seen, worse than the smiles on the faces of the preachers and the doctors and the nurses in my mother's last days, a smile that lied its face off trying to say everything was just fine when nothing was fine. He gave Claire, then me, a quick hug, squeezing so tight I wondered if he was hugging or holding on for dear life, and held me at arm's length. I caught a slight, familiar twinkle. "Don't worry, Kate. I've been pissed on by better than Cash Collins. And I do believe in last laughs. I just have to go lie on mother's davenport for awhile and have a tall cold glass of sweet tea and think." He left us, loping home. I watched him disappear into the shadow of the live oaks and wondered what he would think up, lying on that davenport and sipping tea.

Apparently his thinking had led us to the graveyard and a sack full of dog feces. Tom had lain out of school for a day, not because he had to, he explained to me later, but just so maybe the people who'd laughed at him would worry just a little bit. He'd come back the day after that, greeting the news of Cash Collins' three day suspension with a shrug and a chuckle of his own, drawing a combination of sympathy and head shaking from the students who foolishly imagined that life would just go on, and a few mutters from those who, without Cash there to lead them, somehow looked more dangerous. I worried about what lay in Tom's future with them.

"What are you planning to do with this, Tom?" The bag was nearly full, and soggy in the humid heat. I swore to myself that if the bottom fell out of it I was leaving him there.

"I'm not sure you want to know." He peered down at his collection, nodded in satisfaction, dropped in the spoon and took the mess from me, rolling the top down and sitting down on the edge of a raised vault, "*Mary Campbell, 1919-1937, God's Angel.*"

"Is Claire in on it?" I could never quite get over my jealousy at their closeness.

"No. And I don't want you to tell her. Claire's convinced that people are good at heart, even Cash Collins." He smiled, an echo of the ruined one I'd seen a week before. "Even me. How can you mess with that kind of faith in humanity? But if you want to come, you can." I wasn't sure I liked the dark bond Tom had just acknowledged between us, but I knew it was real, and just ours.

"Count me in."

Chapter Thirteen

We watched the music room after school for several days, until I thought I'd go mad from pure anxiety. He sat, patient as a spider, the bag of shit wrapped in layers of plastic against the smell and hidden in an old leather mail pouch he'd suddenly started carrying his books in, despite a "Nice purse, Miss Carmody" from one of Cash's boys. Cash himself had been subdued since returning to school after his suspension, as if well fed and sleepy for the time being. And on Friday afternoon Mr. Cunningham, the band director, who Tom had told me was "queer as a two dollar bill, you mark my words," had left the music room unlocked so the jazz band could get in to practice before the janitor cleaned and locked it for the weekend. He left, waving to us with a "'Night now; stay cool."

"Stay here and waylay anybody that even looks like they're going to go in there," Tom said, reaching into his bag and pulling out a pair of yellow rubber gloves. He hadn't exactly told me what he was planning to do and I hadn't exactly asked. I was afraid to put words to it, as though by not coming right out and saying we were doing something truly mean we could believe we were caught up in a thing not completely under our control. Heaving the bag over his shoulder, he shifted his eyes back and forth like a spy on a mission and closed the music room door behind him.

I tried to look casual, leaning on the lockers, a book that I couldn't have read if I'd had a gun to my head open in my hands. I was just innocently waiting for a friend, getting in a little homework time, hoping that no one would actually engage me in conversation. I was sure I looked like the lookout at a bank robbery. Fortunately, not a soul came by.

It only took five minutes, but those five minutes took forever. By the time Tom, without the gloves and with a look on his face like he was about to gag, came out and closed the door, I was so scared I almost took off running without him. He stopped me.

"Kate, I want you to go home as fast as you can. Go work the afternoon shift at the café and be sure you complain about it to everybody who passes by. I'm going to go be conspicuous." It wasn't going to be hard. Even though he looked clean, Tom stank. I knew what he was doing; he was placing me away from the scene of the crime and himself right in its middle.

"What did you do?" I was scared for him.

"Go home." He spun on his heel and took off, making a left into the common area, where any after school lingerers were sure to be clustered. Worried, I did as he told me, and sprinted for the café. I slapped Buds and Barqs onto the counter and made change like a machine, and for once not a thing any of the shipyard crowd said could touch me.

Chapter Fourteen

Claire called me that night. "Where's Tom?"

"What do you mean?" Grandmother and Martha were practically in my lap in the trailer's little living room, so I spoke in indefinites. I'd thought about nothing else since he'd turned the corner away from me and into the commons, but had convinced myself he was fine, fine as frog hair, and that he'd come pelting my window later that night. I'd even doped a couple of Vienna sausages, wrapped them in plastic wrap and stuffed them in my bra in anticipation. Martha lay on the floor at my feet, staring at me and drooling so hard Grandmother had declared she was going to have her checked for "the hydrophobie."

"What the hell has happened, Kate?" The fact she didn't call me Cherie gave away her fear. I groped for a way to talk to her without raising suspicion.

"You tell me and we'll both know," I chirped, as if talking about silly girl things, as if we ever talked about silly girl things. To clue her in, I said, loudly, "It's Claire, Grandmother," causing my grandmother's eyes to waver blearily and briefly from the weather report about the latest storm in the gulf.

"Tell Claire I said 'Hey,'" Martha, lying on the floor facing the television with her chin propped on her dog's back, raised one of the black paws and waved it.

"Martha says 'Hey.' Now, give."

"That son of a bitch Cash showed up at my house, standing out at the gate and screaming something about killing Tom. He said he'd destroyed his horn, filled it to the top full of shit. He says the case is ruined and he'll never be able to put his mouth on the thing again no matter how many times he cleans it." An uncontrollable snort of laughter broke through the fear in her voice, and for a moment I felt a rush of pleasure at the perfection of what we'd done. "Kate, he said some horrible things about Tom, called him some names I wouldn't call anybody, live or dead. I swear, if the geese hadn't been there flapping and fussing at him he'd have plowed right through the front door. As it was, Richard and the twins finally went out and got him and took him all over the house, showed him in all the closets and under Gran'mere's bed. You know Richard, he walks spiders out the door rather than hurt them, but he threatened to drown that boy in the river if he ever showed up here like that again."

"Wow." I was wracking my brain trying to figure out how to talk without raising suspicion.

"You mean you haven't seen him at Tom's house yet? I tried calling but nobody but Tom ever answers the phone anyway. Richard and Jean are about to drive me over there to see if he's okay but you're so close and all—."

I kept my voice light by force of will. "I'll see if I can. Grandmother, Claire needs a homework assignment from Tom and they're not answering over at his house. You know how they are," Grandmother had quickly dismissed the Carmodys as too much to deal with and left me to carry rent and messages. "Can I run over there just for five minutes and see if I can get it for her?"

"I guess so. Take the flashlight; it's nearly dark." I stood up and Martha the dog leapt to her feet, dancing and reaching a paw out to me in a way that made my sister frown at me, mad that her companion should suddenly take a liking to anyone other than her. "And take that dog and your sister. That way I know you'll come right back." Grandmother smiled triumphantly.

"Grandmama!" Martha and I yelled it simultaneously, she in delight and me in dismay. Now both Marthas were dancing around the living room. On the other end of the phone Claire was begging to know what was going on, urging me to hurry. It was clear from the look on her face that Grandmother wasn't budging.

"Okay, Claire, I'll call you in fifteen minutes." I hoped we'd be meeting at Tom's far sooner than that.

"Right. We're on our way. Be there in ten."

"Let's go." I grabbed the flashlight and launched myself out the trailer's front door, with girl and dog practically taking air behind me. I strode twenty fast steps down the driveway toward the Carmodys', thinking fast. How on earth was I going to find out what was going on at Tom's without getting Martha and that animal involved? When we'd gotten just far enough away from the trailer so we couldn't be heard and the dusk closed in around us, I stopped and grabbed Martha by the shoulders. The dog made a sound somewhere between a growl and a whine.

"Listen, Martha," I was thinking so fast I wasn't sure what I was saying would make sense, let alone keep Martha away from the Carmodys'. "You know Tom's brother got hurt in the war, right?" She narrowed her eyes, clearly wondering what I was up to. "He's kind of scary. He screams a lot and to tell you the truth, I don't think they'll let you in the house, since some of the things he says are pretty awful." I knew there was a nerve just below Martha's surface, one made of the same memories that kept her coming into my room at night. She'd heard some awful things already during the last few years, and looked as though she wanted to go back to the trailer and the safety of the evening news. But having her out with me had some advantages; if she just went back home Grandmother would get suspicious much sooner, and I didn't know how long it would take me to figure out where Tom was, and whether Cash had found him first. I had an idea, and brightened. "Hey, I know what we can do. Remember when we used to play hide and seek when the mosquito trucks were out?" It was true. In Biloxi, in a life that only went back five years but seemed like another world, Martha and I and every kid in our little trailer park had played hide and seek in the DDT fog from the weekly summer sprayings. While our healthy mother and taciturn father sat on the front steps in the growing dark, watching us and smoking cigarettes after supper, we chased the trucks in the dusk like they were the ice cream man, stalking one another in the sweet, murky soup until we got called in to baths and bed. Martha had run herself giddy in that fog, popping out from her hiding places, yelling "Tag, you're it!" and whooping and howling like a wild thing when she was so little she couldn't stay hidden, and I'd hardly been older than she was now. I wasn't even sure she remembered, but her eyes went soft as soon as I mentioned it, and I knew I had her, at least until it got really dark outside.

Remnants of the pecan orchard still stood and bore fruit between the trailer park and the edge of the Carmody's back yard, an area divided by a huge bramble that looked to me like a combination of blackberries and poison oak. I was sure it was full of snakes and so had been careful to circle around rather than go through the narrow opening that Tom always took. But there wasn't time to be spooky. Now, I led Martha to its edge, gave her the flashlight and said, "You go find a good hiding place while I go knock on Tom's door. Soon as I get the homework I'll come yelling for you. If I have to yell 'I give up' I'll do the dishes for you for a solid week." Martha hated any kind of chores, so I figured she'd rather wet her pants than leave her hiding place, but as an added motivation I hit her where I knew she had the most pride. I added, "I'll bet you can't stay hidden any better than you could when you were little, especially with your buddy there. She'll lead me right to you."

"Will not!" Martha grabbed the skin at the back of Martha's neck and started a defiant march off into the twilight. "You'll never find us, not never!" It was a testament to Martha the dog's love for Martha the girl that she let her haul her away from the sausages that I still had hidden, holding her by the scruff of the neck, even though she twisted and whined and walked on air as they receded to what I hoped was a safe place. They made enough noise, I hoped, to scare away anything that might be lurking in the grass. I felt a pang as I remembered how sweet my sister had been back then, when we'd danced and hidden in the dark, feeling safe, before she'd seen and heard things that had hurt her. But after just a second I slammed that door hard and pushed through the bushes into the Carmodys' back yard.

The Carmodys' house sat high the way most riverside ones did, anticipating the floods that came every few years when a big storm pushed the water from the gulf back upstream, leaving the residences battered but mostly intact. The first floor sat nearly the height of a normal second story, and the second receded up into the gloom. From head height all the way to the ground the underside was protected from becoming a den for a host of Mississippi critters by a latticework skirt, as rough and grey as the rest of the weather beaten structure. The back of the house was dark, the kitchen apparently empty. It looked like it hadn't been lived in for years. I guessed in a way it hadn't.

Locusts were already thrumming into the evening air, telling me the temperature if I knew how to do the arithmetic the way Granddaddy had taught me, singing in a chorus that made the hair on my arms stand up, half in fear, half sheer love. They were loud enough to drown out any small sound I might make, but I was still nervous, tiptoeing and looking about as though expecting to be ambushed. As I walked around the house I saw bluish light shining through the window up above me, diluted and flickering. The Carmodys' television was on as always, its murmur eerily resembling the cadence and tone of the news program I'd just left at home. As I rounded the house toward it, feeling alone in the dark, wishing I had Tom's sure wake to follow, I imagined Mrs. Carmody slumped in exhaustion beside Eddie, her own daily routine with her son leaving her as worn out as my grandmother's with the cafe left her. But out here in the dark I didn't really know anything, and it was driving me crazy. I didn't know where Tom was, or whether Cash was on his way. I didn't know how long it would take Claire and her parents, who, at the moment, I wouldn't have swapped for a gold ticket out of town, to come and make me feel like I didn't have to be the one in charge. I circled toward Tom's bedroom, looking for shells to toss up at the second story window, figuring if he was in there he'd know it was me and not someone with blood in his eye coming to look for him. He'd taught me to do it, after all.

"Hey Kate." Tom's voice was soft, as casual as if we'd just met on a corner on any early summer night. As hard as I'd been looking, I'd still missed him. I jerked so hard that the little pack of sausages slipped sideways, squishing under my right breast and making me shiver. Angrily, wanting to rid myself of any distractions, I fished them out and flung them in a random direction. It was a surprisingly good throw for a girl, as Tom would have said if his mind weren't on other things. The package hit the pavement all the way out on Little Red Road, the sausages rolling out of their binding and coming to rest naked on the gritty street, in the only puddle of streetlight on the short block that ended at the bait shop on the pier. I whirled to face the patch of deep shadow in an angle of the house where the den jutted out, the blue TV light almost directly above. The nook was filled with rakes and shovels and an old lawn mower that wouldn't have provided much cover in the light, but cast a jumble of shadows that confused the eye and did a fine job in the evening. I could just make him out, standing behind a pulled loose section of the rough, unpainted lattice underskirt, arms crossed.

"Tom, for Pete's sake! We've been looking all over for you!" I'd been so scared, and was now so relieved, that it burst out of me, an

117

angry yelp in the dusk. The locusts shut up at once, as though they'd just been a restless audience waiting for the performance to begin.

"Shhh, Kate. Listen."

In the quiet, I heard it; the tick-tick-tick of a hot engine, recently shut off and cooling in the deep shadows beneath the live oak on the other side of Little Red, not twenty feet away. A voice came from that direction. It was as calm as anything. "Carmody, tell that girl if she wants to see you beat to death she's standing in just the place."

Tom had to have seen the Dawg pull up. The dark little alcove was the best place you could be and still watch every direction. He could have easily stood there all night, watching whatever events unfolded from behind the latticework and tools. He'd have seen Cash encounter Mrs. Carmody and Eddie, and would have probably seen him leave with their combined outbursts driving him, and no information whatsoever. Then I'd shown up. From his spot in the corner he'd had an advantage that I'd just taken away from him. Now he stepped forward, arms still folded across his chest, hands tucked under his armpits as if holding himself together. Cash stepped forward at the same time. Tom took another step, now away from the shadows and into the low wash of twilight and TV blue.

"Hello Cash." Tom smiled a smile so broad that it took me aback. For a moment Cash looked confused himself, until Tom casually unfolded his arms and held something out toward him, something too small to see. "Breath mint? I hear you'll be needing one if you're ever going to play that horn again."

Afterward, I couldn't believe I hadn't seen it all coming, like people who are interviewed after surviving being hit by a freight train say they can't imagine why they didn't hear it. I kept running and rerunning the events, the three of us standing there, Claire and her parents barreling toward us out of the night in an attempt at whatever rescue they could pull off, my little sister, who never could stay hidden, and the thing dearest her heart there with her, waiting for me to find them and take them home.

Cash lunged at us like a wild thing, howling. He caught both me and Tom, one in each arm, bearing us to the ground. He kicked at me with his booted feet, catching me under the ribs and making me gasp and roll. He pounded Tom's curled form with his fists, trying to regain his footing in the sandy dirt. In spite of there being a half dozen lawn tools close at hand, Cash appeared intent on just one thing;

wailing away at Tom with fists and feet. He'd have kicked Tom to death I was sure, except for four things. Eddie and the Doucettes were the first two.

The window above us had been closed against the heat and the mosquitoes, the den hovering in the quiet between turning off the air conditioning and opening it to the night breeze off the river. Now it flew open and Mrs. Carmody's querulous voice called out "Who's there? Tom? Who's there?" Behind her I could just make out the growl that was Eddie, the cadence of his curses making them understandable. At just that moment, headlights and a rough roar that could be heard from a block away turned onto Little Red. I watched from my spot lying on the thin, grassy dirt where Cash had flung me, as the camper on the back of the Doucettes' truck leaned hard and the truck fishtailed. For a moment, relief washed over me. The cavalry had arrived. I knew the driver had to be Claire's daddy; I'd been in the back of that truck when he was at the wheel headed toward a rally, and he drove like his tail was on fire. Even Cash Carmody wouldn't take on Richard Doucette in full on help-the-underdog mode. I was ready to feel the relief of a near-but-not-quite disaster, watching the truck plow toward us out of the dark.

The other two things that stopped Tom's whipping, though at a price none of us could have imagined, were Martha and Martha. As I lay gasping, watching the truck approach and praying they'd get to us before anything important on Tom got destroyed, a black blur burst out of the bushes, my little sister in full-out, screeching pursuit. For a split second, before I realized that Martha the dog really did only love two things, and that one of them was about to betray her, I thought she might be coming to leap into the fray and give us a moment to escape. But she didn't. Instead, Martha did what I'd been carefully training her to do for the past few months, so that I could take evening walks with my friend. She charged straight for the sausages on the street.

Richard Doucette threw the truck so hard to one side that I was afraid it would roll over. His instincts, like his daughter's, were just right, but he still couldn't control where a half ton of truck would slide. Just as Martha reached and snatched at the treat she'd grown to trust would come from me, the hubcap of the left front tire hit her full force. She sailed backward, spinning in the air and landing a few feet away, twitching horribly, as though still trying to run, not realizing it was over. At first I thought she was conscious and howling, until I

119

realized that the agonized shriek that split the twilit air was coming from my eight year old sister, who was passing me at a staggering run.

Martha and the Doucettes got to the dog at the same time, Jean catching my sister up and whirling her thrashing, screaming form away from the body while Claire bent over it and Richard rushed the tangle of Tom and Cash. He waded in, stepping over me. Without the least hesitation he grabbed a fistful of boy in each hand, wrenching them apart, tossing Cash like a feed sack and setting Tom on his feet, where he bent over and promptly threw up in the grass. Richard stood between them and stuck out his chest and his fists, the expression on his face declaring him to be the winner of this fight and daring anyone to say otherwise. I thought Richard Doucette must have seen some real scrapping before the pacifist in him had come out.

In all this time, neither Cash nor Tom had uttered a sound, but there was sound everywhere. From above, Tom's mother continued to call out "Tom! Tom! What's going on out there?" Eddie's curses grew louder and more uncontrolled. Martha fought Jean Doucette's embrace, her arms windmilling and her voice eerily crying her own name, almost indistinguishable around her pain. She screamed "Martha! Martha!" until I thought her throat would tear. Her voice blended with the two from above, Mrs. Carmody's plaintive "Tom?" and that of Eddie, who stopped cursing and began to scream himself, an incoherent jumble of syllables that rose and rose until I could have sworn they would tear the dark apart. It was only when his brother began to make noises that had a distinctly out-of-his-mind sound that Tom looked up.

His face was calmer than it had any right to be. He was bloody and dirty, hair wild on his head, a state so foreign to him that it looked like a costume he'd put on, a character who, unlike the amazing Tom Carmody, could be made to eat the dirt of his own yard. His shirt was twisted around on his shoulders from the combined thrashing of his body and his attacker's, its left sleeve pulled away where Richard had wrenched them apart. But even in the dark I could tell that his green eyes were quiet, assessing. As I lay in an odd paralysis that I prayed would release me soon, as Claire cried and stroked Martha the dog's finally still form, as Jean held my sister away from her dog's body, as Richard planted himself, silent and untouchable between Tom and a Cash Collins who now looked like he might cry himself, Tom spoke calmly, as though finally he knew what to do. "I have to call an ambulance," he said, starting for the house's back door, passing us all without a glance. "Eddie's having an attack of shell shock."

"Call two!" Jean yelled out of the semi-darkness in front of the truck. The spell on me broke, and I leapt to where she held Martha, whose limbs shook strangely, stiffly as Jean lowered her to the ground. "Hurry! I think this child's having a seizure."

Time expanded around us, so that suddenly I could examine everyone and everything minutely, from a great distance. I stared at Martha, noting how, stiffened and shaking, she looked much the way her namesake had a few moments before. I watched Jean hold her arms firmly to keep her from hurting herself while she called out to Tom. I saw Cash, deflated and looking toward the Dawg as though about to bolt for it and peel away from the horror he had helped create. I counted the deep breaths that gave Richard away for being more afraid than he looked. I heard Eddie scream and plead for something to stop that wasn't even happening. I watched Tom walking with self possessed steps up the stairs, hurrying but not afraid, and as he opened the door he looked back for just a moment, locking eyes with me, and I knew that he knew exactly what I was feeling. He and I were the best, the very best, at being there without being there, at doing what had to be done while the us, the real us, dwindled down until we were as small as the dot of light on the television when you finally had to turn it off late at night, and just as close to blinking out. I'd spent years in this state, down as close to zero as you can go, holding on with blind tenacity, tenacity without hope, but too afraid to let go. So, I realized at last, had Tom Carmody. Like me, he'd spent a long, long time keeping the alive part of himself down to a tiny ember while waiting to see if anyone would ever again help him fan it back into a real fire. As he wheeled and slammed the door behind him, going to call for two ambulances, and to calm his terrified mother while Eddie screamed, I thought that maybe, when we could, he and I ought to talk.

Chapter Fifteen

I learned later that, even though they still drew attention from the residents of the few houses around Little Red Road and the people who lived around us in the trailer park, having an ambulance show up at the Carmody house wasn't an unheard of occurrence. Eddie's flashbacks were all the more awful for his body's lack of motion, Tom said, as we sat in the lobby waiting area of Singing River Hospital with the small crowd who had been part of our little disaster. We took up so much space that triage nurses and hospital volunteers paced our perimeter, as if trying to decide which of us to tell to stay and which to go home. It was awful, Tom said, to hear Eddie plead and cry and try to fight without any ability to make his body respond, and though she could take his cursing and his demands, Mrs. Carmody couldn't bear it when he went somewhere else in his head, somewhere terrible where she didn't exist at all. Tom had started calling for help not long after Eddie had come home, and now all he had to do, he told me, was say "It's Tom Carmody," and almost before he hung up the phone he'd hear sirens. This time, though, he'd taken them by surprise.

Having two emergency vehicles blare down our little dead end street following the screeching of the Doucettes' truck brakes and the combined cacophony of Martha, Eddie, Mrs. Carmody and Jean, the only ones among us who had had the sense enough to give full cry to the awfulness of what had just happened, was more than the inhabitants of the neighborhood could resist. They appeared as if by magic, clustered in clumps along the side of the street, wearing shorts and flip-flops, housedresses and slippers, some of them still holding remnants of the supper they'd left, chewing thoughtfully on po' boys and chicken legs as they whispered to one another. In fact, the only person, it seemed, who wasn't there, who hadn't come running, was my grandmother. I ran to the trailer to get her. She was asleep in front of the TV, oblivious to anything but her own need for rest. Everything that had happened had taken less time than it took the evening news to run.

"Grandmama!" She started as I yanked the trailer door open, stumbling over the threshold and landing on my hands and knees just inside the door, "Martha got hit by a car and Martha's having some kind of fit!"

Her reaction let me know that I could have done a lot better job of describing the situation. She clutched her heart and jumped from the chair. "Oh dear Lord, where is she? I told you to take care of her! Is she dead? Oh, my God; Oh God!" Her face was ashen as she shoved past me and down the steps, charging toward where the red ambulance lights reflected off the street and the trees. It took me a second to realize that she didn't know which Martha was which. I launched after her, yelling for her to slow down. By the time I caught her, halfway to the circle of streetlight where the little crowd was gathered, she was gasping for breath, trying to run in her mashed-down shoes and uniform, looking like she might just fall down and make us have to call yet another vehicle to the scene.

"Grandmama," I caught at the back of her dress, "It's the dog got hit. It's the dog, not Martha. Martha saw it and Jean says she had some kind of seizure but she's not hurt." My grandmother actually staggered at the news, as though I'd given her permission for a small collapse. We reached the spot together, where someone's red and white checkered shirt had been thrown over the little body on the street. My sister had come out of her frozen, rigid state but was still fighting, her continual cry of her dog's name reduced to a croak. She was being lifted on a stretcher into the back of one of the ambulances. Cash and the Dawg were gone. The kitchen door of the Carmody house stood wide open, blaring light out and looking, at last, alive. I could see the tops of heads through the den's window, bending, straightening. They were probably, I thought, lifting Eddie, heavy and inert, onto another stretcher. It was quiet up there. I wondered if they had shot him full of something.

Grandmother waded into the crowd, not saying a word to anyone but making it clear by the way she clambered into the ambulance with Martha that this child was hers. She traded brief words with the EMT and sat down, stroking Martha's thrashing form and wiping her own brow, firing a look at me as the ambulance doors closed. It confirmed what I already knew. I'd caused this somehow. When she got the whole story, I wondered what she would do, and what she would tell our father, and if, a world away, he would care.

Now she was upstairs with my sister and the doctors, and Mr. and Mrs. Carmody were up there with Eddie. Tom, Jean, Claire, Richard, various members of the Doucette clan who'd come running when they heard, and my grandfather, who shook so hard he looked like he might have to be admitted himself, but who would not go further than the hospital waiting room, sat and tried to figure out how to talk about what had happened.

"It's my fault." I said it simply, as though everyone agreed and were just waiting for me to confirm it. Tom snorted.

"Come down off the cross, Kate Lynn." He still had that calm look, but I flinched at his words. "It's every damn body's fault. It's my fault for screwing up Cash's horn, it's his fault for humiliating me in front of the school, it's his family's fault for turning him into such an asshole, it's your fault for giving a damn about me, it's Martha's fault for falling in love with that dog, it's Richard's fault for wanting to rescue the whole damn world, it's your mother's fault for dying and your father's fault for sending you to live among the Pascagoula. Hell, it's the government's fault for getting us into that shit-forsaken war and causing Eddie to end up a cripple in more ways than one, so give it up. In the great grand scheme of things, you ain't that important."

"What happened to Cash? Where'd he go?" I wondered what kind of person would leave an accident, even if, in spite of how much I'd like to have, I couldn't pin either Martha's troubles on him.

"He just got up and walked away," Richard said from where he sat, one arm around Jean and the other around Claire, who was the only one of us with tears trickling down her face. When she wiped snot on his shirt he just drew her in closer. "He didn't run away; he just walked with his head down like he was going to a whipping. I'd recommend you all leave him alone for a long time." Richard had been the one to talk to the police, who'd appeared along with the ambulances. I wondered what he'd said that had kept them from asking the rest of us any questions. Tom told me later Richard had taken responsibility for the accident, told them how he'd gone to break up a tussle between schoolboys and had hit the dog and caused the chain reaction in the child and troubled young man, and how no one was hurt nor wanted to press charges. From his position as the town communist he must know a lot about talking to the authorities, I imagined. He also, it seemed, knew how to take responsibility without shame. Maybe that was where Tom had learned it.

We sat in the waiting room for hours, eying the elevator doors that led to the upper floors, waiting to recognize someone when they opened. When they finally slid back to reveal my grandmother, leaning heavily against one side of the car, head down and hand on her ample breast as if trying to hold herself together, we all stood up. No one went to her; we waited for whatever she was going to bring to us. She didn't acknowledge us at first; she just shuffled forward, looking as old and as worn out as I'd ever seen her, and sat down heavily on one of the hard plastic seats before looking up.

"Doctor says he don't think it's epilepsy or nothing like that. If it was she would've come out of it different, not still fighting and hollering. He says he wants to do some tests. What in the world happened to that girl?" She shook her head, not really asking the question of any of us but dropping it like a stone on the waiting room floor.

"I'm sorry Grandmama, I am," I didn't care what Tom said; it was me who had deceived her and taken my sister out into the dark. "Is she okay? Is she still calling Martha?"

Grandmother lifted her eyes. When she answered me, she shook her head. "She wasn't saying 'Martha,' Baby." In a place where everybody called everybody by terms like "Darlin'" and "Baby," it had never been in her character to do it. It felt strange and unsettling. "She was saying 'Mother,' over and over, "Mother, Mother,'—like she just now realized your mother was gone." Her voice caught. "It like to broke my heart, hearing her scream for her after all this time. I don't even think she knew I was there. The doctor had to strap her down and give her something to make her sleep. He said when she wakes up she might be fine. We'll have to wait and see. Katie," she looked at me in a way I hated, a way that I recognized from when the preacher and members of the congregation had prayed over our mother as she sat embarrassed but hopeful, when she wasn't yet eaten up and wild-eyed with fever and pain. "Katie, you and your granddaddy ought to go on home. You can't go up to see her anyway. I'll sit with her tonight. At least the café's closed tomorrow."

126

"There's no school tomorrow either. I'm staying." I stuck out my chin, ready to fight if need be. I might not be able to see Martha, but I wasn't going to abandon her.

"I ain't going nowhere," Granddaddy added hoarsely, putting out his Lucky Strike in an ashtray that he'd spent the last few hours filling.

"If you don't mind, Mrs. Lynn, we'll go on." Jean had come over and patted Grandmother's shoulder. "We feel awful bad about the little dog."

"Lord, that dog." Grandmother shook her head again. "Is it still laying out in the road?"

"I moved her. Let me go bury her for you, Ma'am." Richard and Claire had joined us. Tom sat a little apart, listening but still watching the elevator for some sign that his brother was all right. "It's the least I can do. I'm so sorry I run her over, Miz Lynn. She was a fine little dog and I know your girl loved her. I wish I could take it back. I'll bury her out by our place so Martha can come see her if she wants to."

"That would be fine." I knew she wouldn't take Martha to the Doucettes' house, but I thought I could if she wanted me to.

"I want to come too." Claire had wiped her eyes, and seemed ready to carry on, to get her usual handle on things. I wished she would stay with Tom and me, but I didn't have the energy to ask. If she wanted to bury my sister's dog instead, so be it.

"Oh, I almost forgot," Grandmother raised her voice so Tom could hear. "Your mother says Eddie is asleep and they're going to stay upstairs for a while, and for you to go home too."

"Thanks. If you don't mind, I'll stay here with Kate."

She stood up slowly, and surprised me by pulling him to her, patting his back as she gave him the briefest of hugs. "You're a good boy." When she let him go he leaned into her, prolonging the contact. It was the only hug he'd gotten on what must have been as bad a day for him as it was for any of us. "I'll come back down in a while and let you know what's going on with the both of them. Lord, Katie, what am I going to tell your daddy?"

She started back toward the elevator and Tom tugged on my arm. "Come on. Let's go out to the pond and count the ducks."

Chapter Sixteen

We sat outside by the large pond that stretched between the front doors of the hospital and the surface road that ran in front of it, just a chain link fence separating it from Highway 90. It was pretty even in the dark, its surrounding lawn dotted with patches of pampas grass, flower beds and summer-blown azaleas, kept up, a plaque along the lamplit walkway read, by the Wives of the VFW. A few little cement benches faced the water at respectful intervals. We had found the one furthest from the few other people who sat huddled in clouds of cigarette smoke and distressed conversation on one or another of them. Our bench rested in its own little pool of lamplight, surrounded by the fat white ducks and half grown ducklings that spent their days begging handouts from hospital visitors, and their nights sleeping in clumps on the grass. Every summer there were more of them, dropped off by well-meaning parents who'd just had to buy the downy yellow babies for their children's Easter baskets. The new would wear off the ducklings at about the same time the pinfeathers showed up, turning the adorable infants into gawky, snappish adolescents who looked like they were covered with porcupine quills until the new feathers unfurled. Now, in the dark, they tucked their outsized bills beneath raggedly feathered wings and hunkered down in the grass. Not a bit like the Doucettes' geese, they didn't seem to care that there were people coming and going all the time, and I wondered if Easter ducks were bred to be particularly docile and dumb. They looked like lumpy mashed potatoes, I thought, and felt a little guilty as my stomach growled. We'd never gotten around to supper.

Tom hadn't said much since Grandmother had told us what Martha had been crying up in her hospital bed, until the sedative the doctors gave her took hold. He'd just led me outside, away from Claire's family, who were readying to go and deal with Martha's body, and my grandfather, who sat in the corner of the waiting room, sniffling and clearing his throat again and again. Granddaddy wasn't a strong man, but he had a tender heart, and loved Martha as much as he loved me. And in a long spate of not feeling I could count on anything much, I had never once doubted that my grandfather loved me. Unfortunately, it was the kind of love that made him even more helpless as a parent than he already was as a man. He was so afraid of hospitals that he might well have ended up in a bed himself if he'd gone up to see her. He'd never been able to bring himself to visit our mother when she was in the hospital, not when she'd had the operation that kept her there for months and left her unrecognizable to herself and to us, and not when she was dying. And I suspected that, somewhere out here among the little feathered spuds was the one Martha had called "Fluffy" for three weeks the year before. Our mother and father had been furious when Granddaddy had shown up with it on Easter morning and Martha cried for a day when Daddy told her that her duckling had run away. Fluffy was probably somewhere near us this minute, now feathered out and breeding little spuds of his own.

Looking up at the hospital windows, some darkened and some blazing bright even at this late hour, made the hairs on my neck prickle. I couldn't count the times Martha and I had stood outside the base hospital during our mother's many stays, staring up at its windows, waiting for a stick figure to appear in one of them, leaning on our father or one of the nurses, raising its hand weakly, while Martha jumped up and down like a crazy child, screaming "Mother! Mother!" and I made a stiff little wave of my own, trying to smile even as the thought in the forefront of my mind was that I would sleep through the whole night that night, and that someone else would clean her up and listen to her cry. On the nights when her mutilated body failed her so badly that only professionals could persuade it to start working on its own once again, Daddy slept in his bed instead of on the couch and I slept like the dead, both of us saving up strength for our next shift. I knew I ought to feel bad about it, but I had long ago lost perspective on what was good to feel and what was bad. Besides, anything I felt at all was dwarfed beside what she was going through. That much I did know.

"I believe this is the part where I say 'A penny for your thoughts.'" Tom jostled me gently.

"Did you ever lie really still, wondering what it would be like to be Eddie? Not to feel anything? Not to be able to reach up and scratch your nose and to know that it would never get any better and that you'd be like that for the rest of your life?"

He laughed a short laugh. "I don't have to. Remember when I told you that Eddie was really pretty polite when you were around?"

"Uh-huh."

"Well, there are reasons I don't spend any more time in that house than I do. Eddie not only tells me every single day that he hates me for being able to walk and feed myself and feel myself get a hard-on, but that he hates me for wasting the hard-ons I get on the wrong sex. He howls like a mad dog about how unfair it is that a sissy boy's up and walking around while a real man and a soldier lies rotting in his own hell. And then Mother apologizes and tells me how he doesn't mean it, and I don't tell her he's right, that I don't have all those pretty Paul McCartney and broody Bob Dylan posters on my wall because I want to be a great singer someday, but that I'd walk to New Orleans on my knees if one of them would just kiss me on the mouth." He shook his head. "I just can't bring myself to take away both her sons."

"You sound like you wouldn't be her son any more if you told her. Like you'd be dead."

"Kate, you are the only other person I know who gets that there are plenty of things you can be that are worse than dead, and believe me, as far as my family goes, being queer is three or four of them. Now look," he took my hand. "you've seen my whole life laid out like a bad movie while I've just got puzzle pieces to go on where you're concerned. You go along with me and Claire like you're living our lives instead of your own. I kind of get that; don't take offense but your grandparents aren't the most interesting people I've ever been around. But don't you think I ought to have some idea why something like Gator Bill's hobby makes you freak out and your sister starts screaming for her mama and has a foaming at the mouth fit when her dog dies?"

I thought about it for so long that he drew an exasperated breath as if to continue, but I held up a hand before he could speak. "Remember Miss One-legged America?"

"Yes."

"Did I tell you Martha has old pictures of Mother from her Miss Homecoming days hidden under her bed?"

"No."

"She does. I think it's because that's the way she has to remember her. If she remembered her the way she was afterward, it would be like she was betraying her. After, she wouldn't let us take her picture any more. Not a single one. The only pictures of her I have are more than four years old. I get the creeps when I look at them because they tell me lies. They say "This is Sylvia Doyle, the high school beauty queen, the pretty girl in her pretty gown, smiling like she knows you enjoy looking at her and she enjoys it too." I shook my head. "Even the later ones, where she's Sylvia Doyle Lynn, holding me or Martha, when she must have been worn out from taking care of babies or doing whatever she did all day—tell you the God's honest truth Tom, sometimes I think there must be some broken part in my brain because I can't half remember her from back then except for the times when we were all dressed up—she had us fixed up like dolls, smiling and looking like there wasn't anything finer than having your picture taken. Remember that movie star that married the prince, Grace Kelly?"

"Are you kidding me? Mother took me to see *High Society* about a hundred times when it played on Old Movie Night at the Saenger. I was seven or so and I wanted to be her too. It got to where I took particular pleasure in saying 'Hello everybody!' just like Tracy Lord, just so I could watch Eddie twitch."

I chuckled in spite of myself. "Well, that's who she adored, Grace Kelly. She loved her more than she loved Jackie Kennedy, and that's saying something. She loved having a name with a "Y" in each part, just like Kelly and Kennedy. She thought she looked like Princess Grace, and she kind of did, when she did her hair up in a French Twist and stretched her neck out long. She always was big on posture." This last made a lump in my throat. I thought again of the tottering stick figure in the hospital window. "She lit up like Christmas when you pointed a camera at her or when she was talking in what Daddy called her movie star voice, flirting a little with whoever she was talking to. I remember her in church, smiling and nodding to everybody around us while Martha and I itched half to death in all the fuss she made us wear. It was like she'd invented Jesus her own self just to have a theater to go to once a week and act like a star." I was a little shocked at the warm feeling I had in my stomach, as if criticizing her was forging a connection with her that I hadn't expected. "Anyway, it all changed when she came home after the cancer operation. All of it."

"Tell me."

"Christ, Tom."

"Tell me or I swear, I'll never let you help me fill a saxophone with shit again."

I laughed again, ruefully. "You do have a hell of a mean streak, you know that don't you? How do I know you won't use it against me?"

"Because I love you. Tell me."

"All right." He loved me, damn him. I paused again and closed my eyes, gathering her up from out of the shadows. I hated to admit I was afraid of her after all these months, afraid that I might really conjure her and that she might tighten her grip on me once more. I knew I'd been living in twilight since she'd died, one foot in whatever land she still existed in and one in the one in which I longed to really be, with Tom and Claire and the rest of the live world. I wasn't convinced that all the love in the world could protect me if I started really thinking about her.

"You know how they call it Ground Zero when a bomb goes off and everything, all the blown up and burned up things radiate out from that spot?"

"Mmm-hmm."

"I think lives have those too, places where something burns a hole in you and everything you feel from then on out is made by the shape of that hole. Does that make sense?"

"Sure. Eddie's bomb was real; mine was Eddie. Your mother's was cancer and yours was her."

"Yeah, but it's more complicated than that. It depends on who you were before, and what the most important thing in the world is to you, and if that's the thing that explodes. That look she has in those pictures, the look that says that she sees you seeing her, and that the two of you are almost in love over how pretty she is and how good you feel just hanging around her, that's how I remember the best times we had. I mean, she loved me and Martha, but one reason she did was because we loved to look at her too. I used to brush her hair and Martha would rub lotion on her legs when she was so little she just used her left hand to rub because her right fingers were always in her

133

mouth. I don't mean she treated us like slaves; it was just that was the way we loved on one another. We'd sit and watch those movies on TV, Grace Kelly and Natalie Wood and all, and we felt like we had us our own star right there in the living room, one who loved us and made us special too. And then," I fumbled for words, still putting the vision of her off, "she came home one day and said she was sick and they were going to put her in the hospital for a while and make her well. I swear that's all she told us. That's all anybody told us. And she was gone for a long time, for months. From October to May."

"Damn. Where were you all this time?"

"We kept on going. I was almost twelve and Daddy figured that was old enough to do the after school stuff, to take care of Martha until he got home at night. I didn't do much of a job, but he made sure we were fairly clean and fairly well fed even if I was the one who did most of the cleaning and feeding. I was so bad at laundry and bed making that we slept under piles of clean wash on bare mattresses. I cooked so many fish sticks and cans of spinach that Martha gags every time she sees them. We were on base, in the little trailer park they had there, and I swear we didn't leave the yard for the whole time she was gone. The base regulations said the outside of the place had to look spit and polish, but nobody said a thing about regulations for the inside. It was pretty rank sometimes. Not a soul at school knew what was going on. I mean, what do you say to somebody? 'No, I can't come to your house because my mother has cancer and my daddy won't let me leave the house, and you can't come over because it looks like a hurricane blew through'? It was embarrassing. Grandmother came over on weekends and tried to do what she could, but can you imagine my granddaddy trying to run the Rebel? During the week we spent a lot of time just like this, sitting in the car doing homework outside the hospital, looking up at the windows until somebody helped her get up and stand there and wave at us. Germs, you know. Can't have germs on a cancer ward. We talked to her on the phone but she'd always start to cry and say things that didn't make sense and it scared Martha. After a while Daddy said the medicine they gave her made it hard for her to talk and we quit trying. They never did let us visit her, so we really didn't know what she was like until the day they brought her home. And that, that day, was Ground Zero."

"You mean when you saw her?"

"Yes, but like I said it's more complicated than that. We knew she was coming home that day so I got us all fixed up, like she would have done. Grandmother had helped us with the trailer, so it was as clean as it had been in months. I bathed us and washed our hair and put on the prettiest dresses we had, which, to tell you the truth, we had hardly touched the whole time she was away. Daddy wasn't much on going to church and we were just as glad to wear pajamas all weekend. Martha's dress was so short you could see her underwear, but by God that underwear was clean. I knew Mother was coming home and wanted us to look our best, and would take us to get new things as soon as she could. I was so glad she'd be back and I wouldn't have to be responsible any more I couldn't see straight. We were ready hours before she got there, waiting and waiting, not wanting to mess up how good we looked so she'd be proud of us."

"All right. Then what?"

"We spent the whole afternoon standing in the open door, Grandmother griping at us about air conditioning the whole world. There we stood when Daddy's car pulled up and the ambulance pulled up behind it. It wasn't like with Martha and Eddie tonight; it was so quiet no one would have known they were coming if they didn't see them, and the neighbors were probably too polite to make a big show. They just slipped up to the front of the fence and two men opened the back and started pulling this long white thing like a cocoon out of it, one of them holding handles that stuck out the end. It took me a minute to realize it was blankets strapped around her, holding her onto a stretcher. About that time her head appeared, and a man holding the other end. I made ready to smile and Martha started jumping up and down, but then I realized she wasn't looking at us; she was turned looking the other way. She stayed that way the whole way up the steps. Martha was so excited I don't think she noticed; she just kept hopping and calling her all the way into the living room, where they put the legs down on the stretcher and started unbuckling her straps. Martha made a dive for her and Daddy grabbed her in mid air so she wouldn't touch her, and I saw Mother flinch like she expected to be hurt. That's when she turned her head to look at us."

I felt hollow and far away, as though I was seeing her again, feeling the shock that ran all the way to my bones and made me want to throw up. That feeling had been around the edges of everything I'd felt ever since, but now it grew close and big, and I felt as though I was in danger. But I went on anyway, remembering that Tom loved me and hoping he appreciated how much I counted on that love to keep me here.

"You know how sometimes you think you see somebody you know, and just as you wave to them you realize it's a stranger, and it scares you a little bit?"

"I think so. Kind of a Twilight Zone feeling."

"Exactly. Well, whatever it was that came home, it wasn't my mother. I knew it as soon as I looked at her. And she knew I knew it. That was the worst thing, the look in her eyes that told me exactly what the look in mine was, and the effect it had on her. Tom, I swear, she started hating me that very minute. I don't mean she said she did, she never did that. But that thing we had shared, that in love with somebody beautiful feeling, was gone. She was gone. I was gone. We both turned into something completely different that day before either of us said a single word to each other." I was breathing fast and I could hear my heart pounding. I groped for something and Tom grabbed my hands in his, squeezing them so tight they hurt. I was glad; the pain let me know I was with him and not back in that living room staring in horror at the face of a woman who had betrayed me by losing the thing that bound us together.

"What was it?" Tom wanted to know. "What did they do to her?"

"God. They pretty much cut her in half, Tom. They took away her right leg, but they cut off so much of her that she just angled up from where the other leg was. I mean, Eddie gets pissed off about not feeling his dick; at least he's got one. She didn't have anything. They took it all away. They just scooped her out and wrapped a flap of skin from the back to the front and sewed it together. She had a hole in her side where she peed and another one where she shit, and a bag glued over each one that broke loose all the time. That's what we did all night sometimes. We unglued and reglued those damned bags to her side. We helped her put glycerin suppositories into her colostomy—the one for shit—and held a pan under it when it came out, while she cursed us for the looks on our faces and then cried like a baby and apologized for putting us through it. I'll tell you one thing, it sure wasn't like brushing her pretty blonde hair and rubbing lotion on her pretty skin. I still liked to do it, though, brush her hair for her. It was a memory we shared, and every now and then we were a little like

136

before. But it didn't always work. She asked Martha to rub lotion on the leg that was still there once and the poor kid ran screaming. It took me a whole day to figure out that she was afraid if she touched it, it would come off too. Kind of makes Miss One-Legged America make sense, doesn't it?"

"My God, Kate. How long did you have to do that?"

"A couple of years. And that's the hell of it. She didn't get better. She got worse. I didn't know until Daddy told me, when he was trying to explain why he wasn't fighting going to Vietnam, but they, and he, knew all along that they hadn't cured her. She was going to die all along. Nobody told her, and nobody told us, but he spent all that time with that secret, not knowing if the next trip to the hospital, the next pneumonia or infection would be the last one. They all thought that if they told her she'd just give up and go on and die. It must have worn him down something terrible. Hell, Martha and I were just plowing along with our heads down, not thinking about anything. Or I was. Right now I'm a little scared about what was happening to Martha."

"And then she died."

"And then she died." I repeated it as if it was a simple thing, as if I hadn't come home from school one day to find my father standing waiting for us in the trailer door the same way we'd waited for her so long before. She'd been in the hospital again, I'd been sleeping and feeling almost normal, and I'd gotten a crush on a boy named Ricky, who sat in front of me at school. When I saw him standing there waiting I was imagining Ricky asking me to dance, and I was doing a little two-step up the street in front of the trailer. For just the briefest second I thought he'd somehow read my mind and that I was in trouble for being boy crazy. It was a thing Mother had started accusing me of during those last few months. She'd pull me to her and whisper, wild eyed with pain and drugs, that boys were only after one thing and that she'd make me sorry if I started running around while she was sick in bed. That part I wanted to keep to myself, not because I didn't think Tom would understand; he understood boy crazy better than most girls I knew. It just felt unfinished, something I hadn't worked out myself yet, and so anything I told him ran the risk of being a lie. I could tell him one thing, though.

"You know what I felt when he told me? He was standing there; his face was old all of a sudden and his eyes red. It scared me to see him like that, but except for that, the thing I felt was relief. Just relief. I couldn't hurt her any more."

"And she couldn't hurt you."

"I still don't know about that. I mean, the thing about the Pascagoula Indians was that they all did it together. It makes a great story for us to tell because we're not the ones left behind, trying to figure out who we are now if we're not part of something that goes back as far as we do. Sometimes, Tom, I feel like I'm the last of the Pascagoula, standing there on dry land, looking at the spot where everybody who told me who I was, for good or for bad, just walked off and left me. I don't know who to be if I'm not brushing her hair." I buried my face in Tom Carmody's shoulder then, embarrassed that I was crying, not for Miss Homecoming or for the terrible thing that had replaced her, but for me, the last of the Pascagoula, sitting beside him on the shore, hoping he could keep me from drowning.

Chapter Seventeen

They let my sister come home the next day, pale but smiling as she was wheeled out the front entrance by, it looked like, half the nurses at Singing River Hospital. The doctors hadn't found anything wrong with her. Everyone agreed that seeing her dog get hit by a car so soon after losing her mother had just been one too many things for her brain to handle, and that she could stay home for the few remaining days of the school year. Although she made no effort to talk, shaking her head yes or no if asked anything but otherwise paying little attention to what was going on, she clutched a Get Well balloon in one hand and an unfamiliar baby doll in the other. I knew Martha had always hated baby dolls. I thought it a little strange she wasn't acting the least bit upset about Martha's death, but I figured word of her recent orphanhood and her dead dog must have got around, and didn't blame her one bit for taking full advantage of the situation.

Eddie went home too, Tom told me later, taken back in the same ambulance in which he'd arrived and placed back in his hospital bed, snarling at the attendants all the way. I made up my mind then and there that if Grandmother ever wanted anything from the Carmody house again, she could go get it herself. I never wanted to see another sickroom or hear another voice rise in anger or in pain as long as I lived. Something about telling Tom about my mother had given me an appetite for being alive. I wanted to enjoy myself; I wanted to play. School was going to be out in a matter of days and I was in the mood to do something interesting, something that only had to do with the healthy and the living and the full-out foolish.

"Sounds to me like we'd better talk to Claire," Tom said when I told him. "She'd hate to miss out on some real debauchery."

"Boy, am I glad to see you all," she said when we arrived at the Doucettes' house on Saturday afternoon, after I'd worn Grandmother down so she'd agreed to let me go with Tom. She had softened toward him since that brief hug the night before. I left her sitting beside my sister, shaking her head, staring at the empty spot on the floor where the two Marthas had lain in a pile together only a day before. Now, it was all I could do not to look out the Doucettes' windows into the big back yard for the piece of turned earth that would mark where the dog was buried. I'd had enough of graves, too.

"Did you hear about Cash?" Claire's eyes were bright; she was itching to tell us something.

"Do tell." Tom drew his mouth up as though he smelled something foul.

"He's gone. He called here late last night and talked to Richard. "He said to tell the little girl he was sorry about her damn dog and to tell Tom Carmody that if he ever saw him again he was going to kill him, so the best thing was just for him to go off. Personally, I don't think he could face that daddy of his when word got out that Tom had got back at him the way he did. That man's mean as a snake. I almost feel sorry for the boy. Almost."

"But what about school? He can't just stop."

"Aw hell, Cherie, leave it alone." Claire's fierceness startled me almost as much as her news had. "I think Cash is better off without it and it's better off without him. If he's smart he'll get that horn cleaned up and go look up his real daddy up in Nashville." She chuckled. "Can you see him showing up on Johnny Cash's doorstep, saying 'You don't know me but my Mama says you're my real daddy.' That ought to get him a job on the Grand Old Opry, don't you think?" Her chuckle had worked its way into a series of snorts. "Shoot, I never did get a chance to tell him my fake real daddy could beat up his fake real daddy! Go get him, Tom, and let's see who we can send to the hospital this time!" She let out a whoop. Tom whooped right along with her, laughing until he was leaning on her heaving shoulders, gasping for air. It was as though years' worth of tension had finally broken and they had just discovered that they were laughing the last, and best, laugh. I still felt a little bit bad about Cash, but the load that had been lightening since my talk with Tom hitched up another notch and I let myself enjoy a conspiratorial grin. I even puckered my lips

140

and mimed playing an invisible saxophone, sending the two of them off again.

"Now then," Tom said, after composing himself and wiping his eyes on his shirttail, carefully retucking it into the waist of his khakis. "'Cherie' here is itching to get into trouble of some kind. You got any ideas?"

"Well...Richard's going to New Orleans next weekend. I'll bet if we asked him, he'd let us go with him."

Chapter Eighteen

Since I'd never even asked to spend the night at Claire's house before, I had spent the entire week working on my story. I told Grandmother that Claire and I were working on our end of the year project for Mississippi History class, a presentation about the ghosts that everybody said haunted some important state historic sites. My lie was a little bit true; I had taken to reading about them, looking for the one about the Pascagoula, so when I asked her it was easy to fabricate something that sounded believable. I went on and on about what interesting spirits people believed hung around the courthouses and Civil War graveyards that were the centerpieces of many towns, and about the "Devil at the Crossroads" stories that folks up in the delta told, and about the old slave quarters where the ghosts of slaves still cried at night, until her eyes glazed over and she eventually shooed me away with "All right, all right, just tell Mister Doucette to bring you home by tomorrow at suppertime." She'd surprised me by giving in, and even more by sending me off bright and early Saturday morning with a big paper sack full of purple hull peas from the bushel Granddaddy had won in a game of bourre the night before. Communism notwithstanding, she'd obviously seen something in the way they handled the Martha incident that made her trust the Doucettes, and maybe even like them a little bit. She even waved and smiled at Richard when he and Claire showed up in the pickup truck to get me, though she was careful to keep Martha, who sat upright on a corner of the couch as though waiting for something, from seeing the truck.

I walked past my sister and out the door, waving 'bye and swaggering, trying to make her curious, saying "See you later, alligator," hoping she would reply "After while, crocodile," the way we had done since she was a baby and had said "cock-a-doodle" instead of "crocodile," causing our parents and me to fall over laughing and to say it again and again just to hear her. Now she didn't answer. She hadn't said twenty words in the past week, and had spent a lot of time sitting in that attitude of waiting, her eyes glittery and her hands never still, but reaching out to touch the things around her over and over again, like a blind person will. Grandmother had set her up in the one-room apartment attached to the café so she could check on her often, with the television on to keep her company, and she stared at soap operas and cartoons and the evening news with the same rapt attention, as though any minute now she was going to get some important message from them, her fingers all the while tracing the edges of her blanket and the arms of the couch and a cigar box full of newly acquired treasures. Granddaddy had brought her everything he could think of from his forays, hunks of chewy sugar cane that she ordinarily would have fought me like a wildcat for, a piece of box turtle shell he'd found on the side of the road, a package of real Mexican Jumping Beans she'd thrown a full out tantrum for at the Woolworth's last fall, the husk of a locust, a handful of tiny pink shells from the beach. She touched them again and again, lightly, as though each time her hands found them they were a brand new discovery, all the while her eyes never leaving the television screen and the little expectant smile never leaving her face. She was beginning to completely creep me out.

This morning, though, I vowed not to worry about Martha or anything else. What I was about to do might blow up, might get me into more trouble than I'd ever gotten into. It might get me sent to reform school, even to Parchman or Angola, where I heard girls who ran away could end up. The thought of being a Parchman Pigeon or and Angola Bunny made me sick with nervous pleasure.

"Hello Kate," Richard grinned wide as I got in the passenger side of the truck. In spite of a week's worth of Claire and Tom rolling their eyes when I said it, I still couldn't believe he was willingly helping us deceive my grandmother, whom he clearly liked and respected. "How's the little one?"

"She's okay, I guess. No more fits. Still acting pretty weird." I leaned across Claire to talk to Richard, who shifted and nodded, holding his lit cigarette out the window the same way Claire had done the last time I had gone down Highway 90 in this old truck. I thought he was her daddy for sure.

"That little one needs her a Mama."

"I guess." I wasn't interested in Mamas; I wondered how my attempt at a day's worth of freedom was going to play out.

"We're going to get Tom and then we'll go get Bill and Felicia," Claire said. I jumped so hard that Richard chuckled.

"Bill and Felicia are going with us?" After the way I'd acted when we'd visited them, I was afraid they didn't think a whole lot of me. I wasn't sure I was going to be comfortable having them along.

Claire squeezed my hand and went on. "Bill and Richard have a couple hours business in New Orleans, and we can see the French Quarter while they get it done. And there's a surprise, too. One not even Tom knows about." She was practically bouncing on the seat. She had worn a simple T-shirt, shorts and sandals for the day, making her look younger than she did at school, her sophisticated attitude given way in favor of eager anticipation. For once, I felt older than she was.

"You all will have a fine time. After what you been through, you need to see a different piece of the world. Something so pretty it'll make your teeth sing." Richard patted Claire's knee with one hand as he talked, while I tried to sort things out in my head. In my world the kids and the adults, as mixed up as everything had been, had always been on opposite sides of authority. Here was a parent deceiving a parent, or a grandparent in my case, in favor of a bunch of teenagers. A man who was planning a surprise for me, and who was grinning like a possum at the prospect.

Tom was waiting for us by the turnoff to Highway 90, dressed as always in his khakis and tucked in shirt. He had a huge smile on his face and stuck out his thumb as if hitchhiking when he spotted the truck. Just seeing him this happy pulled my own nervousness down a notch. I thought he deserved a little fun, too. Tom's Bugs Bunny act didn't cover up everything. He'd had a hard life, and sticking out the way he did made it pretty certain things wouldn't be easy as long as he lived in Pascagoula. We'd joked about going to New Orleans together and now we were doing it for real, even if it was only for a few hours. I was as glad for Tom's chance to see a different part of the world as I was for my own.

It didn't take me a second to realize there wasn't going to be room enough for everyone in the cabin of the truck if Bill and Felicia were coming along. Claire had obviously been thinking the same. She motioned for me to open my door and gave me a little shove. While Richard fiddled with the radio she and Tom, who'd gone straight to the back of the pickup, tugged at the hatch, swinging it upward. A slightly funky smell wafted out of the shell, causing all three of us to pull faces, but Tom didn't waste any time clambering over the gate and reaching out to haul us up, Claire first, and then me. It was already approaching hot, even at that early hour, and once inside the truck bed the odor was pronounced. Richard slid open the window between the cab and the shell.

"You all want to leave the hatch up and the windows open, go on," his voice piped above the strains of the AM zydeco station way over in Houma. "Sorry for the stink." He didn't say any more. The truck gave a lurch and the three of us grabbed for one another to keep from sliding toward the rear.

There was a long black metal footlocker beneath each of the shell's side windows. Tom stretched out, lounging on the passenger's side, sliding the window open above him, and Claire and I shared the other, doing the same. As the truck picked up speed air rushed through, lifting our hair and whipping it around our faces and into our mouths. Between the open windows and the open hatch, Pascagoula rolled by like a long movie. The morning sun was flat and white against the humid grey-blue sky. The air smelled of salt and decay, a musky mix that made me think of fish and snakes and possums and alligators, and then of Gator Bill's strange mixtures of real and make-believe. I shivered.

"What's Richard and Bill's business in New Orleans?" I shouted above the rush of air. Claire held up a hand. We had reached the Singing River Bridge. I knew without asking that she wanted to wait until we got across to answer. Like every other kid raised in Pascagoula, she wanted to hear the bridge sing under our wheels as we went over the span, a brilliant hum that Granddaddy had always told Martha and me was just like that of the Indians' death song. From my position on the footlocker I could see out the window downriver, past the sand bars and the marsh grass at its edges, past the shipyard's tall cranes and the railroad bridge in the distance, and off toward the trailer, the Carmody house and the spot where people said the tribe had walked into the water. I felt like I was telling Pascagoula goodbye, that this wasn't just a fine adventure or a transgression for which I might get into real trouble, but that I might be leaving something behind, something helpless and sad in the form of my sister, Tom's brother and Cash Collins, even my grandparents and their run down café. I looked across the truck at Tom, who was leaning back, eyes closed, listening to the raucous music flowing back from the radio and the tickling, vibrating hum that I could feel clear through to my insides, and I smiled a smile that felt triumphant . We were crossing the river, and at least for the moment I was leaving my troubles on the other side.

"Richard's helping Bill get started on some of his critters before they go on the road," Claire shouted once we were across. She rapped on the trunk with her knuckles. "Bill's got a guy in New Orleans helps with the first part of the taxidermy, and then Bill does the fancy work when they get back."

"You mean there are bodies in there?" I slid off the box in horror, onto the gritty floor of the truck bed.

"On ice. We lost a big old gander, got its neck caught in the chain link." she said. "He's too old and too tough to eat, even if we could get Jean to clean him and cook him. Real nice wings, though. Wings are always important. Bill has a couple things to load up, too. Richard says he's trying to turn an armadillo into a tank to protest the war. That might not get sold around here but sometimes he sells up north and in California." She pulled me back up beside her. I decided I could sit on a dead goose without too much discomfort; didn't I eat fried chicken at least three times a week at the café? Besides, I wanted to watch the road go by.

I'd traveled Highway 90 between Pascagoula and Biloxi more times than I could count, going back and forth between the trailer and the café. It was a short trip, no more than a half hour's time, but it was full of things I loved to tick off as we passed, somehow reassured that, no matter how much was falling apart around me they remained, more or less, unchanged. I knew and loved all the landmarks—the Gautier Plantation, a beautiful old house on the gulf side of the wide, flat part of 90 outside of Pascagoula, the acres of tall pines that we'd dubbed "telephone pole trees," the crab shack that sat on a pier over the bayou, where we'd gone many times before my mother had gotten sick, and she and my father had danced to Fats Domino on the juke box while I

147

twirled Martha around on the worn linoleum floor until we staggered. I loved the Barq's Root Beer plant in Ocean Springs, the Biloxi Bridge that went thump-thump, thump-thump like a heartbeat under our tires, and, in Biloxi, St. Michael's Church, its round and rippled architecture as astounding as the golden archangel wielding his sword from the baptistry roof. The beach was right across from it on the other side of 90, long and flat, where my parents had brought us to watch the sun set for as long as she could go, even when our father had to carry her across the sand because crutches and wheelchairs were useless in the sand. Shrimp boats and fishing boats and oyster boats lined the piers, as well as trucks like the one we were riding in, their beds filled with ice and their canopies open wide to the salt wind, parked and ready for customers. I always watched for the lighthouse and the Widow's Walk, for the souvenir shop made out of an old shrimp boat and the little putt-putt golf course with the life sized green dinosaur that looked as if it had walked right out of the water onto the sand. Not far beyond that lay the place where we turned inland, away from the water and toward the trailer, where our small world closed in around us once more. I knew the coast from the back seat of my parents' Buick, and from the way it lived in my daydreams. I had no idea what 90 was like the rest of the way to the city they called the Big Easy, and today I was going to find out. There could have been a human body in the locker under my bluejeaned behind and I wouldn't have given up my seat; I was going to New Orleans with Tom and Claire.

When we reached the lot where the winter quarters sat it was clear they weren't going to be there much longer. The canvases with the beautiful paintings were gone, their frames now framing the bustle of activity going on behind. The trailers had drawn in their awnings and the picnic tables were nowhere to be found. There were more semis than there had been before, one of them a slat sided cattle truck. Hay spilled out of its rear and Felicia's elephant swayed at the end of its chain not far from the ramp that led up into it. A large, new red pickup truck towed a horse trailer that bore the circus' banner across its side, as did most of the semis in one form or another. It looked as though in a matter of days they would become a convoy, going from town to town, setting up for a few days, showing themselves to the townies and making what money they could before going to the next place in the circuit.

148

Felicia burst out of their trailer like a little girl, half skipping toward us. She wore a headband Indian style around her pale, fluffy hair and a red and yellow tie dyed T-shirt that hung halfway to her knees over a pair of brown velvet pants and sandals. She looked like a hippie. I couldn't help but grin. People would have a world of confusing choices to make in figuring out what to think about her; even in New Orleans she was likely to slow down traffic. In Pascagoula she'd have stopped it entirely.

"Hey Richard! What'd you bring us?" She ran to the truck, snatched the door open and threw her arms around Richard, who was trying to disentangle himself from the steering wheel and seat. Before I could feel jealous she thrust her arms through the open windows and caught at our hands and arms as though seeing family for the first time in years. Claire opened the gate and she and Tom tumbled out the back, he reaching behind him to grab my jeans at the calf and haul me across the truck bed and out to join them. I looked down, embarrassed, thinking of the way Felicia had stroked my arms while I'd insulted her husband's creations the last time we'd met. I didn't know what to do now. She solved the problem for me by wrapping herself around me in a strangling hug. "Hey girl," she cooed into my ear, "I hear you had you a world of trouble lately."

"That's why she needs her a little R&R," Richard looked at his watch. "Bill coming? We need to hit the road if we're going to be back by suppertime."

"Here I come, man. You could help a little." Gator Bill was approaching, his jagged smile bright beneath the brim of a battered fishing cap, a big canvas bag slung over his shoulder. If Felicia was dressed to attract attention, he was as ordinary as any fisherman on the coast, that is, until you really looked. "Hello Miss Kate. It's nice to see you again. Sorry to hear about your sister."

"Thanks. How do you know about Martha?" I sounded rude and I instantly regretted having asked. "I mean…"

Bill waved a negligent hand while Richard grasped the bag and swung it on to the truck bed. The thump it produced definitely sounded dead. I winced and Bill's smile turned indulgent. "Don't you worry, Miss Kate," he said. "This here armadillo died of natural causes after living a long happy life and having lots of little ones who cried at his funeral." He winked. I could feel myself blushing, but it sounded like we were square. "And Richard told me about the whole thing last

149

weekend." It was strange to think that Claire's father was friends with Felicia's husband. The rearrangement of relationships was hard for me to take in, and left me not knowing how to act.

"Let's git and go, children," Richard jumped into the back of the truck and opened the trunk that Tom had been sitting on. He tugged at the bag, sliding it forward and swinging it up and into the box. The body inside teetered before tumbling in. Richard reached in and I heard him scoop ice with his hands, piling it on and around the bag before slamming the lid and slapping it with his open palm. "Get on in, and let's hit the highway."

"I'm riding in the back with the other children." Felicia seemed to relish straddling the divide I had worried about. She bounded into the truck's open gate like a gymnast mounting a beam and threw her hands up with a flourish, before taking a broad bow. I had forgotten until then that she had some extraordinary talents, ones I had never even seen. Tom, Claire and I followed, me feeling heavier and more earthbound than usual as I clambered aboard. Felicia curled up beside Tom as he resumed his old spot. Bill and Richard climbed into the cab. As we pulled away, she stretched her arms wide. "Ladies and Gentlemen, you are about to encounter wonders the likes of which you have never seen, creatures from your dreams, wishes you once made on a star. Step right up; step right up!" Then she closed her eyes, snuggled against Tom's side, and was asleep before we passed the Barq's plant.

Chapter Nineteen

I hung out the window all the way down Highway 90, only half hearing the conversations passing back and forth between the cab and the back of the truck. We were driving through the wetlands that led out into the gulf, the view as much water as land. Richard drove fast, but the road was quiet, the tall pines and cypress groves whipping by, interrupted by little rusty bridges that hung so low over the inlets that I could have fished out the side window. Now and then short gravel strips led off toward the inlets off the gulf, where rough houses sat high on stilts and boats were tied up underneath. I thought of Jeansonne, the bayou artist who'd made the statue of the Virgin, and wondered what the places were like that weren't close to roads at all.

The closer we got to New Orleans, the more the bayous closed around us, until all I saw was black water and moss-laden trees, their dank smell filling me. I wouldn't have been at all surprised to see a dinosaur raise its head, munching marsh grass like an enormous cow. Though I'd been around bayous all my life, these were a world all their own, one that I had the feeling had looked this way forever.

In spite of its primeval approach, once we crossed Lake Ponchartrain we were quickly in the sprawling outskirts of a bigger city than I'd ever been in, and I tried hard not to let my nervousness show. For all my news-obsessed fantasies about the rest of the world, I was really a small town girl. We'd been in little Mississippi Air Force towns all my life, first out of sheer happenstance, and then because of my mother's illness. While other Air Force kids seemed to come from everywhere—making me far more self-conscious and quiet around them than was my nature, I'd gotten any sophistication I had by watching and imitating. It was one reason I loved Tom and Claire so much; they were smart and funny and different from the common Pascagoula folks. They were another world that lived alongside the one I'd grown up in. The Doucettes, and certainly Gator Bill and Felicia, had given me just a touch of conviction that the way I'd grown up wasn't the way the rest of my life had to be. They made me want to try living in the wider world, whether I was the dumbest girl in it or not. Whether I could or not, I wasn't so sure.

Highway 90 had a name now, Chef Menteur Highway, and had become a wide, flat entry into the city, bordered by wooden fences and stretches of tall marsh grasses. Everywhere I looked there were dredges and cranes, digging beneath the standing water to reach the dirt below. They piled it up into great heaps, making land where there had been none before and canals where there had been shallows. Over the fences I could see rooftops of red clay tile, stretching off into the distance.

Felicia was awake and in full tourist guide mode, tying herself in knots trying to point out things on both sides of the truck as we left the highway for the streets of New Orleans. I scooted to the rear, hung my chin over the gate and watched the city roll out behind me. Tom, Claire and Felicia quickly did the same.

"This is Elysian Fields, this street," Felicia said, indicating the wide road we were traveling. "It'll take us right down to Esplanade and Decatur. I'll get Richard to drop us off at the French Market and we can see Jackson Square and St. Louis Cathedral and Bourbon Street, long as you don't tell your mamas—or in your case, grandmama, Kate."

I drew my head back in for a moment. Claire had called me "jail bait" when we'd visited Gator Bill and Felicia before. I hope they wouldn't insist we turn around and go home. "I don't think there'll be any danger of that, Felicia," I said. "She thinks I'm at a sleepover at Claire's house."

Felicia whistled low, and then shrugged. "Well, all the more reason to have a fine day and get home safe and sound. What if she calls and you ain't there?"

Claire answered, "Jean doesn't know a thing. We'll have to come up with some foolishness to explain why we were gone all day. Unless the truck breaks down and the buses quit running we can get home fine by supper. For all Kate's gran'mere will know we were just out running wild in Pascagoula." She chuckled. "Jean never knows where Richard is anyway; she'll just figure he's off rabble rousing somewhere."

I thought about the possibility of getting into trouble, before I simply decided not to worry. Unless some disaster gave our trip away and my grandmother decided to put Richard in jail for taking me across state lines, an unlikely outcome given how preoccupied she was with Martha, I figured I could get around whatever punishment might come out of our adventure. Grandmother wasn't a whipper, and Daddy was, well, if he wanted to come back from the war to tear me up, he was welcome to try. I mentally crossed my fingers and resumed staring at the scene unrolling behind me.

The street was wide and crowded with a mishmash of houses and small businesses, all set right up next to the sidewalks that lined the sides of the street. Some were as big as the Carmody house and sat as high off the ground, their wide porticoes hung with baskets of ferns and bougainvillea, standing over their surroundings with a look of relaxed superiority. Many of them were long and narrow and painted in shades of white, yellow, pink and turquoise, shell-like colors that folks in Pascagoula would have thought garish. I thought they were beautiful, playful in a way I'd never known grownups to be, much less to shout out to all the world. I could see the fronds of palm trees above the rooftops, and the occasional live oak that spread shade over the lucky houses that sat beneath. Tall shutters were shut against the early heat and air conditioners dripped from side windows. Adults and children strolled the sidewalks and sat on the stoops in the morning sun, fanning and nodding to one another as they went about their Saturday business. It seemed every corner had a Mom and Pop grocery or neighborhood restaurant or bar. The smells of breakfast cooking, mingled with that of old buildings of stucco and brick and wood, made a musty, spicy jumble that tickled the back of my throat.

If Pascagoula had been hot, New Orleans steamed. Sweat trickled between my shoulder blades, even in the strong breeze blowing through the truck's windows. Felicia's and Claire's faces shone, and Tom's hair looked dark and wet, like it had when he'd first appeared at the trailer door, only a few months before. So much had happened since then that I thought I'd become another person, one who didn't really have an identity yet but was taking in everything around me like a new baby does. I was being baptized again in my own sweat. Whoever I would end up being, I was at that moment utterly happy that this day would be a part of it.

"Esplanade, Ladies and Gentlemen; Quarter dead ahead!" Bill, who had spent most of the last hour engaged in an earnest conversation with Richard that had been drowned out by the wind, the engine, the Cajun radio and now Felicia's chatter, peered back at us, his pointed teeth flashing under the shadow of the baseball cap. Felicia bounded to him and gave him a quick kiss on the mouth, his scaly hand resting briefly on the back of her head. I'd gotten used to their odd appearance but I'd forgotten for a moment that they were husband and wife, and I was a little startled to see a girl not much older than me kissing a man nearer Richard's age than mine. It made me feel as sinful and tingly as if I'd kissed him myself. Then she bounded back and was one of us again, half woman, half kid, all confusing in a thoroughly pleasant kind of way.

"Drop us at the French Market, Richard. I got some things to get. How long you going to be?" Felicia was taking charge of the day, setting our plans, making me feel safe as I'd ever felt.

"Oh, couple hours. I want to have a look at Doc's new gaffes, talk a little shop, and Mrs. Hopper's real particular about having people stay for dinner." From his expression I got the feeling he looked forward to Mrs. Hopper's cooking as much as he did to seeing Doc. "She'll probably load us up with etouffe and her famous bread pudding with bourbon sauce to take home. Lord, that woman can cook!"

"Well, give her my regards, and see can you get us a quart of oysters for supper," Felicia replied, the two of them just an old married couple talking about supper. "I'm going to run by the square and see if Louie-by-Day has changed his mind about coming on the road with us. Why don't you pick us up at two—Richard, will that give us time to see Bayou Eau Claire?"

So much for the old married couple. I knit my eyebrows inquiringly at Tom and Claire. I had heard more unfamiliar names in this short bit of conversation than I had in weeks; my life in Pascagoula wasn't exactly a hotbed of strangers. Tom just shrugged back, but Claire's little smile led me to believe she knew at least something that neither he nor I had gotten.

The dwellings had gotten closer together as we'd approached Esplanade. As we turned off the wider thoroughfare and onto a narrow one, on the left they'd become one, a long, uninterrupted stretch of shared walls and varied edifices, natural brick beside painted stucco, their changing colors and materials marking where one business or home—I was having trouble telling what was what—left off, and the next began. Most were two or three stories high, the second floors sporting balcony rails of iron filigree, each as distinct as a lady's lace. Many of the balconies had tables and chairs and pots of flowers and vines that had grown through and around the railings. They were perfect for sitting and watching life go by on the streets below. The balconies' undersides were hung with signs advertising the shops. Most of the doors were covered with shutters, some opened for customers, some shut, mysterious and quiet. On the left at the turn was a large brick building with a lush lawn, surrounded by an iron spike fence. I was so taken by it that I forgot to watch where we were headed. Then I turned my head, and caught my breath.

We were passing an open market, its roof broad and high. Shoppers packed the aisles that ran between rows of tables underneath. Tables and awnings spilled into the street, each one laden, some with things I could identify, purses and candles and racks of postcards, jewelry and T-shirts. Some had things I recognized but had never seen in the flesh before, feathered and beribboned ceramic masks and brass water pipes, real alligator skulls, sticks of incense and posters of Jimi Hendrix and Janis Joplin and Bob Dylan. I poked Tom and pointed. He nodded, his eyes shining, his Bugs Bunny cool completely gone.

The merchants stood or sat in the heat, laughing and talking to customers and fanning themselves, showing their wares, taking money, making change. The truck crept along between the buildings and the open market, one of a line of vehicles that made their way through like a slow parade, meandering into and out of the wafting smells of incense and spices and the strains of street jazz and zydeco, played by little duos and trios, each with its own little gathering and its own hat or instrument case on the ground.

If I'd thought Felicia's hippie clothing would attract attention in New Orleans, I was wrong. While her white skin might give some people pause, there were lots of people dressed in ways I'd only seen on television, with hair that would have made my father go blue-faced. In my first five minutes in the city I'd seen more fringes and flowing dresses and bright, colorful shirts than I'd seen in my entire life. Either a lot of these people had come from other parts of the country, or I had seriously underestimated my Southern peers.

"Stop here!" Felicia shouted, reaching out and unfastening the gate's latch before Richard had lurched to a complete stop. "We'll meet you right here in two hours' time. My love to Doc and Mrs.Doc!" She was down and striding into the crowd so fast that we had to scramble to catch her. Claire grabbed Tom and me each by the forearm and tugged, leaning into the bodies packed around us. I looked back at the truck, feeling a sudden rush of fear that we'd never see them again, but Richard grinned and waved lazily as they pulled slowly away. He clearly thought Claire was going to be just fine, and that I would be just fine right along with her. Comforted by his confidence, I turned around and plunged into the French Market.

From the perspective of the truck, the market had had the air of a performance, something I could enjoy at a safe remove. Now, as Felicia plowed ahead and Claire pulled me in her wake, the closeness threatened to overwhelm me. For the millionth time in my life I cursed the gene that had made me short; I was in a sea of shoulders, wading through armpits, many of which had a distinct call. Except for the Mardi Gras parades I'd been to when I was small enough to be hoisted on my father's shoulders, I hadn't been in a crowd this large, ever. Some nervousness that had been planted in me by my family's tendency toward caution with strangers made me touch the pocket of my jeans, where I had put the twenty dollars, all of it in quarters, that I'd saved from my tips at the café. I'd wanted to have eating and drinking money, and something to call home in an emergency, but more than that I wanted to buy something that I could look at at night when I listened to the radio. I wanted to remember that I had been in the very place the music came from, that New Orleans was real, and that when I could I'd be heading back here "like a babe to the bosoms," as Granddaddy would say.

"Come on, slow poke!" Claire's voice drifted back to me from a startling distance away; she'd let go of my arm when I'd slowed to check my pocket. As I pressed to catch up, a deeply tanned, sweaty man's face inserted itself between me and my friends.

"Hey, Little Sister, you got a cigarette?" He was smiling a smile I knew; I'd seen it in the café just before I'd dropped a glass of iced tea in the smiler's lap. He grabbed my forearm where Claire had held it just moments before, but in a grip determined to hold me back rather than pull me forward.

"I, uh, I don't smoke." I cocked my head back, trying to get enough distance to look at him. He was dressed in jeans and a vest, shirtless, with multiple strands of love beads around his neck. His hair was longish and tangled, held at his nape with a strip of cloth, and his face was greasy, the pores on his nose filthy black. I'd noticed with pleasure that there were people in the crowd at the market who were dressed hippie style, but now that I could see closer, a lot of them weren't cute like Felicia was. They were dirty and ragged, looking more like street beggars than the young people I'd seen flashing peace signs or protesting the war on TV. The man who clutched me was nothing like those friendly, peace-loving hippies. He looked like I ought to put as much distance between him and me as possible. "Let me go!" I tugged, but he had me in a firm grip, the crowd around us oblivious, pushing us closer together and separating me from my friends.

"C'mon, Little Sister, how about some spare change? I'm starvin'. I got some weed. I know where there's a party. We could have us a time."

"Let me go!" I couldn't think of anything else to say. I pulled my arm, something at the back of my mind wondering why I was as weak as a baby. Tiny black gnats seemed to be swarming in front of me. "Let me go!"

"Hey Brother, what's happening?" Claire's bright face appeared at my side, grinning with all her teeth, staring straight into the young man's eyes. "You need something?"

"Well, hey back." He leered at Claire, his grip on me tightening. "I was just telling your girlfriend here I could use a smoke. Or you and her could come back to my pad and we could play some cards. You all know how to play strip poker?" He winked and licked his lips. I flinched, but Claire's hand popped up between her face and his, brandishing a cigarette that seemed to have come from thin air.

"Thanks for finding this one for me; she gets lost all the time," she said. She lowered her voice and leaned into him, saying in a stage whisper, "It's from the syphilis. Five years now, can you believe it? It's awful she got it so young. It's eaten into her brain."

He let go as if I was white-hot, snatching the cigarette and stepping back into the path of a weaving, red-faced man who muttered

"What're doin', you hippie freak?" Claire gripped my hand and pulled in one direction as he seemed to just fall in the other, frantically rubbing the hand that had gripped me on his vest before disappearing into the kaleidoscope of bodies that shifted around us. The last glimpse I had of him, he was staring at that cigarette as if trying to decide whether he needed it bad enough to risk the possibility of catching the disease from smoking it. Almost immediately we were with Tom and Felicia in a little clear space in the crowd, behind a group of little boys who were tapping to beat the band to the tinny jazz tune blaring out of the tape player on the pavement beside them. I thought for a minute that Claire was leaning down to watch their flying feet. Then I realized that she was doubled over laughing.

"Oh my God! Oh my God did you see his face?"

"Whose face? What happened?" Tom and Felicia were looking from Claire, who just kept hiccupping and saying "Oh my God" over and over, to me. I'd been as glad to see her as I'd ever been to see anyone in my life, but I was downright embarrassed about what she'd said about me.

"Cherie just got propositioned by some asshole back there and I told him she had the syph! You should have seen him—he just about peed his pants!" I felt a smile quirking at the corners of my mouth. It had been pretty funny. Felicia stared at the two of us for a moment and shook her head like an indulgent mother.

"Can't take you anywhere." She stretched her neck and looked around her, getting the lay of the land. "I want to get some produce at the farmer's market, but let's go find Louie-by-Day at Jackson Square first. He's got all the good gossip, and he'll tell you your fortune for a small fee."

"Louie Bidet? What the heck is a Louie Bidet?" Tom asked.

"By-Day. Louie-by-Day." Felicia said it slowly, word by word. Tom just frowned deeper.

"What is he by night?"

"Louise."

She was off again, leaving the three of us to stare at one another for a moment before running to catch up. I didn't know about Claire; she seemed more unshakeable all the time, but I had the feeling Louie-by-Day was going to impress the daylights out of both me and Tom Carmody.

I hated to have to hurry through the French Market; I could have stayed all day just wandering among the stalls and looking at the unimaginably old buildings that lined the other side of the street. Felicia assured me that we'd linger long enough for me to do a little exploring on the way back to where Richard and Bill would be picking us up. "No sense carrying things we don't have to," she explained, and it made sense. Besides, I wanted something that would be just right, not the first thing I saw. It had to be special. So I broke into a half-walk, half-jog to match Felicia's long-legged stride and kept my eyes taking in all they could, hoping I could remember enough to write it all down when I got home.

We wove through the thinning crowd at the market's edge, across the street between the slow-moving cars and under the awnings of the buildings on the other side. Felicia, who had talked about hardly anything but food ever since we'd entered the city, played guide in her own fashion. "This is Central Grocery—ever have a muffaletta? If you survive the first one you'll never be happy 'til you get another. Whooee, don't those shrimps smell good? Over there's the Café du Monde. It's famous. We've got to get some beignets and chicory coffee before we go home. I'll even buy. Cover you with so much powdered sugar you'll look like me!" She was so happy she almost shone. I wondered if it was because she attracted so little attention here. I had noticed peoples' heads turning as we walked by, but it wasn't a lasting kind of attention. Felicia's albinism was just one outstanding thing in a place where wonders shouted from every sidewalk.

Then we were at Jackson Square, staring over the wrought iron fence into a swatch of green, surrounded by palms and bushes. Out of its center rose the statue of Andrew Jackson on his rearing horse, hat waving at the city as if in salute. Behind him, making even the general small by comparison, St. Louis Cathedral rose right into the blue sky, its steeple clock reading almost noon, the spire looking like it could spear the clouds. No matter whether I wanted to keep up with Felicia; it stopped me in my tracks. I felt Tom beside me, and heard his intake of breath.

"My God," he said, and sounded like he meant it. "You could put a dozen Our Lady of Sorrows in there." He turned to Felicia. "Can we go in?"

"You can," she nodded, "but I got business. Tell you what; you all go on in. See how there's painters and fortune tellers and what-not all around the square? Louie-by-Day has a table set up down at the far corner in front of the benches just before you get to the Café Pontalba; that's his regular place. You all go on and look at the cathedral and walk around the square and meet me there in a half hour. You can't get lost if you don't lose sight of the square."

She took off without another word. Tom, Claire and I all stood for a minute, watching her lope toward the far end of the square, her white skin and downy hair radiant. Tom sighed. "That girl just gives off happy. If I'm ever as comfortable in my skin as she is, I'll consider my life a total success."

"I ever tell you how I met her?" Claire murmured, watching Felicia's retreating form. "She tried to go to school. Three years ago. Her mama and papa rented a little house over on Colville Street for the winter and enrolled her at the junior high. She lasted one whole day before they formed a ring around her after school. They called her "White Nigger" and "Baby Eater," and the boys pulled her shirt down to see if her titties were as pale as the rest of her." She shook her head. "Richard won't let me go to the places he goes, the ones where it's dangerous to be a Negro, and people say things and do things to hurt people just for the pure-dee hell of it, but I saw it that afternoon while we were standing there waiting to be picked up to go home. I stood with her and caught some hell too, "Commie pig" and "White Nigger Lover" and the like, but they all knew me and knew I'd be back the next day and we'd go on. But they just drove her on out. When Richard showed up I thought he was going to get himself arrested for sure; he was that mad at those kids. They scattered like little mice when he came tearing around the side of the truck, and he just picked her up and put her in the seat and told me to get in, and we waited. Pretty soon her Mama and Papa showed up, two grown up versions of her, as pale as the moon. They shook Richard's hand and mine, like I was grown, and took her home. She never did go back, but Richard and Jean and them got to be good friends, and so did me and Felicia. She never blinked, never changed expression the whole time they were doing it, and she never said a word about it then or after." Claire turned toward the massive cathedral, looking up at its huge spires. "She married Gator Bill about a month later. I always wondered if she was trying to be a regular kid just once and what happened made her decide she really was circus."

"Lucky her," Tom said wryly. "What're the rest of us supposed to do?"

Claire looked at him for a minute before shrugging. "Change things."

Chapter Twenty

St. Louis Cathedral was the biggest, most beautiful room I'd ever been in, and I wanted out of it immediately. It wasn't that I didn't like the way it looked; the vaulted ceilings with paintings of a King and the baby Jesus, with Joseph and Mary glowing like they were lit from inside, the rows of tiny candles that Tom whispered to me were just like prayers that kept on going long after the person who'd prayed them was gone, the places where you could kneel down and put your knees on a padded rail and pray right on the back of the pew in front of you, and the unbelievable stained glass windows, all those things were a wonder, and looked like they cost more money than I'd ever see in my life. But in Pascagoula, though I hated to admit it, I'd fallen a little bit in love with simple Our Lady of Sorrow, and with the terrible, sorrowful Mary there. Here the Christ on the cross and the Virgin with her Child looked as though they'd never had an ugly day, much less suffered the way Negroes or queer boys or albino kids or girls who lost their dogs and their mamas did. They looked like something I could never, ever hope to be, and I was dead tired of that. If I was looking for life, and for the real way it comes and goes, I knew where to find it, for better or worse. And it wasn't here.

"I'm going outside," I whispered to Tom, who had crossed himself with holy water and was staring upward with a face that told me how much his raising was fixed deep in his heart, and Claire, who had put one of the little napkins that were in a pile beside the holy water on her head, and who looked impressed by the place in spite of herself. "I'll go around the right side of the square toward where Felicia went. I want to see all I can in the time I've got to see it." The two of them just nodded, and I went out into the midday light.

163

The street that ran between the square and the cathedral was as slow moving as the others. I stepped easily between the cars and to where the vendors lined the square, to stand in front of a row of little tables and carts that sat under a variety of bright umbrellas. They were both alike and different, as if there was an agreement among them, even though I could see all kinds of services being offered, as to what you had to do and how you had to look. There were no tables full of goods. There were artists, palm readers, readers of cards, and a few men who conducted tours of the French Quarter and other parts of New Orleans. The open shutters of the shops that lined the other sides of the streets around the square were festooned with wares, from bird-bright kites to antiques to souvenirs, but the street vendors clearly were a special breed. Deciding to work my way from left to right, I walked up to the first, a broad black woman sitting with a tiny girl, who perched on her wide lap and sucked a popsicle that dripped purple down her chin. The woman was rubbing a piece of charcoal into a work in progress, a stylized portrait of Martin Luther King. Around her, propped against the cart that held her supplies and the legs of the easel on which she was working, were similar images, one of a distinguished John Kennedy, another of Elvis, lip curled and brows lowered, a third of Marilyn Monroe, her smile wide and innocent. Though they were far better than anything I or anyone I knew could have done, I thought they looked more alike than they should have. Something I couldn't name was missing. The others I couldn't identify. These were people, with the kind of expressions people actually had. I liked them, even though I had never seen a one of them before.

"These ones were done from photographs," she answered what I'd been thinking, indicating a small picture of Martin Luther King tacked to the top corner of her drawing.. "Trouble is, folks pose when they get their picture taken and hide what they're really like. You sit down now, let me do you." She grinned up at me, wiping her palms on her skirt, which was smeared with black from the charcoal and purple from the popsicle. The little girl matched the grin with a wet one of her own, and held out her treat to me. I shook my head at the offer and she popped it back into her mouth. "You got a pretty face, ought to smile a little more but right pretty. Let me draw you, you don't like it you don't have to pay me a thing."

"I don't think I'd have the money to pay for it anyway. Besides, I've got to meet somebody."

"Oh go on, sit down, child." She pulled the tacks from the corners of the picture, whisking it under her chair and setting up a blank surface in its place. "I'm tired of working on poor old Dr. King; need me somebody I can talk to while I work. I can do you in ten minutes' time; you wait and see. You got five dollars?"

"Yes." I slid onto the folding chair facing the woman's, and she started whipping her stick of charcoal around on the blank page without taking a look at me. "How can you draw me without looking at me?"

"Oh, this is just the roughing out. Everybody from Jesus to Boo here—," she nodded at the girl, who was imitating her strokes, waving the popsicle stick in the air, "everybody has the same basic shape; oval head, two eyes, mouth on the bottom," she winked and went back to making her quick, sort movements. "It's the details make us different. Now you—turn your head just a little that way—what's your name?"

"Kate."

"Pretty name. I got a cousin who's named Kate, works down at the Camellia Grill—you ever eat at the Camellia?"

"No ma'am."

She cocked an eye at me, slowing for a second. "You got nice manners, too. As I was saying, you got this little line runs between your eyebrows, like you probably look at things kinda hard. Bet your Mama tells you 'Kate, you quit scowling like that; your face will freeze.'"

I could tell she was waiting for me to laugh. When I didn't, her hand stopped making marks on the paper. "Now I know I said something wrong. I just don't know what." She began rubbing the paper with her fingers in between touching it, now more gently, with the charcoal.

"My mother's dead." I said it, and waited for the look. Instead of the typical wince and the pity I both liked and loathed, she just pushed out her lower lip and nodded. "It's a terrible world sometimes. You got a daddy?"

"Vietnam."

"Where do you stay?" She'd leaned forward, working the portrait with both thumbs, arms encircling the girl, who giggled and bounced.

"With my grandparents." It all sounded so simple when I just said it. Not necessarily lonely, not necessarily tired. "Me and my sister. Her dog got killed too."

"Mm-mm-mm. Ain't that awful." She shook her head and kept working, looking at me, looking at the paper, looking at me, making a stroke and rubbing it in. Strangely, I had the feeling she heard me, was really paying attention even thought she hadn't tsked or acted as though she was shocked by my answers. It was nice. I relaxed.

"Now there you go; I told you, you got a nice smile. Smile for me pretty, gal." I let out a long breath, and let the smile take me. For two or three minutes I sat looking around at the wonder of Jackson Square in the noon sun while she worked, as relaxed as I'd been in quite a while.

Looka here." She put the charcoal stick down, swiped her fingers onto her skirt and turned the drawing to face me. It was a rough sketch, the marks slashed onto the paper and the rubbing rough, but after a remarkably short time the perfectly believable face of a girl my age and with my hairstyle had been created. She stared out at me from the smudged paper with an expression I struggled to take in.

"That's me?"

"Sure as I'm sittin' here. You don't like it?"

"It's not that. She looks—she looks like the two halves of her face don't fit together. She's smiling with her mouth but not with her eyes. No offense."

"None taken." She leaned back, again looking from me to the portrait, nodding in affirmation. "That's you all right. You know, when you look in a mirror or get your picture taken you strike a pose too, just like these folks here." She waved at the celebrities at her feet. "That's why I like to talk to somebody while I draw them. Might not have the distance between the eyes and the set of the nose just right, but I generally get the person down pretty good. You look just right for a girl who lost her mama and whose daddy is gone off and whose little sister's dog got run over."

"I didn't say she got run over." I didn't know if I was disgusted or fascinated by what this woman was telling me was my own face. Maybe she was one of those voodoo women; maybe she could read my mind. I stood up and stepped back. "How'd you know that?"

166

She shrugged, sliding the child off onto the ground with one hand, grunting a little as she stood. "That's what happens, most times. See here; you give me three dollars for this one. Spend the other two on your sister. Let her know you care how bad she feels." She picked up a flat, bright red paper bag and slid the portrait into it, holding it out. "See you don't mash into it. That charcoal will rub right off. Put some hairspray on it when you get it home. That'll help keep it right."

I looked at the bag for a long minute, but she didn't pull back an inch. Finally I dug in my pocket and produced a handful of change. I counted twelve quarters into her hand.

"Looks like you and my cousin got more in common than I thought," she chuckled as I took the bag gingerly by its corner. "Always can tell a waitress. They're lousy with pocket change."

"Thank you. For the drawing."

"Thank you for the face. I hope your life gets a whole lot better."

"Yeah, me too." I smiled, almost reaching up to feel whether the smile made it to my eyes. Then I turned and began looking for my friends.

I'd only been in one place before where you were supposed to ignore it when someone was calling you, but it didn't take me long to realize that if I answered every "Hey, come here, let me talk to you a minute," or "I got just what you need over here" I'd never make it through the gauntlet that ringed the square. The voices sounded so much like the men at my grandmother's café that I felt myself drawing up, ready to be angry. Then it dawned on me that they were a lot more like Felicia and Gator Bill, part of a very old guild. They didn't care about me. I was a town girl whose only purpose was to part with some of my money. The woman who'd made the drawing had probably made thousands of them and knew how to talk to each potential customer so that she would seem to know them. I only had her word to take for how I looked, and she'd gotten my two most troublesome things out of me in a very short time, convincing me she was able to see my inside because it was on the outside.

I slowed my stroll down the street and took time to see what each stand had to offer before shaking my head and moving on. There really were beautiful paintings at some of the stands, scenes of the French Quarter and the surrounding country, trees dripping Spanish Moss and old pirogues tied in front of bayou shacks, looking romantic and beautiful rather than poor. I was sorry I didn't have the money to buy one for Grandmother; she didn't have many pretty things. I was enjoying myself so much looking at them I reached the end of the row without realizing it.

I found Felicia at almost the same time that Tom and Claire found me. I heard their excited conversation behind me as I walked up to the last stand at the corner of the square, across from the Café Pontalba and next to a cart that looked like a giant wiener on a bun with a sweaty, dangerous looking man standing behind it and a red and white striped umbrella tilted at a wobbly angle over its steaming silver compartments.

Felicia turned from the person she'd been talking to, who sat half obscured by his own umbrella as though shielding himself from the crowd rather than thrusting himself into it as the other vendors had done. Long legs stuck out from underneath, ending in skinny, flip-flop clad feet. The toenails on those feet were painted a brilliant red. "Well, hello, Jailbait," she chirped. "I see you all have been enjoying yourselves, buying up the whole town."

Tom and Claire had obviously spent a little time playing on their own. Each of them was sporting a design painted onto their face, Claire's an elaborate unicorn and Tom's a bright yellow flower. He was swinging a long strand of pink glass beads with a crucifix attached, I assumed from the gift shop I'd passed on the way out of St. Louis Cathedral. In his other hand was a wad of Spanish Moss, doubled over and with a scrap of bright red cotton cloth wound around it, making a kind of crude doll. He waved them both at me happily. "Rosary beads and a voodoo doll; I got it covered all ways!"

A low, throaty laugh came from beneath the downturned umbrella. "I bet you do, darlin'. I bet you do." A hand extended, palm down. I still couldn't see the person attached to it, but the hand itself invited a good long stare. It was long fingered and knobby-knuckled, with the longest, reddest fingernails I had ever seen. They curved so far beyond their fingertips that I couldn't imagine how their owner ever did anything useful. I'd read that in China that kind of fingernail meant that you were too high class to have to do anything for yourself, but I doubted that could be the case here among the vendors.

Claire stepped in front of me and took the hand, clasping it the way she would any girlfriend's, leaning low to get under the edge of the umbrella and saying "You must be Louie. I'm Claire Doucette, this is Kate Lynn, and Father Voodoo back there is Tom Carmody. We are all pleased to make your acquaintance." She stood up again, eyes twinkling at Felicia, who stood casually off to the side.

"Thank you, Claire Doucette. I'm pleased to make yours." A body wriggled from beneath the umbrella and unfolded for what seemed like minutes before coming to its full height. "And yours," the head, crowned by the noon sun, nodded in my direction, "and especially yours," it nodded to Tom as I moved next to him in order to get the sun out of my eyes. I heard Tom swallow twice before he nodded, saying nothing. As my eyes adjusted I understood why he'd had a hard time answering.

Louie-by-Day was the most beautiful man I had ever laid eyes on. It wasn't just that he was pretty, or that he was feminine; to tell the truth I'd seen more feminine looking men in Pascagoula, on the rare occasion that Tom had pointed them out to me, speculating on whether they might be homosexual or were just girlish looking by a trick of nature. Louie-by-Day, however, had clearly worked to look as much like a woman even while dressing like a man as he could. If I'd had to guess, I'd have figured him for nearly thirty, but doing everything he could to look younger. His pale face was astonishingly smooth, almost flawless, his hair long enough to be drawn back in a short ponytail. It was bleached blonde, the dark roots just beginning to show, the dry ends poking out at angles. His eyebrows were plucked and shaped, arched delicately above brown eyes that looked taut, as though pulled back at their corners. He was thin to the point of being a little gaunt, a characteristic that worked against his femininity since it made his joints and the edges of his jaw protrude, and didn't do a thing to hide his Adam's apple. A form-fitting light blue T-shirt, the face of a geisha peering coyly from behind a fan painted across its front, stretched over faint traces of ribs, its cut down neck revealing a sharp collarbone.

If Louie had come close to looking like a woman, he had completely achieved smelling like one. The air around him practically shimmered with perfume, a bright scent that reminded me of flowers and oranges and made me, without thinking, lean closer and open my mouth to smell it better. I wondered what it would smell like on me.

I realized after a moment that the way I was taking him in could be considered rude, except for the fact that he had practically struck a pose for us. Besides, he had hardly registered me at all. His mouth was quirked at Tom as if waiting for him to say something.

169

Tom, for the moment, wasn't obliging. I sympathized. If anything could make Tom Carmody squeak, it would be Louie-by-Day. After a long moment in which no one said a word, Louie blinked slowly.

"Hmmph," he deliberately turned back to Claire, shifting his weight to his other leg, thrusting out a bony hip in tight blue jeans. "Cat appears to have gotten Father Voodoo's tongue." He reached out a hand to play with her hair, catching strands of it on his nails and running them through to their ends. "Felicia was just telling me that you all are on your first very brief trip to this fine city. It breaks my heart," he emphasized by putting his hand on his chest, "that you only have an afternoon, otherwise," he turned back to Tom, "Louise could show you a night in New Orleans you'd be talking about for years to come." He reached out to touch Tom's head in the way he had Claire's. Tom stepped very carefully backward, reaching out behind himself with the hand that held the voodoo doll and balancing in front with the one holding the beads. His Bugs Bunny cleverness had evaporated, leaving me feeling strangely betrayed. I'd gotten to count on Tom to be sure when I wasn't, and I had the feeling I'd just seen the place in him that wasn't sure of anything at all.

"Mr. Louie, is it okay to ask you about Louise? Felicia said you're Louie-by-Day and Louise-by-Night." Claire could ask a question better than anyone I knew. She didn't sound rude or nosey, and there wasn't a hint of disrespect in it. Felicia, who hadn't said "boo" since she'd introduced us, continued to watch, maybe, I thought, enjoying not being the center of attention for once.

"Certainly, honey, and you can leave off the misters and misses." Louie swung the umbrella deftly until it leaned to the rear and sat down on a lawn chair, beside a card table spread with an Indian batik bedspread and several colorful silk scarves. A deck of Tarot cards and a chart bearing a hand crossed with many lines lay on the surface. He rested his elbows on the table and, with a graceful motion, propped his chin on the back of one hand. The other drummed red nails on the table. "Ever since I can remember when, I've loved being pretty. I used to stand in my mother's closet, inhaling the perfume off of her clothes, rubbing my face in her silks and satins. My mother knew her silks and satins, I must say. She never told me no, not even when I started trying them on and spending hours in front of her mirror, playing with her makeup and perfume, styling a look for myself." He sighed, turning back to Tom before continuing. "You

170

know, in the theater long, long ago all the women's parts were played by men. Juliet was a boy in Shakespeare's day. Had I been born in ancient Japan, I would have practically been the object of worship. As it is, I have a small but pleasant job, singing at the Club Desire on Bourbon Street three evenings a week. By day," he indicated the spread in front of him, "I carry on the profession handed down to me by my mother, who had second sight and the purest heart in Louisiana, God rest her soul." He crossed himself and Tom reflexively did the same, blushing when he realized what he'd done.

"Oh good! Can you tell my fortune?" Claire plopped down in the chair opposite Louie, the way I had sat while having my drawing done. "What would it cost?" She extended her hand. "Can you read my palm?"

"Honey, I can read anything. Palm, tarot, tea leaves, bumps on your head, tell you your future and all the secrets in your black little heart. Five dollars." Five dollars seemed to be the standard rate for services. "But since you're friends of Felicia's, I'll do three for twelve, a dollar discount each."

"Not me, thanks," Tom murmured evenly. He looked strained, worried, as if he was afraid something he didn't want to know would be revealed for all of us to see.

"Shoot, honey, you ain't got a secret in the world," Louie answered, his smooth voice low and gentle. "You and I are cousins, you know. Animals of a similar species. Birds of a feather, only I get to wear my plumage on the outside. Don't worry, little cousin. It gets easier and it gets harder, and there ain't a damn thing you can do about it. That's *your* fortune, come Jesus, voodoo or kiss-my-foot." He reached out his long arm and took Claire's hand, leaning over her palm. "All right, you two for seven skins and Felicia buys me a Sazerac." Tom looked a little less anxious. He even edged forward as Felicia and I leaned down, straining to see what Claire's hand would reveal.

Louie-by-Day looked at Claire's hand for a long moment before running a red nail down her palm. "This line here is your life line, honey. It can tell you about the life you've led, and about the one in your future." He studied for a moment. "See how it goes all the way down here? You should have a long life, longer than most. Looks like you'll marry young, and then marry again old. See this little line here, and all these little bitty lines way down here? It looks like you'll have one child when you're young, and a whole bunch of children when you're kind of old for it." He looked up, shrugging. "Well, my mother was near forty when I was born, and I turned out all right. Looks like you'll do all right with money, too; see this little pyramid where the lines cross?" He looked up at Claire, who was frowning a little, not looking all that pleased with what she was hearing, "But it won't be for a long time yet either."

"Well, thank you, I guess. So, one bad marriage and no money for a long time." Claire's thanks sounded distinctly disappointed. She tried to pull her hand away but Louie's tightened around her wrist, his other hand folding her palm closed, pulling it close to his chest and holding it while he closed his eyes. He looked like he was listening to something, taking her pulse perhaps. All of us stood there, perfectly still, even Felicia, as if we were suddenly in our own little bubble while noisy New Orleans went on all around us. When Claire began to look nervous he drew a deep breath and let go, opening his eyes fuzzily.

"Water. There's a whole lot of water around you. You're a good swimmer, honey. You don't have to be afraid." He withdrew his hands and shook his head at the frowns on all our faces. "Hey, you're lucky. Sometimes all you get for your money is 'You will meet a tall, handsome stranger.' Which you won't, by the way." She stuck her tongue out at him. It looked more tease than insult, but she still seemed irritable. He grinned, and shooed Claire out of the chair before indicating for me to sit down. "Let's see what you got, little girl."

I felt a flutter in my stomach. I suddenly realized how afraid I was. I was afraid that Louie would look into my palm, gasp and turn away, having seen in the future the kind of thing I had already been in the middle of for way too long. He might see me dying the way my mother had, and that idea scared me so much I couldn't even let it all the way in most of the time. But I also wanted something good to hold onto, an assurance that nothing bad would ever happen to me again if I was just careful, if I just kept watch and did all the right things. I sat down and laid my hand on the table. Louie picked it up.

"Whooee, that's one sweaty palm. Well, a little sweat won't hurt me, though I do try to avoid doing it myself. Let me look." Claire, Felicia and Tom leaned over me the way we had over Claire, as if a vision, clear to all, was going to appear in the middle of my hand. Louie's perfume closed around me like a curtain. I felt myself twitch,

172

and his grip tighten in response. "Hold still; I'm not going to hurt you. Hmm, look at all those lines. Either you have a complicated life for such a bitty thing, or you do a whole lot of dishes." He looked up at me. "Are you a twin, by any chance?" I shook my head. "Well, you must have a complementary soul somewhere, somebody you're all tangled up with. Your lifeline looks like two lines connected real tight. You have a long lifeline too—oh, honey, are you okay? You want me to stop?" I hadn't realized how bad the tightness had been until it let go in a hiccup. My eyes were full of tears, but I shook my head, pushing my hand further into Louie's. He looked at Felicia, who nodded, and went on. "You have a long lifeline, too, but all of your lines are kind of thin and crisscrossed. Makes you real hard to read. Lots of people around you, coming and going out of your life. Lots of things happening, lots of decisions. Or it may just be all those dishes. You might want to stop that for a while and come back. I'd sure think about that other soul, though. It seems to keep other things from being seen, like a big old shadow."

"What about children and college and tall, dark strangers?"

"I'll be honest with you. I can't tell. You could have it all or nothing at all. Wish I could say more, but Louie never lies."

He folded my hand the way he had Claire's, pulled it to his heart and closed his eyes. The feeling of quiet came over me again, Louie's face smooth and inviting. I was so caught up looking at him I jumped when he opened them. "Huh." he remarked with a look of vague curiosity, "Well I'll be dogged. Water again. You all go swimming together?"

"I can't swim," I said, embarrassed.

"Me neither," Louie replied. "Never did learn. There's no dignity in it, flopping around like a fish, plastered down hair, no clothes on to speak of. You might want to hang onto your friend here when you all are around water. She does better with it than you do. Well," he dropped my hand and rubbed his on the legs of his jeans, "That's all I can see. You all ought to come back when you're older and have had a few more marks made on you. I am a wonder with middle aged women." He sat up, stretching, and caught sight of the bag in my hand. "That looks like one of Miz Amen Samson's pictures. She loves those red paper sacks. Can I see?"

I extended the bag, holding it by the corner. He took it carefully, sliding the drawing out, face up. Felicia whistled low, while

173

Tom and Claire said "Wow" simultaneously, drawing the sound way out.

"What?" I looked down, trying to look at it as if I was seeing it for the first time.

"She got you, all right." Tom looked back and forth from the charcoal to me, eyebrows raised, head nodding.

"No kidding." Claire traced a finger in the air over the drawing's surface. "That's you to a "T"." Felicia nodded in agreement.

Louie held the drawing up beside my face, pushing his lips out and nodding too. "You should be flattered, Kate. Miz Samson doesn't take to everybody, but when she does there isn't anybody can do you better. You take care of this; one day you'll be glad you have it. Shoot, her work's famous in New Orleans. She's been here on the square longer than anybody I know." He carefully slid the drawing back into its red bag. "It was Miz Amen Samson first showed me Louise. I was just a skinny little thing, not nineteen years old, new to this town and no idea how to make my way. I was walking by her stand, just down where she is now, and she shouted out, I can hear it like it was yesterday, 'Hey boy, come over here let me draw your picture. I need somebody to talk to. You don't like it, you don't have to pay.' Before I knew it I was holding a drawing of a beautiful woman who looked just like me, could have been my twin sister." He stopped for a moment, thoughtful. "You know, Kate, you and I might just be cousins, too. I was an uncertain child until I let Louise have her way with me. Now the two of us are happy as two peas in one beautifully put together pod." He threw back his head and laughed, before handing back the bag and waving both hands as if to shoo us away. "Felicia, you can owe me the Sazerac. Take these children on out of here; I'm not circus material and you know it. I'm a New Orleans girl and always will be. But you, cousin," he looked at Tom through lowered lashes, "come see me again whenever you want. No strings. I'll be your Auntie Louise and introduce you to society. Now pay me and go on home." Louie wouldn't take our money directly; he flicked a finger toward the table top instead. Then he embraced Felicia, surprising the rest of us by lifting her off the ground in a bear hug before sitting down and swinging the umbrella around to obscure his face once more.

Felicia shook her head. "He sure does know how to make an entrance and an exit, doesn't he? Show business all the way. What a hug! I'll smell like him for a solid week. Well, let's get those beignets in a sack and go wade back through the market. Richard will skin me if we're not there when he gets back."

Claire was still staring into her hand as we followed Felicia back toward the Cafe du Monde. "Do you think he knows what he's talking about?"

"Beats me," Felicia settled into her long-legged lope. "I don't much go for it, myself. But I like the hell out of Louie, and I think he'd make a fortune for the show. He could sing and tell fortunes, and would give King George a run for his money in the blow-off, too. There's some Mississippi country boys would fall slap in love with Louise."

Chapter Twenty One

We left the beignets for the ride home, though both Felicia and Claire thought it regrettable that we couldn't eat them hot and with lots of chicory coffee. They made a dark grease stain that soaked through the sack Felicia now carried and made my mouth water, but I wasn't about to give up a trip through the market to eat or argue.

"This way," Felicia directed us into the flow of the produce market, a pungent place with a concrete floor and one big, crowded aisle that ran down its middle. Along the sides were early summer foods, iced shrimp and fish, lettuces and tiny carrots, peanuts and potatoes that had wintered over somewhere, fresh baked loaves of bread, bottles of home made hot sauce and strings of andouille sausages. The heat was made less fierce by a row of fans that hung from the ceiling, stirring the midday air and cooling my face when I looked up.

Felicia drifted among the stands with the rest of us trailing behind. She bought green tomatoes, a bottle of hot sauce and a couple of sausages before turning to the three of us who straggled restlessly behind her. "See that Sno-Ball stand over there? If we meet there in fifteen minutes you all can go look around, see if there's anything else you want to buy."

We scattered before the words were out of her mouth, trying to stay close to one another at first, but each eyeing the tables that attracted us. Tom had stuffed the beads and voodoo doll in his shirt pocket, where they hung out like strange plunder from a treasure chest. I watched him without him knowing it as he slid his fingers along the edges of T-shirts and handbags, and refrigerator magnets that looked like lampposts and read "Bourbon Street." But the crowd was even thicker than it had been before, and I realized that if I spent all my time watching out for him and Claire I wouldn't see anything of the market. Besides, Amen Samson said I should get something to make Martha feel better. I didn't know what that would be; even thinking about my sister sitting on that sofa, staring at the TV and fiddling with her cigar box of treasures took some of the pleasure out of the day I was having. Maybe if I brought her something, I would get it back.

Fifteen minutes wasn't much time. I had to be careful about what I got, since anything that screamed "New Orleans" would take a lot of explaining at home and I wasn't at all sure she'd lost her taste for blackmail. Martha wasn't a girly girl. I'd never known her to care how she looked, so pocketbooks and love beads were out. She hated baby dolls, and I knew I'd be uncomfortable if she carried the hand-sewn Mammies and babies that sat propped on several of the stands when she was around Butch. Besides, I had twelve dollars left, I was hungry, and I might find something else for myself.

In the middle of a table loaded with votive candles and bright, painted wooden animals, I saw a bowl filled with what looked like the charms that had dangled from a bracelet my mother had worn, and that I knew now rested in my sister's stash beneath the bed. Martha had loved the tiny piano, the Ten Commandments so small you had to have a magnifying glass to read them, the miniature graduation cap from high school, the teddy bear with green glass eyes. They'd been just the kind of things any girl I knew would get when something important happened. These charms, though, were the strangest I had ever seen. They looked like something out of a Cracker Jack box, tiny tin images of animals and people, and even pieces of people—arms, hearts, ears and legs, each with a tiny loop for hanging. I could dip my hand into the bowl and hold a hundred of them. I knew as soon as I saw them that they'd be perfect.

"Hola, Senorita. You like those?" The man behind the table put down a sandwich he'd been about to bite into, wiped his hands and waited.

"What are they?" I reached out a finger and touched the top of the pile, feeling the metal shift under the slight weight.

"Go ahead; you can pick them up and have a look," he said. "They're Milagros, for praying." I drew my hand back.

"Good grief," I sighed, "Is everything in New Orleans for praying?"

The man let out a loud, short "Hah!" People all around us stopped what they were doing and glanced at us before going on with their business. "Yes, that's right. Everything is. Prayer for the sick, prayer for luck, prayer for lovers, prayer the sun won't fry your head. You pray, Senorita?" The skin around his eyes scrunched up into a mass of wrinkles when he smiled. I shook my head.

"No, not really." I smiled wryly. "But I wish a lot."

"Same thing." He reached out and scooped up a handful of the charms, picking one up and laying it on the red cloth that covered the table. It looked like a tiny house, like the ones I had drawn before we had lived in the trailer. "See? You wish for house, you wear this. If you pray to saint, you give to the statue of the saint." Beside it he dropped an eye and an ear, so small I leaned down to see the detail more clearly. "You want someone to see you, hear you, you want to see or hear better, you wear these." The Milagros began to fall faster, several pattering onto the cloth. I made out an arm, a heart, a sword, and, to my delight and shock, a leg and a tiny figure of a dog. I pointed to it.

"Do people pray for dogs?"

"Sure they do. But sometimes it's not the thing, but what it means. Dog means good friend, somebody stays by your side. Pigs mean money because they're fat; fish too—see? The scales look like coins. You eat black eyed peas and greens on New Year's Day, Senorita?"

Of course I did. I nodded.

"Same thing. Peas look like coins, greens look like folding money. Now, what you wish for?" He spread the rest of the Milagros onto the table top and stood back, folding his arms.

"It's for my sister. Her dog got hit by a truck." I slid the dog away from the pile. "And, uh, her dolls keep losing their legs." I figured that was explanation enough for her Barbie problem. I slid a disembodied leg next to it. "And she doesn't talk much," a pair of open lips joined the other two. "And she sucks her fingers," a hand might help. "And she can't sleep, and she's afraid of blood, and—." I pulled more and more figures out of the pile, eyes, a heart, a cupid so small I could barely make out his bow and arrows, because I wasn't sure she knew anybody loved her. The more I thought about Martha's problems, the more they seemed to grow, until I had a pile of twenty in front of me. I stood in front of the sum of our troubles, as exhausted as

179

if I'd had to heave the real things and not their miniatures into a humiliating pile in front of the man.

He stood there for several seconds before asking "That all?" as if there could possibly be more. I nodded. He moved the bowl aside and swept the pile off the back edge of the table into a plain white envelope, folding it in half and holding it out to me.

"How much?" I fished my pocket and clutched the handful of quarters I came up with.

"Quarter apiece. You got five dollars?" I snorted, counted out the change and took the envelope. I was about to ask the man if he'd ever heard of anyone's Milagros wish coming true, but he'd already picked up the sandwich and was chewing away, gazing down the row of tables as if I'd vanished into the hot, aromatic air. Cramming the envelope into my pocket, I headed for the Sno-Ball stand and, I hoped, something to eat.

Claire was already at the stand, happily munching on a rainbow colored mound of crushed ice and clutching a large bag out of which stuck something rolled up and wrapped with a rubber band.

"Guess what I found!" She bounced with excitement. Between the colorful snow cone and the unicorn painted on her face, she looked like a happy three-year-old.

"What?" I ordered my own cone, my favorite banana flavor, counting one more of my dwindling supply of quarters onto the Sno-Ball stand's counter.

"It's a poster of the amusement park at Pontchartrain Beach! Shows the roller coaster and the Dark Rides and everything. Man, I'd like to go out there, but this is just about as cool. I can put it on my wall and torture Jean about my real daddy!"

I stopped before I'd even nibbled my cone. "Claire, do you really think Richard isn't your real daddy?"

She grinned, showing blue and purple gums. "You want to know the truth, Cherie? Gran'mere's been telling me all my life that Jean was crazy in love with Richard since she was about twelve years old. He was her Cajun beau who lived on the bayou and brought andouille and biscuits wrapped in newspaper for school lunch. She only had one fight with him all that time, and then she did go out with that Merchant Marine guy for about two dates before Richard showed up one night, crying like a baby and promising her he'd do anything she wanted if she'd marry him. They got married right away, and Jean

180

always said I must have taken hold right on their honeymoon because I came real quick, a little bit early in fact. What Gran'mere didn't think about was that I could count to nine as well as she could and I knew where babies came from since I was a little bitty thing, and to tell you the truth I don't think anybody knows for sure if my real daddy is Richard or that sailor." She shrugged happily, turning up the white paper cone and slurping the last of the juice out. "Richard's my daddy in every way that counts and I purely love him, but I just can't help keeping it on their minds a little bit. Man, I get that look in my eye like I might feel bad about being a woods colt and I get away with murder. Now where have Tom and Felicia got to? Richard and Gator Bill are going to be here any minute."

I couldn't think of any questions about Claire's parentage that seemed worth asking. She sure seemed peaceful about the whole thing, like she could play a trick on her mother and father that might last a whole lifetime and they'd put up with it.

Several quiet minutes passed, me crunching away at my snow cone and Claire bouncing restlessly, before she jabbed me in the ribs and whispered "Well will you look at that!"

I almost choked on the ice I was chewing. If ever a Panama hat and a silk scarf could look both completely ridiculous and completely wonderful on anybody, that body belonged to Tom Carmody. He hadn't spotted us yet, and the way Claire grabbed my hand let me know that she loved seeing him unawares as much as I did. He wove through the crowd like a young lord, nodding to people, smiling and strutting as if he was leading a parade. The Panama was cocked a little to one side. The scarf, knotted around his neck and tucked into his shirt front, was bright purple, green and gold, Mardi Gras colors. I had never seen him look so simultaneously cocky and innocent, as if he was more himself in that strange costume in New Orleans than he had ever been in Pascagoula. It made me proud and scared, as though I was looking at a newborn baby. In that hat and with that happy strut, Tom couldn't have looked more carefree, or more queer.

He spotted us when he was half a block away, his smile brightening as he swept the hat from his head and bowed low, sashaying up to us in with a heel-toe dance step. Claire let go of my hand and curtsied. "Damn, boy, what got into you?"

"I don't know what you mean," he replied, his voice casual, but I noticed that he was sweating and blushing so hard his freckles had almost disappeared. "I'm just dressing for the occasion. Besides," he stepped back, gazing out over the French Market as if he owned it, "If it was good enough for Tennessee Williams, whose real name was Tom, by the way, it's good enough for me."

I wondered where on earth he had come up with that, but Felicia was on us before I had time to ask, tearing straight by, tossing bags at us and crying "Run! There they are! Catch them, Tom!" We juggled armloads of produce, Claire and me struggling to protect our own purchases, and took off after her toward the corner where Richard's truck was just about to turn out of sight. Tom whipped the hat off of his head and sprinted past us and toward the truck, whooping and waving the Panama, catching and passing Felicia, then catching the truck and pounding its fender. As we jogged behind him, Claire huffed "I still want to know what happened to that boy."

I thought maybe I knew. Tom's wake was filled with the scent of Louie-by-Day's perfume.

Chapter Twenty Two

"Claire, where are we going?"

We'd been driving away from New Orleans for fifteen minutes, staring out over the wet bayou land from the elevated highway that led north, munching beignets that tasted wonderful even thought they were cold and the powdered sugar had taken on a fair amount of grease. Claire, Felicia and I had talked about things; people we'd seen, what we'd bought and what we wished we'd bought, pausing to watch out the back of the truck as the waterways and marsh grasses and Spanish Moss-laden cypress passed below us. I could barely believe we'd been gone from Pascagoula for little more than half a day. I felt as though I'd taken a trip to a foreign land, my feelings a mixture of the pleasure of seeing things that I had hardly imagined and the shocked realization that, up until now, the most interesting places I'd ever been had been inside my own head. The thought made me nervous, as though I'd spent my whole life wrapped in a crazy quilt, put together out of bits and pieces of things I didn't understand and things I'd just plain made up.

Richard answered my question from the cab of the truck, where he and Gator Bill sprawled, relaxed and quiet. I was aware that the smell of beer drifted back to us, a smell I knew well since the café seemed to be drenched in it. "I told you, Chere, we're going to go see something pretty. We're going to—," and he said something that I didn't understand. I raised my eyebrows at Claire and Felicia.

"He said we're going to Bayou Eau Claire," Claire answered. "It's where Jean grew up. It's where she lived her whole life until Richard took her away just before Gran'pere died. She won't go back, says it makes her too sad. Neither will Gran'mere, so Richard likes to go check up on it every once in a while."

I thought for a minute. "Eau Claire?"

She nodded. "'Clear Water.' There's a spring and a little lake there that's as fresh as can be in the middle of a whole bunch of brackish bayou. Richard taught me to swim there when I was a little bitty thing."

"Did they name it after you?"

She snorted. "No, silly, other way around. They named me after it. People from the churches used to come there to get baptized in the lake because it was so pretty and still. When I was born Richard carried me right out in the water and said, 'This place belongs to you and you belong to it, so it's fitting you have the same name. Richard is what you'd call a romantic."

I had a sudden thought. "Hey, do you think that's what Louie was seeing? Clear Water?"

Claire looked at her palm as if it held the answer. "Might be. I guess we'll never know."

"How'd you like Louie, Miss Kate?" Gator Bill turned around and I could see a faint blush on his rough cheeks. I hoped he and Richard hadn't had too much to drink. "Honey, did you talk him into anything?"

"Course not," Felicia said. "You knew I wouldn't. He's happy as a clam in New Orleans even if he is so skinny and poor you can see his backbone from the front. Louise loves New Orleans and he loves being Louise. I don't see anything prying him away any time soon."

Once we'd gotten into the truck Tom had been as quiet as I'd ever seen him. The smell of perfume still hung in the air but it was hard to tell if it came from Felicia or him. Now he looked up. "Are there a lot of people like Louie in New Orleans?"

"Depends on what you mean by 'like Louie.'" Felicia replied. "You mean men who dress like women? Yeah, there are whole reviews on Bourbon Street. Some are better than others. Louise is pretty good from what I've seen, but they kind of have to sneak me in the back doors. I mostly get to hang out in the Ladies' Room as lookout while he and the other performers get dressed and undressed. I swear, I know more about how to fold and tape and hide male equipment than a girl my age should." She winked at me. "You're not the only jail bait in the world, you know."

184

"That's not exactly what I mean," Tom spoke softly, hugging his knees, his voice smooth but hard to hear over the truck's engine. He'd laid the Panama on one of the trunks, the scarf wrapped around it like a hat band. The doll and the beads lay on its brim. He looked odd, like a light in him that had always been there, but that had flared bright earlier in the day, surprising us all, had dimmed to nearly nothing.

"You mean homosexuals?" Claire, as usual, said it bluntly. Tom nodded.

"Well, one thing's for sure, it ain't Pascagoula," Felicia replied, before turning back to Bill. "I got us enough fresh goods to last us a few days. You get the oysters?"

"Yup, on ice back there in the trunk. Got some etouffe for you children to eat when we get to Eau Claire, too, and some cold drinks. We'll have us a picnic."

"A fast one," Richard chimed in. "It's only another ten minutes north, and we can go the back way home instead of back through New Orleans, cut off a little time that way. Be home before you can say 'Jack Rabbit'."

We rode in silence, each of us, it seemed, working out the day in our heads. Felicia reclined on her bags of groceries on the truck bed, eyes closed, baring her white midriff to the sun streaming in the shell's window, hanging her feet over the gate and waving them in the breeze. Claire lay with her head on Felicia's shoulder in a comfortable companionship I envied. Even though they looked nothing alike, they looked like sisters.

Tom, though, still looked thoughtful and a little sad. He'd picked up the pink beads and was examining the silver cross that hung from them, dangling it in front of his eyes and squinting as though trying to see the tiny figure that hung from it better. I wondered if he was praying, and if he was, for what. On impulse, I pulled the envelope full of Milagros out of the back pocket of my jeans where I'd stashed it. Rummaging through the pile I found what I was looking for; the tiny cupid with his bow and arrow.

"Tom, here." I pressed it into his hand. He frowned down at it. I explained about praying or wishing for love and how you gave the little image to the saint you prayed to, to remind them after you were gone. It was like the votive candles, I said, only this never went out. Maybe, I said, he could pray or wish or whatever it was he did, that he'd figure out how to just be him and love who he loved, no matter

185

what. To my shock and dismay, tears welled up in Tom Carmody's green eyes. He didn't say anything, but fastened the loop on the little cupid to the one holding the crucifix, so that Jesus suddenly had a tiny, armed cherub fluttering beside his head.

"Thanks, Kate. You're the best. If I was into girls you'd be the girl I'd be into."

"Oh, sure," I grinned, "first you want to marry me and run off to New Orleans, and now that we've run off to New Orleans you don't want me any more." I leaned forward and kissed him on the forehead. "Let me be the first to make your prayer come true and love you anyway, no matter what."

"Amen and amen," he nodded once, firmly. Then he slipped the beads into his shirt pocket and sighed, wiped his eyes and, smiling his sly smile, very quietly reached a hand beneath the lid of the trunk under his window and dropped a piece of ice into Felicia's belly button.

Tom might have gotten injured in the eruption that followed if Richard hadn't suddenly swerved sharply to the right, yelling "Whoa, Nellie!" as Gator Bill whooped.

"I damn near missed the turn-off!" he called back. "It's getting so grown up I couldn't see it."

The three of us climbed back on top of the trunks to stare out the windows, Felicia taking the opportunity to, as my grandfather would have said, slap Tom upside the head. He continued to smile as we jounced down a narrow stretch of crushed shell road, jerking our heads back as brambles and the occasional tree branch whipped past the windows, so close it felt as though they were reaching in to grab at us. I couldn't see much; trying to keep my red sack from getting wrinkled and my backside on the trunk took about all the effort I had in me. Behind us, a little dust rooster tail kicked up, to be quickly dispersed as the branches narrowed the gap again.

Suddenly, as if we had been squeezed out into the sun from the little road, we were in the open, in a wide clearing of short, scraggly grass and patches of sandy soil. There were no fewer than five live oak trees, so old their branches bent nearly to the ground before reaching up again, the Spanish Moss that clung to them moving like slow grey smoke in the breeze. Four of them surrounded a huge, battered house that looked as if it had been a wonder at one time. Its white paint was flaked but enough remained for it to look fairly grand,

186

much nicer, I thought, than the Carmody house, up 'til now the biggest house I'd had more than a passing interest in. It didn't sit as high as Tom's house, but spread wide beneath a sharply sloped roof whose line was broken here and there with windows, and even a door leading out onto a tiny balcony on the second floor. My favorite part, though, was the porch, which wrapped around the front and both ides and looked as if you could spend most of your life sitting there. I wished that there were rocking chairs and glasses of sweet tea waiting for us, as there must have surely been when the place was full of people and cats, surrounded by geese and the occasional baptismal crowd. Even now, ferns and bushes crowded against the edges of the house and porch, overgrown but not awfully much so. I thought the place looked like no one lived there, but it hadn't been entirely forgotten either.

The fifth oak sat on the bank of what could only be the lake Claire was named for. It lay at the base of a gentle slope, about thirty yards in front of the house, and stretched, wide and still, off into the distance. A pier jutted out not far from the tree, and a little flat bottomed boat, its wood so weathered it looked as though it was becoming part of the ground, lay upside down at its base. I was sure that the view from the porch was beautiful. I could imagine sitting there after supper, staring out at the water, feeling the breeze and hearing the Spanish Moss whisper as it passed through. I couldn't imagine how anyone who had lived there could move into the cramped, goofy chaos of the Doucettes' house in Pascagoula. Jean must have gone plumb crazy when her daddy died to have left here.

Claire's head was next to mine as I looked out the window and the truck rolled to a stop. "Not bad, eh?" she said, with a satisfied sigh. "Come on. Felicia got to be the guide in New Orleans; now it's my turn. Watch out for the fire ant beds, though. They spread like crazy when we don't keep them burnt."

"And keep an eye out for snakes!" Richard yelled after us as the three of us walked toward the front of the house. "Ain't been a flock of geese to worry them for years."

"Yeah, yeah," Claire waved him off. "The rats probably keep the snakes away anyway."

"Fire ants, snakes, rats. Well hell, I just can't wait to check this little bit of heaven out," Tom said wryly.

Once we were on the porch, though, he shook his head in wonder. "Now this is the place to wear a Planter's hat and look out over the property. Richard was right. It's really pretty."

"Mm hm," Claire sat down on the top step of the porch, brushing away a vine that was trying its best to grow from one side of the stairs to the other. "It used to be pretty inside too, but I don't even go in any more; it's chewed and mildewed and all the furniture's gone and the wallpaper's falling down. I like it out here. I remember it pretty well too, from when I was little." She pointed toward the tree that grew beside the lake, its long branch reaching out over the water. "Richard made me a rope swing. He used to push me so high I'd go way out over the water. He used to tell me that if I believed hard enough I could let go and I'd turn into a white heron and fly away. I'd turn loose and plop into the water and he'd laugh and say 'That's alright, Cherie. This time you turned into a fish. You'll get it next time.'"

Richard and Gator Bill had pulled the truck up beside the lake, and were hauling things out of the cab. Bill had a box and a brown paper sack, and Richard the threadbare blanket that had covered the seat of the truck. He spread it out on top of the upturned boat beneath the tree and beckoned for us to join them.

"Hallelujah, some actual food!" Felicia leapt from the porch and trotted down the little slope. By the time Tom, Claire and I followed, she was rummaging in the sack, pulling out Ball jars full of food and setting them on the makeshift table. She produced paper plates and plastic forks, and began dishing out Mrs. Hopper's famous etouffe.

"None for me, Darlin'," Bill patted his stomach. "You wouldn't believe what that woman made us eat. I think I'll go lay on the pier and enjoy the view." He took a pull on his beer and started out over the water, stretching and yawning. "Come join me."

"Not me," Felicia lifted her shirt to show her midriff, which was a surprising shade of pink. "I got to stay out of the sun; that little bit in the truck about gave me a sunburn." She nodded toward Bill. "You all go on and eat out there if you want."

"I got to go look around the house, but I'll be back for a swim," Richard replied before striding up the rise toward the porch.

"Um, isn't it dangerous to swim right after you eat?" I asked around a mouthful of etouffe that was so good it made my eyes roll back in my head. Felicia had handed me a hunk of French bread and a root beer, and I decided I couldn't have asked for better.

Claire snorted. "That's an old wives' tale. I been swimming since I was three years old, before, after, and during some meals when I could get away with it, and I ain't had cramp one. How about you, Tom?"

"Well," he had taken just a couple of spoonfuls at first, but quickly spooned a large pile from one of the jars, "I must admit Mother didn't encourage it, but I never paid much attention. Eddie used to throw me in," he stopped, a faraway look in his eyes, "and I don't think he ever stopped to ask if I'd just had my dinner."

We sat in silence for a while, drawing out the meal, listening to the little sounds the water made, Claire, Tom and I stretched out in the sun and Felicia with her back against the live oak, in the deepest part of its shade. I was drowsy and as relaxed as I'd been in a long, long time, watching the sun make colors on my eyelashes, feeling the gooseflesh rise on my arms when the occasional insect buzzed close to my ear. I drew a deep breath and let it out, thinking that this was the way I wanted my life to be, as simple as an afternoon by a lake. If I could have that, I could relax.

We felt Richard charging down the hill before we heard him, the thud of his bare feet pounding by our heads just as he yelled "Last one in is a union buster!" I jerked my head up just in time to see him go off the end of the pier in just his blue jeans, kicking his feet and flailing his arms wildly as he flew, dropped, and made a magnificent splash. Claire was on her feet in an instant, kicking off her sandals, jerking her shirt off over her head and dashing in her shorts and bra after him, screaming as if she was being chased by the devil. Tom watched her go, licked the last of his food off of his fork and stood up.

"You coming?" He tried to look casual as he unbuttoned his shirt but the blush once again gave him away. I felt a little embarrassed seeing his chest, hairless and with nipples that were pinker than any girl's I'd ever seen. Knocking the loafers off of his feet, he checked carefully to see if his pockets were empty. "I gather skinny dipping is out of the question?" I knew he'd have died before he'd have taken off anything else. He held a hand out to me but I shook my head.

"You know I can't swim."

"'Can't' never could, Kate Lynn. Come on; we wouldn't dream of letting you drown. Your grandmother would kill us all."

"No, Tom. I can't." I felt an old fear rising up in me, one that I had never been able to overcome. My father had tried to teach me to swim a few years before, on one of our rare trips to the Keesler Air Force Base swimming pool. He did it the same way, he said, that his uncles had taught him when Granddaddy couldn't. He'd sneaked up on me as I trembled at the edge of the pool, trying to get up the nerve to ease down the ladder into the water, and thrown me in. I'd sunk like a stone, the chlorine burning my eyes and nose and lungs as it rushed in, my arms and legs so heavy I couldn't make them move. He got to me before the lifeguards did, hauling me out and slapping my back over and over again as I puked up water and snot all over the cement. I could still see the look in his eyes when I began to cry. I was useless, not at all the child he wanted me to be. I'd been terrified at the mere thought of being in water over my head ever since.

"I'll bet if you asked him, Richard would teach you." I thought about it for a moment, imagining Richard, patient and smiling and telling me I could fly like a white heron or swim like a fish. I couldn't risk disappointing him too. I shook my head.

"Hurry up, Tom!" Claire's voice rose out of the water. I could see splashes from off the end of the pier and imagined her and her father playing together like two otters in the warm, clear water. It clouded my day considerably. Tom, however, just shrugged and took off running, screaming "Cannonball!" before leaping right over Gator Bill's prone form at the pier's end, drawing up his knees and disappearing below the edge. A geyser of water fanned up, soaking Bill, who leapt to his feet.

"Aw hell, Tom! Look what you gone and done!" He shook himself like a dog, flapping his arms and slapping the air, before stomping back toward us.

"Uh-oh," Felicia moaned. "there just might be hell to pay."

"Why? What's wrong?" I stood up and backed away as Bill passed us and continued up the hill, looking like thunder, disappearing around the side of the house. "Where's he going?"

"Looking for a faucet, I expect." Felicia stood beside me as Tom, Richard and Claire straggled up to us, dripping and shivering.

"I'm sorry, Felicia," Tom said. "I didn't know he'd get upset."

"He'll settle down in a little bit," she replied. "Don't tell him I told you, but Bill's scared to death of getting an infection. He don't talk about it, but his skin gives him all kinds of hell. He worries about

190

it all the time. He keeps covered and won't go near a lake or a river. He likes his water civilized, he says."

"Does he know 'civilized' around here is just a well that's probably the same as the lake?" Claire said, wringing her hair out and pulling on her shirt.

Felicia shrugged. "Don't matter. I think it's just the only way he can be mad about the way he is, and like he can do something about it. He'll rinse the lake out of his shirt and feel better."

"He gonna be okay?" Richard ran his hands through his wet hair, slicking it back, and started toward the porch where he'd left his shoes and shirt. "We got to go."

"He'll be fine. Come on and help me, Kate," she began gathering up the remains of our dinner. "You all get dried off as much as you can and let's get on back. I've got livestock to feed and we've got packing to do. Bill won't hold it against you, Tom. Part of him knows he over reacts, but he's got to make a big to-do over it to hang onto his pride."

By the time we had everything loaded, Bill was stalking back from the rear of the house, his baseball cap pulled low and his hands jammed into his pants pockets. His shirt, far wetter than the lake had made it, clung to him. Tom stood uncertainly by the truck's passenger door, the rest of us having been herded toward the rear by Felicia, who said Bill would probably be better off if he could say something without any of the rest of us right there. We tried to look like we weren't watching, but it was hard not to. Bill walked up to Tom and the two of them stood, heads close together for a moment, before Bill stuck out his hand. Tom took it solemnly and they shook, evoking first the memory in me of the roughness of Bill's skin, and then, as if bubbling out of nowhere, the first time Tom and I had met on the trailer steps, it seemed years ago.

"Tom says the handshake was invented by the ancient Greeks, to show they trusted each other. Only they didn't shake hands—,"

I made it into the truck before Tom got to me, impressing myself by leaping onto the lowered gate with, I imagined, almost as much grace as Felicia. Tom bounded up behind me, Claire and Felicia close behind. Felicia had spread the blanket over the bed of the truck so that Claire and Tom, who were still sopping wet, wouldn't pick up too much of the dirt from its surface. Bill and Richard took their places and, bouncing and jouncing, we started back out the little road. Out the back of the truck we watched the branches close in behind us once again, and Eau Claire was gone.

"How often do you come here?" I asked Claire, who stared out the back of the truck with a wistful expression..

"Maybe twice a year. We left when I was six. Richard had gone off looking for construction work, and while he was up north he joined the Communist Party. Gran'pere got so mad he threw us all out, said we could never come back until Richard came back to his senses or Jean left Richard, one. Jean said if he wanted to make up with her he could come to her, and a few months later he had a stroke and died. Gran'mere came to live with us and neither one of them will come back. That's almost ten years. They sold off most everything to take care of Gran'mere's bills and I guess the bayou's taking back the rest. I think Richard loves it more than Jean does."

"Yeah, Chere, but I love your mama more," Richard called back from the cab. "She say come home, we come home, but not before. Her mama's one stubborn woman and my Jean's just like her. I'm just the caretaker." He shook his head and accelerated hard as we took the main road. "Well, hold onto your hair back there; I'm gonna make tracks, get us home."

"Richard?"

"Yeah, Kate?"

"Thank you for showing me such a pretty thing. I loved it."

"You're welcome, Kate. You remember it's there and you can go back any time you want. You all can. I'm the caretaker and I say so."

Claire leaned back, smiling. "Commie through and through," she said, proudly.

Chapter Twenty Three

Richard was right; we were home by supper time. He was so nervous about it that he barely let us say good-bye to Bill and Felicia, who were pulling out within the next few days and wouldn't be back until after fair season. "We might even pick up a Halloween gig," Bill said, baring his pointed teeth. "Gator Bill can scare the Blessed Jesus out of the young'uns in a Haunted House."

"Well, be safe. Call us when you think about it," Richard said, hauling the bags and assorted foods out of the truck before climbing back into his seat. The rest of us stayed in the bed, hugging Felicia over the gate, clasping Bill's rough hand.

"You all take care of Jail Bait; and you tell your little sister to keep her chin up and we'll bring her something special when we come back," Bill said.

"Okay, I will." I felt a pang of jealousy in spite of myself. Martha was on everybody's mind these days. She'd better not turn out like Eddie, I thought, and then mentally bit my tongue. I didn't want to think about what kind of person thought that kind of thing.

We rode back across the bridge in the evening air, Richard driving alone up front with the radio off and the three of us in the back suddenly out of conversation. When we pulled up at the corner where we'd picked Tom up that morning I had the feeling the day was unwinding, leaving me looking the same but with so much more of the world inside me that I couldn't help but be changed.

If I was changed, Tom Carmody was transformed. He and Claire had lost their face paint in the lake and his hair was slicked back and stiff, making him look older than he had this morning. He didn't smell like Louie-by-Day's perfume any more, but I expected we'd both remember the flowery, lemony smell of it for a long time.

"Well," he said, holding the Panama by its brim and scuffing his feet like a shy boy, "you two have a good slumber party. Paint your nails and do your hair and listen to the radio and watch Morgus the Magnificent and get too scared to sleep. Don't worry about me; I'll just go tell Eddie about my day."

"Sorry, Tom," Claire said. "Even Jean and Richard won't let me have guys sleep over. Even you. Call me tomorrow." Then she added, "I had a really good time. I'm glad you came."

Tom smiled. "Me too. And Kate, thanks for the milagro. I hope it works."

Chapter Twenty Four

I had no idea what Martha did with the nineteen other Milagros. I'd given them to her the Sunday night I'd come home from Claire's, hoping, I supposed, that she'd suddenly light up and be herself again, but she had simply stared at the shiny pile of them lying in her hand and dropped them into the cigar box with the jumping beans and the coins and the box turtle shell. I had the urge to choke her, to slap her so hard she'd scream and tell on me and I'd be grounded for the rest of the summer. I was afraid that she'd found the place I'd gone to when I'd narrowed down to just about nothing, when things had been too hard to be in the middle of, and the thought that she might not come back, and that it was my fault, made me desperate for her to show me something else, some sense that she was going to be okay, and that I could stop thinking about her for a while. Instead, she went back to staring at the television and I went off to my final week of school. After all that had happened, tenth grade ended so quietly I hardly felt it.

One morning a few days after school was out, when I had managed to talk Grandmother into going off to the café for the breakfast rush alone by promising her that I would look after Martha if we could just stay at the trailer with our own things instead of in the café's cramped apartment where we kept nearly nothing, I lay in my bed, listening to the low murmur of the television coming from the living room. My sister had gotten up and gone with her cigar box to watch Captain Kangaroo, a habit she had reacquired now that she didn't spend her mornings with her dog. Granddaddy had shown up a few days before with a pair of round-tipped scissors and a great big pile of magazines, and she had taken to cutting out pictures and adding them to the collection in her box while she watched. I was relieved to see her doing anything that looked remotely purposeful, and as I lay there I thought I might go in and see if there was any sense in what she was cutting out.

If this was Captain Kangaroo, though, he'd gotten awfully serious all of a sudden. All I could hear coming from the other room was a low masculine voice that seemed to be saying the same thing over and over.

"Martha! What are you watching?" I yelled from habit, not expecting an answer. I was surprised, then, when she appeared at the bedroom door. She spoke as if she was talking in a foreign language and saying the words phonetically, not understanding what they meant but just repeating the sounds. What she said nearly made my heart stop.

"Presidential candidate Senator Robert Francis Kennedy has been shot," she intoned. "Senator Robert Francis Kennedy has been shot."

"Oh no!" I sprang out of the bed, nearly knocking her over as I dashed for the living room. It couldn't be. But it was. The news anchor spoke in a voice that sounded as though he was talking from the bottom of a well. His eyes were haunted the way Walter Cronkite's had been when I'd watched him saying the same things about Robert Kennedy's brother. He said that Robert Kennedy had been shot the night before, in the kitchen of the hotel where he'd given a speech, and that he was in the hospital, and that no one knew if he would live or die.

"Oh, Martha," I said, sinking onto the couch and doubling over until my head rested on my knees, "what on earth are we going to do?"

The telephone rang. I tugged Martha back from where she sat, so close to the television that if I answered it she'd be between me and the information I was struggling to take in. She let me pull her onto the couch beside me without resisting. She sat upright, watching intently as the news showed a camera shot that swung wildly among a crowd of people and an ambulance pulling into a hospital emergency room. If the sight of an ambulance so soon after having ridden in one had any effect on her, she didn't show it.

"Hello?"

"Hey. Are you watching the news?" It was Tom. He was out of breath. It sounded as though a riot was going on in the background.

196

"I just started. I can't believe this!" I kept trying to convince myself, even though I saw the footage being run over and over again, that what I was seeing wasn't possible. There was craziness in it that made me want to draw the curtains and hide.

"I don't suppose you could get over to Claire's?" I realized that that must be where Tom was calling from, that the chaos in the background was the sound of a large group of people, screaming words I couldn't make out but I could imagine. "I swear, I think Richard's gone a little insane."

I could believe it. After Martin Luther King's assassination, after he had gone off to Memphis and seen, and for all I knew been a part of, the rioting that went on there, Richard had worked even harder than he had before, eking out possible voters not only in Pascagoula, where the pickings were about gleaned, but in Mobile and Pensacola, bigger places that he said had more organization and more chances of getting people to register and to vote for the last hope he had to latch onto. That hope had been Bobby Kennedy.

"Oh Tom, I can't. I've got Martha here, and Grandmother swore she was going to call and check on us every time she got a break. Why? What's he doing?"

"He's packing. He says they're moving away from here. Says he can't stand it any more, there's nothing he can do around here except get him and his family killed." Tom's voice was so strained I had trouble understanding it, but I understood that he was saying that Claire might be going away, and that was more than I could bear.

"Tom, you have to stop him!"

"Me? He's got women and children screaming at him in two languages and it doesn't seem to be making a difference. I don't know what I could do. Here," his voice grew faint as though he'd turned away from the receiver. I heard him say something indistinct, and then Claire was there, sounding like I'd never heard her.

"He can't do it!" She cried into the phone. "Kate, who would do such a horrible thing? Why is everybody killing everybody? He can't make me go!" She started to sob. I felt as though I was listening to a child, not the level headed girl I knew.

"Claire?" I gulped, suddenly afraid she was going to vanish overnight. "Claire, maybe he'll be okay. Maybe it'll all be okay." I didn't know if I was talking about Bobby Kennedy or Richard. In the background the shrieking went on, over the sounds of the television and Martha's repetition of the terrible phrase.

I thought fast. I couldn't just sit here feeling helpless and disconnected while this terrible thing went on all around me. "Claire, I'm going to walk Martha to the café. I'll see if I can get over there. Richard can't do this to us. He can't."

"Well you better hurry, Cherie, because he damned well says he's going to."

All the way to the Rebel Café I practiced what I was going to say to Grandmother, but when I got there it was clear it didn't much matter what I said or did. The café was empty. I could see my grandparents and Linda the waitress through the front window, sitting and drinking coffee alone. When I tried to open the front door, it was locked.

Linda opened the door for us, whispering "Butch up and quit," as though it was a secret she was keeping from my grandparents. "She called this morning and said she'd come back when her folks was as welcome to sit at these tables as anybody else."

I guided Martha to where Grandmother and Granddaddy sat. He looked ashen and she looked grim. "Butch quit?"

She nodded. "At least, Sarah Parsons quit. That's what she said, that Butch took the job and she was glad to have had the job but Sarah Parsons wouldn't let her work here until Enoch Parsons could walk in the front door and eat at a table same as anybody." She shook her head. "And that just ain't going to happen."

"How come you didn't just sell coffee and donuts? Or cook yourself?" I knew every penny counted; I'd seen Grandmother work we she was sick, when she was dead tired and when she'd had to fill in on the rare occasions when Butch had been unable to come in. She hadn't called me to fill in for the breakfast shift. She and Granddaddy were just sitting in a locked up café, smoking and drinking coffee from an urn that held a hundred cups.

Granddaddy put his coffee cup down so hard that Linda jumped right out of her chair. She murmured something about clean dish towels and went into the kitchen.

"I'll tell you why we ain't open," my grandfather's voice growled out of his mouth in a way I'd never heard before. "Goddamned niggers, that's why. We open those doors and in they come. They want to ruin us. They know Goddamned well that if a one

198

of them sits down in here we might as well lock the doors. Not a white man will come in here, and niggers ain't going to keep us in business."

My skin crawled. I didn't have any illusions about his feelings toward Negroes; he'd embarrassed me now and then when, in the same kind of stupor in which he'd tell me about the Pascagoula Indians, he'd hold forth with a tale about a "good nigger" he'd known or laugh in delight at the old movies on Dialing for Dollars, where the whole point of having black characters seemed to be so that they could sing and dance and make the white ones look smart by comparison. But I'd never heard this kind of anger from him, toward anybody.

My grandmother slapped her free hand down on the table. He stopped without saying any more. He raised his coffee cup to his lips again, hands shaking so hard he slopped coffee onto the table. She put down her own cup and sighed. "Katie, before you get to thinking you're better than we are, you think about how you get the food that goes into your mouth. Your granddaddy's right. If—if they start coming in here we can kiss this place goodbye. I got to feed you and clothe you and your sister, and this is the way I've got to do it. So before you go getting on your high horse you think about that."

I didn't know what to say. Then I remembered why I was here. "Grandmother, you know why Butch didn't come in? Robert Kennedy, I mean?"

My grandmother drew in a big breath as though she was going to say some last straw kind of thing, but then she deflated and just sat there, her cigarette burned down between her fingers. "I know," was all she said. I figured it was worth a try to ask her.

"Claire's daddy is really upset, Grandmother. He says they're going to pack up and move away. Please, I want to go talk to him."

She looked up. "And just what do you plan to say to him?"

"I don't know, that people here need him. That moving away won't make things better."

"For who? I expect moving away would make things a lot better for them, and for us. I know you like Claire and I know they was good to us, but we don't need them Doucettes stirring up more trouble than we've already got. Nice to you children or not, if you ask me they should have moved a long time back."

I felt anger rise in me, and before I could stop them, the words came out in a rush. "How can you say that? What about us? What

199

about me and Tom? Jesus Christ, is that all anybody knows how to do, to just take off and run when it gets too damned bad?"

"Girl, you better watch your language. I let you go around with that girl and that sissy boy because you've had enough trouble in your life and I thought having friends would take your mind off of it, but if this is what she and Tom Carmody teach you it might be just as well she's going."

If I had looked in a mirror at that moment I knew what I'd have seen. I'd have seen a face gone red except for right around the lips, where it would be pale white from my teeth being clenched so tight. My fingernails were digging into my palms. I couldn't breathe. I knew as well as I knew my own name that if I didn't turn around and walk out of the Rebel Café I would die right there on the gritty linoleum floor. I didn't say another word, but spun on my heel and strode out, my grandmother's "What do you think you're—," cut off by the slamming of the door. Once outside, I ran. Even this early in the morning it was hot and humid. I had to stop and walk, gasping and sweating, before running again. In a half hour of running and walking, I made it to the Doucettes'.

I could hear the house long before I saw it. The geese were going wild, honking and honking, and above them, even louder, I heard what sounded like the whole Doucette family, all yelling at once. I doubted the flock in the yard, upset as it was, would let me in without coming after me. Leaning on the gate, I yelled for Tom, hoping he was still there and could hear me over the riot. The screen door opened after a moment and he stepped out, his body wedged between two huge, open umbrellas. Using them as twin shields, pirouetting to keep them between himself and the thrashing, bleating birds, he came for me. In spite of my distress, I had to put my hand over my mouth to keep from laughing.

"You look like you're trying out for the ballet. Goose Lake."

"Oh, grow up," he snapped at me, batting at the big gander that kept trying to reach under the rim of one of the umbrellas to get at him, and unfastening the gate's latch. "You get your butt nipped a couple of times, you get smart. Now come on, but don't expect to get a word in. It looks bad."

He was right, it did look bad, but though I hated to admit it, it also looked a little comical. Richard Doucette wasn't a big man; he was dark and stringy, strong in the way that men who have grown up

200

working hard and eating poorly can be. At the moment he looked as though he was trying to tear the house apart singlehanded, pulling open kitchen drawers and dumping their contents into a box on the kitchen table, snatching the toaster plug from the socket and tossing it beside a pile of little dented appliances, all the while trying to reclaim parts of his body from the yowling pack of women and children that were hanging off of every part of him. Although I'd been a little uneasy about his beer drinking with Gator Bill, I didn't imagine him to be like my grandfather, starting early and ending when he could no longer stay awake. He must be sober, but he was yelling and snarling at his family in a combination of English and French, and if the French words he was using were anything like the English ones, I was being treated to some world class cursing. And Jean, Claire, Francis, Marie Therese and Regina were right in there, if not matching him curse for curse, at least matching him in intensity, tossing things back onto counters as quickly as he turned from them, regardless of what popped off of them in the process, pulling his hands away from the refrigerator and cabinet doors, hanging off of his legs as he tried to walk. Even in the middle of the chaos it wasn't hard to see that no one was in danger of hurting anyone else; it reminded me of the people at a funeral, desperately trying to keep a grieving, hysterical family member from hurting himself in his pain. On top of the noise in the kitchen, the three or four cat fights that were breaking out in sympathy and the muted but distinct squalling of the geese outside, loud bursts of static from the back made Gran'mere's presence and disturbance as much a part of the fray as everyone else's. The squall had stirred up so much cat hair that it looked like the cottonwoods were in bloom. I looked at Tom, standing there watching openmouthed, and fought the hysterical urge to laugh outright. Instead, I did something I had never done before in my life, though I'd wanted to a million times a day. Drawing in the biggest breath I could, I screamed at the top of my lungs.

The effect was wonderful. The Doucettes froze like a diorama, just for an instant, before the pile of them lost balance and collapsed to the floor. Cats ran in all directions, disappearing under furniture and down the hall to Gran'mere's room. Tom, who must have heard enough shrieking from Eddie to make him immune to anything, simply shifted his weight to his other leg, pivoted and looked at me without changing his awestruck expression.

"Stop! Everybody just stop for a minute!" Once I started yelling I couldn't stop, even though the place had gone dead quiet. "Richard, please. If you go off—if you take Claire off, what will Tom and I do? We can't do anything without her. She's part of us. You're all part of us."

Richard had begun shaking his head as soon as I started talking, even as the pile of arms and legs untangled themselves into members of his family. Jean pulled herself up with an expression of mangled grace, limping toward the sofa on Francis' arm. Claire and her sisters helped one another up. Claire stood, chin out, her face only a few inches from his as if daring him to start up again. "Miss Kate," he began, his voice tight as the cords in his neck, his breathing heavy. "I know you and Claire are good friends. I couldn't be happier she's found good, reasonable people in this God forsaken place, but I can't stand it no more. I am dog tired. When I was a little boy I lived poor—you just ask my Jean over there. We was no supper poor sometimes, raggedy pants and shared shoes poor, and I swore to my Mama and Daddy that if I ever got to where I had a little bit I'd help others get some too. So I did. I joined a union when I started carpentering, and it was fine to hear folks talk like I thought, that everybody ought to have a living wage, and after a while it just made sense that if they had a right to work they should have a right to live where they wanted and to vote for the people they wanted. In Louisiana and Mississippi that means helping black folks, and I've done what I can around here. I got to tell you, it ain't much of a life for making friends and feeling like you're among your own, but I kept going because my family likes it here and I could read the papers and watch the TV and I knew there was a movement, not just me, trying to make things better, here and in other places too. But now," he shook his head, sagging against the counter. He looked beaten, his eyes sunken. "I don't know what I'll do later on, but for now I say 'uncle.' They can have it; they can have the whole stinking world. I just want to go home."

"What do you mean, 'home'?" Claire stood her ground. "This is my home. This is home to all of us. If you want to run off back to the bayou, go on. We don't need you. We'll be just fine without you!" She stomped off to her bedroom and slammed the door, leaving me and Tom standing there with her family. I was suddenly uncomfortable, my link with the Doucettes broken by Claire's retreat. But I couldn't just go with things the way they were.

"What if he's okay, Richard? Maybe he'll be okay."

He shook his head again. "Don't matter, Cher. I got to go. Claire, Jean, the rest, they don't want to go with me, it's up to them." He turned to Jean, who was collapsed on the sofa between Marie Therese and Regina. Francis sat on the floor at their feet. Even Gran'mere had gone quiet. "It's up to y'all. Me or Mississippi. But I'm for Louisiana soon as I can git." He strode past me and Tom, who was still oddly silent, and went out the door, shushing the geese, who seemed to know to get out of his way. I heard the truck crank and roar away.

Claire's door opened and she edged out, her expression as pinched as my grandmother's had been. She walked over to her mother and dropped onto the floor, laying her forehead in the woman's lap. "Mama, what are you going to do? Please don't let's go. Everything I've got is here." I'd never heard Claire sound like a little girl before. I thought my heart might break then and there. Tom gripped my hand and squeezed, tugging me toward the front door. We walked out as if we were leaving forever. The geese parted and let us pass.

Senator Robert Francis Kennedy died the next day. We watched his funeral alone, Martha and I, on the trailer's television, while Grandmother cooked and Linda waited tables, the menu shortened to burgers, sandwiches and fries until she could hire a new cook. I refused to go back into the café when the "Reserved" signs appeared on every one of the tables. While it was a fact that the short lunch rush filled every seat, and that the same men tended to sit at the same places for their meat-and-threes every day, I doubted that a single one of them had ever eaten at a restaurant before that had a sign at his place stating that it had been reserved for him and him alone, and I didn't hesitate to say so. Grandmother threw a fit, telling me that she just couldn't understand how I could be so ungrateful when she worked herself half to death keeping food in our mouths and clothes on our backs. I said I knew about the Social Security checks she got every month and the money our father sent her. She threatened to keep me from ever seeing Claire or Tom again. I asked her when she planned on sleeping. She promised to tell my father the next time he called. I said I'd tell him myself, and if he wanted to whip me all the way from Vietnam he was welcome to try. I went on strike, silently pledging to myself that, while I wouldn't run out on Martha the way Richard was threatening to do with Claire, I would make it clear I thought what they were doing was wrong and I wouldn't be a part of it. While business at the Rebel Café went on, I sat silently with my sister and watched the slow funeral parade go by, the blue hatbox from my mother's closet on the sofa between us.

A week later, Richard Doucette was gone. It was just a temporary separation, Claire said, when we met at the ruins of the old boat. He needed to figure things out, and Jean was just as determined as the rest of the family that she wasn't going to leave her house and her geese and her cats. Sometimes, Claire said, you had to compromise.

"Did it ever occur to you how scarce fathers are around here?" Tom made his point even as we sat not a hundred yards from where his own father sat in the bait and tackle store. "Welcome, Sister Claire, to the Pascagoula Society of Fatherless Children."

Claire rounded on him. "Don't you dare say that! Richard did not run away! He said he'll call person to person every night and ask for himself so we know he's okay without having to pay the phone company for it. He's going to send money as soon as he finds work. There's always work for a good carpenter. He said he'll tell us if he's going to come back here to live before school starts in September so I'll know whether I have to keep working. But he will. He'll come back."

I turned. "What do you mean 'keep working'?"

Claire sat up straight, as though trying to look older. "I got a job. Come Saturday I'm the new ticket taker at the Saenger Theater. All of us are getting jobs to help out. Francis is going to deliver papers and keep playing the trumpet, and the girls are offering two-for-the-price-of-one babysitting, which is a good idea because they have one brain between them. Jean's looking in the want ads, and is even thinking about selling some kittens if it doesn't kill her. We're all pitching in. It's a good thing we can't sing; we'd be putting on concerts like the Osmond Family." She had look of determination and happiness that was a little too bright, like she was selling something she wasn't sure she believed in.

Tom, who had been buffing his fingernails against his pants leg since Claire had yelled at him, looked up. "Can you get us in the theater for free? I'm dying to see *Funny Girl* when it comes out."

Claire snorted. "You bet. I'd consider it a revolutionary act. 'Course, if I get fired you'll have to explain to Jean, and she's had it up to here with the revolution."

I frowned. "When will you be working? Weekends? When will we see each other?"

"Of course I work weekends. And every afternoon until closing. I get Mondays off." She gave a shrug that looked half resigned, half boastful. "Had to happen sometime, Cherie. Can't live a life of leisure forever."

"And you'll stop when Richard comes back?"

She hesitated. "I don't know. Maybe. Or I might look for something full time. I'll be sixteen in October. I kind of like the idea of joining the working class."

"But, school." I sat back down, my hands cold. I was vaguely aware of my heart beating in my ears. Tom continued to look down, his face still. He'd been unnaturally quiet ever since the morning at the Doucettes' house, and it worried me.

"Let's wait and see." Claire smiled and put her hand on my knee. I didn't know which made me madder, her superior looking smile or Tom's cool. Both of them had the same effect.

I stood up again, slowly, and nodded. "I have to go."

"Already? I was thinking of walking to the beach." Claire's smile faded a little. "I don't have so many days left to mess around."

"I have to look after Martha," I replied, not looking right at either of them, but somewhere in between. "I'll call you later. Say hello to Richard for me, when he calls."

"I will, Cherie."

I nodded to Tom, who nodded back, eyebrows lowered. Then I walked to the Rebel Café, took an apron off the peg in the kitchen, and, in front of my astonished grandmother, started taking orders.

205

Chapter Twenty Five

I decided to stay home for the rest of the summer, to work in the café and to let Claire Doucette and Tom Carmody know that I would be perfectly fine without them. I lasted two weeks before I called Tom.

"About damn time." He sounded happy to hear from me, but there was an odd reservation in his voice.

"I know," I sighed. "It's not you. It's Claire. But it's not really Claire either. It's just that I was getting to like the idea of being a normal kid in high school doing normal high school stuff. I liked sneaking off to New Orleans, doing something my folks don't know about. I've never done that. I'm disappointed."

"You want to go walking with me tonight?" I felt a stab of joy followed right away by a stab of guilt. It would be the first time we'd walked since Martha's death. Without the little black dog there sneaking out would be a piece of cake, a fact I couldn't have hated more.

"I'd really like that," I replied. "Can you come after midnight? And don't tap; I'll just meet you outside. Martha sleeps like a cat these days."

"Sure. Meet me on your side of the bushes behind my house." He still sounded strange, distant.

"Okay. Uh, Tom, have you seen her? Claire?"

"Of course I've seen her. You're the one not talking to her."

"Is she okay? Is Richard calling?"

"Every night. By now every operator in the country probably knows Richard Doucette isn't home. I'm surprised they haven't called out the dogs." This was the Tom I knew. I really smiled for the first time in two weeks. Maybe he was talking to me after all.

"Tom?"

"Yes?"

"Do you think he'll come back?"

"Call me a fool, but I do. They'd all die rather than be apart. If they didn't feel that way they wouldn't all be so stubborn about how much they don't need each other. Claire's having a ball at the theater, sitting up there in the ticket window like she owns the town. She can see and be seen by everybody that drives, walks or crawls down Market Street. I know everybody that's dating and who's sneaking around on who."

"She isn't upset with me?"

Tom laughed so suddenly his voice broke, something I realized was happening less often. "Oh hay-ull no, Cherie. Claire's just as sure you'll come back as she is that Richard will. She's just sitting there in the biggest window in Pascagoula waiting for you."

I thought about trying a little of the remaining paregoric on Martha to make sure she'd sleep through my sneaking out that night. Even though she'd taken to having to be cajoled into eating, and I was pretty sure Grandmother was worried enough about it to let me feed her ice cream for dinner, and that I could sneak it in without her knowing, I couldn't bring myself to do anything else to my little sister. Instead, I helped her bathe, even adding a little of the bubble bath I'd bought for myself because I'd liked the word "Frangipani" on the bottle. Then I curled up with her as though I was going off to sleep myself, and waited for what seemed like hours, until Grandmother watched the ten o'clock weather report and shuffled back to the trailer's back bedroom. I had my radio, a flashlight and a copy of Edgar Allan Poe stories that I knew I shouldn't be reading before going out in the dark. They kept me company until I heard Grandmother's deep snores. Then I slipped out the front door and trotted through the uneasy darkness to where I'd dared Martha to hide so I couldn't find her, just a few weeks before. She'd sure managed to do that. She was so hidden I wasn't sure I'd ever find her again.

Tom was standing by the bushes in the bright moonlight, his arms folded. He was wearing the scarf he'd gotten in New Orleans, holding its end to his nose. He looked sheepish for a moment before saying "It smells like Louie, see?" and holding it out for me to smell.

"Mm-hm. He was kind of wild, wasn't he?" I had a feeling it was important what I said, but wasn't sure how I felt about Louie-by-Day. He'd been interesting and a little funny and a little frightening. I had put him away in my head the way I had put Amen Samson's drawing of me away in my diary at the bottom of the toy box. I reeled a little every time I thought about either of them.

"Kate, can I tell you something?" Tom started walking, skirting the puddle of light where Martha had died. I appreciated that, and thought for the thousandth time how much I had grown to love Tom.

"Of course you can," I said, falling in behind. "Anything." He was headed toward the pier by the bait shop. I could smell the funk coming from the water, and shivered a little in the night breeze. Pascagoula Indians, Edgar Allan Poe and Louie-by-Day combined in my head. As I sat on the pier beside Tom and swung my legs over its side, I had the unbidden image of a red nailed hand reaching up and snatching me down.

As if he knew what I was thinking, Tom hooked his arm through mine and peered into the water. "Feeling like the last of the Pascagoula again?"

"I guess so. Sometimes I wonder if every time somebody does something that takes them away from me I'll feel that way."

"Like Claire getting a job?"

"You know it's not just the job. It's changing from somebody I know and understand into a stranger, into somebody who's so different from me that I don't know her any more. My mother did, and Martha did, and even my granddaddy now—I always knew he was a drunk, Tom, and somehow he's both the sweetest person on earth and has the kind of ideas about black people that make me cringe, but I never thought it was as bad as it is. It's like I don't know him. And Claire—I thought Claire would do something great. She's the bravest person I know. She talks back to her daddy and goes where she wants and Cash Collins couldn't touch her. You saw the way she reacted to Louie's palm reading. She wants things to happen. She thinks she is somebody. She doesn't want to quit school and turn into some hick waitress with no life. How can she be thinking about that?"

"It sounds like you have a little crush on our Claire, Cherie." Tom's eyes glinted in the moonlight. "Or maybe it's just hero worship. You're right, though. She's not like you and me. Did you know she says she's slept like a baby every night of her life? She's never once come out walking with me. She doesn't need to, even now. Hell, she believes so much that everything will turn out okay that she even makes me think so every once in a while."

"So you're saying that I'm imagining Claire's life will be terrible if she quits school, and she doesn't?"

"I'm saying Claire's got the best chance of anybody I know to come out okay, because she believes it. The whole damn family does. They're like your Indians, all walking into whatever they're walking into together, nobody left on shore." He stopped, let go of my arm, and leaned far over the river water, so far I worried he'd fall in. After several moments he said, "Here's what I want to tell you. When I went back to see Louie, that day in New Orleans, he gave me his business card."

Tom fished in his trouser pocket and came up with a worn card. It looked as though it had spent considerable time in that pocket. I smiled when I saw the geisha behind her fan on its bright pink surface. "Louie was something else. I'd sure like to see Louise sometime," I said, holding it up so the moonlight gave me a better view.

"So would I," Tom said. "That's why I'm going to New Orleans tomorrow."

"Beg pardon?"

"Really. See that phone number? It's Louie's place in the Quarter. I've been talking to Louie ever since we came back. He lets me call him collect from pay phones. I'm going to spend the weekend. He's going to introduce me around."

"What do you mean, introduce you around? You mean he's going to help you meet other homosexuals?"

"No, he's going to take me to meet the mayor. Of course he's going to take me to meet other 'homosexuals'." I didn't like the way his words echoed mine.

"Well what would you call them?" I could feel my face coloring. It seemed to be the end result of every interaction I had with people these days.

"How about 'Mary'? Fag? Did you know that you're a fag hag? That's what they call girls who hang around with fags." I couldn't really see Tom's face, but his voice was even more pitchy and tight. I didn't know what to do or say. He seemed to be mad at me for

210

just being there. After a few tense, quiet minutes I couldn't keep quiet any longer.

"Tom, I don't know how to talk to you about this. I just don't want you to get hurt. Are you sure Louie's okay?"

"What, you think he's going to pop my cherry?" He snorted.

"I don't know. I don't know it's not popped already. It's just that Louie's older. I guess I just remember that guy in the French Market who made a pass at me. He scared me. He wasn't some boy I was in love with who—"

"Who what?" He rounded on me. "Who took you to the prom? Who sat in the Saenger Theater with his hand up your skirt? Just where do you think we are, Kate? Honest to God, I have lived in this town all my life, *all my life*, and I know a bunch of guys who are probably queer, but even if we do give one another a curious look now and then I have never talked to a single one of them. I'm scared to. You might have to go through your grandparents and your daddy to have a boyfriend, but I have to go through all of Mississippi. Do you think I've wanted to go to New Orleans all these years just to get away from Mother and Eddie? I love you, Kate Lynn, but I'll go crazy if I don't go. I'll be back Sunday."

"What are you going to tell your mother?"

Tom looked at me as if I was the stupidest person he'd ever met. It hurt. "I'm not going to tell her a thing. I'll just be sure she's got everything she needs to take care of Eddie so she won't want me to go to the store for her, and she'll forget all about me. I could be dead in my bed for three days and they'd walk around just wondering what that stink was. Look," he said. "Louie's no chicken hawk. You don't have to worry."

"Chicken hawk?"

"That's a man who's into boys. Chicken. Me." He tapped his chest.

"Oh." Tom had been talking to Louie on the phone at night, learning a new language, moving away. "You sure? Because I'll worry about you, whether your mother does or not."

Tom sat up and wrapped his arm around me tight. Louie's perfume wafted into my nose. "I love you for that. For a lot else, but if you don't mind, mostly for that. I'll be gone one night and will come back and amaze you with stories of debauchery. But I'll stay safe, I promise."

211

"You'd better. You're the only homo friend I've got."

"Couldn't be a fag hag without me!" He stood up and tugged me up after him. "I got to go." I held out Louie-by-Day's business card, but he shook his head. "Keep it. I know the info backward and forward."

Tom walked me back to the bushes beside the field. I didn't know what to say, so I just hugged him and walked toward the trailer. I looked back once to see him standing there watching me. He raised his hand and held it there, waving, and then disappeared into the shadows.

I let myself back into the trailer and slipped into my room. Martha lay in my bed with her mouth open, as asleep as if I had given her the paragoric. Her eyes jumped behind their pale lids. I wondered if she was dreaming of her dog, or her mother, or me.

I slid the closet door open quietly, raised the lid of the toy box and fished beneath the pile of toys, all of them now discarded by both me and my sister. My hand found the journal and I pulled it out. Turning on my flashlight, I tugged Amen Samson's drawing of me out. For a long time, I stared at the girl whose smile didn't go all the way to her eyes. Then I tucked it and Louie's card into its pages and closed the lid.

Chapter Twenty Six

The next afternoon I asked Grandmother if I could take Martha to see *Yellow Submarine* at the Saturday matinee at the Saenger. When I told her it was a cartoon she was pleased, and even offered to drive us. I said no, that it would be good for us to stretch our legs even in the heat of the early afternoon. I figured that keeping her from knowing that, not only was it about The Beatles, who she thought were "nasty," but that Claire was running the box office, would ensure that Martha and I made it all the way into the theater. My grandparents and I hadn't exchanged a word about either the Doucettes or the *Reserved* signs, but discomfort hung like the ever present cloud of cigarette smoke in the café's air. I was used to it with Grandmother, but I missed Granddaddy like crazy. Even when he was in one of his tipsy fogs, he was strangely distant and silent. It seemed everybody in my family had stopped talking, and my friends were rapidly finding other lives. I was so lonely I thought I'd die.

It was hot and sticky as we meandered the ten blocks past the high school and to the theater. Martha was hard to keep on track; whenever anything caught her eye she went toward it, ignoring both cajoling and threats. By the time I saw the little box office, with Claire sitting in the big window under the marquee and laughing with a couple of kids who were buying tickets, I was sweating and exhausted from herding her. I grabbed her wrist and tugged her the last half block, barely slowing when her flip-flops bent and twisted and made her stumble along. We arrived at the ticket window as though we'd been dumped there, disheveled and out of breath.

When she realized we were there, Claire's smile got even wider. "Well, if it's not the Lynn sisters," she beamed, leaning forward

213

to direct her words at Martha, who ignored her completely, fixing her attention instead on the brilliant colors of the Peter Max poster that advertised the movie. "Hey Martha, I'll bet I could talk my boss into letting me have that for you if you want it."

"Yes!" Martha nodded enthusiastically. She traced her fingers around the edges of the little submarine that floated beneath the images of the Beatles and read the legend "It's all in the mind, y'know!" I jumped at the sound of her voice.

"Martha!" I grasped at anything I could think of to make her say something else. "How about if you get us the tickets? Here's the money." I might as well have been talking to the poster. "Do you want some popcorn when we get inside?" She didn't even look at me. Claire and I exchanged looks. She shrugged.

"I'm glad to see you, Kate," she said, counting my change and handing me our tickets. "I've missed you. Why don't you call me?"

"I thought you were working in the evenings," I replied, wincing at how snappish I sounded. "and I'm working in the café in the daytime, so—"

"So you're mad," she sighed. "I'm sorry. But I'm not sorry I took the job. If we all hadn't found work we might not be here at all."

"But, quitting school is just crazy. You don't want to do that."

"If I do quit, I'll get my GED. I can go to the junior college, get a better job and work for the money to go on. It won't be that hard, and Jean and Richard are all in favor of it. Richard says I might become a lawyer, work for—how does he put it—justice for the little fella." She shrugged a second time. "I'm just not that interested in high school any more. If I have to go to one more pep rally or one more assembly on how 'marijuana is the match, heroin is the fuse, LSD is the bomb' I swear I'll gnaw off a limb. I want to be in the real world, where things matter."

"Y'all want to hurry it up? I'd like to see the cartoon they play before they play the cartoon," a young man's nasal voice called from behind us, to a chorus of giggles. A line was forming, many of them people I'd seen in school but not a single one who'd have said a word to me unless, like now, they wanted me to get out of their way. Claire cocked an eyebrow as if to say "I rest my case." If I hadn't been so miserable I might have been tempted to agree with her. But I knew that, small and unimportant or not, I was going back to PHS in the fall.

"I'll call you, okay?" Claire said brightly. "Let's do something Monday. We'll call Tom. And I'll get Martha that poster." I nodded, and pushed Martha none too gently into the theater. All through the movie she sat smiling, now and then bringing her fingers up in front of her face like fans, peering through them, sometimes wriggling them toward the bright images as though she herself was drawing them and setting them in motion. She looked as if she was as much in the world of Yellow Submarine as she was in Pascagoula, Mississippi. I sat slumped in my seat, staring at the screen without seeing, wondering what was happening to Tom in New Orleans and to Claire right here. One thing was clear; they were in motion and I was stuck, alone in the dark.

That night, in bed, I lay and watched Martha trace her fingers in the air as if playing the movie over again in her head. "You really liked it, didn't you?" I murmured.

"We all live in a yellow submarine, a yellow submarine, a yellow submarine," she sang softly, the most I'd heard come out of her mouth in weeks. I smiled.

"Yep. It's all in the mind, y'know," I replied.

The phone rang. I bolted upright. We never got calls this late unless something was wrong. I heard my grandmother answer the bedroom extension, her voice first fuzzy with sleep, then rising in irritation, saying "No, he's not here! Why would he be here at this hour? Try the Carmodys'. No, I don't know the number. Yes, operator. Goodnight."

I leaned back, a smile widening on my face. Tom had let me know he was fine, and was thinking of me all the way from New Orleans. Reaching under my pillow, I tuned my transistor radio to WTIX and pretended he was listening to the same song there that I was listening to here in Pascagoula. Before long, Martha and I both drifted off to sleep.

Chapter Twenty Seven

It turned out that it didn't matter how much Tom loved me, once he spent the weekend with Louie-by-Day, his life changed to one I could never really share.

"I brought you something," he said when we sat on the trailer steps on Monday night, just the way we had on the first night we'd met. He pulled a series of photo booth pictures from his pocket. Two women, a blonde and a redhead, mugged for the camera in a series of four shots. They both wore heavy makeup, bright blouses and enormous glittery jewelry, the blonde in blue and the redhead in green.

"They look like they're from Dallas," I said. "You know, high hair and too much make-up. Who are they?"

"Who do you think?" Tom traced his finger over the face of the blonde. "Let me give you a hint; if it wasn't night time you wouldn't recognize him."

"Louise?" My mouth dropped open. Oh my God, Tom, he looks just like a woman! Did he give you these? Were you there with him? Does he really look that much like a girl?"

"Oh I was there with him, all right," he wiggled his eyebrows and tapped the picture. I looked again, hard.

"It's you!"

"I know! Don't I look gorgeous?" Tom pulled the photos out of my hands and gazed at them happily. "You have no idea how much fun it was! I got to go to the club and the girls made me up and let me watch from backstage, which is really just the end of the bar near the ladies' room where everybody gets ready. Felicia was right; even I learned more about what the male anatomy can do than I ever knew. Louise's act was so wonderful she gave me chills; it was like watching a magic show where you pop Louie into a box and this gorgeous creature pops out. Guys were just screaming, they were pounding the tables. I went out to the lobby pay phone to call you and I swear I was afraid somebody was going to come up and proposition me right there." He grinned. "How'd Grandmother like getting a collect call from me?"

"She hated it. But I loved it. Then what?"

"Then we went out after the show and Louise took me to three different parties. One of them was in, I swear, the biggest house on Esplanade, in a courtyard filled with lanterns and a pool full of beautiful fish and a portable bar made out of a door they took off its hinges. There was a high wall around the courtyard, and so help me, the top of it was covered in broken glass and razors and all sorts of things to keep anybody from climbing over. The owner has this party every year, calls it his "Wall Party." Everybody brings things to add onto it, beautiful pieces of glass, and razors they've tried to kill themselves with in the past year—anyway that's what Louise told me, but she's pretty dramatic when she gets tipsy. And, you won't believe it, Claire, the party ended when somebody fired a gun, so help me! We might've shrieked like girls but then we tore off our heels and ran like the boys we were!" He laughed, his eyes bright and oddly pretty, as if there were still traces of make-up enhancing them. "I even had what Louise called a Baby Sazerac, mostly ginger ale but with enough rye and bitters to make it interesting. I have to tell you, Kate, leaving a lipstick print on a glass is pretty sexy."

"So you liked it?" I didn't know if I was fascinated or frightened. "Do you want to be, you know, like Louise?"

"Tomasina by Night?" Tom laughed. "Nah. I had a great time, but I have no future whatsoever as a drag queen. Louise says when I talk I sound like mules farting, damn him, and I don't want to spend my life doing hair and makeup and lip synching Diana Ross. If I was going to sing I'd want to sing for real. We just went out like it was Mardi Gras and strutted our stuff. And in case you're wondering, I still have my cherry. For now, anyway."

I looked again at the two pretty creatures in the photos. "You did more in a night than I've done in my whole life. Are you going to go back?"

"Of course. Whenever I can. This might sound silly, but if I know I can go there, I think it'll be a lot easier to be here. Maybe it's my version of Bayou Eau Claire."

"Yeah," I said quietly. "I hope I find some place that feels like me. Seems like everybody, you and Claire and her family and even Bill and Felicia have a place where they know they can be themselves."

"I hope so too," he said, "but I think you have to figure out who you are first, all by yourself. Not somebody's daughter or sister or friend, just Kate Lynn, with her ass hanging in the breeze. Then you'll find someplace. 'Course, then you'll have to trust the rest of us to love *you*, no matter what."

Chapter Twenty Eight

Summer went on without any more dying. Hurricanes scared us a time or two but none made us leave home. Claire was only around on Mondays when I couldn't stay up late because of the breakfast rush, so we couldn't spend much time together. Tom told me more and more worrisome stories about his trips to New Orleans, and since I was afraid to think about how much he loved being the person he was there instead of being the boy I knew, I decided to dedicate myself to trying to connect to something in Martha, in the hope of getting her to wake up. I cut out pictures from the magazines Granddaddy brought and we pasted them onto big pieces of cardboard cut from the boxes that the café's supplies came in, making such fantastic collages that they even made Grandmother smile. I bought her a set of drawing pencils and a watercolor set at the dime store with some of my tip money, and she took to it right away. The only thing that bothered me was that every single picture she drew or collage she made had a dog as its centerpiece. The ones she found in magazines might be collies or Dalmatians or anything, but the ones she drew looked more and more like Martha, as though her memory of her dog was becoming more solid instead of fading. And though I hated to admit that my mean, blackmailing little sister could do anything better than I could, in fact could do something really well, her drawings were becoming more and more interesting looking, as though not only Martha the dog but the world that Martha the dog lived in were blossoming, while Martha the little girl faded away. As the summer went on toward the beginning of the school year I began to think that, like Claire and Tom, the old Martha was gone for good.

My grandmother must have thought the same thing, because in August she finally told our father what had happened. She'd already told him the bare bones of it, the next time he'd called after Martha had spent her night in the hospital. She'd explained how Martha's little dog had gotten run over and how somebody had called an ambulance because she had had a "fainting spell" at the sight of it, but for three months she had covered over the fact that Martha had become a little pleasantly smiling ghost. The fact that he only called every couple of weeks or so, and that ever since he had been gone Martha had been so intimidated by having to say "over" so he could switch the radio transmitter back and forth that she'd been practically tongue-tied, had helped keep our secret. And I had helped, joining in without any prompting from Grandmother to protect my father from worrying about his daughter. I told him when he asked that she was "fine as frog hair," and that she said to tell him she missed him and wished he would come home soon. I told him she was getting to be a real artist, and left out that she didn't do anything else. I wasn't sure why I didn't want him to know; I felt somehow that he'd left her in my care and I'd done no more good with her than I had with my mother. At the same time, I was mad that I had to do it at all while he got to go to a place so far and so different that I expected he bought whatever we said about being okay, just so that he wouldn't have to think for even a minute that maybe he should have stayed around. I envied him so much that at night I often dreamed about being where he was, in a jungle filled with bright birds and trees so tall they looked like green sky.

But Grandmother had reached her breaking point, and she finally told him everything. She shooed me away from the phone in the café while she talked, as though she could say anything I didn't already know. I suspected she didn't want me to see how upset she really was, but it had become obvious since Butch had quit and she'd been working in the kitchen that she was near an edge. She seemed too tired to do anything except shuffle through her day and fall asleep almost immediately at its end. She'd even stopped dying her hair, and I was shocked that the roots I'd been convinced were Indian black were coming in grey. She'd almost quit having anything to do with Granddaddy at all, the mad rolling off of her whenever he was there, drunk and helpless as always instead of pitching in in any way she could appreciate. She'd had no use for his gifts for Martha, pushing her lips out and scowling whenever he showed up with a pretty set of

222

beads for her to break and glue onto her pictures or a new flower, which he showed me how to press between the pages of my mother's old family bible and give to her. He was there less and less as a result of Grandmother's anger, and for the first time I actually thought about the two of them as people who had thoughts and feelings that went between them and held them together the same way other men and women did. Though I'd never given it much thought before, I was afraid that they might break up from the strain.

"Kate, your daddy wants to talk to you," she called back to the kitchen, where I'd been loitering, trying to catch meaning in the sound of her voice rising and falling. A feeling of dread filled me. I dragged my feet toward the phone, she waving for me to hurry and hissing, her hand over the mouthpiece, "I told him how she's acting, but you don't have to make it no worse." I nodded, took the phone and waited pointedly for her to leave the room. She did, but not before wagging a finger at me. I wondered if, like me, she was listening from the kitchen.

It didn't matter. As soon as my father said, "Katie, what in the Sam Hill is going on there? Over," my brain shut down, just as if he'd pushed a button.

"I don't know. Over."

"What do you mean you don't know? Your grandmother just told me your sister is acting like she's lost her mind. I want you to tell me what she's doing. Over."

"Okay, uh, she, uh, you know, she doesn't do anything much. She just watches television and draws pictures. Over."

"I thought she was having some kind of fits. Your grandmother made it sound like she needs to be in a mental hospital, ov—."

"NO!" I hadn't waited for him to switch the transmitter but it didn't matter. He would certainly hear most of what I was almost shouting. "You can't do that! She's not having fits; it was just that one time. She's fine! I'll take care of her! I do it anyway; I feed her and wash her and sleep with her and don't let her wander off. We're fine. We can take care of ourselves!"

He had waited until I ran out of steam before he spoke. When he did, it sounded like lead. "You wash and feed her? How's she going to go to school if she's so bad off you have to wash her and feed her? Uh, over."

"She'll be okay. She just got upset about the dog and, you know, mother and all. She'll come out of it. She will. Over." I wanted to slap myself for revealing how helpless Martha had become. I had ruined her, and now I was saying things that might wind her up in a mental hospital, all alone. I vowed that it would be over my dead body.

There was another pause, so long that I repeated "Over," in case he hadn't heard.

"All right," his voice had a tone of defeat that I remembered all too well. It made my skin crawl. "You look out after her. Tell your grandmother that I'll call back as soon as I see what I can do. Over."

"What do you mean, what you can do? Don't do anything to her, Daddy, please. Over."

"Just tell your grandmother. I got to go. Over."

"Yessir. Over."

"All right. Bye. Over."

"Bye. Over."

The phone clicked, and he was gone. I stood with the receiver in my hand, in the dark café, until my grandmother appeared, gently guiding Martha ahead of her and seating her at the table nearest the phone, at the backmost corner of the room. Martha smiled up at the brightly lit Budweiser sign that hung on the wall above the table, a snowy winter scene that rotated behind a pair of Clydesdales pulling a sled.

"What did your daddy say?" I watched the big, strong horses against the white backdrop, for a moment as mesmerized as my sister was. I wished I could go there, I thought, and take her with me. Neither of us had ever seen snow. It looked cool and calm. I imagined us sitting on that sled, dashing through the snow, like the song said.

"Kate, answer me! I don't need two of you acting the fool."

I turned my eyes down to meet hers. I might have gotten myself in trouble with my reply except for the look in her eyes. They were deep in shadow, as red-rimmed as if she had been crying, though I'd never seen her shed a tear. Rather than being mad at her, I was afraid once more that we might really be too much for her. I sat down and rested my forehead on my arms.

"Grandmother, I'm sorry," I said from the well of my arms. "I'll bet you never thought you'd be stuck with us like this."

There was a long moment of quiet. I looked up to see her stroking Martha's hair, a tender and strange gesture for her. She was looking at her as if she longed to comfort her, but didn't know how. Martha sat there as if nothing was in the world except the Budweiser Clydesdales, and I found myself envying her the way I had when she'd sat in our father's lap sucking her fingers after our mother had died, while I stood apart, watching them share their loneliness. Now, it seemed, Martha had found a way not to be sad or lonely, and a small, mean, miserable part of me wished it was my hair being stroked, even as I knew I would never let it happen. I was so lost in the thought that Grandmother's voice startled me.

"I'm not mad at you, Katie," she said. "You didn't make any of this happen. Sometimes I'm not too crazy about your daddy going off and leaving you, but I'm not mad he left you with me. Y'all are my grandbabies. Did you know when you were born I was happy as I could be to have a girl grandbaby, even if I didn't have an idea in the world what to do with you. Your granddaddy was so smit that he said you was his doll baby, started calling you 'Doll' right then. He carried you around as much as your mama would let him— he didn't drink as much back then but enough so she didn't trust him. But he'd have died rather than seen you two hurt," she continued stroking Martha's hair and looking at her, but the tenderness in her voice reached out and warmed me as well. "We both would have. You're right I didn't plan on this. I planned on you having a mama and a daddy and all the things a perfect baby girl ought to have. I thought I'd be the grandmamma who spoiled you rotten and sent you home. But it just didn't end up that way. So all of us got to do what we got to do. I mostly try not to think about it, and I'd advise you to do the same, though I doubt you got it in you. You're like your mama that way. She fussed over everything."

I shook my head. "I'm not like her," I said. "I don't want to be."

She frowned, saying, "You could do worse. I know better than you think I do how she got, but she didn't mean anything by it. Sometimes I think you're ashamed of the whole lot of us."

I shook my head, guilty about how much truth there was in what she said, then sat up straight, breaking the moment. "Daddy said to tell you he would call as soon as he sees what he can do. What do you think he means?"

"Well," she patted Martha one last time and stood up, straightening her skirt and stretching her back. "He told me he's going

225

to see if he can get what they call a 'compassionate deferment.' He's
going to see if they'll let him come home."

Chapter Twenty Nine

      While we were waiting to see if our father would come home, Martha and I started school. The doctors said that it would be good for Martha to go, that being around other kids, the kids she'd known the year before, might make her come back. She'd always gotten good grades, even when our mother was sick, even last year when she was in a new school and with no mother and father at all, but since we'd been in Pascagoula she hadn't said two words about friends or what went on there every day. She'd had Martha, and hadn't seemed to want, or need, anybody else. I doubted that she would discover a brand new interest in her classmates, but I hoped she would, along with everybody else.

      Grandmother talked to the principal and the third grade teacher about Martha, and assured them that she would behave and wouldn't distract the other kids. After the first three days the principal called and asked her to come into his office when she picked Martha up after school. She called PHS and said I should leave sixth period early and come along so she could talk to the teacher while I watched Martha. She sounded nervous, and I thought she might just want somebody who was used to schools to come along.

      The teacher told Grandmother that on the first day Martha sat in her desk, gazing with what looked like attention as the lessons were written on the blackboard, but had shown no interest in participating in anything. She had gone quietly anywhere she was taken, but made no effort to leave her desk unless she was guided. The teacher was so nervous she might wet herself that she took her to the girls' room every hour. On the second day, the teacher asked if any of the kids in class wanted to help take her to lunch and recess. A couple had volunteered, but had quickly gotten tired of spending their time on the sidelines of the kickball and hopscotch games and left her standing by the chain link fence. When the class came in from recess, the teacher had spent several panicked minutes before she found her walking down the sidewalk, two blocks from school, on the street that led to the trailer. "I can't watch her all the time. They can't watch her. It's not reasonable to expect little kids to have that much responsibility," she said. I choked back a snicker, thinking she had no idea how much responsibility a kid could take on if she had to, but Grandmother didn't say a thing.

"Then today she did this." The teacher held out a schoolbook, something called "Our Animal Friends." Most of the pages had big holes in them where pictures had been torn out.

"She does like animals," I murmured, holding Martha's hands as she reached to take the book and, I supposed, find more things to rip out of it. "Can she keep what she tore out?"

"Katie!" Grandmother snapped before turning back to the teacher. "I'll pay for the book," she said, fishing in her old handbag and coming up with a checkbook.

"It's no problem, Mrs. Lynn," the principal, a big, red-faced man who blushed all the way through his crew cut, said, "but this isn't the place for Martha. Maybe a special school."

"And where will we find one of those? I sure ain't heard of none around here," Grandmother said, standing up and pulling Martha close to her. "Is that what you do? Give up on children who need you? What am I expected to do while I work all day? What do I pay taxes for if my grandbabies can't go to school? Well you can both kiss my foot. Shame on you. Shame!" Holding my sister close, she sailed like a ship out of the room, leaving the principal and teacher looking as if she'd shot them dead and they just hadn't fallen down yet. Once I recovered from the shock, I took off after her, catching the two of them halfway to the car. I danced in front of them, opening the door for Martha and following her into the passenger side.

When Grandmother got in, I burst out, "That was the best thing I've ever seen! Whooee, you told them off good!" I bounced up and down, feeling the power of what she'd done surge through me. "Did you see him turn red? He looked like a big ol' tomato! I thought his head was going to blow up!"

Her lips twitched. She put the car in reverse and backed carefully out of the elementary school parking lot. "Hmph," she said. "Talk about my grandbaby while she's sittin' there like she's a stick of wood. They can kiss my foot all the way up to my butt."

I whooped in delight and surprise. When we'd gone a few bocks Martha reached under her T-shirt and pulled a stack of papers from the waistband of her shorts. They were the pictures she had torn out of the book. She looked up at me and I thought I saw a look of satisfaction in her eyes. I knew we wouldn't be seeing the inside of that school again.

As for the start of my own year at PHS, I didn't know what to make of it. My life in Pascagoula had been so caught up with Tom Carmody's and Claire Doucette's that, except for what happened with Cash Collins, nothing last year had made much more of an impression on me than this year did on Martha. I didn't care a thing for the PHS student body, the football team, the teachers or any of its activities. I was just faking it, moving through and acting a part while most of me was trying to figure out what really mattered to me at all.

I was depressed, though, about Tom and Claire. I was more alone than if the two of them had died, because I could see them right in front of me, walking away to places I couldn't imagine, much less follow. Richard hadn't come home yet, but Claire's sixteenth birthday had passed with a spaghetti dinner at the Doucette household and a real live call from Richard, person to person to her, that made her grin more than the Joan Baez album I bought her or the Indian bedspread Tom had brought from one of his trips to New Orleans. She chatted with him about things she hadn't told me, that she was trying to get a job with a lawyer friend of his, filing records and getting lunch and making copies, and that she was learning to type and would be good at it in no time. Watching her eyes sparkle as she dished spaghetti to her siblings, balancing the receiver on her shoulder and mouthing to Jean that she'd give her the phone in just a minute, I couldn't imagine her in Mississippi History class, suited up and playing softball in gym class, bopping down the hall in her Claire way, cool and above, but very much a part of, high school life. She had graduated in a way that I wondered if I ever would.

Tom was still in school; he even sat in front of me in home room, but something in him had become more open about his true self, and high school was becoming a trial I wasn't certain he would withstand. Even though he'd had his place in Pascagoula school society for his whole life, the people around us were all changing, finding boyfriends and girlfriends, taking a lot of pride in their places as the popular, the smart, the losers, and, like me, the not-really-there. There were a few guys who I imagined fit Tom's description of the "probably homosexual," but they were like he had been when I first met him—something I couldn't quite describe, that would be easy to deny if challenged. Last year Tom had been much the same, but now something he'd always held at arm's length seemed to have a firm grip on him.

One Monday morning he came in bleary-eyed and so scrubbed his face glowed, but with clearly smudged eyeliner around his eyes and the now-familiar waft of perfume pointing him out like an accusing finger. He collapsed into his seat after flashing me a wink and a grin, propping his chin on his hands and sighing loudly. I could see looks and gestures happening around us, a limp flip of the wrist here, a quick and obscene jerking up and down of a fist there. When the bell rang there were open laughs as boys and girls minced past him, one of them knocking his bare ankle in its loafer hard enough to make him wince. He made no comment, not his old smart-aleck dismissal nor any indication he cared. He just got up and drifted out into the crowd in the hall. I caught up to him as we headed to first period.

"Tom, go look in the mirror. You still have makeup on. You're going to get in serious trouble!"

He grinned at me languidly. "Oh, I hope so, and the sooner the better," he said, poking me in the rib with a finger not completely free of nail polish. "But okay, I'll go see what I can do to hide my glory." He sighed. "Too bad you're a caged bird; you could go with me some weekend. I could show you some things!" He continued down the hall in front of me as I stopped in front of my classroom, waving lazily over his shoulder, whistling "I Feel Pretty" as loudly as he could.

It took two weeks for him to show up with a black eye and a split lip.

I gasped as he sauntered into homeroom, eyes flashing, and dropped into his desk. Conversation around us stopped. People who, the day before, had done nothing but look at or comment about him now stared at their desks. No one smirked or whispered behind their hands. The teacher continued to write out the day's schedule on the blackboard, oblivious.

I touched his shoulder and he flinched a little before turning around and smiling the new slow, flirtatious smile. "Tom," I hissed, "what happened? Who did that? Did you tell your mother?"

He nodded his head. "Yes I did, Cherie," he drawled under his breath. "I told the whole family I got into a fight after school, told them 'You should see the other guy!'" He ran a finger under the puffed eye and down around the lip. "I think it was the proudest day of their lives, well, after Eddie getting paralyzed, of course. Can't say the Carmody boys aren't real men now, can we?"

"Who did it? We have to tell the principal!" I was yelling in a whisper. I could almost feel the blows landing, as if they'd beaten my face along with his.

"No we don't. We don't tell anyone, understand?" He reached out and grabbed my wrist so hard it hurt. I stared dumbly at it, unable to believe that somehow I'd ended up on the side opposite Tom in the matter. "The official story here at school is that I was diving in the river and plowed my beautiful face into its shallow bottom. Good story, huh? Just one of the boys out swimming, had an accident and will be perfectly fine." He turned around in his seat, before turning back, briefly. "Oh, and of course I'll mend my sinful ways and go back to pretending I'm nothing, just the way it's always been, just the way it'll always be. But," and he grinned his Bugs Bunny grin for just an instant, "you and I know different. And you won't tell a soul, right? Because honestly, Katie, either my life or somebody whose life I'll surely take if they lay a hand on me again depends on it."

I nodded. "Not a soul," then added as the class was called to order, "I love you Tom. I'm sorry." He winked his unswollen eye and turned around, and we began living the lie that we never stopped, not as long as I was there.

It wasn't long. A month later, our father came home, announcing he'd already found us a house in Spokane, Washington, where he'd been reassigned so he could find help for his mentally ill child. He took us away from Pascagoula, Mississippi so fast I didn't believe it was really going to happen until I saw the tears in my grandfather's eyes. He sold the trailer to a shipyard worker and it stayed right where it was, furniture and all. We packed the things that mattered and gave or threw away the rest. We wrapped the things that reminded us of our mother and carefully placed them in a big moving barrel, the little blue hat box at the bottom. I made sure Martha had all her drawings and collages and art supplies, and I had my mostly empty journal with the drawing and Louie's business card. Our father, who still couldn't seem to believe that Martha had greeted him with a wan smile and gone right back to the painting of a black dog she was doing, and could go whole days as if she lived in some other universe next door to ours, asked if we were sure we didn't want our toys so many times that I got impatient with him, finally asking which one of us he expected to play with them, the pissed-off teenager or the zombie kid. It made him mad, but he stopped asking, and I thought he might finally be catching on to what his daughters had been doing while he had been gone.

Chapter Thirty

On the day before we left Pascagoula, Tom, Claire and I sat by the ruins of the old boat, watching the sprinkler pull water out of the river and spray it over the rotting timbers.

"I wonder how many times that water has cycled over that wood?" Tom mused, holding his hand under the spray. "Every year, over and over, always the same."

"It's a river, Tom," Claire said, wryly. "That water's probably been everywhere from the North Pole to the Panama Canal. It won't even look at Pascagoula in the rear view mirror on its way out."

"Like Katie, here," he reached over and put his wet hand on mine. "I'm going to miss you. Who will I go walking with at night? Write to me. Come back and visit. Don't go." He looked as miserable as he had in the chapel of Our Lady of Sorrow months before, lost and ready to declare his love rather than be alone. I knew, though, that there were already people in his life that were more important than I was.

"Richard's coming home," Claire said quietly, grinning when I yelped and clapped my hands. "He called and said he guessed he'd have to find a way to live with us if we wouldn't go with him. He said it was too easy being a bachelor; he needs a challenge. I think he just misses seeing his oldest daughter grow up."

"Oh, so now you're his daughter?" I tried to match her wry tone, but it came out sounding irritable and envious. It was a fact that my relationship with my father had, for a very long time, felt like a stiff partnership built around taking care of someone else, first my mother and now Martha. I couldn't even miss him any more; I'd given up on telling him how I felt about things or wanting him to take an interest in me. He was just an itch between my shoulder blades that I couldn't scratch.

Claire must have heard the envy in my voice. She slid an arm around my waist and said, "Richard's going to hate like hell that he didn't get to say goodbye to you. He always said to me, 'That Kate Lynn will be something special someday; I just got a feel about her.' I think that's one reason he wanted you to see Bayou Eau Claire, you get to him."

A lump rose in my throat. "I thought it was, you know, to make up for Martha."

She shook her head, squeezing my waist and giving me a little shake. "Cherie, everything ain't about your mama or your sister. You better figure that out; I don't want to have to tell Richard you didn't amount to anything." She stood up, drawing me up after her, and threw her arms around me. "I have to go to work, and if I stay here I'll cry and my mascara will run. You write to me, girl. I'll write back. We'll get together again. I still got to teach you to swim, right?"

I choked out, "Right." She let go of me, slapped Tom on the back, and, tossing an "Au revoir, Cherie!" over her shoulder, set off toward the old truck and her job.

"Looks like it's just you and me," Tom murmured. "I don't want to say goodbye and I'd sound like an idiot speaking French. I don't know what to say."

"That's a first," I grinned, swallowing the lump that I knew wasn't going to go away. "What would the ancient Greeks have done?"

He looked at me for so long I felt my face heat up. Then he pulled me close and kissed me, the way he had under the statue of Mary, who looked as though she had lost the most precious thing in the world. He held me out, examining my face hard before shaking his head ruefully. "The ancient Greeks would've wished to God you were a boy."

We both burst out laughing. Then he turned and walked away. I stood and watched him go, my hand under the spray from the Pascagoula River that kept the ancient boat from rotting to dust. I wondered if there were molecules of the Indians in that water, bits that had traveled wherever the water had gone for hundreds of years. I wished I had heard them sing their song so I could take it with me to

Spokane, to whatever life I was going to, so that, no matter what, I wouldn't be alone.

It was almost dark. The frog chorus was just beginning. I listened to the sounds of night in Pascagoula for the last time, the water slapping Mr. Carmody's pier, the dogs barking from far away, kids yelling in some twilight game from off toward town. I stood there until I knew my father would want to know what had kept me, and I wouldn't have a chance of making him understand.

Cupping my hands under the spray from the river, I let them fill. I raised the water to my mouth, and drank.

Chapter Thirty One

We had been in Spokane for two months when the box arrived. I had written a few letters to Tom and Claire about how strange everybody at school was and how much I missed them, and they answered me, Claire saying how she had found a boyfriend at the lawyer's office who was twenty two and who she might have to break up with because he was talking about getting married, and Tom speaking in code about his long distance girlfriend Louise, and how much he liked visiting her when he could, just in case somebody else saw the letters. Halloween had just passed, and our father had taken more of an interest in it than he had ever done before, taking Martha to get a costume that he'd ended up picking out for her—a nylon princess dress and mask that made me wonder if he was living in as much a fantasy world as she was. She'd worn it when he put it on her, plastic mask and all, but all it had done was made her look more like a puppet than ever, and I had the feeling he was as creeped out by it as I was. He signed her up for what special classes he could find, but speech therapy and tutoring in math and reading didn't have much of an effect when your pupil perfectly echoed your words when you told her to and said nothing else, and drew the answers to all your math questions in numbers of dogs. It made me laugh out loud, but he got mad at me, just the way he had when neither of us had been able to stop my mother from slowly falling apart. He began going out at night after supper, ordering me to have us both in bed by ten. I was worried that we were as much too much for him as we had been for our grandmother, and I stayed awake nights wondering what would happen if he gave up on us too.

The mailman brought the box on Saturday morning. Martha and I were watching The Beatles cartoon from the living room floor, with a big bowl of Alpha-Bits on the rug between us. I spooned cereal into my mouth and hers alternately, ignoring her fishing in the bowl with her fingers to spell out the soggy words "Martha, Beatles, submarine" on the sheet of paper in front of her.

"Nice one," I said, pointing at the last word. "Bet those teachers would have a stroke if they saw that." At the knock I leapt up, hoping that our father hadn't waked, glad that he slept like a stone. The times when he was there and I felt safe, but was in his room asleep so I didn't have to tiptoe around him, were my favorites.

The box was big, half the size of a coffee table, but was only a little heavy. I dragged it into the living room, casting a fast glance down the hall to assure myself that the door at its end was not going to open, and then gave it my attention. Martha was right beside me. She pointed to the address.

"Hey, it's for you! And it's from Pascagoula!" I picked at the tape until it came loose, and pulled up the flaps. There, on top of a pile of white packing paper, was a letter addressed, not to Martha, but to me. It said "Miss Kate, please read before looking in box."

I snatched it up and closed the box quickly, straddling it while Martha pushed and pulled at me, trying to get it open. "Wait just a minute! This says I have to read it first. Maybe it's fragile or needs directions or something." She stopped, clearly waiting for me to read the letter out loud. I cleared my throat and began.

"Dear Miss Kate," it read in a tight, printed hand, "That day we went to New Orleans, Richard and me had a plan. I know how you feel about all this, so you look and decide what you want to do, but we thought it might help your little sister. Felicia says hello and she hopes we see you again someday. Me too. Sincerely, Gator Bill"

"Uh, Martha, why don't you go—," I started. She responded by plowing into me with her full weight, knocking me backward onto the floor and wrenching the box open. She threw the paper in all directions for a moment, and then stopped still, her mouth hanging open. Then her eyes rolled back, she began to shake, and she dropped to the floor.

"Martha! Daddy! Daddy, come quick!" I screamed, leaping around the open box and grabbing her. The door down the hall opened and our father, wearing only his boxer shorts and T-shirt, came running. He looked around the room for an instant, frowning at the paper and spilled cereal, before his eyes found Martha. He grabbed her up and laid her on the sofa, saying her name and patting her arms, yelling for me to go get some water and to call an ambulance. I didn't move. I had caught sight of what was in the box.

It was Martha. Gator Bill had taken my sister's dog and turned her into one of his creatures, and in the process had made her into something I imagined he really did think might help a little girl hurting for her lost friend. The little black head was the same, eyes bright, the little muzzle almost smiling, the body sitting as if waiting for her mistress to come home. But on her back, slightly unfurled, as if caught just in the moment before stretching out full, were two enormous white wings. He had turned Martha into an angel, into something that could never die. I didn't know if it was the sweetest thing I'd ever seen, the stupidest, the craziest, or all three.

"Kate, what did I tell you to do? Move your ass!" My father roared at me, but then turned back to my sister as she slowed her thrashing. I still couldn't move; from where I stood I was the only one who could see both Marthas, the one in the box and the one beginning to take deep, gulping breaths and to push hard against our father's chest. Looking stunned at the sudden change in her, he scooted back, leaving her room to launch herself off of the sofa and to the side of the box, where she knelt, her eyes wide. He started to stand, but I thrust out my hand with such force that he stopped, looking at me as though the relationship we'd had for my whole life had suddenly shifted and I had the right to tell him what to do. I thought that was right; I'd seen my sister through something he'd been absent for, and in my mind he had given up his right to simply give orders rather than be a father who listens as well as talks. He might never be Richard, but if he wanted anything from me he had to accept me, and both Marthas, for what we had become.

Martha reached into the box and stroked Martha's head, then her back, then her wings, while I explained to him about Gator Bill and his magical way with taxidermy. Then I told him about Tom and Claire and Felicia and Richard and Eddie and Butch and Cash Collins. As I went on, I got louder and faster. I told him about the whole time he had been gone, about Martin Luther King and Bobby Kennedy, about Granddaddy's drinking and Grandmother's exhausted care, and how much I hated Mother for dying and him for leaving, and how I didn't know if I would ever forgive either one of them. By the time I was done, I was crying so hard I had to sit down on the floor with Martha, who had taken her old friend, under our father's horrified but paralyzed gaze, out of the box and put her on her lap. When I was done, he cleared his throat, shook his head, looked at the Marthas, looked at me, cleared his throat again, and then stood up, went back into his bedroom and closed the door. On Monday he began making calls to find someone to come in and help with Martha and the housekeeping. He never mentioned the things I'd said to him, and neither did I. He got a part time job in addition to his Air Force one, and sometimes we went for days without seeing him. Martha kept on going to school, carefully positioning her dog by the front door every morning so they could greet one another when she came home. They spent all the rest of the time together, my sister creating a life for her companion out of everything she could find. Now all her dogs were Martha, and all her Marthas had wings.

Grandmother called not long after to say she and Granddaddy were closing the Rebel Café and moving back to where they had family, to a little town near Jackson where there were no shipyards and no breakfast rushes, and no worrying about who would eat with Negroes. With them gone, I had no idea if I would see Pascagoula again. I wrote fewer and fewer letters to Tom and Claire, until our time together receded to something I sometimes dreamed about and that tugged at me at unexpected moments. I grew up and moved away from my sister, her dog, and the year we had all shared without quite knowing where I wanted to go. It stayed that way for nearly forty years, until she and Martha came to live with me, and Tom Carmody sent us his message:

"You said you'd always love me, no matter what."

Part Three

2005

Chapter One

"Oh hell, Kate, do I have to repeat it?"

"Well you sure haven't lost your flair for drama," I felt for my chair and sat down heavily. "Would you mind telling me what you're talking about?"

Tom sighed and coughed again. "God—I've had this conversation in my head for years, on and off, and all of a sudden I'm tongue-tied. It isn't like me. Kate, a lot happens in any forty years of living. I don't know what yours has been like; I hope it's been wonderful. Mine has."

"It has? Then why are you—"

"Because it isn't any more," he said, so softly that I pressed the phone to my ear harder, to capture the thin words. "You aren't married, right?"

"Right," I answered, suddenly ashamed that I wasn't.

"Well I was. I was as married as the world would let me be, until two years ago," he said. "Almost thirty years!" I could see his red hair, and the grey eyes that glinted in the moonlight when we'd sat on his father's rickety little pier. Thirty years was suddenly a concept I couldn't grasp.

"Who—what happened? You're not married anymore?"

"I'm a widower. He died, two years ago last April."

"Tom! I'm sorry."

"Thank you. His name was Lawrence. He was a banker—can you imagine? I thought I would end up with some wild gay Quarter Rat who'd bleed me dry and abandon me, and damned if I didn't find myself a sweet, serious suit—," He broke off. I couldn't tell if it was emotion or the 'cold.' "with a flair for money. We never even knew

243

who got it first; just that things started happening, simple diseases were worse than they ought to be. Lawrence couldn't get near a germ without catching it, and he was a fitness freak. I got pink eye. My gums bled. I got thrush, for Christ's sake! I thought only babies got thrush. Of course we knew immediately, but we spent months trying to hide it, trying to hide ourselves. It was the cruelest thing in the world, having to hide again, after all those years with friends and lovers and a place where we didn't have to pretend anything to anybody. But before long it really couldn't be hidden. Everybody was so scared, and then everybody was so sad, and then everybody was sick or in love with somebody who was sick, and we were just two more after a while, trying to face the unfaceable with some modicum of sanity and grace."

"So, what you're telling me—you got—you're saying you're HIV positive?" I could barely bring myself to say it, as if the words themselves had the power to hurt him. He quickly put that notion to rest.

"No, I'm saying I've got full tilt, immune system blowout, every microbe in the known world fighting over who gets to munch on me next AIDS, darlin'. I've fought it for years, and I've seen it kill the love of my life and more of my friends than I can count and I've held it off longer than any of us thought possible. But it's finally got me. I've got so many things coming apart and breaking down I can't keep up. And I'm tired of trying. Kate, you'd better get used to the idea right now that if you're going to have anything to do with me at all it's going to be the whole package, and it's not pretty. I've got Kaposi's Sarcoma on my chest, I'm as desiccated as a mummy, my lungs fill up at the drop of a hat, and I bleed when I take a crap. But I'm still me, and I remember us when we were just pretty children and how special you were to me, and I want you to come see me so bad it just may have been keeping me alive, even after my sweet Lawrence is gone."

"Jesus God, Tom," I whispered, my arm suddenly almost too heavy to hold the phone to my ear, "there isn't anything? I mean, there are drugs—,"

"Not for me, Cherie. There were for a long time, but not anymore." Hearing him call me by the nickname Claire Doucette had given me almost forty years before made me dizzy, as though I was falling down the rabbit hole of my own past. "I've done it all, the whole antiretroviral cocktail, plus a few herbal things and some voodoo my doctors would shit bricks if they knew about," he broke

244

off, laughing, wheezing, before drawing a deep breath. "Hey, did you notice I don't squeak anymore?"

"Congratulations," I said. "Did you stop when you got your full growth or is it just a nice side effect of the disease?"

He barked a stronger laugh. "That's my girl; spit in the bastard's eye. I knew you had it in you. I remember, Kate. I remember what you said about your mother, how she was, and I knew you'd understand. Everybody around here has gotten all weepy and quietly determined, as if they just have to keep me going long enough for Jesus himself to show up and tell me to pick up my bed and walk. I swear if they don't let me go I'm going to take about half of them out with me."

"Are you telling me you're really thinking of killing yourself?" I could hear myself from a distance, while part of me tried to walk backward, into a place I hadn't been for a long time, a place I suspected Martha was probably the mayor of by now. I fought to stay with Tom, to be who he thought I was, to spit in the bastard's eye.

"Actually I like to think of it as killing this horror show of a disease, sending the demon back to hell, as it were. The bad news is, I have to go with it."

"Okay, this is a lot to take in, Tom. I mean, I need to think about this. My God, I'm so sorry."

"I know. And I understand. You've got to remember, this is only news to you. I've been living with the shadow hanging over me for years, and with the reality of it while Lawrence was dying. I was relatively okay then, at least physically. Now I'm not, and I don't want things to end that way. He—he didn't know me. I couldn't comfort him. Hell, I couldn't even recognize him, long before that wonderful body of his finally gave up. I want to die while I can still say goodbye and know who I'm talking to. I know I'm assuming an awful lot about how you turned out, and hell, I don't know that this whole 'let's look up our high school semi-sweetheart' impulse isn't some drug-inspired psychosis at work. You'd be shocked at some of the things I think. But one way or another, Kate, I'm not going to be here a lot longer, and I've carried you around inside me all these years as somebody who really believed she could love me no matter what, and who talked with so much feeling about the Pascagoula Indians and not being left alone on shore. Remember?"

"I remember."

"It got me through, sometimes. Hell, it's one reason I never looked you up before; I was too afraid you'd be completely different from that kid who was half crazy from seeing so much then, and so might be able to help me figure out something just as crazy now. I was afraid you'd gotten normal. I knew if you called me you'd at least be the Kate who remembered how amazing it was to see New Orleans that first time and who wished me a life with love in it. Lawrence was that wish come true, but the time for wishing is over. All I've got left is doing. But, vain thing that I am, I want it to mean something to somebody, and I figured maybe it would be all right if you and Claire and a few other people I love were with me. Will you come?"

"What about the people around you who are waiting for that miracle?"

"Don't worry. Nobody takes what I say seriously anymore; I didn't invent this idea, you know. The fellow who answered the phone—Bunny—he's my nurse. He's heard me howling about this for months and thinks my sudden desire to see old friends is a healthy letting go and also might keep me going a little longer, the cheerful bastard. You'll like him. But we do have to keep this between us."

"And Claire?"

"Honey, I'm wearing out here; I need to stop. Claire will be here. Now, will you?"

I sat for a long moment, looking around me. I could see my entire life from that chair, the computer where I ventured out into the world for the benefit of others' creative lives, the locked library where I kept all my facts and certainties, the kitchen where I made the meals that I ate more or less alone, the stairway that led up to Martha's whole world, a world I maintained, but could never share. "Yes, I'll come," I said, and felt a tension in me let go. My heart pounded as though it had just now remembered how to beat, and wanted to give it all it had. "I don't know how we'll do it, and I don't know if you realize what you'll be getting into with Martha, but we'll find a way."

When he started to speak again, it was clear Tom was crying. "Thank you, Cherie. Thank you. Oh, I'm going to see you again! I'm so happy! Don't worry about getting here; I'll have arrangements made. Someone will drive you all the way. But Kate, it will take days; you have to get ready now. All time is borrowed time."

Chapter Two

By the time the limousine pulled up to our little house on Whidbey Island, Tom and I had had half a dozen short conversations. I told him about Martha and her fierce attachment to the stuffed body of her namesake. I explained as best I could about Martha Land, and how her only interest in things in this world was incorporating them into that one, halfway hoping he'd see how futile the whole idea of travelling was and change his mind. He seemed weaker with each call, less interested in answering questions. He just kept saying "Come." He had taken care of everything, he said. We would have a wonderful trip.

I had spent the week tying up loose ends in the present, while the past unrolled in my mind as though it was happening all over again. Andy Gerald wasn't thrilled with me telling her she'd have to look up her own facts for perhaps as long as a month, but my contracts always had clauses for unannounced time off "for health reasons," in case something happened with Martha. The few other projects I was working on were the same—a biographer squawked a little, but couldn't convince me that his Magnum Opus on the life of Charles de Gaulle preempted my emergency leave.

As I cleaned out the refrigerator and arranged for mail and newspaper delivery to be stopped, I realized how little relied on me, how few things in the world would miss me if I was gone. There were no pets to board, the only dog in the house having lost the need for food and walks forty years before. The yard was wooded, no lawn would need mowing, no non-native plants would require non-native care. I kept no houseplants; I had told myself that it was pointless, that Martha would have snatched any leaf or flower that caught her eye and moved it into Martha Land, but I knew I could have dissuaded her if I'd really given it a try. I couldn't speak for Martha, but except for my library and the little blue hatbox that I still kept high in the back of the closet, I wouldn't miss a thing.

I was worried about how Martha would take to the limousine or its as yet unknown driver. I'd been talking to her, mostly shouting up the stairs, about what she could bring and what would be waiting for her when we got back. I told her about how long the trip would be and promised her we would stop every night and that, while we couldn't bring any paints in the car, her pens and pads and scissors and magazines would be right where she could get at them. I warned her again and again that she the things that were part of the car had to remain part of the car. I even filled a cigar box, twenty generations down from the one she had had as a child, but her favorite container still, with tiny figures, beads and metallic paper and bits of mosaic tile, anything I thought might keep her going during a week on the road and could be scraped off the car at the end. In my own cache I put the bottle of sleeping pills I had been prescribed, but had been afraid to take or to give to Martha, and a bottle each of gin and tonic. If worse came to worse, I told myself, one of us might get some relief. I put the pink rosary in my pocket, just barely resisting saying a "Hail Mary, full of grace," if only for luck.

We were ready hours before the car was to arrive. I had scrubbed, combed and dressed Martha, insisted she eat, packed a box full of easily opened and easily cleaned up snacks, and checked and rechecked the suitcases. Two were filled with the closest we could get to appropriate and bearable clothing for August in New Orleans, and one with everything I had assembled to keep my sister happy. Martha had wandered around anxiously, picking things up and putting them down, before hiding in the studio under threat of her life if she covered herself with paint before we left. I expected she was huddled up there with Martha, rubbing and talking to her in a low, incomprehensible croon, the way she did when she was really upset. I wasn't sure how she was going to take being separated from her companion, even though I was equally sure that the stuffed Martha, who had weathered the past years remarkably well but still lacked a shocking amount of fur and looked brittle, as if a wing or a leg might drop off at any minute, needed to stay right where she was. I had talked to her about it until I was sick of it, and was troubled at how thoroughly she had ignored me. By the time the firm knock came, announcing our driver's arrival, I was exhausted and wishing I could call the whole thing off.

I opened the door to find a startlingly handsome man of about my own age standing there. Behind him sat a car the length of a school bus. It was black from stem to stern, with tinted windows that hid its inside so well that anything happening in there would never be seen by those even standing nearby. Even as I whistled in shocked admiration, I chuckled inwardly, thinking that, even in dire straits, Tom Carmody had known what he was doing.

"How do, Ma'am," the driver stuck out his hand. He didn't wear a uniform; instead he wore a crisply ironed yellow polo shirt with a tiny appliquéd crawfish on its breast and navy blue, sharply creased slacks. A blue baseball cap, brim neatly curled, covered what looked to be a thick head of silver hair. The cap bore the legend *Big Easy Rider Limousines, New Orleans*. He looked fresh and capable, and I couldn't imagine that he knew what he was getting into. "I'm Jim," he said. "I'm taking y'all to New Orleans, if you'll let me."

"Jim, I'm pleased to meet you. Please come in." I stepped back. He passed me and I caught a whiff of cologne. It could have been named "Southern Gentleman" for its resemblance to all the cologne I had smelled on dressed-up men in my childhood. It was the counterpoint to "Fisherman's Funk," the sweat-and-Jim Beam combination that my grandfather, Mr. Carmody and the myriad men who only dressed up for weddings or funerals sported. Men in the Northwest wore no scent at all. Jim had been in my presence for all of thirty seconds and already I was in a world I hadn't seen for decades, but that I knew down to my cells.

"This all you're taking?" He indicated the bags and box. "Have mercy; I don't know a woman can go to the can with that little luggage—oh, 'scuse me. I didn't mean to be rude."

I smiled. "No offense taken. So, would you like some, uh, coffee or something?" I waved my hand toward the kitchen, suddenly alien in my cleaned-up, packed-up house, as if it was impatiently waiting for us to leave so it could go on about its business. Jim shook his head.

"We'd better hit the road. I told Tom I'd have you there in five days, tops, and he said make it four if I could." He looked at me from eyes that had gone soft and sad. "It would be a good idea. He's awful sick."

"You know Tom? Other than driving?"

"I do. He's a good friend. We've worked together, one way and another, for a lot of years. Tom's good people." He reached for the nearest suitcase. "Might as well get these loaded, then." As he stood, his eyes focused on the stairway leading up to the studio. "You'd be Martha, I'm guessing," he said.

My sister stood scowling, still wearing the T-shirt and jeans I'd coaxed her into but obscured enough by the stairs' shadows so that I wasn't sure she was free of paint. One thing was perfectly easy to see, however, and I sighed. She had Martha clutched high in her arms, the half unfurled wings curling up on either side of her face, the little black muzzle pointed outward, doubling the unfriendly stare. I groaned.

"I've been trying all week to explain that she can't bring that damned dog," I said, sitting down heavily.

"Why not? We got room. Don't look like she eats much." He reached into his pants pocket and produced a tiny yellow cardboard camera, the kind that used film that you mailed off once the roll was done. "Tom told me about you, Martha, and showed me your pictures," he said, sauntering to the foot of the stairs. Martha took a step backward and up. "I know this is going to be a long trip, so him and me hatched an idea. Since we'll be going through a lot of pretty country, I thought you might like to take some pictures of Martha along the way. When we get there we'll get them printed up and you can use them any way you want. C'mon outside and I'll show you how to use it."

Martha's eyes fixed on the camera while mine rolled upward. She shifted Martha to one arm and came down the stairs, her hand out. Jim pulled his arm back and slipped the camera back into his pocket. "It's time to go," he said, turning and hoisting the suitcases. "Miz Lynn, get what you want to take with you and I'll put these in the trunk. Martha," he called over his shoulder, "let's get you and your friend fixed up. We got a ferry to catch."

My sister marched, dog in arms, down the stairs and out the front door. For a moment I stood with my mouth hanging open, thinking that his trick might work, before reality set in again. Grabbing the last of the bags I joined him at the car's enormous trunk, where he was neatly storing the luggage.

"Uh, Jim, I appreciate what you're thinking with the camera and all," I began, as he lifted my bag and tucked it in with the other suitcases, one that I assumed was his own, and a large cardboard box. "but Martha's just as likely to take that camera apart as use it. I don't guess I've ever seen her take a photograph in her life. That's why I've got all this stuff," I indicated the suitcase still on the ground. "It goes with us on the seat so maybe she'll let your car alone."

"How many of them do you think she can take apart before she gets tired of it?" he asked, reaching into the trunk and flipping up the loose flap of the cardboard box.

"Jesus Christ," I murmured. "How many are there?"

"Tom said get fifty, so I got fifty," he replied, pulling out three more and handing them to me. "Whatever she decides to do with them, it's going to get us off this little island, and then it's 'Katie bar the door!'" He slammed the trunk with gusto. I burst out laughing, shaking my head. "You better go lock up. I don't expect to stop before Boise."

I hustled back to the house and took a final look around. The disarray at least looked clean; no dirty dishes and no food left to rot in the refrigerator. I thought that I could easily set fire to the place if it wasn't for the trove of Martha Land works upstairs.

I found Jim and Martha sitting amid a tangle of yellow cardboard and a ribbon of black film on the porch. She was running the film through her fingers, holding it up and examining the holes at the edges. Jim looked up, eyebrows raised. "She's fast," he said. Then he pulled a second camera out of his pocket, pointed it at Martha the dog and snapped the shutter. "Now you have a picture of Martha beginning her trip to New Orleans," he said. My sister's eyes narrowed. "Take it apart and the light will expose it and ruin it. Keep taking them and you'll have the whole trip in pictures. Let's set her in the car and get her there." He stood up and walked to the car door, opened it and waited.

Martha looked up at me. "Come on," I cajoled, "I need for you to do this. Tom needs for you to do it. Please."

She stood up and carefully picked up the ragged little dog, carefully holding it so the wings wouldn't be crushed. "All right, we'll go," she said, walked to the car door, and placed her on the seat. She held out her hand for the camera. Jim handed it to her, she deftly

251

snapped a shot of Martha perched there, wound the film to the next stop, and climbed in after her.

"Well I'll be damned." I hurried after her and climbed in. "Jim, take us to New Orleans," I said.

"Be there before you can say 'Who dat?'" he said, closing the door and climbing into the driver's seat. "Sit back, ladies," his voice now came from a speaker in the ceiling of the massive car, "and let me fill you in on the amenities in this fine luxury vehicle. Big Easy Rider Limousines feature all leather interiors, a fully stocked bar, in this case stocked with a variety of sodas, juices and snacks and a small but tasty assortment of wines and hard liquors." I mentally ticked off the gin in my suitcase. "Overhead is a TV with DVD player and just underneath the seat you'll find a drawer full of DVD's. Tom said you'd like 'Yellow Submarine,' Martha, and I just threw in a few other things I had lying around. There's satellite radio and a bunch of CD's, but I have to confess the music leans heavily toward one band. There are some blankets and pillows if you want to sleep. If you think of anything else you need let me know." Then he dropped his professional voice and said "Really, Miz Kate, I'm going to get you all there as fast as I can. I promised Tom we'd make it in five days tops and that's going to take some mean driving. But he promised to wait for us, and from what I can tell, that's no picnic either."

Chapter Three

In all the fantasies I had had about travelling to New Orleans with Martha, I had never had one that featured me being bored out of my mind. Jim was up front driving and Martha, as it turned out, was happy as could be, as long as she could run Yellow Submarine over and over again and draw scenes of Martha in a long yellow car, first in the forest, then in the mountains, then in dry, scrub country. At first it was clear she was mirroring what she saw out the window as we crossed Washington, but the more she watched the cartoon the more her drawings took on the character of Peter Max's work, until she had woven her companion into an only slightly distorted version of the film's plot.

"You realize we'll never be able to sell those," I said around a mouthful of potato chips near the middle of our second day. "Not an editor in the world would fight off the lawyers."

We'd made it to Boise that first day, staying in a motel that I instantly fell in love with for its sheer sparseness and its general distrust of mankind. Once I had unplugged the telephone and internet connection and given them to Jim to keep, there was hardly anything that wasn't either bolted down or designed to be stolen. If an ashtray or Gideon Bible went missing, I reasoned, they could call Jim. He had made it clear that he was handling the bills and everything else, and that we were to simply relax and enjoy the ride. I appreciated his efforts, but if he thought that I was going to get to watch anything on the DVD player other than Yellow Submarine, he hadn't figured on my sister. As long as she was sitting on the car's long back bench, wrapped in a blanket with her dog, watching the movie and creating the saga of Martha as the fifth Beatle, all was well. Let me try to watch, listen to or do anything else, and she began to fiddle with things. As soon as I realized that she was using the knobs of the stereo to press round indentations into the paper, which she then colored over like rubbings I'd seen of memorials and tombstones, I gave up. Now we were halfway to Denver and I slumped on the side bench, dejectedly eating my way through the snack supply and wondering if I could drug her to sleep without her knowledge. Martha had sensitive taste buds and a child's attitude toward medicine, and I still imagined that that dog was staring at me accusatorily after all these years; I doubted I had the nerve to try.

I finally decided I couldn't take it any longer. I had tried calling Tom from the hotel on the first night of the trip, but the voice I knew as "Bunny" had said that he wasn't up to talking. "I'm sorry, Kate," he nearly whispered, his voice catching. "His breathing's bad. We're keeping him comfortable but he's not able to carry on a conversation right now. He'll be happy to know you're on your way, though. I'll tell him. It'll perk him up." I'd called a couple more times, out of nerves, but had gotten the same response. "Hurry." Finally I decided that any company I was going to get would be right here.

Jim and I had maintained a professional, courteous distance so far, helping one another at rest stops, him setting the stuffed dog up wherever Martha could not, and watching her snap away with the yellow cameras. He was solicitous and kind. He never commented on the strangeness of her photographs, though I was unnerved by the scenarios she set up and recorded whenever we stopped. In spite of the fact that we were going through countryside that neither she nor I had ever seen, and that, when I wasn't in too irritable a mood to pay attention, was often breathtaking, she had an agenda that had nothing to do with documenting Martha's road trip across America. Instead, if we were at a rest stop or gas station, she carefully took the dog to any unoccupied car and laid her down beneath the front tires, in effect reenacting her demise, until people began to look at us a bit too hard and I could persuade her away. At a scenic overlook in Utah she had insisted on propping her so precariously on the rail of an overlook that Jim took his belt off and rigged a strap so the dog wouldn't fall hundreds of feet down a red rock mountainside. He and I were like estranged parents swapping off child rearing duties. Near the end of the second day of our trip, when I found myself sulkily singing along

254

to Mean Mister Mustard through a mouthful of dry Pringles, I decided something had to give.

"Jim?" I scooted up to the window that separated him from the back of the car and tapped gently. It slid down.

"Y'all need a pit stop?" he turned down the stereo, a jazz CD that I didn't recognize but that sounded good.

"Not exactly. I'm kind of used to having something to do," I said, "and Martha and The Fab Four are about to drive me insane. Could I come up and sit with you for a while? I promise I'll watch her like a hawk and tell you if we have to pry her off of anything."

"Sure," he answered. "I'm a little tired of listening to myself sing up here anyway. Let me find a place and we'll pull off. Maybe we can find a nice river for her to drown Martha in," he chuckled.

"Don't give her any ideas," I replied, suddenly feeling as happy and self-conscious as if I'd asked a boy out on a date. Jesus, I thought. If the simple act of riding in the front seat with the grownups made me this jittery, I might ought to think about what my life had become.

I explained to Martha that I was going to sit up front for a while, and that I would come right back if she wanted me to. I said we would leave the window down so we could hear her if she needed anything. I told her that if she did anything at all to harm the car I would throw her dog out the window.

"No you won't," she said, her eyes darting back and forth between the TV screen and the paper she was rapidly drawing on. It was clear she didn't care whether I was there or not. Somehow, though, I couldn't stop reassuring her.

"Okay," I said, as Jim took an exit and pulled the limousine into a gas station parking lot, "I'll be right up front. You know how to get a soda or—" I ran out of steam as the car stopped, and finally just pushed past her to open the door. She craned her neck when I went between her and the screen. I slammed the door, marched to the front of the limousine, and got in.

"You look a little bumfuzzled," Jim said, folding a map that had been lying on the seat where I now sat.

"Yep, that's just what I am," I replied. "Just do me a favor and talk to me, all right? And for God's sake don't do it in an English accent." I looked around me. The car was opulent, but spare. There were few clues about this man, no photos of family taped to the visor, no books or papers, nothing dangling from the rearview mirror. "Is this your car? I mean, do you own the service?"

Jim shook his head. "Naw, fella named Jay Thibeau owns the service. He's a good friend of Tom's, has been for a lotta years. You really don't know a whole lot about Tom, do you?"

"No, I don't," I said. "Tom and I were friends during what we thought was the most awful adolescence ever experienced. We had a real bond. You know how there are a few people you knew when you were growing up that you always mean to look up, but you're afraid you'll find out they turned out terrible and you want to keep them like a bug in pine resin, just the same as you knew them? That's me and Tom. Actually," I sighed, "that's me and a lot of people."

"Like Claire?"

I stared at him. "Do you know Claire too?"

"I do," he said, slowly, glancing at me and smiling briefly before looking back at the road. "Known her for quite some time."

"Is she still down there? In Pascagoula? In New Orleans?"

"Not exactly. I hear you went out once to her place. Bayou Eu Claire."

"Oh my God. Claire lives at Bayou Eu Claire?" It suddenly hit me that I was really going to see people that had, over the years, become stories to me, that wonderful, funny Claire Doucette, who I'd idolized, who I'd so often wanted to be, was just a couple days' ride down the road. A lump rose in my throat.

"She does," Jim answered my question. "There's a lot Tom didn't tell you, I guess. That's where he is, out there at her place. That's where we're headed. They moved him out there a couple of months ago, when he decided there wasn't anything else they could do, or that he wanted them to do. Claire's—well, he couldn't be in better hands."

"You mean I've been calling Claire's house all along and she hasn't spoken to me?"

"Don't worry about it. Claire does things her own way. She's excited you're coming. She'll talk to you when you get there."

I glanced behind me to be sure Martha was occupied, and said, "You sound like you can fill me in on more than I realized. You said you and Tom worked together. How is that?"

Instead of answering, he reached out and punched the button on the CD player. The jazz band I had heard before took up a tune I didn't know, but that sounded like pure New Orleans, bright and bouncy and lusty all at once, horn heavy, an invitation to strut.

"Hear that?" He tapped the steering wheel, keeping time. "That's my band, The Jazz Revelators. We been playing Tom's club about once a week for a lotta years. Hell, he was the first one to give me a job when I got back."

"Back from where?"

"Oh, I spent about fifteen years tom catting, playing horn all over, getting in trouble, drinking too much, screwing around with my life, 'til I decided to sober up and try to make something of myself. Quit being a son of a bitch—no offense. I gave up drinking and I do try to live a good life, but I've never quite conquered cussing."

I waved my hand. "None taken. You say you went back. So you grew up in New Orleans?"

He took a deep breath. "Noooo," he replied, "actually I grew up in Pascagoula. Went to PHS. Did a world of hurt there too."

"Really? But you're about my age. Did we know each other?" A low buzz started in my head, like a voice calling from far away. I strained to hear it. Suddenly Jim's features began to change, the hair darkened, the thick, middle aged body became rangy, the benign features twisted into a handsome, angry sneer. I sat up straight and grabbed the dashboard as though I needed it to keep from falling over. "Cash," I said dumbly. "You're Cash Collins."

He shook his head. "I ain't been Cash Collins for years. That was my mama's boy, her crazy dream. Like to have driven me crazy too, between her and my old man. It took me quite a few years to decide that staying mad at them kept a chip on my shoulder that was as good a prison as Parchmen. Hell, I'm damned lucky I didn't end up in Parchmen, some of the things I did. But one day when somebody asked me my name I didn't say 'Cash, what's it to you?' I gave them the name on my birth certificate. I said "I'm James Collins, and I'm pleased to meet you" instead. Once I did that, I got the urge to make amends, like that AA says, to let James Collins make up for some of the things Cash did. I kind of walked it backwards, telling a few women I was sorry for running out on them, playing a few make-up gigs for when I was too wasted to do a halfway decent job of playing the horn—I still play the saxophone," he smiled brightly, "but I never could bring myself to put my mouth on the one you and Tom fixed up for me. I cleaned that sucker up and traded it in at a pawn shop for one half as good but way less likely to make me puke."

"Tom didn't say a word," I said. "When were the two of you going to tell me?"

"I wanted to do it, been wanting to since Tom told me he'd talked to you. I've been waiting a long time, probably putting it off out of fear of what I'd find out. I lit out quick after the night when I started that fight with Tom, but I called back, you know, to some of my boys, to find out what happened to Eddie and your sister and the dog and all. Last I heard the dog was dead and your sister had gone plumb crazy—I'm sorry, Miz Lynn; I don't mean that. It's just what they told me. We was kids, you know?"

"Kate."

"What?"

"Name's Kate, not 'Miz Lynn,'" I said. I settled back into the seat, feeling the road rumble as we flew headlong down the road. We rode in silence for a few minutes, before I said "I always figured it was me."

"You? What about you?"

"I was supposed to be looking out for Martha, and I wanted to just be a kid instead, with teenaged drama and regular kinds of fights and all. When you hurt Tom at that debate and he wanted to get back at you, I hate to say it, but it was the most normal, simple thing I'd done in years, or at least it felt that way at the time. I had a friend, we were doing things together to get back at the bad guy—that's you—when neither of us could do jack about what was really hurting us. It felt pretty good. It was exciting and powerful. I just didn't count on her," I jerked my thumb back over my shoulder. "I probably should have thought it through better, but I was busy feeling like one of the only two lost lambs in Pascagoula, me and Tom. So if you want to be responsible for breaking Martha, get in line."

"Oh, I didn't say I was responsible," he said, looking at me again, just for an instant. "I was responsible for being an asshole and trying to make Tom Carmody suffer, but what happened to your sister came from a lot more than just me. Or you. "

"You do therapy on the side?" I wrinkled my nose in a sneer I hoped didn't look too harsh. As stunned as I was that he had once been the terrible Cash Collins, I liked Jim so far, and I wanted him to like me. But I disagreed with him on this.

"Nope," he answered. "But it does look to me like you could use a break."

"I heard that," I said. "And I'm just betting that what we're headed into isn't going to be it."

"Well, I can't say for sure what it's going to be," he said. "I only know two things. Tom's sicker'n hell and is ready to die, and the weather channel said there's another one of those big-assed storms out in the gulf. I reckon only the Lord knows the rest."

I sighed and shook my head. "Damn, it's strange to hear you talk like everybody I grew up with. It's like hearing a song on the radio I haven't heard since I was a kid, but I could join in and sing it right along with you, lyrics, tune, everything."

"Yep, same old things," he smiled ruefully. "Music and dying and shaking your fist at the weather and taping up the windows anyhow. Hasn't changed a bit. Welcome back."

"Thanks," I said. "Maybe. How bad's that storm? Bad?"

"Maybe."

Chapter Four

Martha knew we were getting close before I did; she suddenly lost interest in her DVD and her drawing pad, now a pile of cut, glued, drawn and painted depictions of Martha in her Peter Max world that had left Jim speechless. She rolled down the window and drew a deep breath, placing her dog on the seat beside her and leaning out, as if she were the happy canine with her face in the breeze. I opened my mouth to tell her not to lean too far, and the hot wind hit me. It smelled like home.

"That's bayou for sure," I said. The scent of the flat, close piney woods we had been travelling through, angling more and more southward through Louisiana since we'd left Dallas that morning, had taken on a note of brine and rot. "We must not be more than half a day out."

I tucked Martha's pile of work under an Andy Gerald novel I had spotted at a truck stop in Oklahoma City and impressed Jim with, not only by showing him my name in the acknowledgments but by swearing on a stack of bibles that I hadn't the faintest idea what the plot was. I had bought it and tried to read it in the car, but gave up, finally admitting that I was too nervous to do much of anything but ride herd on my sister and make frustrating small talk with him. He kept fiddling with the radio, obsessing about the hurricane that he said might be coming to meet us, and getting more and more reticent about answering my questions about Tom and Claire and what I would find at Bayou Eau Claire, finally saying "Kate, you are a fine woman but you are getting on my last nerve. I wish I could say something to make you feel better but I can't. You have just got to see Tom and Claire and everything, and if you don't want to be there I will personally drive you back to that island. But it'll be after. I've made my promises to Tom and I intend to keep them. We need to get home, so let me drive." Then he clamped his mouth shut and would only answer me in short sentences. I got mad until I realized he was probably doing some impressive holding back. Although I itched to ask what he meant by "and everything," I'd left him alone for most of two days.

Now, though, I was too excited to keep to myself. I scooted forward, out of the whipping air, and tapped on the raised glass. It slid down silently. "Hey," I said, apology in my voice.

"Hey," he said back.

"How long, do you think?" I was keeping it short, though I was dying to jump up and down like a kid.

"Oh, not too long. I told them to expect us for supper." He smiled at me in the rear view mirror. "How're the girls back there?" He'd taken to Martha's dual identity with an ease that filled me with gratitude. I promised myself to give him the pile of drawings from the trip if he wanted them.

"They're good," I said. "Got a few cameras left and I've still got all my hair, so I'd count the trip a wild success."

"Knock wood," he said, rapping his knuckles on his head. It looked like we were square.

Martha and I both spent the afternoon gazing out the open windows, watching the land change more and more to water and sandy, scrubby earth. I was shocked at the heat and the dankness of the air. I had lost my acclimation. But I couldn't bring myself to roll up the dark windows and separate myself from the first wisps of Spanish Moss and the palmettos and that wild, fecund smell; I knew this country. I knew the trees and the slate blue sky and the flatness of the road and the seeping water at its edges. I knew the nature of the road kill, the crushed armadillos and the occasional burnt-rubber waft of unfortunate skunk. I was in as deep a dream as my sister, the sights and the smells erasing decades. I thought that if I looked in a mirror I would see, not a middle aged woman with a grey braid and a deep frown line between her eyebrows, but a brown haired girl, on her first trip through the primitive beauty that led toward an adventure, her friends at her side. How on earth, I wondered, had I let her get so far away?

The shadows were getting long when Jim called back, "There's the turn-off, just ahead. We're here."

We turned left where, in another lifetime, we'd turned right, and were enveloped in a wash of shade, the trees arching overhead and dappling the car, the ground and our faces with bits of gold and deep green. The road was wider than I remembered, but just barely. Jim drove slowly, the massive car becoming not just a means of getting us somewhere, but the stately entrance of two—or three—or four—important characters into a play. I felt self-consciously important showing up in this massive black thing, with the spectacle of Martha and Martha at my side, driven by a man who'd been thinking about making amends to us for most of his life. And I felt terrified that I would let everyone I was about to see down, that whatever Tom wanted from me would be too much and I would end up hauling my sister home, as Jim had said, "after," having failed a friend's dying wish.

We slid out into the open gently, the drive now extended all the way up the little slope and to the front of the house, where it bent into a circle around a swatch of grass and a bed of flowers of wildly disorganized design. Jim tapped the horn twice, and a cacophony of echoing honks sounded from somewhere I couldn't see.

"Hallelujah, they've penned the geese, "Jim said. "I can manage a lot, but those sons o' bitches have got it in for me in an unnatural way."

"You're joking. She's still got the geese?"

"Oh yeah. Only about half a dozen, thank God. She does have some restraint with the geese, at least. Hope you like goose eggs. She puts 'em in damn near everything."

The words "some restraint" sounded like there was some meaning behind them, but I didn't have time to think about them. Claire's house—or cluster of houses—spread out in front of me like a little settlement. Besides the house there were three other buildings that I could see. Two cottages with porches of their own and tall, open French windows on either side of their doors flanked it, and a building that looked like it could be a barn, a workshop, or a combination of the two stood off at some distance to the side and near the woods that surrounded the clearing. Its wide double doors were flung open, its interior dark. All the buildings were nicely painted, the main house in the stately white I had imagined it the last time I had sat on its porch, the two cottages a shade of peach that reminded me of the houses in New Orleans. It was hard to see from the angle where we were sitting, but it looked as though a mural ran the length of the big building by the woods, something with a lot of yellow and red. A pile of rusted metal, at least five feet high, sat beside it, smaller pieces trailing off as though they had broken free and were escaping through the straggly grass. The live oaks were still there but the buildings were wound among them, each of the cottages seeming to have claim to its own. The trees' branches were dripping with wind chimes, whirligigs, bird feeders and things that looked like their whole purpose was to glimmer in the sun. The biggest bottle tree I had ever seen, much bigger than the ones in Butch's old neighborhood, stood like a totem in the middle of the circle where the flowers grew, the multicolored glass bottles stuck on its branches challenging the petals to out-brilliant it. Half a dozen people bustled around, some of them waving as we drew up and then going about their business, as though having a fifteen-foot-long car cruise in on the evening air was the most natural thing in the world. A smoky fire burned in a pit situated in the center of the grouping, its peppery smoke making my nose itch.

"Jim, what is this? A camp? It looks like a bed and breakfast blew up."

He snorted a laugh. "You're not far from the truth. Every time I see the place they've added something. I think they had a plan once, but it kind of got lost in Claire not being able to say "No." When I get the heebie-jeebies from all the riot that's usually going on, I go down there." He pointed.

On the other side of the car, down the slope, lay the lake, the live oak, and the pier. Where the overturned boat had held our afternoon etouffe, a pair of picnic tables, set in an L, angled around the base of the tree. The pier had been rebuilt; it had a wide deck with several weathered Adirondack chairs gathered under an enormous umbrella, and a rope swing hanging from the furthest tree branch near its end. It looked calm, like a place where you could sit and think.

One of the chairs was occupied. I could see a halo of short white hair over its back. I wondered if it was Claire. It wasn't.

"Cherie! Cherie, you're here!" She was on me before I realized she was there at all, leaning in the window of the car and wrapping me in a hug so hard that bugs swam before my eyes. I hugged back, breathing in a mixture of sweat and soap, and a peculiar little tang of something that seemed familiar. When she gave me breathing room, I drew back and looked into the crinkled blue eyes of

Claire Doucette. She might be more wrinkled, but her hair was still long, impossibly blonde, and her freckled face was as open as a flower, her smile full of spark. She wore a bright blouse and jeans, and a pair of wide, flat sandals that I had long associated with the words "earth mother," and a smile that I had dreamed about. Sometimes over the years, when the world had seemed particularly sour, I had thought I'd made her up, and here she was, possibly the least run-over looking middle aged woman I'd ever seen. As far as I could tell she was Claire all the way to her bones, and right now she was crying like a baby. I cried right back.

"Claire, I can't believe it!" I pulled her in close again, and then held her at arms' length. "You look so wonderful. And you're here; it's so strange; I feel like I'm coming back to earth from a trip to outer space."

She wiped the tears from her face and flung them, a gesture so familiar that for a second I saw her young again. I shook my head. "You made it in time," she said, her expression mingling sadness with the joy. "Tom's a complete mess, but he's as tough as ever. It's going to be a tonic for him to see you. It sure is for me."

"Y'all want to get a move on so I can get some supper?" Jim was standing behind her, smiling as if he was responsible for our happiness. "Let's get those suitcases in the house. Lord, my behind is worn out from that car seat. And Kate, you might want to have a look at your sister."

I had been so caught up, I hadn't realized that the door on the opposite side of the car had opened and Martha had gotten out. Dog clutched under one arm, a wing arching over her shoulder, she was headed straight for the lake.

"So that's the famous Martha," Claire called, propping her chin on the roof of the limo as I leapt out the door and ran after her. "Need some help?"

"No, I got her," I puffed, rounding her just as she got to the pier, and grabbing her arms. She wriggled hard, trying to break my grip. "Stop it," I said, "you can't go down there by yourself and I want to see Claire and Tom. Later, Martha, we'll come down later, I promise."

"No! No!" She shoved me hard enough to break my grip, almost knocking me off my feet, and started around me again. I was shocked; Martha could be stubborn but, in the confines of our little house there was seldom need to coerce her. I simply arranged things around her, accommodated rather than fight. Even on the journey of the past few days we had mostly been in the confines of the car or a series of unassailable motels and rest stops, and I had let her watch her movie and draw, to stay deep in Martha Land because that was the easiest thing to do. Now we were in a place full of irresistible dangers—rusted metal, deep water, unguarded fire and the numerous strange people and things that lay around us. I had no idea how to deal with her. For all Bayou Eau Claire's eerie familiarity, I was in a place I knew almost nothing about, and over which I had little control. All the fear I had been avoiding washed over me.

"Oh, let her come on," a feathery voice called from the chair at the end of the pier, "I'll look after her. We'll watch the lightning bugs come out together."

The white head rose above the back of the chair and the face turned toward us. It shone like a milky moon in the waning light.

"Felicia." It was I now, not Martha, rushing toward the end of the pier. She was on her feet, arms stretched wide before I got to her. She swept me up in an embrace that almost lifted me off of my feet as Martha passed us and stopped, looking out over the rail and into the water.

"See? She just wants to have a look. And I want to look at you." She ran her pale blue eyes over me and nodded. "How've you been, Kate? Last time I saw you, you were just a child." She laughed. "Me too, I guess, even if I did think I was the most grown up person on the face of the earth."

"We're fine," I said, keeping one eye on Martha and taking in the older version of the graceful, self-assured girl who had astonished me in so many ways. I looked back toward the house and the car, where Jim and Claire were rummaging in the open trunk. "Where's Bill? Is he here too?" I wondered how he would look, whether he had kept the pointed teeth or found some treatment for his scaly skin. How would Gator Bill look if he was just Bill?

Felicia shook her head. "That no good bastard ran off with a hoochie coochie dancer, must have been just a couple of years after you left."

"Bill? But he seemed like he adored you. I thought you were happy."

"We were; we were real happy," she replied. "But Bill wasn't born circus. He always wanted to believe he fit in on the outside, and when this cute little thing came on with us and took a liking to him, he just couldn't resist. Before I even knew there was anything going on, he took off with her. Last I heard they were in Las Vegas. So there I was, right about twenty years old and all of a sudden by myself with nobody to mother or to keep me away from trouble. So I got in trouble. But that's a story for another time. I've mostly done real good, and I'm good now." She looked at Martha, still perched at the edge of the pier. "Don't tell me that's that dog Bill and Richard fixed up. Does she carry it around like that all the time? I can't believe it's still in one piece. He always did do good work, though. Remind me to—"

"Are y'all going swimming or coming up to the house?" Claire's voice interrupted from the car. "You did come here to see Tom, didn't you? Let's go see if he's awake, and then we can have some supper and catch up."

"Go on," Felicia said, "I'll bring Martha along in a few minutes. You go see Tom. He's been counting the days."

Chapter Five

"Claire, I'm scared," I said, as we walked up the stairs to the wide porch.

She took my hand and squeezed. "I would be too," she said. "Have you ever known anyone who died from AIDS?"

"No. To tell you the truth, I haven't even known anybody who was very sick from anything since I was a kid. Just my father, I guess, but it wasn't like we spent any time together."

"Really? He remarried?"

"No, never did."

"So who took care of him?" She stopped, her hand on the door. Inside it looked dark and cool. I wanted to be in there, not out here under her quizzical stare.

"The U.S. Air Force took care of him," I said. "I take care of Martha."

"Hmmm—." I didn't know what to make of the sound, but didn't have time to think about it. She continued. "Well, we're taking care of Tom, but he's miserable. Come on."

It was the first time I'd been inside the house. Claire had claimed it was too decrepit to go into when we'd been there as kids; only Richard went in to do the bare maintenance that kept it from falling apart all the years it sat empty. Now, it was anything but empty.

Half a dozen people were clustered together on an assortment of sofas and chairs, in front of a large television screen. The room was growing dark; it was the time of evening when locusts sang and mosquitoes came out. I suddenly realized why the low, smoky fire was going. It was an old trick to keep mosquitoes away. I hoped it worked; DDT had gone out of favor a long time ago, and in a place like Bayou

Eau Claire I expected that, as Granddaddy would have said, they carried knives and forks.

"Who are they?" I whispered to Claire as we passed by without pausing for introductions or causing anyone to look up from the screen. On it, a weatherman was pointing toward a map of the Gulf of Mexico and the states—the states we were in the middle of—that ringed it. A whirl of cloud almost the size of the gulf itself rotated slowly in its midst. "What are they doing?"

"I'll introduce you later. They're watching the Weather Channel. Don't you know? It's the CNN of the South. They want to see what that hurricane's supposed to do," she said. "It ran through a little bit of Florida and is picking up steam. Hurricane watching's still the regional pastime. Silly name for this one, though. Sounds like an ice skater's coming through."

"Oh yeah? I've been in that car with Martha for a week. What'd they name it?"

"Katrina."

Chapter Six

"It's possible, just possible," he sighed, "that you are going to break my heart."

Claire tugged me to the foot of the bed in the darkened room. "He says that a lot in his sleep," she whispered, smiling at the figure on the bed, one I could hardly see amid the surrounding arrays of flowers, cards, stuffed animals, baskets and other obvious gifts, many of them unopened. "I don't know if it's a memory of some tragic breakup or the best pickup line I've ever heard."

The room was large and comfortable, the window open, its gauzy curtains puffing in and out as though the room itself was breathing. There was little furniture, the hospital bed in its center taking up much of the space. I could see the top of an IV stand amid the bouquets and presents, its line leading down to the bed. The white top sheet had been tented so that it hovered a few inches above the body lying beneath, keeping the air off but touching nothing. The wispy voice I had heard on the telephone came from beneath it.

"Claire? Is that you? It's too dark; I can't see."

"Hey Baby," she responded softly, sliding up the side of the bed. "It's barely evening. You've been sleeping. I brought you a present."

"Oh, I hope it's a dirty book," he said, his voice a little stronger. "Bunny's been torturing me by reading me nothing but literature, though hearing Papa Hemingway in his voice is worth a listen. I keep telling him I prefer 'The Old Man and the Semen,' but he won't listen." He coughed a wet cough that was too weak to do any good. Claire turned to me and beckoned. In spite of the fact that every muscle in my body ached from tension, I found the strength to move forward. I reached into my pocket, where I had kept the little pink rosary, replacing it there with every change of clothes, for the duration of our trip from Washington.

"Claire brought me and I brought this," I said, leaning forward and swinging it in the air above his chest as Claire switched on the bedside lamp. "Oh, Tom." I said it before I could stop myself.

The face smiled through cracked lips. In the light he looked like a mask that had melted to sharp peaks and dark hollows, his skin waxy and oddly shiny, his eyes sunk so deep I couldn't read them at all. "'Oh Tom' is right," he said, "Hell, you should see me on a bad day, Cherie. I'm great today, aren't I, Claire?"

"Absolutely," she said, putting on a pair of surgical gloves, dipping her little finger in a tin of salve and rubbing it across his mouth. He winced. "I'm sorry; I didn't mean to hurt you. Can I help you move up a little?" He nodded. A slight, handsome young black man stepped forward from where he'd been sitting in an armchair by the window. He wore a light blue scrub suit and flip-flops, his loosely curled hair pulled back in a short pony tail. He nodded to me, a sweet, sad smile just brightening his face, before turning to Tom. Between them, he and Claire grasped the sheet and slid it upward, the man sliding another pillow underneath the sheet, clearly trying to brush as little of Tom's skin as possible. Tom broke out in a sweat, but kept smiling, looking at me with eyes that were still green, and that, as soon as he was settled, took on a wry flash that reached down deep inside me. He was clean shaven, his hair white and cropped very short, the freckles I had loved standing out against skin drawn so hard against his cheekbones that they looked about to break through.

"Tom," I repeated, as though I had just now caught sight of my old friend in the body on the bed. "It is so good to see you." I lay the rosary on the bedside table and leaned forward, examining him. "Damn if you don't look like your daddy."

"Oh hush, Kate! What a thing to say to a dying man," he waved weakly. "I don't want that thought lingering with me as I go to my grave." The young black man brought a cup of something and tried to put a straw to his lips. Tom turned his head away. "Quit it, Bunny, I don't want that vile concoction. Kate, they want me to drink those terrible meals in a can so this body will keep on torturing me. Now that you're here I can say no with impunity." He put his hand on the young man's gently, and continued, "But a little ice would be nice. I'm sorry I'm not a better patient."

"You're fine," Bunny replied, turning to go for the ice. I saw him press his lips together as if in pain himself, once Tom couldn't see his face.

"So, other than a truly frightening resemblance to my daddy, how do I look?"

I didn't know what to say. Memories of my mother came back like a cool avalanche, distant, unsettling. I remembered the feverish sweat and the suffering in the eyes, the hint of something animal behind the effort to stay sane. I remembered the thin cough that did no good, and the blood on the Kleenex afterward. I hadn't thought for a long time about how my mother had looked the last time I had seen her, when she had gone into the hospital and no one had thought that two little girls would be better, and not worse off, if they could visit their dying mother. She had been terrifyingly sick, but not as sick as Tom was now.

"Does it hurt a lot?" I bit my tongue. I should be saying something reassuring, comforting, not asking my dying friend the questions I had never asked my dying mother.

"Like the very devil," he said. "I was afraid to go on—too much of the drip before you got here. I was afraid—I'd go so far I— couldn't get back." His words were becoming staggered. He closed his eyes, exhausted. I frowned at Claire, who tapped the IV bag.

"We can increase the morphine dose," she said. "He'll be more comfortable, but it's hard to know what they'll do at this point. He might just be unconscious."

"And I did so— want you to be here, Katie," he sighed, almost inaudibly. "Tomorrow we'll have—our meeting—and then I think it's time to go."

"To go? You mean—,"

"To Front Street. To the river."

"What?"

"I'm going home. I'm going—to join the Pascagoula."

Chapter Seven

"You're not serious," I said around a mouthful of cornbread, embarrassed at how wonderful it tasted to me when Tom had lost interest in food. Claire, Jim, Felicia, Martha and I were gathered around a big table that sat in the middle of the kitchen. Bowls of fresh corn and butterbeans steamed in front of us, sliced tomatoes so ripe I could smell them from across the table lay on a platter beside bread and butter pickles and whole green onions. My head swam, half lost in overwhelming sensory memory and half trying to take in the fact that we were sitting there seriously talking about letting Tom Carmody drown himself in the Pascagoula River.

"Well, Tom is serious, that's for sure," Claire poured sweet tea and set a glass in front of Martha, who sat staring at her plate as if she had never seen food. "Bet it's been a while since you've eaten this good, hasn't it, Martha? Here, try this ham; it's the best in Southern Louisiana." She speared a slice onto Martha's plate, and to my surprise Martha picked up her fork and knife and cut herself a piece, putting it into her mouth and chewing, then smiling and nodding. Claire nodded back once, and turned to me as if that job was taken care of. Claire continued, "You got any thoughts on the matter, now's the time to voice them, before we talk to Tom tomorrow."

"Thoughts? I don't know what to think." I rubbed my forehead, running my fingers along the furrow between my eyebrows that had been there since Amen Samson had sketched my fifteen year old face. "My God, he looks terrible." Tears sprang into my eyes. "I can't believe any of this. It hurts just to see him. I know him and I don't. I know you all, and I don't," I gestured around the table. The sixth chair sat empty. If this had been an ordinary reunion among old friends Tom would be there, eating and, I imagined, wisecracking his way through the meal. "Doesn't it sound crazy to you? Doesn't AIDS do that sometimes, cause dementia? I mean, what's the point of all this?"

Claire looked at me for a long moment. Felicia and Jim were quiet, watching the two of us as they ate, now and then exchanging a glance. Martha continued to nibble, though she was arranging her beans, corn and pieces of meat into a pattern on her plate. "For who?" Claire asked. "For Tom? For me? For these guys? Or for you? Seems to me that's all that matters, whether it means anything to you."

"Look," I said, fighting to keep down the anger I was beginning to feel. "I'm new here. This is all going too fast."

"She's right," Felicia said. "We've all been tangled up in this for months, ever since Tom brought up the idea. You remember how we reacted then? " She turned to me. "We didn't want to believe that he'd done all he could, that he was going to die of this thing. Once we did, though, Claire and me were willing to do whatever he asked us to. Jim, here, took some time to come around."

"I'd rather wrestle an alligator naked than try to stand up to those three," he said, shaking his head. "But I said I'm in, and for Tom I'm in."

Felicia went on. "You need to know, Kate, how it's been all these years. We've got history, Tom and Claire and me."

"I'm sure you do, but—,"

"You know I told you I got pretty lost for a while after Bill left. Out there in the living room's a man named Sam, thirty five years old this September. He's mine, mine and somebody else's, and I don't know whose. It was that bad. When I knew he was coming I left the Biggers Brothers and the things I had started doing that would have killed us both if I'd kept them up, and moved to my mama and daddy's. They were hurt, but like I told you once, they were practical people. We were all a little shocked when Sam was born as average looking as could be, and it kicked in something in me that wanted him to have a life on the outside, where he could have friends and go to school and not have to explain to any living body his mama's skin or that he didn't have a daddy." She smiled a sad smile. "So I thought, now how could I give him the kind of life I couldn't have? Who could help me? So I gave him to Claire."

"You what?" I looked from one to the other of them.

"That's right," Claire nodded. "There I was, dropped out of college after a few semesters because I just plain hated it. Much as I wanted to, I couldn't focus on just one thing. Outside of being a Doucette, I didn't know who I was. Richard had finally talked Jean into coming back here after he'd fixed it up. I moved here too to get my shit together, and here comes Felicia with the most beautiful, smartest five year old boy and the damnedest sob story any of us had ever heard, and I swear Richard fell ass over teakettle in love with him. He'd have killed Gator Bill if Felicia had asked, and he'd have disowned me if I'd said no. So we just claimed him. Got him a fake birth certificate and he became Sam Doucette Carmody. Put that boy in a parish school and I'm telling you, he just flew. He's the light of our lives, Sam is. I do believe Richard thought he was his real granddaddy, the way he fussed over him. Gave him anything he wanted. By the time he was in junior high he'd decided to become a lawyer like I'd thought I would, and he hasn't looked back. He's working for a firm in New Orleans that specializes in discrimination cases. There isn't a black or gay owned business in New Orleans will take his money; he's damn near famous already, both for being an advocate and for being Tom Carmody's boy."

"Tom's boy? Sam Carmody?"

"Well, yeah, being a bastard wasn't going to work in his favor none, and Tom fell just as in love with him as we did, and wanted to be his guardian right off, to be sure he had the money he needed and no one could challenge it. Sam's really the reason Tom worked so hard to make a bunch of money; it wasn't just luck. This was way before Lawrence, you know. So we got married."

"Whoa, now. You can't be serious."

"As a heart attack. Of course," she grinned, "it was literally a marriage in name only. If you look at the records it seems Tom and I got married in nineteen seventy two, the year before Sam was born. We had a phony marriage and a real divorce. Of course the divorce settlement was very generous. I got major custody and Tom agreed to a big old child support payment every month, which we put in trust. That's how he met Lawrence, in fact. He handled the trust."

"Are you telling me that somebody filed a phony marriage and birth certificate just so Felicia's son could be—could be—," I couldn't find the words.

"So he could be everything," Felicia said. Or at least, so he'd have a chance at it. Richard and Tom both would have moved heaven and earth for him. A little payoff to the right people, and believe me, Richard knew the right people, and we all gave him what we didn't have. He can go anywhere, do anything, be anybody. He could be president."

"With a communist mother and a gay father? The South must have come a lot further than I thought."

"Kate," Claire said, "he needed me. How could I say no? How can I say no now?"

Jim raised his eyebrows at me. "Didn't I tell you?"

Chapter Eight

"I'm delighted to meet you, Miz Lynn," Sam Carmody held my hand in a firm grip, his warm brown eyes looking down at me from a considerable height; he was far taller than Tom or Felicia or Claire. The two of them stood beside him, pure adoration on their faces. "Daddy and my mothers have told me you were an important part of their lives back in the day. I'm glad you can be here now." His voice was deep and smooth, his accent careful in the way that educated Southern men's often were. "Mother," he turned to Claire, "I have to get back to New Orleans first thing in the morning. That hurricane looks bad and I don't trust the staff at Miss Eddie's to properly prepare the place in case they lose power. You need to make everybody quit sitting around and board up. We're way inland, but it doesn't mean there won't be things flying if it comes ashore close by." Claire nodded, a look of deep sadness in her eyes. Without a word she walked out the front door, for the first time looking like an ageing woman. Sam watched her go, before turning back to me. "I'm camping at Daddy's apartment above the club as of tomorrow. Miss Eddie's is tight in the Quarter, but will need care if the hurricane comes in. Jim has put your things in my room upstairs."

"But, where will you sleep tonight?"

He looked at me evenly, as if measuring very carefully what he was about to say. "I am going to spend the night with my father," he said. "I am going spend the night telling him I love him, in the event I don't see him again."

"Then you know?"

He took my hand and squeezed gently. "I know that life ends. And I know I love him, and will miss him when he's gone. That's all I

279

want, or need, to know." He patted my arm the way Claire had done earlier, walked to Tom's room, opened the door softly and slipped inside.

"Ain't he something?" Felicia whispered close behind me.

I nodded. "He looks like a good man. Does it bother you he calls Claire 'Mother'?"

"Oh, he calls me 'Mother' too," she said. "Funny, isn't it, back when we were kids it seemed there was a shortage of parents. Now we're a bunch of hens with just one chick."

"Speaking of chicks, where's Martha?" I looked around nervously.

"She's in there with Jim and the others, her and that dog, watching them try to figure out where the storm will hit," she said.

"You don't know Martha," I said. She's not going to sit and watch TV. She'll take the place apart."

"I'll tell them to keep an eye on her and call you if need be. Jesus, girl, you aren't the only one who can wrestle a middle aged woman and a dead dog. Why don't you come out to the lake with me and Claire? The breeze keeps the mosquitoes off and we can talk some more. Let me pour you a glass of this good red wine."

Claire was waiting for us. I could smell her cigarette smoke long before we reached the water. "Hello Cherie," she said. "Your head spinning around yet?"

"Just about. I guess you all know your arrangement is a little, um, unusual."

"Really? I always thought it made perfect sense. What's mine is yours and what's yours is mine, and if you need it and I've got it, hallelujah."

"But what if someone finds out about Sam?"

"Oh good Lord, Cherie, half of New Orleans knows about Sam. What we gave Sam wasn't legitimacy, what we gave him was power. And a generous heart. And a sense of outrage at the injustices dealt his fellow man."

"The gospel according to Richard?" I smiled. "I don't know how to ask this but to ask it; where is everybody—Jean, Richard, your brother and sisters?"

"Well," she let go a plume of smoke that caught in the breeze and swirled away. "Francis and my sisters are in various states of disarray, married and divorced, living up north." She laughed, then said "Look, the lightning bugs are out. Anyway, Gran'mere died before we came back here, hollering through that bullhorn to the end. We buried it with her. Jean got kind of strange after that—remember how she was, absent minded and sweet but always managed to get her way? Well, over time it seemed those geese and those cats—not a one of the cats left, by the way; I'm a neutering fool—meant more to her than any of the rest of us did. I think that might be one reason Richard took to Sam the way he did; Jean just plain forgot the rest of us existed. She was sweet and vague and nobody had any idea she had a lump in her breast until it was too late. She died ten years ago."

"Oh Claire, I'm sorry."

"Me too. I feel bad about it to this day. But she didn't. If anybody ever reached what you could call a state of grace, Jean did. She just sort of faded out, in a clean hospital bed with all of us around, loving on her. Not like Tom, who has to do it his way to the end." She smiled a rueful smile. "He is a piece of work, our Tom. I can't imagine life without him."

"What about Tom's folks? What about Eddie?"

Felicia chimed in. "Tom's folks have been gone for years, too. They were just old, you know. Tom told me that Mr. Carmody passed just sitting in that shop like always. Customer walked in and there he sat, dead. Tom called his mama regular, but I don't think he could stand to go over there much. Since he had the money he hired home health care for Eddie and her both, but once she passed too he had him moved to a nursing home, where he is to this day."

"Jesus. What'll happen to him after, you know…"

"We're leaving all that to Sam," Claire chimed in. "He's executor of Tom's will. I hate to say it, but Eddie is my limit. Poor bastard. I understand he's calmed down some, but he never did forgive Tom."

"For being gay?"

"For being all right, I think. Tom told me he never even told him he had AIDS because he couldn't bear to give him the satisfaction." She shook her head. "What a family. Well, who haven't we covered?"

"Richard?"

"Oh he's fine as frog hair. He's over in Pascagoula, supervising some repairs on the Carmody house. Tom still owns it. You'll see him when we get there."

"Richard's alive?" My old crush came back in a rush of pleasure and relief.

"Sure is. Sam calls him Gran'pere; can you beat it?" She smacked her hand against the arm of the Adirondack chair. "He's almost eighty and looks sixty, still fights the powers that be and still swings a mean hammer, though really he just supervises these days. He's going to bust an artery when he sees Martha. He wanted to kill Gator Bill over that dog but Bill finally convinced him it could help. You never did catch on that she was in those chests in the truck when we went to New Orleans, did you?"

"That was Martha?" The funky smell of the truck came back to me, and my nervousness about sitting on what I'd thought was a dead goose. I blushed in the darkness, remembering how I had reacted to Gator Bill's "critters" when I had visited the circus. If I had known what they were up to I might have had a chance to object before Martha ever saw her dog turned into something that looked like magic, and things might have turned out differently.

"You mad?"

I thought for a minute. "No. I don't think Martha made her crazy; she just gave the crazy a shape all its own."

"Quite a shape it is, too. Once we realized about the books Tom made us buy every single one of them. It's hard to believe that quiet little thing in there does that. But I guess you never know what shape your crazy will be, eh? You can pretty well tell I've been reclaimed by Bayou Eau Claire and so has Felicia."

Felicia nodded. "I could give my boy away but I never could leave him. Claire let me stay whenever I wanted to, and eventually I just stayed. Richard built me a house, the one back there closest the barn. I even kept a pony or two til I got too old and my bones got too brittle to trick ride. I'd have brought the elephant if they'd have let me have her."

"Claire, you mean?"

"No, the Biggers Brothers. Claire would have let me; she can't say no to anything. Except Eddie. So what about you? What have you been up to for, well, forever?"

I didn't know what to say. I thought of my little house on Whidbey Island, sitting still, no plants that needed watering, no pets that needed feeding, no husband or children who were waiting for me to call. I thought of the silence and the insomnia and the evening wine,

wine that, drunk alone, didn't have half the flavor of the glass now in my hand. I thought of the cigarettes that I had hardly thought of at all since we'd left and that Claire's smoking didn't make me crave. And, for some reason, I thought of what I had told Tom Carmody long ago as we sat by the pond at Singing River Hospital, that I didn't know who to be if I wasn't brushing my mother's hair.

"Nothing, really," I said, staring out over the black, quiet lake, where the lightning bugs flashed, seeking one another out in the night. "Nothing much at all."

Chapter Nine

"Sam and I have done all he'll let us to make him comfortable; if you're going to talk you all better do it now." Bunny stood over us as we sat at breakfast the next morning, another mouth-watering meal that rang bells from my distant past, prepared by a young woman I hadn't met, but who moved through the kitchen with a familiarity that had to have come from experience. I hadn't worked out who the people were who came and went at all hours, but it seemed to happen naturally and I didn't have the strength to ask about them. I had other concerns on my mind.

Exhausted after my talk with Claire and Felicia the night before, I had hauled a caterwauling Martha upstairs and into the bed we shared without asking any more questions. Once we were away from Jim and the others she began exploring Sam's room, opening drawers and examining books with an intensity that worried me so much I had done what I had been avoiding doing for the whole trip. I crushed a sleeping pill between two spoons and stirred it into a cup of hot chocolate. Then I lay beside her as she snored, wide awake under the stare of Martha the dog, who sat in a leather chair by the open window as though she was about to take flight over the lake. This morning my sister was bright-eyed and I had added exhaustion to the swirl in my head.

"Thanks, Darlin'," Claire answered Bunny, standing up and wiping her hands. Felicia rose too. Jim looked up from where he was sopping a biscuit through a pool of molasses. "I don't need to talk about anything. I'll stay here with the Marthas," he said.

"You sure?" Claire asked.

"I'm sure."

"Me too," Bunny added, picking up a clean plate and beginning to fill it. "You all know where to find me if you need me."

When we entered the bedroom, Sam was sitting in a chair beside the bed, his forehead resting on the white sheet beside Tom Carmody's emaciated form. The tented sheet was lower, revealing more of Tom's torso. His hand was on Sam's head, his fine boned fingers barely stroking the dark hair. The contrast between Tom's pale hand and Sam's warm, alive, almost swarthy complexion made me grab the door frame tight. Whoever his father was, I thought, he deserved a blessing for Sam's presence at this moment. At the sound of our entry Sam looked up, his eyes swollen but glowing. Saying nothing, he raised his father's hand to his lips, kissed it, and, with a hug for his two mothers and a promise to keep up with us by telephone, he went out.

The room was bright and already warm, shut off from the air conditioning that kept the rest of the house cool during the day. Tom lay propped higher than he had been the night before, an oxygen line beneath his nose the only difference I could see. If anything, he looked worse in the daylight, but when he smiled I saw Tom once more.

"They treating you all right?" His voice was a raspy whisper. He tried weakly to clear it, accepting a sip of water that Claire jumped to give him. Felicia kissed the tips of her fingers and blew the kiss to him. He barely puckered his lips in answer. "They introduce you to Sam?"

"Boy did they," I nodded, wondering where to stand, what to do. "That's some scheme you concocted, but he seems like a good man."

"He's our immortality," Tom said. "He's here because of all of us. I love him something fierce."

"So Tom, here we are," Claire said, and stopped. For once she looked as at a loss as I felt.

"Yes," he said, looking at each of us, his eyes shining. "the women in my life. My God, the irony. Too bad Louise couldn't be here." He broke off, coughing softly.

"Louise? You don't mean Louise by Night?" I hadn't thought about Louie by Day for years. In spite of myself I felt a tingle in the hand he had stared into when I was fifteen. "He must be eighty by now!"

"He died, Kate," Tom said. "Louie, Lawrence, my friends, my enemies, my lovers; Louie was one of the first, when nobody knew anything except something was mowing us down, and it could be caught. It was terrible; not a funeral home would bury him." He shook his head, wincing.

"Louie wanted to be buried as Louise, in his finest, with a jazz funeral and a party that would burn that club he sang in to the ground," Claire said. "He wanted to be buried beside his mother, who loved him. He never did have any more money than he did when we met him, and all his friends were dirt poor, even Tom back then, but everybody took up a collection, the artists at the square too. Hell, we even got one of the social clubs to throw in. It didn't mean a thing."

"We lied to him," Tom said. "We told him it was arranged. We sat there night after night when he couldn't sleep and we told it to him like a bedtime story." A tear pooled beneath his eye. "We helped him pick out a gown and a white coffin with the most shameless red satin lining you ever saw—he said it looked like he was going to meet Jesus in a Red Velvet cake. He loved it. Then we put him in a cardboard box and burned him instead, because that's what—that's what we could get. And it cost every cent just to get that." He smiled. "We did have that party, though. And we did scatter his ashes over his mother's grave. Or at least we did it with half of them. A little smidgen of the other half got mixed in with every Good Old Boy's entrée served by every gay waiter at every fine dinner club in New Orleans."

"I don't guess we have to tell you whose idea that was," Claire said, carefully wiping the tear from Tom's cheek and throwing the tissue in a trash can beside the bed.

"There were so many," Tom said, his voice cracking. "So many who got turned away, whose families didn't even show up, not to take care of them and not to bury them. I decided then that if it ever happened, when it happened, because I knew it would, that I would die when I wanted, the way I wanted, with people who gave a damn about how dying ought to happen, and who would understand why it was important to me. You're not the last of the Pascagoula this time, Katie. I am. And I'm damned if I'm going to let this thing win."

"The car's ready to go whenever you want to, Tom," Felicia said. "Jim's surly but he's ready. But I have to tell you, there's a hurricane in the gulf and people are already evacuating. They might stop us if we wait too long."

"Of course," Tom said, his words light as the curtains blowing in and out with the breeze. All of us leaned closer to hear. "Is tomorrow soon enough? After all this trouble, I still want one more night."

Claire reached out and stroked his sweating forehead. "I think so."

"Tomorrow, then. We go tomorrow."

Chapter Ten

"We'll be going east, away from where it's headed," Jim said. "I talked to Richard and he says the Carmody house is boarded up, the generator's got gas, and we're out of our fucking' minds, and I can quote him on that. But he's waiting for us there. 'Course, he might be going a little senile himself."

The late morning was mind-numbingly hot, the sky full of thunderheads, but nothing seemed out of the ordinary for late August in bayou country. It was hard to imagine a hurricane was on its way. We'd been meandering around the grounds of Bayou Eau Claire, Jim, Felicia, Martha and I. Claire was, as Jim said, "fussing," going back and forth between where the limo sat parked in front of the house and the boxes of things she and Bunny had decided were necessary for us to make the ninety minute drive to Pascagoula without Tom having to suffer too much. Bunny had made it clear he wasn't going to go and, as Sam had, he would only talk about what we were planning in the vaguest of terms. "I'm Tom's friend and employee," he said, "and the last thing he's going to have to do before he leaves that room is to fire me, because as his employee I can't turn my head if he's doing himself harm. But I guess I'm ready for that. Besides, I need to get on home too; my mama needs me to help her and my aunties get out of the Faubourg Marigny. The ladies don't drive."

"Bunny's been teaching Claire how to take care of Tom," Jim said, "how to regulate the meds and deal with the catheter." He shook his head. "This is the last thing we ought to be doing, moving him around like that. We could cause an infection—," he broke off and burst out laughing, the laugh tinged with horror. "Oh dear God," he said, running his hands across his eyes and over his face, as if trying to wake up, "what are we doing?"

"Forget God," Felicia replied. "We are playing God, and if God exists and he don't like it, then he can come down here and stop us. And if he does, I got a few questions I'd like to have the answers to, because he has laid some serious shit on this little group, and if he's trying to make a point, I sure as hell don't see it."

In the steamy morning I was getting my first real look at Bayou Eau Claire. The place reminded me of old farms I had seen up in the delta, where carefully tended lawns and gardens shared space with random piles of accumulated history. A couple of young women, one the one I had seen in the kitchen at breakfast, bent over a row of bean plants in an enormous and beautifully kept garden at the rear of the clearing, throwing weeds into the large pen that held the dozen geese. The birds barked and squabbled over the greens, flapping their wings and raising a little cloud of dust. A man I hadn't seen before carried sheets of plywood from the back of a pickup truck, stacking them beside the houses. I knew this routine. Boarding up before a hurricane was a sight that Gulf Coast children grew up with. I found myself praying the guilty prayer of every Gulf Coast native, the one that went "Please let it come on shore somewhere else." So far, that "somewhere else" looked to be the mouth of the Mississippi, closer to where we now walked than to the Carmody house in Pascagoula. I hoped that, as Jim had said, Bayou Eau Claire was far enough inland so that things would simply fly, and not flood. I was trying hard not to think about Pascagoula.

"Martha, don't go in there!" Felicia rushed forward to stop my sister, who was headed for the open door of the barn. "It's old and dangerous; the floor's half rotted through."

"Remember the Woolworth's in Pascagoula?" I called out. "There might really be gators under the floor around here. And that junk pile is a perfect place for snakes to get in out of the heat."

Martha stopped and looked from the barn to me, to the pile of metal at its front, and back at me. I could almost feel her itching to explore the tangled mass. "You stick your hand in there you're going to come up snakebit for sure," I went on, putting as much doom in my voice as I could manage. "They might have to amputate." Martha turned pale and made a one-eighty away from the barn and back toward the front of the house.

"Jesus Christ, Kate," Jim said. "Did you have to scare her to death?"

"Yes, yes I did," I snapped. "Look, I've been handling her twenty four hours a day for most of my life, and if it works, I've done it. I've had my phone disassembled three times, my clothes cut to ribbons, and the light switch unscrewed from the wall with the power full on. I know she's not stupid but she's so far away that I don't know what she sees, hears or knows. I love her and I am grateful to her for what she has done for me, but you don't know what it's like, so don't go off on me for how I do it. I want to be sure she doesn't sneak off and go in there when my back is turned and this is how I know to stop her. You want to take care of her, you do it your way."

Jim sucked his teeth for a few moments. "I did okay with her on the way down here, right?" He said. "Do you trust me?"

As annoyed as I was with him, I had to admit he had been remarkable with Martha, patient and accepting and gentle. I nodded.

"Then you all go do your thing," he said, turning and trotting after her. "I've got to check out the inflatable boat before we pack it. She'll stay with me on the pier. I'll watch her like a hawk. We'll be fine."

I nodded again, feeling a lump rise in my throat. Cash Collins, about whom I had thought some terrible things, had turned out to be a good man. "Thank you, Jim," I called after him. "And I'm sorry."

"No big thang," he called back, as he disappeared after her around the front of the house.

"I should have asked him to marry me," Felicia grinned. "I think he's in love with Claire, though, although he wouldn't admit it if you tortured him. Come on, I'll show you my place."

The house was a tiny shotgun, the windows and door on the front and back situated so the breeze off the lake would blow right through. The three rooms lined up, a living room that held a couple of comfortable chairs and not much else, a kitchen that looked barely functional with its tiny stove and miniature refrigerator and a sink barely large enough to wash a teacup in, and a large bedroom filled with circus memorabilia, a large and lovely bed covered in pink mosquito netting sitting squarely in its center.

"I eat in the big house," she explained, "and I don't do a lot of entertaining. I do love to lay up in the bed though, reading and playing the queen. And now and then I find me some company," she winked.

"Claire has had some fine men pass through from time to time, I don't mind telling you, and well, you know, I am exotic."

"Felicia, who are these people? What are they doing here? Do they live here?"

She turned her palms up. "Oh, they're mostly people Claire or Richard meet, folks who need a leg up for some reason and who they're pretty sure won't try to walk off with the place or deal drugs out of it. People with, as Claire says, a lot of community spirit. We've had everything from writers to laborers to what Richard calls 'political refugees.' They don't scare me, but every now and then I worry about what they might attract. The Klan still exists, you know, and Louisiana politics ain't gotten any more liberal in your absence. They just hide their prejudices better. But Claire's the eternal optimist. 'What can possibly go wrong?' she says. I expect she'll have it on her tombstone. I just hope she dies an old, old lady. I can't imagine a world without her."

We had dragged the two chairs out onto her little porch. As we talked she rubbed sunscreen into her white skin and I sipped a glass of tea so sweet I smiled, remembering Gator Bill saying her tea would make your teeth sing. I felt his absence, sorry that, even if he had turned out to be a son of a bitch, I most likely would never see him again.

"Felicia, do you ever miss Bill?"

"Oh, not much," she said, stretching her legs out in front of her, checking for missed spots. "Besides, if I do I can always go out to the barn."

"What do you mean?" No sooner had I got the question out than I was interrupted by shrieks from the direction of the lake. "Oh no, what's happened now?" I leapt up, my knees creaking but enough fear running through me to let me half-walk, half-run around Claire's house and toward the water.

I couldn't see Martha. All I saw was water rising in a little arc from below the level of the pier, accompanied by someone yelling and another sound, one that hadn't untangled itself into anything I understood. Felicia at my heels, I half ran, half waddled down the slope and out onto the pier.

Martha the dog sat in one of the Adirondack chairs, staring out over the scene in the lake. A pile of clothes lay on the pier beside her. A bright yellow inflatable boat moved lazily through the water, Jim

Collins, in a baggy plaid pair of boxer shorts, perched on one of its seats. He faced the rear of the craft, waving his arms in the air as if conducting an orchestra, singing, lustily, a largely improvised version of "Yellow Submarine." At the boat's rear, holding onto a pair of handles and kicking a plume of water into the air, were Claire and Martha. As near as I could tell, neither of them had a stitch on.

I grabbed Felicia's arm. "Dear Lord," I said, my voice high and pinched with panic, "she can't swim! Don't let her let go; she can't swim!"

"Looks like she's doing all right to me," Felicia said. "She swims about as well as Jim sings, with enthusiasm if not much grace. Long as she hangs on she'll float." She reached down and hauled Martha the dog out of the chair, depositing her on her side on the pier, legs and one wing jutting stiffly into the air, before taking her place. "Besides, you think Claire and Jim would let her drown? Sit down here and enjoy the show."

I dropped into the chair beside her as if my strings had been cut. Jim paused long enough in his song to wave and shout, "Hello Kate! Come on in!" before launching back into "and we swim beneath the waves, in a yellow submarine! Everybody!"

Claire and Felicia joined in the chorus, Felicia pounding out the rhythm on the arm of the Adirondack chair the way Claire had pounded it the night before. Martha didn't sing, but she had a smile on her face the likes of which I hadn't seen in a long time. She looked like she was really there, splashing like a kid and looking, really looking at Jim with something close to adoration in her eyes. I felt the muscles in my forearms contract, as if to reach toward her, to snatch her up should she let go. But I couldn't save her. I couldn't swim.

"Martha, come out!" I shouted. "Jim, Claire, please get her out of there; she's going to drown! She'll take you down with her!"

Jim shouted to Martha. "Do you want to come out?"

"No!" she shouted back.

"The lady has spoken," he yelled up to me. "Claire's got her, and Claire's a good swimmer."

"That's what Louie by Day said," I said softly. "Remember?"

"Sure do," Felicia said. "He told you that you should stick close to her because she was a good swimmer. You might think about trying it out."

"I can't!" I wailed. The sweat that poured down my face came not only from the heat, but from a mix of fear and humiliation. My crazy sister, the one I had been sure would live in Martha Land forever while I devoted my life to making up for having put her there, was doing something that I couldn't. She was changing. I stood up, my knees so weak I could hardly raise myself from the deep seat. "I have to go inside; I think I've had too much sun. I feel a little sick."

"Okay," Felicia said, pausing to shout encouragement to the group before adding, "If you don't hear anything you'll know everything's okay."

I turned to walk back to the house. On the way I passed the cast-off Martha, looking frail and impossible where she lay on the pier.

Everything was catching up with me, the strangeness of this place, the difficulty with sleep, the lack of control I had over anything, now even the sister I had done practically everything for and who appeared to be doing just fine without me. Martha had hardly been out of my care for so long that I felt disoriented, as though a limb was missing. I shuddered at the thought. I needed something to do, some way to feel useful. I decided to see if Tom was awake. I tapped at the door of his room gently, and when I heard a sound from the other side I went in.

"Hello Kate."

I barely heard him, but Bunny, who was at his side fiddling with the IV, beckoned me to come in, and then left, whispering "He's pretty comfy but he'll be drowsy. Sing out if you need me." I drew a chair up to the bed. A whoop and a peal of laughter came through the open window. I fought the urge to run to see if my sister was safe.

"Are they having a party out there?" he asked, "I wish I could see. I feel like I've been in this damned room forever."

"They're teaching Martha to swim," I said, finding the words hard to believe even as I spoke them.

"Sounds like fun," he replied. "Remember when we all jumped in and I splashed poor Gator Bill? Too bad he turned out to be such a prick, although I guess he got us Sam. Now there's a man loves to swim; Richard taught him to go right off that rope swing out there. I guess I have to wait 'til tomorrow to go swimming. How about you? You aren't joining in?"

"You forgot that I can't swim," I said, feeling old shame warm my face.

"Still? I'd have thought some fine man would have shown you how. Don't tell me you're still afraid."

"Of what? Swimming or fine men?" I joked, but then looked away. It was hard to look into Tom's concerned eyes.

"I'm sorry," he said, his hand sliding down to touch mine. I tightened at his touch, and he said "It's okay. It's hard to catch."

"That's not it," I said. "It's just that now that I've seen everyone I feel bad I didn't take the trouble to know you all these years. I think I convinced myself you all weren't as important to me as you were. Or more likely that I wasn't as important to you. I didn't know Sam, or you when you were—,"

"Alive?" He chuckled. "It's okay, Cherie. I know that, if I'm lucky, tomorrow will be my last day on earth. You've missed a whole lot. I've done my screaming and crying and begging and praying and being an asshole. It might be the drugs talking, but once I decided to do it this way, I'm all right. And I'm glad we know each other now. It's funny though, I always thought you'd go off like a pistol soon as you weren't cooped up."

I shook my head. "Me too. It was all I could think about. But I didn't. I don't know why; I just meandered, like I was lost without a guide. Then Martha came along and I realized what she could do and it's like I assumed the other half of her life, the half that deals with the world. Sometimes I think it takes both of us to make a whole person."

"That's no way to live, Katie," he said. I could hear the effort in his voice as he tired. "Not for either one of you."

"Maybe not, but she needs me to protect her and I don't have a choice."

"But she's the one out there swimming," he said, closing his eyes. "Are you sure you got it right who's protecting who?"

Chapter Eleven

"Wake up. Wake up. Wake up." Martha pushed me back and forth, making the springs squeak in Sam Carmody's bed. I groaned. I had fallen asleep only a few hours before, after listening to her breathing for most of the night. To my astonishment, when I opened my eyes she stood beside me, wearing the clean shorts and t-shirt I'd laid out on our packed suitcases the night before.

"Who got you dressed?" I asked, sitting up and wincing at the ache in my back. She didn't answer me, but lifted one of the cardboard cameras to her eye and snapped. Before I could protest she picked up Martha the dog and went out the door.

This was the day. Everything was ready. We had made certain the night before that all we had to do today was get Tom, our supplies and the inflatable boat into the limousine and go to the Carmody house in Pascagoula. Normally the drive would take little more than an hour and a half, but Jim, who had been calling everyone he knew to monitor the hurricane, said that we needed to get a move on as early as possible, just in case. "They're talking about closing the bridges, and I can't guarantee the roads ain't bumper to bumper," he called up the stairs as I pulled on my own jeans and shirt, grabbed my shoes and the ones Martha had left beside the suitcases, and began hauling them out the bedroom door.

"Where are you taking those?" Claire came out of her own bedroom, tucking a blouse into her cut-off shorts. She had a backpack slung over one shoulder. "We don't need all that. We've got the boat and everything we need for Tom, but Richard has the house stocked. Worst case we'll be back here in a couple of days. Here," she ducked back into her room, emerging with a wad of canvas, which she pitched in my direction before trotting down the stairs, calling out to Jim and Felicia as she went. It was a duffel bag, plastic lined and heavy, smelling faintly of mildew and bleach. I stood looking from it to the two suitcases, stunned into immobility until Claire called up the stairs for me to get a move on. I had never seen her good humor so absent; she sounded like a general giving orders to a green and irritating soldier. Her brusqueness stirred me, however, and I quickly opened and rifled the bags, tossing toiletries, shirts and underwear, and, on impulse, a wad of colored pens and a pad of paper for Martha into the canvas sack before shoving the suitcases back into the bedroom and shutting the door.

I met the others at the limousine. Jim was cramming things into its vast trunk. Felicia and Claire's backpacks were already inside, along with the tightly rolled inflatable boat and a pair of collapsible oars, several jugs of water and an ice chest full of food, "in case we get stranded somewhere other than Tom's house." Martha stood watching him load, now and then raising her camera and snapping a shot. When she perched Martha on top of the heap in the trunk, he paused for just a moment, saying "Go ahead, but only one," before handing her not only the dog but a large paper sack. "Here's the rest of your cameras," he said. "Keep them with you because we might not be able to stop." Martha nodded and climbed into the car, bag, dog and all. She reached up and turned on the DVD player, frowning when nothing happened. "I buried that damned movie," he muttered to me out of the corner of his mouth. "I'll tell you where you can dig it up once this is all over and I've had a ten mile head start for home." After one last check of the trunk's contents, he slammed it shut, turned to us and said, "All right. We've got everything we can take. It's time to get Tom."

By the time we got to Tom's room Claire's and Jim's sense of urgency had taken hold. Instead of tapping and entering quietly, the entire troop of us, including Martha, camera in hand, dog left behind in the car, swarmed into the room. Tom was dressed for the first time, lying on top of the covers in a pair of gauzy but elegant looking pants and shirt, a pair of flip-flops on his thin feet. The shirt's loose sleeves were rolled up, the IV line extending from beneath one sleeve. He was sweating and his breath came fast and shallow, as though drawing every breath was like running a mile, but deep in his tired eyes a light shone. Bunny was at his side as always, but his usual sweet demeanor had been replaced by one of alarmed determination.

"You don't have to do this, Tom," he said, rounding on us as we came in. "None of y'all has to make a show of this man's dying. It ain't right. He needs to stay right here and go down easy, not trucking all over God's earth in the middle of a hurricane. It's supposed to be bad, Tom. I don't want to think what you all might be getting into in that big old house of yours, so close to that river." His teeth caught at his lower lip. Tom reached out and patted him the way he had done to me.

"Leave it alone, Bunny," he said, halting between almost every word. "I know you don't understand. And if any of these good folks want to stay here I won't mind; it's not fair to put them in the way of that storm. But I've come this far and I want to go on, and I can't do it alone. I can't even walk, Bunny. You know what they say about hell or high water? I think I've seen enough hell and I'm ready for the water. I'm doing like you said. I'm firing you, darlin', right here and now. Go take care of your aunties and tell your mama I love her boy something fierce. Thank you for everything. Now go on." He sounded as though he was talking to a child. Once he had done speaking, he lay spent, his muscles slack. Bunny stood looking at him for a moment before bending down, kissing him on the cheek, and striding out without a look at any of us. Martha raised her camera and snapped a photo of him as he passed by.

"Poor thing; he's been through so much," Tom said. "I don't know how many people he's seen off. I'm glad he's gone. No matter what happens, tell him I went easy as peanut butter pie. He should have that."

"Tom, I'm going to carry you to the car now unless you tell me otherwise," Jim said, pushing past us.

Claire followed, gathering up the IV bag and holding it high, and the urine bottle, holding it low. "Are you comfortable? I can put something in the line."

"I feel as all right as I can. I do believe I'm having one of those rallies you hear so much about," Tom replied, his strained voice belying his words. "But be careful, Jim. I've got sores in places you wouldn't believe. I swear, my hurt hurts."

Jim nodded, and, reaching down, folded the light blanket on which Tom lay over him. He did the same on the other side, swaddling him in a soft, white cocoon before lifting him, seemingly effortlessly, into his arms. "Damn, Tom, you don't weigh nothing a'tall," he said quietly. "He's hot as fire, Claire. Can't we do something?"

"We've given him all we can," Claire said. I've got wipes in the car to wipe him down. Tom," she said, "I do believe that what we're doing to you is going to prove fatal, whether you change your mind or not. Are you sure, one hundred per cent sure, you want us to go?"

"Lord, I am. Are you? Everybody?"

The house ticked in the silence. But one by one, we all said it, except for my sister. "I am." I knew when I said it that it was final. We wouldn't turn back.

Martha lifted her camera and snapped a photo of Jim holding Tom in his arms. "Well hello, Martha," Tom said. "I'm pleased to meet you at last."

Felicia had been quiet all this time. Now she reached out and picked up the pink rosary from where it lay on the bedside table. Tom reached out for it, and she placed it in his hand. "Louie called you Father Voodoo when he saw you with that rosary in one hand and that voodoo doll in the other."

"Well, the voodoo doesn't appear to have worked," he smiled, leaning back in Jim's arms. "but I'll hang onto this, just because," he faltered, "because my mother wants me to. Please let's hurry, Jim. I'm so tired."

The residents of Bayou Eau Claire hustled about like an army as our little procession walked down the stairs and to the car, Jim and Claire in the lead, Felicia running around to open the door on the near side and climbing in to assist in getting Tom situated on the long bench seat at the limo's side, Martha taking photos, and me feeling useless. There were men hauling the Adirondack chairs off the pier and the picnic tables from under the live oaks on its bank, heading with them to the barn. The women were in the garden, picking rapidly.

Claire came to stand by my side as I watched. "They're going to get in everything they can in case the wind gets bad enough to throw it around. Once we're gone they'll turn the geese loose. Jim hates those geese; he's probably hoping by some miracle they'll blow away." She sighed. "I hope it's okay. I love this place like I love my daddy. I don't know if I've missed an opportunity by staying here or had one I don't appreciate enough."

"Let's go, children," Jim said, opening the driver's door. "I hear this thing's supposed to make landfall sometime after midnight. If you want to go through Biloxi on 90 we got to do it now before they start turning folks back."

"I figured you'd like to see it again before it gets blown away," Claire said.

"You think it's going to be that bad?"

"Hell, Cherie, do we ever know? I think we've all been riding a wave of luck since Camille. It's just sitting there, a thing you pass by every day without realizing how wonderful and fragile it is, just like this place. Like Tom. Like all of us. Might as well go give it some love on the way through."

As we pulled out the long drive and away from Bayou Eau Claire, the sense of purpose that the group had held dwindled considerably. I sat on the short back seat, Martha and Martha on one side of me and Felicia on the other. Claire sat on the long floor beside Tom, watching the IV bag swing from a hook she had rigged in the ceiling. Tom lay propped on a stack of pillows, his head back and his eyes closed, the strain etching his face. I could see the muscles in his jaw work. He licked his lips but when Claire offered him a straw he turned his head away from the water without comment. She looked back at us, her brows knit.

Jim's voice came over the intercom from the front, though the window between the sections of the car was down. "We're going to be on I-10 for most of an hour and then I'll drop down to 90, if they'll let me. You might be shocked at the change, Kate. The place is lousy with casinos. I guess it's good for tourism but it don't look the way it used to."

"Richard'll give you an earful about those boats," Claire said.

"What boats?" I asked.

"Oh, that's what they call the casinos in Biloxi. They used to literally be boats, went out beyond the twelve mile limit to gamble back when the Baptists ran the show. Then the government decided it was a pretty good deal so they wrote that as long as it was on the water and not land it was a boat and legal to gamble on. Every damn one of those casinos, huge things, is built on a barge and tied up at a dock. Craziest thing I ever heard. But that's capitalism for you."

I smiled at hearing an echo of the old communist in Claire. Then I had a thought. "What happens to them in a hurricane?"

301

"Guess we'll find out if this one hits hard enough. To tell you the truth, I'm just as glad we're going on to Pascagoula. We'll be up the river enough so maybe it won't blow us away.

"It won't." It took us all a moment to realize that Martha had answered.

"I hope you're right, girl," Felicia said.

We settled back into silence as Jim negotiated the flat roads, eventually coming to a highway entrance. "Oh, hell," he said, slowing to a crawl.

The evacuation was underway. Cars stretched as far as we could see in both directions, as if people weren't sure which way lay escape. I had a moment of realization that this entire highway system had been built around the time I left the Gulf Coast, before I ever drove a car, and I didn't know where any of it led.

"Where are they all going?" I asked.

"Just away from the water," Jim replied. "I've talked to folks going to Mobile, to Baton Rouge, up into Mississippi and Louisiana to wherever they can find a motel or a relative or even a parking lot that won't blow away. They're shifting all the lanes in the city to go out, so maybe Bunny and the old ladies will make it before things get too bad.

"Claire?" Tom's voice was barely audible over the engine. He seemed to be weakening by the minute. "Don't do me like Louie, please," he whimpered. "Don't lie to me. I don't want to go to Mobile. I want to go home."

"I swear. We all swear." Claire looked about to break. Felicia leaned forward.

"Hey Tom, remember the last time we were all together on the road between Pascagoula and New Orleans? Katie here was jail bait and that bastard Bill and Richard had cooked up that scheme about Martha—," she broke off and looked sharply at my sister, who, to my surprise, looked back. Felicia looked as though she was trying to decide something , and went on. "Martha, did anybody ever tell you the story about what happened to you and your dog?" I shook my head at her, trying to signal for her to stop, but she went on. "You like stories about Martha, right?" Martha nodded, a line etching itself between her eyes that looked so much like the one between mine that I reached up and touched my brow. "Well, they tell me when you were just a little bitty thing your mother got very sick, and she died. You remember?" Martha took a moment to nod again. "And you remember when you moved to Pascagoula and you had a dog that Tom said was named Martha, like you?" Martha nodded again, reaching out to lay her hand on the head of the stuffed, winged animal at her feet. "And you remember when Martha got hit by Claire's daddy's truck?"

The nodding stopped. Martha began to look around her frantically, suddenly absorbed in the buttons in the leather upholstery, reaching out to touch the etched glass bottle that sat in the rack in the bar. Without thinking I slapped her hand away.

"You don't remember that, do you?" Felicia said. "To tell you the truth, neither do I. I wasn't there. But Kate was. And Claire. And Tom. Kate didn't tell you?"

"Felicia, I don't think this is the time," I said. "We've got enough on our plates, don't you think?"

"Always do," she said. "The plate is always full, if you're lucky. I get the impression you've been trying to keep an empty plate. Why is that?"

I had long forgotten the bluntness in Felicia's nature. I had liked it as a girl, had admired how adult she seemed and, I had to admit, it had made me feel special to have friends who were as strange and interesting as she and Bill had been. But now it grated. She had been peripheral to the love I felt for Tom and Claire, and I had to remind myself that Martha and I, and not she, were the strangers in this group.

"Don't judge me, Felicia," I said. Claire looked up from where she sat by a now sleeping Tom. "You had a mother and a father and a husband and a child and places you felt like you belonged. I had a dead mother and a father who gave up on us after she died and Martha here, who, in case you haven't noticed, *is* a full plate. I feel like I've spent my whole life just putting one foot in front of the other while all y'all did things however you wanted, safe and secure and assuming the world was your oyster and nothing bad would happen. Even this," I gestured toward Tom, "you treat like it was a part of something bigger than the horrible thing it is. Like you're still in the circus, creating some grand kind of show." I stopped, embarrassed at how far I had let my anger and pain go. I had forgotten that she was the girl who had been driven out of school for the color of her skin. "I'm sorry. I shouldn't say that."

"No, it's all right. You're right. I do think of this as part of some grand show. It's the way I was raised. You aren't the only one who's seen some things you shouldn't have, I just saw them in a different way. My mama and daddy and the Biggers Brothers taught me to take control of things if I could. But it's not out of a lack of respect, not for any of it. I love it. I love the whole crazy thing when I stand back and look at it. I mean, look at us. Most folks would think all of us a couple bricks short, in one way or another, whether it's displaying yourself in a freak show or loving your own sex instead of the other one or making a whole 'nother reality out of a stuffed animal. Come to think of it, you and Claire are the most ordinary ones of us all, but she seems happy with it. She's the ringmaster." She laughed. "Bill was right about you, Claire. You're running the show after all."

Claire stretched out her legs and leaned her head against the side of the seat where Tom lay. "I don't know that I'm always happy, but it's what I was raised to do too," she said. "Richard always said I could do anything I wanted to, and that it was helping people out when they were down that mattered. Might be what he wanted me to do, but it tickles me to do it. Hey Kate, did I tell you Richard and I did a DNA test a couple of years ago? We got a wild hare and decided to see if he really was my daddy after all."

"Oh Claire, really? And?"

"When we got the result in the mail we stared at the sealed envelope for a while and then held a ceremonial burning out at the fire pit. Best fais do-do we ever held."

A slow grin spread over my face. "You people beat all."

"Well hell, if we don't who will?"

Chapter Twelve

It took us four hours to get to Biloxi. Tom's brief excitement had been replaced by restless, almost ceaseless movement, his breathing interrupted by a shallow cough. He had stopped talking, seeming to focus inward, far away from us. We took turns trying to lift him to help clear his lungs, massaging his arms and legs where we could. Claire checked the catheter and shook her head worriedly. "I don't know if it's blockage, dehydration or what, but he has all but stopped peeing," she said, pulling off the gloves she had put on for the examination. Tom whimpered when she touched him, and she said "I'm going to raise the morphine, Tom. Just a little."

"But I want to go home," he said, looking at her as if seeing her for the first time. "Can you take me home? I want to see Mother."

"All right, we're taking you home," she answered, "We'll be there soon. Don't you worry." She leaned forward to Jim and said "Make this thing fly as soon as you can. I've got to give him more morphine and he's sliding. It'd be a damn shame if he didn't make it to Pascagoula awake after all he's been through."

"The road looks good up ahead and I've got the flashers on," Jim said. I felt our speed pick up as the cars thinned. "I'll bet we turn a few heads, this big old thing barreling down the road in front of a hurricane."

The weather was still hot, humid and surprisingly mild as we finally turned toward the coast. It was early afternoon. Jim had kept up a stream of calls to Richard and was assured that once we hit Biloxi Beach we could indeed open up and fly. When we rounded the last curve, crossed the Bay Saint Louis Bridge and I saw the gulf, my heart leapt harder than I could have ever imagined it would.

"Martha, look," I said, rolling down the window and letting the gulf air wash over us. "Remember? Bay Saint Louis, Waveland, Gulfport, Biloxi, all in a row. Remember all these places?" Without thinking I reached out and took my sister's hand. To my surprise she let me hold it as we both gazed out over the grey water. There were whitecaps on the surface, and the water churned beneath a sky that grew darker and darker toward the southern horizon. The rain was coming. Wind whipped the palms back and forth as if uncertain about which direction to blow. Gulls dipped and pushed against the air, struggling to remain stationary before giving up and letting the gusts carry them, first high and then low. A pelican stretched its wings from atop a piling in the water, opening its deep sack of a bill. Boats of all kinds, from little catamarans to top-heavy, lumbering shrimp boats bobbed so hard they almost hung suspended in the air when the water's surface dropped. Even over the engine I could hear clanging as rigging and stop lights and signs twisted in the wind. The streetlights were illuminated against the encroaching dark, but I could still see the green of the live oak trees and the enormous houses that sat beneath them, glowing white and brick red, set far back on lush lawns facing the ocean, their porches broad and fern filled, azaleas and palmettos and tufts of pampas grass whipping in the yards. Most of them had plywood over the windows. Though nearly every one was dark and abandoned, they sat solid and ancient looking as the oaks that had shaded them for decades.

The little coastal towns blended into one another seamlessly, but it was Biloxi that drew the memories forth. I smiled as we passed things I knew, the white lighthouse and the Edgewater Inn and the miniature golf course that, miraculously, still sat on the beach. I gasped at the "boats," the Beau Rivage and Hard Rock and Treasure Island and other casinos that blocked the view of the gulf. I felt a pang of regret that it had taken an extraordinary plea to get me to come to see a place that, connected to painful memories or not, was deep inside me. I longed to see Biloxi on an ordinary day, a day when the roadside stands sold snowballs and trucks stood open and full of fresh catch, and I vowed that, once I had a chance, I would eat crabs and walk on the sand and buy something at a souvenir shop, something shell pink that said "Biloxi, Mississippi," and would make me think of something besides how bad things had been when I had lived here.

We rode for a long time, Martha and I staring out through windows rolled down just far enough so that the wind stayed mostly outside, until Jim said "There's the bridge. Say goodbye to Biloxi." The last thing I saw as we left was the round, rippled architecture of the church of St. Michael that I had loved so as a girl, the archangel with his raised sword still standing atop its baptistery, as it always had and, I hoped, always would.

"Not much to see 'til we get to Pascagoula," Felicia said, reaching past me and pushing the button that slid my window up. "You couldn't find where we used to winter over if you had to; it's all Popeye's Chicken and tanning salons now. Twenty more minutes and we'll cross the Singing River."

"There's a new bridge," Claire added. "Well, not *new* new, but since you left. Remember the sound that old bridge made? The new one doesn't do that at all. I can't believe they didn't keep the singing, but that's folks. They just don't appreciate things." She broke off, chuckling and shaking her head. "Damn, I sound old. You'd be surprised, though, Pascagoula hasn't changed all that much. The shipyard's about all on this side of the river now, they have a new high school and ours looks like it's been bombed, and I hate to tell you but both the trailer park and your grandparents' place are vacant lots. But the Carmody's house looks pretty much like it always did, better I hear since Richard's been working on it.

I thought about the fact that the places I had lived in Pascagoula were gone, and I wasn't surprised that I didn't much care. I had never thought of my own things as lasting, only those I had connected with others. "What about your house?" I asked.

"No idea," she said. "It's funny but since we moved I've had no desire to see it. I guess my home wasn't so much the place as it was the people. We'll take the tour in a few days if you want."

"Claire?" Tom spoke for the first time since before we had turned south into Bay Saint Louis.

"Yes, Baby?" She sat up on her knees, looking up at the IV and putting her hand on his forehead. "We're almost there. Do you want some water?"

"Almost where? Where are we going? Where's Lawrence? No, I mean where's Sam? I want to tell Sam something. I want him to fix my will. He's got to fix it so Eddie's okay."

"Here, have some water. You already did that. Sam's got everything taken care of. Eddie will be fine. Everything's going to be fine."

The new Singing River Bridge arced up high in the air, unfamiliar and uninteresting. I looked out my window toward the south, toward the railroad bridge, still stretching in the distance the way I remembered it. Though I couldn't see, I knew that once we left the bridge we would turn and ride along the river toward town, toward Our Lady of Sorrow, toward Tom's house and the vacant lot where once my grandmother had slept in front of the television and I had sneaked out to walk at night with my friend. We would be at the place where Martha had died. My throat grew tight and I clenched my jaws to keep from choking. I dropped my face into my hands.

"It's going to be all right. We've got you. It's going to be all right," Claire's voice cooed from beside Tom. I hoped that she was talking to both of us.

Chapter Thirteen

"Hello mes amis! We been waiting and watching! Come up; come up. Boys, come down here and help these people out the car. Hurry now, these boys got to git and go theyselves. They got family to tend to." Richard Doucette shouted from the front porch of Tom Carmody's house as we pulled the limousine right into the yard and close to the stairs. The wind was kicking up, the live oaks that had dropped their acorns on the porch every year since I had been a teenager rattled and tapped against the plywood that covered all of the house's many windows and bumped the railing of the upper porch that ran across the house's second floor. I looked across the road, still small and unpaved, to the short stretch of empty pilings where Mr. Carmody's bait shop and the pier had once stood. It was closer than I recalled. The river in which Tom Carmody imagined ending his life seemed as confused as had the gulf. The water swirled and fought the prevailing wind that pushed it in the wrong direction. Looking at it, I could see clear problems with Tom's idea, in the storm the prevailing current could carry his body the wrong way. A moment of realization about what we were doing swept over me and I shuddered.

A scramble of young men burst out of the house behind Richard and dashed down the stairs, clapping Jim on the shoulder as he jumped out of the driver's seat and opened the trunk. There were four of them in all, all young and quick, and in a few seconds the contents of the trunk had disappeared back up the stairs and into the house.

"Whoowee, looks like you're ready for Noah's flood," Richard called down. "Come up here, Kate Lynn and let me look at you and Martha."

I'm not sure I would have recognized him. Richard, on whom I had had a crush that had become a warm memory over the years, had gotten old. As I mounted the stairs he got smaller, until he stood not much taller than I, a grizzled, only slightly grey man with a neat little goatee, whose brown eyes snapped from the middle of a mass of crinkles that almost hid them completely. His clothes were a little bit formal, as though he had acquired not only dignity but a little money over the course of his life. He was as weathered as the house we were entering, although as I got used to the idea that he was no longer the father in his rabble-rousing prime but an aged man with the look of having spent a lifetime in the hot Gulf Coast sun, I had to admit he was still attractive. I still felt a twinge of pleasure at coming near him. When he enveloped me in a bear hug I didn't hurry to pull back; there was still something about Richard Doucette's sure charm that made me feel safe and a little daring. I could see how he would be a hard father to let go of, blood relation or not.

"We got the house all ready, fixed like Tom told me, Claire," he shouted down. She waved from the back of the limousine, distracted by the chore of getting Tom out. To me, he continued, "You sure grew up, didn't you? And Martha." he extended a deeply tanned hand to my sister, who stood at the foot of the stairs, clutching her dog and looking around her anxiously. "Come here, Cherie, it's all right. I ain't going to bite you. Not with that ferocious beast guarding you. Come on."

She stared up at the two of us, then moved closer to Jim, whose rear half stuck out the back door of the car as he worked to help move Tom. When she bumped him I heard a muffled "Move, Martha!" from inside. Startled, she stepped up a step, her face sliding into the bland smile that I knew so well. Martha, who had spent an astonishing amount of time reacting to the things around us during the past few days, retreated a few steps into Martha Land once more.

"Richard, my sister has some problems," I began, but he waved me off.

"Jim told me she's a little broke down, but you don't need to worry. We'll see she's took care of," he said, reaching out once more toward where Martha stood gazing off into the middle distance. I noticed then that he leaned heavily on a beautiful, polished wooden cane. His hand rested on the base of a deer antler at its top, honed and set at a perfect angle, its points curling up around his wrist.

"Ain't I a dude?" He grinned, holding the cane up for me to see. "Won it in a game of bouree. Come on, girl; we need you out the way." He beckoned to Martha with his free hand. She focused on him at last and slowly came up the stairs, shifting Martha to one arm and raising her camera to take a photo of me and Richard. "Lord a mercy, that dog," he said. "That Gator Bill sure talked me into some stupid shit back in the day." He backed the three of us up to clear a space for the slow procession of Claire, Jim with Tom in his arms, and Felicia, that now inched up the stairs. "I got better though, and he got gone. Left some interesting things behind though. If he hadn't broke Felicia's heart we wouldn't have Sam, and if he hadn't made that animal, well, who knows?"

I hardly heard Richard. I was distracted by how floppy, how colorless Tom looked. His eyes were closed and his head lolled against Jim's shoulder. Richard stopped what he was saying, murmuring "Oh, sweet Jesus," as they passed us. He and Claire exchanged a look that was full of hurt before he said "Take him upstairs. He didn't want to be in there where his brother was, so we got his old room fixed up."

It occurred to me for the first time that I had never seen Tom's room. His need to be away from his home and my unease around Eddie and his mother had kept us on the pier, by the dessicated boat that might or might not still lie down the road beside the river, at the Doucettes' house, at Our Lady of Sorrow, anywhere but in the shadow of Eddie Carmody and Tom's mother's disinterest in her younger son, who would come home only after they were gone. I had heard him call out for his mother during our journey to Pascagoula. I wondered what it meant. Was it the return of early memory, of the time when she had dressed beautifully and taken him to movies where he had learned to love bigger than life women in his own way? Was Tom crying out from love or fear? I didn't know any more than I had known how I cried out for my own mother, before I had stopped reaching out for much of anything at all.

We followed Jim up the worn staircase that led to the second floor of the Carmody house, Claire attached to Tom by her IV bag and bottle of yellow fluid following close behind. Felicia went next, then Richard, and I herded Martha. By the time I made the landing everyone else had entered the room at its head. I was the last one through the door. My eyes widened as I looked around me.

In contrast to the house's weather beaten exterior, Richard had made Tom's room beautiful. Many times bigger than the room I had shared with the Marthas, it ran the length of the house's front. Its enormous French windows and a door that led onto the second story porch overlooked the yard, the road, and the river. Richard had left the windows and door uncovered, though plywood panels lay ready on the floor of the porch outside. The walls were freshly painted in light blue and pale rose, the sheer white curtains tied back so that the light made the walls glow. The old floor had been polished, and deep white rugs arranged beside the bed and in front of the loveseat and several chairs that were gathered in a group on one side, in anticipation of our arrival.

The bed itself, slightly raised, faced the windows. The quilt and sheets were drawn back, allowing Jim to gently place Tom, who moaned softly, onto its pillowy surface. I smiled at the painting above the bed, a primitive tableau of a house and pond that looked as though it had been painted by a talented child. It was clearly Bayou Eau Claire, with two men and two women, one of whose skin was very pale, all standing in front of the house and waving, their faces open in enormous smiles. The name "Sam" was painstakingly printed in the lower left hand corner.

"I did it just like he asked me to," Richard said as we looked around. "He said the rest of the place could go to hell but he wanted this room to be the last place he saw, and he wanted it nice for his friends. That's us all." He nodded, tapping the cane on the floor for emphasis. "Mostly it wasn't no big thing, but that there did give me a little trouble. "Tom," he said to the wan form on the bed, "you have no idea how much money I had to give and what kind of promises I had to make to get her here just for a few days." He raised the cane and pointed over my shoulder, to the corner beside the rightmost window, behind me. I turned, looked, and had to reach out to grab Claire for support.

Our Lady of Sorrow stood on a pedestal across the room from where Tom lay. The face I had sometimes wondered if I had imagined looked down at him as it had on the day he sang to me and asked me to marry him so we would never be lonely any more. All the loss and pain in her expression, the pain of a mother for her lost child, was directed at him, her hands extended as if he had just slipped from them and gone.

No one said a word, but Claire nudged me and, when I looked at her, nodded ever so slightly toward the bed. Tom's eyes were open. He stared up at Our Lady of Sorrow, transfixed, his lips parted, smiling, tears leaking from the corners of his eyes.

"I made it, Mother" he whispered. "I'm home."

Chapter Fourteen

"When in doubt, fix supper," Richard said as we rummaged around in the kitchen of the Carmody house. I had risked leaving Martha upstairs with the others just so I could spend some time alone with him, still guiltily fascinated by his presence. "As you see we're roughing it, no stove and just this old refrigerator for the cold goods. I reckon we can live on crackers and beans and hoop cheese a few days if we have to. I got enough ice and water to last a little while." He opened a bottle of beer and took a long pull. "You know, Tom says he left this property to Eddie in his will, with the stipulation that the house be torn down and the land sold off to pay his bills. I didn't do nothing but fix it up enough to stay upright and have a working kitchen and that room upstairs. The rest is pretty near empty. Was a nice old place once, but I think it's got bad juju from all it's seen. Best it goes, just not tonight." He stared out the window, toward the streetlight that still illuminated the spot where his truck had killed Martha. "I sure am sorry about your sister, Katie," he said. "I didn't ever know her like I did you, but I talked to your granddaddy now and again after you all left. It broke his heart to lose you all, his two dolls, he would say. Never was the same. Neither one of them was. I wish— you know—I always felt like if I hadn't run over that dog—" he broke off, shaking his head. "Ah well, wishing don't make it so. It's good to see you both, even if I would trade it for this not to be happening."

"Richard," I said, "should this be happening? Why on earth did you and Claire and Felicia agree to do this? It's murder, legally, assisted suicide at best. We could all go to jail."

"I'm doing it because he asked me to," Richard said. "You didn't know me when I was a young'un, but I was so mad about being poor I figured I was going to change the world so nobody would have to go through that. Took me a while to realize I wasn't just doing it for other folks, but so's I'd feel like I had a reason to be here too. But to tell the God's honest truth, I wasn't that good at it. When you all were children, the year all that killing was going on, I swear I like to have died right along with them, with Martin Luther King and Bobby Kennedy and those children at Kent State and the convention and all. I just went crazy from not being able to make sense of it. I near about left my family over it, near about gave up my child up there," he looked upward toward where Claire hovered over Tom's bed. "When I came home I decided that I might not be able to stop all that was wrong in the world, but I did vow that if I could just help the people I loved, then that's where I would start and hope it would ripple out from there. All my young'uns were about grown by then, and after my Jean passed they did what they were supposed to do, went off and made families of their own. All but Claire. Then Sam came along, and I guess it all went to him, all my hope for better, for a world where you can say who you are out loud, and say how you want to live and how you want to die, and not be beat nor killed nor driven out for it. That's all, Kate. I just think it's better if people live and die how they want to. If that's wrong, then I'm doing wrong, but like everybody else, I guess, I just did the best I could."

"You're brave," I said. "I wish I was as brave as you."

"Well, you're here, ain't you? Seems plenty brave to me."

Jim came in and looked into the refrigerator, producing a soft drink and turning on the portable radio that sat on the kitchen counter. It crackled and sputtered. "We best all be brave," he said. "That hurricane's turned north. It's coming in slap across the coast. Category three, maybe four by morning. We'll be feeling it good in a few hours. If you're the praying kind, you might throw up a word."

"We're in real danger, aren't we? This could get us all killed," I said.

"I hope not," Jim answered, "but I do believe we're in for more than we imagined." He glared at Richard. "Typical." He leaned his forearms on the counter, his head drooping almost to its surface. "I swear, if I live through this I'm going to listen to nobody ever again but my own self."

316

"You probably live longer that way," Richard said, hoisting a tray in one hand, leaning on the cane with the other, "but you gonna be lonesome."

We carried the supper, bread and cheese and cold cuts, sodas for Martha and Jim and two bottles of good wine for the rest of us, up to Tom's room, where we sat and ate, listening to the growing wind rattle around the corners of the house, talking quietly about other storms, Camille's destruction the year after Martha and I left Pascagoula, Betsy's many years before. When it was too dark to see outside at all, Jim and Richard boarded the windows and bolted the door. Richard had taken the trouble to cut a small square hole in each sheet of plywood, so that we could look out into the storm. While they worked, aware it might be my last time outside, I stood on the porch in the whipping wind and the first band of stinging rain, squinting toward the river, which sounded more and more like an oncoming train.

When the lights flickered, we readied the hurricane lamps that Richard had set around the room. We took turns listening to the radio downstairs so as not to disturb Tom, who slept surprisingly quietly beneath the gaze of the Madonna, and watching Claire watch him. Martha had long since fallen asleep on a couch cushion on the floor, Martha beside her, as though no time had passed at all since she was eight years old and nose-to-nose in the living room of the trailer with the little dog to which she had given all of herself. Only the wings gave her away.

Morning was breaking when the electricity went off. The house shivered steadily in the gusty wind, now and then thumping as something struck its wooden side. We lit the lamps and took turns peering out at the rising water, all but Claire, who hadn't left Tom's side all night. In the flickering light of the hurricane lamps they looked like something from another time, a death watch by lamplight. She stared at him with such intensity that I drew a chair up beside her.

"What are you thinking about?" I asked.

She rubbed her eyes as if I had wakened her, and smiled wanly. "I'm thinking about Tom, about how he's been a part of my life like nobody else has, part brother, part partner, part friend, part pain in the ass. I know you used to go out walking with him at night sometimes; he told me you all went to the church together. But I also know he went there all the time, by himself, to visit that statue, like he was looking for something—a little like your sister, I guess."

I nodded. "He told me he used to talk to her when she was just stored in the church, before somebody broke the original and they had to use her."

Claire chuckled. "He told you 'somebody' broke it, huh? Don't you know by now that not much happens by accident with Tom? When he gets a notion, watch out. I was so glad when he fell in love with Sam, and then Lawrence. It gave him people to do things for, and who loved him for just who he was. He deserved it, he deserved to see love in somebody's eyes, not just sorrow, and it was pure pleasure to see." She sighed. "He just got to me, you know? I know Jim likes to say I can't say 'no,' but I can. But not to Tom. Never to Tom."

"Can I ask—I mean, I don't actually know what we're going to do here. Did he tell you what he wanted? Is he going to stay like that now?" I looked across the bed to where he lay sleeping, mouth slightly ajar, breathing shallow and slow. "What are we going to do?"

She sighed, stretching her back. "From what I understand, this could go on for days. It's just what Tom didn't want. If that God damned storm wasn't going on we'd have come here, hopefully with Tom awake enough to say good-bye, and all of us would tell him what he meant to us and how much we love him and how he'll be a part of all we do from now on, and how we'll tell any babies Sam might have about their wonderful gay gran'pere Tom Carmody. Then we'd have carried him in that little boat downstream and pushed morphine into that line until he was hardly breathing at all, and weighed him down and slipped him in. Now, I don't know. This sounds morbid as hell, but if he went into the river now he might end up washed up in the delta, and I don't think that's quite what he had in mind."

"So what are you going to do?"

"I'm going to wait." She reached out and fingered the filled syringe that stuck out of the line that extended down to Tom's bruised, thin arm. "I've been sitting here all night trying to decide whether to just reach out and do it. But he might not die. Then what do I do?" She caught a sob and, for the first time, I reached out and drew Claire Doucette to me and held her tight while she cried for Tom.

By noon we knew we were going to survive Katrina by luck alone.

"Dear God, look at that water come," Jim said from his station at the window. "I can't see right down to the car but I bet it's about to float. Y'all better thank whoever built this house up off the ground

318

because I do believe it's going to be under a considerable piece of that river."

As if in answer, a blast of wind shook the structure and, in spite of its plywood cover, a window broke downstairs. Martha jerked awake and grabbed her dog, looking around at the lamps and the shadows as if genuinely frightened. Her hands began to tap the edges of the cushions and to fidget with the fringe on the rug. The house shifted and cracked.

"Here, Martha, look," I said, grabbing the duffel bag and dumping its contents onto the floor. I picked up a handful of colored pens and a pad of paper from the pile. "Here. Draw, Martha. It'll be okay." She pulled the pens and paper to her without looking up, flipped open the pad and began sketching rapidly. I could immediately see the outline of a dog on the paper.

Another crack came from downstairs. Richard stood up. "We got to get stuff up here or it's like to float off," he said. "Everybody come grab everything you can from the kitchen. Even if we make it through all right we might be here longer than we want to without food or water." He grabbed a lamp, gave one to Claire, and limped out, the rest of us fast behind.

Later, I told myself, the way I had when my sister had become the way she was, that if I had been thinking, if I hadn't been scared half to death, if we had been in the middle of anything familiar, if I had had one night's sleep in the past week, I would have realized what we were doing. I would have made certain that, frightened as she was, Martha came with us down the stairs and into the kitchen. But I didn't. I left her alone with Tom and Our Lady of Sorrow, right in the middle of Martha Land.

We were all in the kitchen, grabbing things from the cupboards and stuffing them into our emptied backpacks and the duffel bag Claire had given me, emptying the refrigerator, now dark and warming, into the ice chest with what little ice was left. Richard struggled with the boat and the portable inflator before handing the former to Felicia with instructions to get it upstairs. She nodded and left.

"The water's lapping at the door," Jim called from where he could see through the hole in the plywood covering a living room window. "I'd say that's near ten feet. God help anybody in a one story." He grabbed one end of the rolled up boat and Richard the other, both grunting as they struggled it toward the stairs.

The sounds of the house were terrible; it groaned and popped as if in pain. Now and then something smashed against its side, or, more alarmingly, its roof. The wind had voices. It cried and screamed, and, oddly, dropped to a low, tender croon before rising to a snarl and hurling something against the building again. There was another sound too, a moan that played over and over, like the deep groan of a bass fiddle. When I stopped what I was doing and cocked my head, Richard said "Them live oaks is crying in the wind. The littler limbs will probably break clean off. They likely all going to be dead before this is over." Until that moment I wouldn't have imagined anything terrible enough to make the live oaks cry.

In the storm's roar none of us had heard anything from upstairs. But five minutes after we had come down, as water began to seep under the kitchen door, we heard Felicia cry out. In that moment I realized that I had left Tom alone with my sister.

Martha had simply done what she always did when she was intent on making something manageable out of the unmanageable. She had climbed right over Tom to get to the beautiful child's painting on the wall, to make it part of something only she could see. She had pulled its heavy frame off of its hanger and fallen backward with it onto the floor. Along the way she, or the painting, or Tom's own displaced arm, now hanging off the side of the bed, had pushed the plunger of the syringe that Claire had carefully inserted into the IV line. The entire syringe full of morphine had gone into him. Martha sat unharmed on the floor amid the picture frame's shattered pieces, Sam's painting spread out in front of her, calmly drawing in Martha, wings full spread, soaring into the sky over Bayou Saint Claire. The little pink rosary hung, swinging, across the outstretched hands of the Madonna.

Chapter Fifteen

It took Tom Carmody a half hour to die, long enough for us all to tell him that we loved him and that we were sorry it hadn't worked out the way he'd planned, and to run out of things to say. He never opened his eyes nor gave us any sign he heard us, so we touched one another constantly, holding one another as we watched him go. I had, for once, left Martha alone, just picking up the broken glass and pieces of picture frame around her and letting her work on Sam's picture while the wind tore at the house and the surge rose. The room stank a little from the water downstairs, but it appeared we were going to be high enough; it reached two-thirds up the walls on the first floor, where it stopped. After a few hours Jim said he thought it was slowing down. The house still creaked, but it seemed it would hold.

I couldn't stop staring at my friend's still face in the flickering lamplight. All the fear and confusion I had felt for the past few days had stopped still and I was quiet inside, as if something in me listened for a sound from far away. I wasn't afraid of the storm and I wasn't afraid of what would happen afterward. I was curious, but not about the answers to everything as I had always been. For once I was more curious about the questions.

"You okay, Cherie?" Claire put her arm around my shoulder as we stood at the foot of the bed.

"I think so," I answered. "I can't decide about this, if it went wrong or all right. It wasn't what he'd planned. He didn't get what he wanted."

"Oh, I'm not so sure about that," she said. "I think he just wanted to be first for a change, the most important one. He wanted us to love him enough to try. He needed that as long as I knew him. But then, don't we all?"

"But Martha—,"

"Oh, pooh, Martha. She's as innocent as that hurricane out there, innocent as the cancer that ate up your mama and my mama and the virus that killed our Tom. Not a one of them means it, as much as we'd like somebody to shake our fist at and say that if it wasn't for them we could make everything just fine. I never did much believe in God but there is something to that old saying 'Man plans, God laughs'. We can't help but try to make things turn out like we want them to, and sooner or later if we're lucky we get to see what a truly loveable bunch of fools we are."

"So what are we going to do with him?" Felicia joined us. "We've come this far; it seems a shame not to give him what he wanted now."

Richard, who was stretched out on the couch watching Martha draw, said, "I been thinking about that. All this water that's been pushed up is going to have to go back sometime. We could still blow up that boat and send Tom with it. I expect once he gets a good start, he could go all the way out into the gulf before it drops him."

We washed Tom the way Richard, who had seen it done when he was a poor child and they'd buried their own, showed us. At first I was afraid to touch him; when I looked at him I saw my mother, and me at fifteen, horrified and relieved and confused. But after watching the way Claire and Felicia and Richard caressed his face and his long, thin limbs, whispering to him and one another as though they were comforting a child before sleep, I reached out and stroked his hair, his cracked lips, remembering the photo of him and Louise by Night in lipstick and rouge, at the beginning of the journey that we were about to end. Then I took the little pink rosary from the Madonna's hands and, after giving Jesus and the tiny cherub a kiss, placed it in Tom's. "No matter what," I said softly.

Once we were done Claire and Jim wrapped him in the bedclothes, even laughing together as they used duct tape, the only thing they could find to strap them around him, to hold the blankets in place. We nearly had to hold a still upset Felicia back when Martha left her picture and placed her dog beside him on the bed, snapping one photo before grabbing her again and returning with her to the altered scene of Bayou Saint Claire. She had added figures in such close imitation of Sam Carmody's childhood style that it almost looked as though Jim Collins and I were part of the original.

"Where are you in that picture, Martha?" Jim had asked. She had pointed to the winged dog in the sky. "I see you. I'll bet you see me too, even if you won't admit it," he said, and returned to Tom. Martha followed him with her eyes, watching him for a long time before going back to her work.

As the wind dissipated, Richard opened the door and stepped out onto the upper porch, tapping gingerly with his cane in case it wouldn't hold. "Railing's about gone," he called back into the room over a roll of thunder. "but I believe she's safe enough. Dear Lord." He fell silent, then added "Y'all better come look. I do believe this is what the end of the world will look like."

Chapter Sixteen

We sent Tom Carmody off in a way that might not have been much like the Pascagoula Indians went, but when he'd been fifteen the sheer strangeness of it would have made him blush with pleasure. He left us on the outgoing surge when the water had retreated enough for us to go down to the ruin of the first floor. We lay him in the bottom of the inflatable yellow boat, swaddled in the blankets from his bed, his head on the pillow on which he had died. Then we launched him from the front porch of the house that would soon be bulldozed, leaving nothing of the Carmody family but the live oak trees that would indeed survive the storm. Jim and Claire waded out neck deep in the black, swirling water, tethered to the porch with ropes out of Richard's building supplies, holding onto the flooded limousine and pushing the boat with broken off limbs until it floated free. When it finally cleared the bank and caught in the river current, we all let out a breath. "It better last a while," Jim said as we watched the boat bump its way through everything in Pascagoula that could float, "because if they find him, Richard, there's going to be more explaining than even you can handle."

"I doubt it," Richard replied. "Look around you," he indicated the broken puzzle that had once been Pascagoula. "There's gonna be so much that people can't figure out that he could walk back right on the water and nobody would ask too much."

It took a long time for the little boat to dwindle down the river, but we stood watching it, every one of us, even Martha, who, as Tom disappeared, snapped one last picture of him, saying "Yellow submarine" before turning back to the house. Now I really am the last of the Pascagoula, I thought. Though I was embarrassed, I caught myself hoping for a snatch of song on the diminishing breeze.

The next day we walked out of what was left of Pascagoula. We locked the house tight though we doubted there was any point, and carried our backpacks and the duffel bag stuffed full of clothes, Martha's art supplies and leftover cameras and as much food as we could haul, not sure that what we were walking into was any better than what we were walking out of. The water had gone out as fast as it had come in. The weather was beautiful, the sky bluer than it ever was on an ordinary day. I looked up a lot, because to look anywhere else was too terrible. As it was, we had to climb and stumble our way through the debris of every life within miles of us. If it hadn't been for Richard and the river we wouldn't have known where we were at all. Pascagoula, and, I would later learn, Gautier, Ocean Springs, Biloxi, Pass Christian, Waveland and Bay Saint Louis, looked as though it had been picked up and dropped from the sky, landing in random piles in a rain of silt and mud. Houses so ordinary they had only registered in my mind as background when I had lived there lay smashed, defiled, dishonored as though the victims of a child's rage. I couldn't help but wonder about the Doucettes' house, the theater where Claire had sat watching all of the town pass by, the graveyard where *Melissande DuChamp* had lain for centuries and Tom and I had begun the chain of events that had shaped the lives of my sister and me. It was unthinkable that so much might be simply and finally gone. Even though I had come to agree with Claire about the absence of malice in elemental things, it was hard not to want there to be someone of whom to ask 'Why?"

It seemed I wasn't the only one with those feelings. By the time we reached Highway 90 there were a surprising number of people walking with us and asking just that, in numbed, awestruck voices. To tell them the storm was innocent didn't seem right. For once I became as quiet as Martha, who was so befuddled by so many little pieces and shards around her that she didn't pick up a thing. She just walked, holding her dog by a tattered wing that looked as if it would come off with just one more puff of wind. Every now and then she reached out to Felicia, who carried the rolled up painting that her son had made and that Martha had claimed as her own, and patted her arm. I wondered if there was the slightest chance she was saying "I'm sorry."

326

The National Guard, and a few volunteers who were loading up any vehicle that moved with stunned people just wanting to get away from the sanity shaking world around us, said they could help us far enough north so that Jim could call someone to come and get us. The reports from Bayou Eau Claire were good; things had flown around as Claire had predicted they would, but everything was standing, and the geese had come home. Richard clapped Jim on the back and promised him a goose egg omelet for breakfast.

A few days later, we sat on the pier overlooking the lake.

"It doesn't seem real," Felicia said, tilting the umbrella and rubbing more sunscreen into her arms. "Everything I do feels like it's in slow motion, like my body is doing what it does while the part of me that sees and hears things is mostly back there with Tom and the storm, seeing it like it was and seeing it how it could have been and wondering if I saw it at all. Do you think that's what it's like for her?" She pointed at Martha, dressed in one of Claire's swimsuits and wearing an orange life jacket, dog paddling in the lake between Claire and Jim.

"I think it's like that for all of us," I said, turning my head to feel the warm sun in my ear. It felt wonderful. "She does it better than most because she can make something out of it, but I don't know that I've been any more in the world than she has. I've spent my whole life wishing for things to have been different instead of doing it myself, because I hated what had happened to me. When Bill left, you sort of went off to some fantasy that you thought would make things all right, didn't you?"

"That I did. Liquor, men, you name it. I got lucky as hell. I didn't die, I got Sam, and I had people to go to that loved me, no matter what."

We exchanged a long look before I turned back to watch my sister. "She seems to get better here," I said.

"Claire says so too. Says you all ought to stay. That other house back there will empty out sooner or later, and you and Martha could move in and work from here. We got internet too, you know. 'Course once Martha realizes Jim doesn't live here she might not take to the idea," she chuckled.

"Oh, we couldn't. That's not possible," I said.

"What's not possible?" Richard came up behind us, cane thumping the boards of the pier, and sat down on the wide arm of Felicia's chair.

"Oh, Jail Bait here says she and Martha can't join our little commune."

"Why not?" he said. "You better hurry and get dibs on some space, though. The city's in a world of hurt and the coast ain't any better off. It's unbelievable. They's about a million people needs a place to be and food and drink, and I'm tracking down everybody I know can lend a hand." He shook his head as if to clear it, then smiled brightly. "Damned if I can't raise an army of do-gooders still. I sent the boys off to Baton Rouge with a list of phone numbers long as your arm, people I knew from way back when we was hell bent on revolution. Now they got people bringing food and water from all over the country. That storm didn't blow us away and those government bastards ain't gonna drown us. We'll show them how it's done, by God!"

"I believe you will," I grinned. "I knew you could talk people into just about anything, but getting Our Lady of Sorrow to let you borrow the Virgin Mary impressed even me."

For the first time since I had met Richard Doucette, when I had had a crush on him for being the kind of father I wished I had, he looked defeated. "Well, I guess I should tell you all this one thing," he said, shaking his head. "I lied to Tom about borrowing that statue. I went down to the church and flat stole that thing after everybody had lit out. I just didn't want Tom to know they turned him down. He wanted so bad to believe they accepted him after all these years. I swear, when I can get back to Pascagoula I'm bringing her here. Lot of people will be needing somebody to talk to after what they—what we—been through. She came out of the bayou, she can come back to the bayou."

"Richard," Claire had swum to the edge of the pier. Thirty feet out, Martha clung to Jim and squealed. "Just how many people did you tell they could come here?"

"Oh, a few…" he gazed off into the middle distance. She rolled her eyes, then slapped the life jacket Martha was no longer wearing up onto the pier. "Cherie, she said, "it's time you jumped in this water with me."

"Oh, no," I shook my head. "I can't."

328

"Can't never could, Kate Lynn," Felicia said, reaching out and placing her hand on mine. "You think we'd let you drown? We love you."

"But, my clothes are too heavy!"

"Shuck 'em," Richard said. "You think me and Jim ain't seen women's underpants, you seriously underestimate us." He tugged me out of the chair. "Let an old man sit," he said. "You put on that jacket and give that rope swing a try. Let go at the right time, you just might turn into a heron and fly."

At that moment, I wasn't anywhere but on that pier. I wasn't the girl who only felt all right in the shadow of a broken homecoming queen, or the teenager who'd been left behind by her dying, or the woman who had stopped living her own life for a sister who might just do fine without her. I was just Kate Lynn, and Kate wanted to swim more than she wanted to stay on dry land. Quickly, more quickly than I had ever done anything, I dropped my jeans and shirt, buckled on the life vest, and grabbed the long rope that Claire had brought to the edge of the pier. I drew it back and placed one foot on the knot at its end."

"Come on, Kate! Come on!" It was Martha, my sister, calling to me from the water. I looked around. I didn't see Martha the dog anywhere. Taking a deep breath, I dashed toward the pier's rough edge, swung hard, let go, and flew.

Epilogue

I found the envelope when I went out to check the mail. I sat down at the kitchen table amid the packing boxes and instructions for the house's new owner, and tore it open. A photograph slid into my hand, along with a single page.

"You ought to see the place," it read. "Richard's got half of Louisiana living here, and organizing them to get out and help the other half. Martha's fine, painting and making artwork out of everything that's not nailed down. She's telling the stories of everybody that's come here for shelter, listening to what happened to them and putting it all down on paper or canvas or the side of that old barn, whatever she can find. They're so good Sam thinks he can get her a gallery show in the city.

Richard built a grotto by the lake. The Lady looks down at that water like she's looking at everybody who got taken by the storm. He was right, people light candles by her feet and pray and cry like they're going to die, but after a while they get up and try to go on. As for me, every raindrop that hits that water I hope there's a little bit of Tom in it, coming home.

We haven't found Martha yet. I was starting to wonder if she was just a dream we all dreamed until Jim got those pictures developed. You might want to have a look at this one. After that, go! Take Kate Lynn out and show her the world. Don't hold nothing back, as my daddy would say. We'll be here whenever you want us. Love, Claire, Felicia, Jim, Richard, Sam, Martha and Tom."

I looked at the photo for a long time. Martha had taken one last shot of Tom Carmody when the two of them were alone, before she had climbed onto the bed to pull Sam's painting off the wall. It seemed he had had a rally in the end, after all. In the photo Tom held the syringe connected to the IV line in one hand, his thumb on the plunger. With the other hand, over the defiant, impossible figure of Martha the dog, he blew us a kiss goodbye.

Acknowledgments

I once let a woman read my palm, and asked her if I would get rich from my writing. She replied, "Honey, you'll have more riches than you can put in a bucket."

Here are my riches:

My husband Michael, whose help and simple patience while I ran around like a chicken with its head cut off cannot be praised enough. I couldn't have asked for better.

My sons Justin and Andrew, who put up with my mothering and whom I love more than I thought I could love anyone.

The talented women who have read, reread, edited, suggested, laughed, cried, encouraged, modeled strength and talent, and brought me down to earth more times than I can count. Allison, Carol M., Carol P., Elizabeth, Susan, you are the definition of the word "friend."

My sisters Melissa and Marletta, the only ones who know the things I actually plucked from our lives in that little town and the things I just plain made up.

Bob Bergman, without whom neither the book nor its author would have gotten this far.

CPSIA information can be obtained at www.ICGtesting.com
Printed in the USA
BVOW021211261211

279158BV00005B/33/P